A WONDERFUL
WELCOME TO OZ

L. FRANK BAUM

A WONDERFUL WELCOME TO OZ

THE MARVELOUS LAND OF OZ, OZMA OF OZ & THE EMERALD CITY OF OZ

*Selected and with an Introduction
by Gregory Maguire*

Illustrations by John R. Neill

THE MODERN LIBRARY

NEW YORK

2006 Modern Library Paperback Edition

Introduction, "Traveling On?" and "Let's Talk About Oz" copyright © 2006
by Gregory Maguire

Biographical note copyright © 2003 by Random House, Inc.

Published in the United States by Modern Library, an imprint of The Random
House Publishing Group, a division of Random House, Inc., New York.

MODERN LIBRARY and the TORCHBEARER Design are registered trademarks
of Random House, Inc.

LIBRARY OF CONGRESS CATALOGING-IN-PUBLICATION DATA
Baum, L. Frank (Lyman Frank), 1856–1919.
A wonderful welcome to Oz / L. Frank Baum ; selected and with
an introduction by Gregory Maguire ; illustrations by John R. Neill.
p. cm.—(Modern Library classics)
Summary: A collection of three adventures in Oz, including the sequel to
The wizard of Oz, Dorothy's return to Emerald City under its new ruler,
and Aunt Em and Uncle Henry's visit there with Dorothy.
Contents: The marvelous land of Oz—Ozma of Oz—The Emerald City of Oz.
ISBN 0-8129-7494-8
[1. Fantasy.]   I. Maguire, Gregory.   II. Neill, John R. (John Rea), ill.
III. Title.   IV. Series.
PZ7.B327 Wol 2005
[Fic]—dc22   2005054038

Printed in the United States of America

www.modernlibrary.com

2 4 6 8 9 7 5 3 1

L. Frank Baum

Lyman Frank Baum, otherwise known as L. Frank Baum, one of the world's most celebrated children's authors, was born to Cynthia Stanton and Benjamin Ward Baum on May 15, 1856, in Chittenango, New York. His affluent parents arranged private tutoring for the delicate young Baum, who had been afflicted with a heart condition that shortened his brief schooling at the Peekskill Military Academy in 1870. As a teenager, Baum wrote and printed a house newspaper, *The Rose Lawn Home Journal.* He seemed to have found his professional calling early in life, and other journals of his creation followed. In 1874, however, he joined a theater company and became an actor.

That Baum had two vocational passions was apparent, although his career path remained unclear for years; he found a measure of success with both newspaper reporting and acting. He joined the Union Square Theatre of New York City in 1878, and in 1882 he organized his own company, wrote a dramatic script, and played the lead in the acclaimed *The Maid of Arran.* That year Baum also married Maud Gage. With the birth of their first son, Frank Joslyn, in 1883, financial stability became increasingly important. Poor accounting caused Baum to lose a chain of theaters given to him by his father, forcing him to join the family business selling Baum's Castorine, a grease made from crude oil.

Baum's first foray into book publishing was a curiosity. *The Book of the Hamburgs,* his nonfiction book about breeding Hamburg chickens, was published in 1886. A second son, Robert, was born that year. The family fortunes declined after the death of Baum's father in 1887, and in yet another career change, Baum moved to a small prairie town in the Dakotas, where he ran a general store called Baum's Bazaar for two years. In 1889, a third son, Harry, was born, and soon Baum returned to writing and newspaper publishing. He operated *The Aberdeen Saturday Pioneer,* where he penned a popular column titled "Our Landlady," until the paper failed. In 1891, a fourth son, Kenneth, arrived, and the Baums relocated to Chicago, where Baum landed a reporting job with *The Evening Post.* He also held, over the next few years, secondary jobs as a traveling sales-man. Indeed, he was ever occupied—even as his first children's book, *Mother Goose in Prose,* was published in 1897, he concurrently founded *Show Window,* a journal dedicated to store window-dressing. He also wrote and self-published a volume of poetry, *By the Cande-labra's Glare.*

The success of Baum's second book of children's verse, *Father Goose,* published in 1899, demonstrated that he could be a best-selling writer. Beautifully illustrated by Baum's longtime collabo-rator, William Wallace Denslow, *Father Goose* was a prelude to Baum's masterwork. In 1900, *The Wonderful Wizard of Oz* found sub-stantial popularity among readers, and critics too valued Baum's vibrant characterization. Full of hope and optimism, Baum had cre-ated the first American fairy tale. That pivotal and productive year also saw the publication of *The Army Alphabet, The Navy Alphabet,* and *A New Wonderland for Children,* as well as a collection of his *Show Window* articles, *The Art of Decorating Dry Good Windows and Interiors.*

More children's books followed, including *American Fairy Tales* and *The Master Key,* but none achieved the celebrity of the Oz book, which gained even more fame as a stage adaptation in 1902. Al-though Baum endeavored to widen his literary efforts (he never meant to publish a series), the intense demand for fiction about the magical land of Oz was overpowering. In 1904, he published a sequel, *The Marvelous Land of Oz* (later known as *The Land of Oz*). Baum also completed other works of juvenile fiction during this time, notably *The Woggle-Bug Book* and *Queen Zixi of Ix*. His romantic adventure novel for adults, *The Fate of a Crown,* was one of the many books he wrote under a pseudonym.

In 1907, he returned again to Oz with *Ozma of Oz. Dorothy and the Wizard of Oz* appeared one year later, followed by *The Road to Oz* in 1909, and in 1910 he published what he intended to be the last in the series, *The Emerald City of Oz.* The Baums moved to a house they named Ozcot in California. Investments in failed adaptations of his stories, however, forced the prominent writer to declare bankruptcy in 1911, also the year of publication for *The Sea Fairies. Sky Island* followed in 1912. Financial pressures and appeals from readers for new Oz stories motivated Baum to write *The Patchwork Girl of Oz,* published in 1913. His play *The Tik-Tok Man of Oz* enjoyed a favorable run in Los Angeles that year and was adapted to book form as *Tik-Tok of Oz* in 1914. Between 1915 and 1919, Baum wrote one Oz book per year, of varying literary quality—*The Scarecrow of Oz, Rinkitink in Oz, The Lost Princess of Oz, The Tin Woodman of Oz,* and *The Magic of Oz.*

Though Baum remained a highly productive writer, his health waned. On May 6, 1919, he succumbed to his longtime ailments. The last in the Oz series to have been written by its creator, *Glinda of Oz,* was published in 1920. Baum's publishers then hired another writer to sustain the popular series for future generations of readers. The 1939 film version of Baum's original Oz novel showcased his incomparable imaginative power for a wider audience and ensured the beloved classic's place in American mythology.

SOURCES

Rahn, Suzanne. *The Wizard of Oz: Shaping An Imaginary World.* New York: Twayne Publishers, 1998.

Riley, Michael O. *Oz and Beyond: The Fantasy World of L. Frank Baum.* Lawrence, Kan.: University Press of Kansas, 1997.

Rogers, Katharine M. *L. Frank Baum, Creator of Oz.* New York: St. Martin's Press, 2002.

Twentieth Century Literary Criticism, volume 7. Farmington Hills, Mich.: Gale, pp. 11–12.

CONTENTS

Introduction

Welcome to Oz

Gregory Maguire

If you say, "I was a bookish kid," then, for the bio-flick of your life, the director relies on Central Casting to locate a slope-shouldered boy with long lashes and a weak chest, sporting horn-rimmed eyeglasses four sizes too large for him. Or a girl with a dewy vastness in her expression, and a satin sash, and preternaturally clean fingernails. Or someone to whom both those descriptions apply, gender at that age being largely irrelevant.

I *was* a bookish kid, and no slave to Charles Atlas—and I did wear glasses. And do. But my nails were dirty, my T-shirts scuzzy, my fingers stained with watercolors, my curly hair buzz-cut into submission and further flattened because I taught myself to carry my library books home on my head like an Ashanti woman coming home from the village well.

It's an accurate metaphor, if far-fetched. To a ten-year-old reader, dismally stuck in the baking heat of the city for most of the summer, the public library *was* a village well. And what I brought home on my head nourished me like water.

By then, I was aware of the dozens of worlds not only beyond the neighborhood of Pine Hills in Albany, New York, but beyond the navigable margins of the horizon. I made weekly visits to Neverland, Wonderland, Prydain, Narnia, and the 100 Aker Wood; to the mansion of Malplaquet and the manor house at Green Knowe; to 17 Cherry Tree Lane in London, where Mary Poppins came and went; and to the Victorian villa at 40 Walden Street, Concord, where the Hall children had their magical adventures in Jane Langton's books.

Later I would discover the Inferno, Middle-earth, Atlantis, Camelot, Attic Greece, Prospero's island, Gormenghast's castle, and Dickens's London. And later still I would return—like an expat making a sentimental journey home—to the wells of the library to learn about places newly discovered since my prepubescent years: Hogwarts, Earthsea, Joan Aiken's alternate England, and the thousand thousand lands implicit in Philip Pullman's magnificent cycle. Pullman proposes that all possible histories—those with magic and those without—lie adjacent to one another, or even nestled within each other. His is a Unified Field Theory of otherworlds: There isn't one, but an infinite number.

In one of those infinite worlds lived I, saddled with lovingly tyrannical parents who endorsed reading and who only rarely let us watch TV. In another of those worlds lived the Scarecrow and the Tin Woodman, Glinda and the Wicked Witch of the West, the Wizard, and Dorothy, and Toto, too.

It seemed we inhabited incompatible, mutually exclusive zones. Yet no matter how many times Dorothy left Oz at the end of the first book, I had only to open to the front again to bring her magically back, riding that twister sidesaddle. And to bring myself back, too.

◇ ◇ ◇

The bookish kid grows up to learn all sorts of things that children's books don't generally reveal. Being able to satisfy one's wanderlust for the world at hand, however, doesn't quell the appetite for the strictly literary sojourn.

With my U.S. passport, I traveled as far as the laws of this globe—and my finances and courage—allowed me. With my library card, I also returned to the haunts of my youth—the literary fantasies of childhood—to be nourished, or occasionally disappointed when my destinations seemed smaller, shabbier, less wonderful than I had remembered. More as an act of nostalgia than anything else, I began to order and compare the magic lands I loved.

The nineteenth century was a golden era of literary fantasy. Not the first, mind you, but the first for an educated middle-class audience. Literary fantasy in its nascent forms promoted nationalistic self-identification, and served also as a corrective to the ills of filthy early industrialism. The Romantic era of Wordsworth and Keats and Shelley in England, and, in a sense, of Washington Irving and Poe in the new world, had primed readers to appreciate the magic of the domestic märchen collected by the Brothers Grimm in Bavaria and published in English in 1823. Shortly thereafter, building on a seventeenth- and eighteenth-century tradition of original droll fables circulated in ladies' salons, Hans Christian Andersen popularized the obscure subgenre of the "literary" fairy tale—the fanciful story invented out of whole cloth, intended to evoke magical tales of antiquity and barnyard common sense alike: Ovid and Aesop, the ballad and the New Testament parable. *Could* there have been a Lewis Carroll or a Charles Kingsley in the mid-1860s without a Hans Christian Andersen in the 1840s, or an L. Frank Baum by the turn of the century without a Lewis Carroll before him?

Certainly *Alice's Adventures in Wonderland,* published in 1865, counts obliquely as a literary progenitor of Dorothy in Oz. Both in the United States and in England, *Alice's Adventures in Wonderland* and *Through the Looking-Glass* were two of the bestselling children's books of the century. It would not have escaped L. Frank Baum, who was unabashedly interested in commercial success, that the story of a fanciful voyage to a land of nonsensical wonder had made its author buckets of money.

But despite the obvious narrative similarities—plucky girl slips accidentally into magical landscape, returns—the story of Oz was invented by a different artist, in a different country, for a different purpose. Wonderland is a dreamworld; its inconsistency and absurdity are signal characteristics of the hypnagogic state. Oz—especially as depicted in Baum's first and best Oz novel—is a land of comic incongruity, a pell-mell stitching together of fanciful set pieces that nonetheless adheres to principles of cause and effect. Practicality and common sense are just as strong as magic. The homely virtues of self-reliance and good cheer—as well as courage, smarts, and a kindly heart—are the main supplies one needs to face down humbug wizards, wicked witches, and pomposity and small-mindedness of all sorts.

(Incidentally, J. M. Barrie conceived of making a play out of his Peter Pan notions as early as 1901, after seeing a London stage production of *Bluebell in Fairyland*. By 1901, the surprising success of *The Wonderful Wizard of Oz* in the United States might well have come to his attention. Neverland would be made out of scraps of a child's imagination—the pirates and Redskins and mermaids, the flying and the fairies, and the fate of being brilliantly, happily, temporarily orphaned—all heartfelt desires of safe middle-class children. I've never heard it said that Neverland owed anything to Oz, and I don't think it does. But how interesting that so much mapping of dreamscapes was going on nearly simultaneously, when the twentieth century would all but blast the notion of the innocent childhood to smithereens.)

✧ ✧ ✧

The history of the surprising success of *The Wonderful Wizard of Oz* can be found elsewhere. It is a book that I loved and puzzled over, and one that I happily plundered for raw material when writing my own novels for adults, *Wicked* and *Son of a Witch*.

Mostly by its annual airing on television between the late 1950s and 1980, the famous 1939 MGM film *The Wizard of Oz* secured in the public mind a pared-down (and in some ways more coherent) version of Baum's original lolloping tale. It worked its Technicolor magic on me, for sure, as it was one of the few films aired on TV that I was permitted to watch. But for many young viewers in the 1960s and 1970s, the film effectively eclipsed rather than enhanced the reputation of the Oz franchise—fourteen books by Baum himself and, at this writing, some thirty-five more or less authorized additions to the series. And that's not even mentioning the heretical revisionists like Geoff Ryman, Philip José Farmer, myself, and others. (Chapter two of Edward Eager's children's novel *Seven-Day Magic* is worth seeking out.)

This volume exists to help redress that balance. In the first decades of the twentieth century, thousands of American children waited for their annual holiday gift of the latest Oz volume. They knew there was more to Oz than Dorothy's classic shipwreck-by-cyclone. While Baum was not overly concerned with the history of Oz—the lapses and contradictions prove his attention strayed from time to time—he was tirelessly inventive as regards the spectacle, the curious and the novel, the quaintly bizarre. The books are uneven in quality, and none of them is as tightly plotted as the original or the sequel. But once readers discovered Oz, they seemed content to enjoy the largely picaresque nature of the later books. New characters continued to amuse, and if in time the original characters, reappearing, seemed stodgy, worn about the edges, and more sentimentally inclined, no one minded.

There is this truth. Anyone who travels is torn between the sexy and dangerous temptation of the unknown on the one hand and, on the other, the comfort and solace of the familiar.

✧   ✧   ✧

The current volume collects three of Baum's additional Oz novels and includes a brief extract from a fourth.

The Marvelous Land of Oz (sometimes called *The Land of Oz*) was written following the success of the first stage version of *The Wonderful Wizard of Oz*. The 1904 novel is generally lighter in tone, a bit more vaudeville, than the sober *Wizard,* which for all of its detractors (and there have been quite a few) had the virtue of being written in American plain-style, with few flourishes or cloying "heartfelt" moments. Baum was a competent writer, but in *Wizard* he had a better idea than he deserved, and he was possessed of enough good sense to write simply and to let the story speak for itself.

The Marvelous Land of Oz is written by a more confident hand, and the occasional glimpse of dreaded "facility" begins to show. In the first sequel, Dorothy has not yet made her reappearance. The

Scarecrow and the Tin Woodman are the familiar characters, and Baum used them partly because in the 1902 stage version of *Wizard*, two magnificent vaudeville performers, Fred Stone and David C. Montgomery, had brought those characters to new life. (I know how Baum felt, having seen the same thing happen while watching the stage musical based on *Wicked.*)

In *Land*, the orphan boy Tip helps put down a revolution in the Emerald City, and the royal Ozma is recovered from her hiding place. While Ozma seems more gutsy when still in her disguise, she matures into the closest thing to a goddess that the unrepentantly secularist Baum ever devised. More on this below.

Ozma of Oz followed in 1907. The volume deserves attention for the solidification of Ozma as a kind of youthful materfamilias— part Lady Liberty, part Gibson Girl—and for the introduction of new characters possessed of grit and gumption. Baum had not yet sold out to the notion of Oz as an all-purpose "fairyland," a literary theme park. (That temptation was strong, and Baum couldn't always resist it. The further along the series went, the more prone was he to depicting Oz as a sunny Utopia, a kind of Big Rock Candy Mountain where little went wrong. Narrative crackle occasionally became a bit muted.)

My household edition of *Ozma* dates from 1927, when the original illustrator, John R. Neill, supplied a new cover illustration, giving Ozma the aspect of a seasoned habitué of gin joints. I'm told collectors call it "the slinky Ozma." It forever confused me as to Ozma's age—was Ozma Dorothy's mystic Oz-ish twin and soul mate, or Dorothy's elder and better? Baum says the former, but this crucial bit of artwork confounded me early on, and I never recovered. Ozma is a mystery—or many mysteries.

In *Ozma* we see the return of Dorothy, though she seems more prone to faintly self-righteous platitudes than she used to be. With her is Billina, a robust hen originally named Bill but renamed when her gender became more apparent.

While *Ozma* is lighthearted in ways, Baum also suggests subjects darker than those usually found in books for the young. Part of the plot hinges on a king who, having sold his wife and children into slavery in exchange for the promise of a long life, commits suicide. Another royal figure, Princess Langwidere, keeps a number of pretty severed heads in glass cases, which she can fix on her own neck as the mood of the moment dictates. The contrast between the royal characters with no true centers and those commoners, however humble, who know who they are and win out is a motif that runs through much of the Oz canon.

The main events of *Ozma* take place in Ev, somewhere to the south—or west—or east—of Oz. (Baum wasn't consistent in Ozian "jogerfy.") Dorothy meets up with the terricolous Nome King, a fanciful creation and a formidable enemy, although the magic belt she takes from him becomes a bit of a crutch in Baum's later Oz books.

The third full selection of this anthology is *The Emerald City of Oz*, where the Nome King meets with his comeuppance. *Emerald City* is suffused with an elegiac quality, as Baum intended his sixth Oz novel to be his last. Like Arthur Conan Doyle before him, however, Baum found that the audience for his creation had grown too powerful, and would not let him escape. He wrote eight more Oz novels, to my mind none the equal of the first six.

The Emerald City of Oz unfolds with two narrative strands. One involves a military threat and the other a comic jaunt-about; the plots mimic each other slyly. The Nome King convenes a coalition of the willful and decides to invade Oz by burrowing under the deadly desert. Dorothy returns, too, this time with an incredulous Uncle Henry and a bracingly peppery Aunt Em, and they make a Cook's tour of Oz, meeting up with the Cuttenclips, the Fuddles, and other indigenous populations happily ghettoized for their own comfort and protection.

The third novel in this anthology reveals Baum's admiration for what Lévi-Strauss, in other contexts, called bricolage: the art of assemblage. Notice how many of the populations are "created" somehow: the Whimsies with their pasteboard mask heads; the Cuttenclips, animated paper dolls; the Fuddles, a three-dimensional puzzle people. Baum seems to be saying that we are in the act of making ourselves up—and possibly of making fools of ourselves.

For all its trappings of royalty, Oz is a place for the self-made creature; the Tin Woodman retires to a Tin Castle, the Scarecrow to a
manor shaped like an ear of corn.

Yet Baum knew he intended to close down the series with this
book, and it seems fitting that the enemies of Oz fall prey to an en-
forced senility and sweet forgetfulness. The nepenthe offered as a
kind of dea ex machina suggests Baum's own ambivalence about
being involved with Oz any longer. Anyone who has read C. S.
Lewis's *The Last Battle*, with its reunion of characters, its final triumph of good over evil, and death itself proving to be the real ac-
cess to the most magical world of all, may hear an eschatological
tone in the sonorities that bring *The Emerald City of Oz* to a close.

❖   ❖   ❖

Dear reader, be warned: I'm about to talk about a significant plot
element in *The Marvelous Land of Oz*. Via Internet chatter about
Wicked the musical, I have come to understand the concept of a
"spoiler"—sounds like a certain unsavory Oz type, doesn't it?—the
egregious giving away of a plot twist. I don't care to spoil this volume for you, so if you'd rather wander in Oz without the road map,
read these novels first and then come back to catch the conclusion
of this introduction.

❖   ❖   ❖

There. Is the room clear of all but the initiated?

At the end of *The Marvelous Land of Oz* we come upon one of the
most astounding episodes in all of children's literature—the meta-
morphosis of the plucky lad Tip into the genteel, feminine Ozma.
Gender shift or sex change? Mutilation or cosmetic enhancement?
Reconstructive surgery—or seeing not through a glass darkly, but
face-to-face?

Of all the transformations in Oz—and shape-shifting is a time-
worn trope of legend and lore that Baum used repeatedly—this
conversion from boyhood to girlhood, Tip tipped into Ozma, is the
most jaw-dropping. Tip resists the suggestion, but for the good of
the country he accedes, at last. Questions of cross-dressing are not

to the point; nor do I interest myself, here, in the reasons why Oz has become a metaphor for the safe and welcoming home for which gay men have long longed. I speak merely in terms of reader response, then and now, among children and adults. What are we to make of the sacrifice Tip makes—if it is one—for the good of the nation? Is Oz, after all, a little bit more about politics and the nature of a just society than the rollicking, episodic, comic narratives suggest?

In the opening of this introduction, I suggested lightheartedly that the gender of a reading kid is irrelevant. I leave adult readers with this conundrum: As you wander through these pages and pages of Oz, does it matter much to the plot that Dorothy is a girl and not a boy? Does it matter to the catalogue of improbable characters Dorothy meets—or to Tip, for that matter?

"Your riches are the only riches worth having," exclaims Ozma at the end of *The Marvelous Land of Oz:* "—the riches of content!" What is this? *Contentment?* Is that what we wanted all along? What about brains, or courage, or a heart, or even our sister's shoes? Contentment seems to me a dangerously inert state. Better you should feel awkward in the gender you were born in! Contentment belongs in the next county, in the next growing season, in the next crisis well met, the next disaster survived. America knows this—or used to.

As Baum attempted to wrap up his affairs in Oz, he became a bit sillier and more sentimental; he lost the brisk no-nonsense tone of *The Wonderful Wizard of Oz,* a tone of the sensible Midwest. I think that he worked better, wrote better books, when times were leaner and his own riches of content hadn't been underwritten by the riches of commercial success. His heart's desire was in the yearning. There's a reason we all think of the song "Over the Rainbow" as the national anthem of Oz. Without yearning, we have nothing to strive for, and Baum—and young America—knew full well that the richest savor in life is in the yearning, not in the securing. The chief goal of the up-and-coming American citizen has been to perfect the Art of the Strive.

Roger Scruton, the British philosopher, wrote: "The consolation of imaginary things is not imaginary consolation." In asking oneself why the horizon of an imaginary landscape has such a strong pull on readers young and old, one might do no better than considering the differences between consolation and contentment. Consolation supposes an existing wound, a grief that might never be healed but that might be survived. Contentment supposes a full recovery with no scars, perhaps even no memory of the catastrophe—a sweet nepenthe, splashed by the Water of Oblivion from the Forbidden Fountain.

We lucky adults who can return to childhood magic—in our dreams, in our rereadings of beloved books—we have survived childhood, and the scars still throb from time to time, reminding us of a different life. We are the more bruised, and the luckier, for such memories.

So welcome to Oz, or welcome back. Despite the occasionally saccharine sensibility, despite the reliance on puns (and it should be noted that children love puns more than adults do, for puns help them feel clever), L. Frank Baum has mapped out the only true American wonderland. One hundred years on, Oz is still as wide as a continent. It is as silly and dear and frightening as the twenty-first century. If there truly is no place like home, then travel abroad is the next best thing.

Returning to a charmed landscape last seen in childhood may just reawaken in you a sense of what it was like to long for a magic land of your own. Welcome to it. Welcome to Oz.

—

GREGORY MAGUIRE's novels include *Son of a Witch* and *Wicked: The Life and Times of the Wicked Witch of the West* (the inspiration for the Broadway musical *Wicked*). Maguire, who writes for children as well as adults, has lectured on art and literature both here and abroad, and is an occasional reviewer for *The New York Times Book Review*.

A Note on the Text

The texts and selected illustrations in *A Wonderful Welcome to Oz,* an original Modern Library omnibus edition, are reproduced from the original American editions of L. Frank Baum's classic novels: *The Marvelous Land of Oz* (Chicago: Reilly & Britton, 1904), *Ozma of Oz* (Chicago: Reilly & Britton, 1907), and *The Emerald City of Oz* (Chicago: Reilly & Britton, 1910).

The original editions are not always consistent on matters of punctuation, spelling, and capitalization, and while certain words have been standardized to the form used most frequently (for example, "grey" for "gray," "farm-house" for "farm house," and "Woggle-Bug" for "Wogglebug") and obvious typos have been corrected, the publisher has allowed a number of inconsistencies to stand, in order to preserve the original flavor of L. Frank Baum's earliest printed editions.

The Marvelous Land of Oz

Being an account of the further adventures of the

Scarecrow and Tin Woodman

and also the strange experiences of the Highly Magnified Woggle-Bug, Jack Pumpkinhead, the Animated Saw-Horse and the Gump; ✤ the story being

A Sequel to The Wizard of Oz

By

L. Frank Baum

Author of Father Goose-His Book; The Wizard of Oz; The Magical Monarch of Mo; The Enchanted Isle of Yew; The Life and Adventures of Santa Claus; Dot and Tot of Merryland etc.,etc.

PICTURED BY

John R. Neill

The end-papers from life poses by the famous comedians, Montgomery and Stone.

CHICAGO
THE REILLY & BRITTON CO.
1904.

Copyright 1904
by
L. Frank Baum

Published, July, 1904

AUTHOR'S NOTE

After the publication of "The Wonderful Wizard of Oz" I began to receive letters from children, telling me of their pleasure in reading the story and asking me to "write something more" about the Scarecrow and the Tin Woodman. At first I considered these little letters, frank and earnest though they were, in the light of pretty compliments; but the letters continued to come during succeeding months, and even years.

Finally I promised one little girl, who made a long journey to see me and prefer her request,—and she is a "Dorothy," by the way—that when a thousand little girls had written me a thousand little letters asking for another story of the Scarecrow and the Tin Woodman, I would write the book. Either little Dorothy was a fairy in disguise, and waved her magic wand, or the success of the stage production of "The Wizard of Oz" made new friends for the story. For the thousand letters reached their destination long since—and many more followed them.

And now, although pleading guilty to a long delay, I have kept my promise in this book.

L. FRANK BAUM.

Chicago, June, 1904.

To those excellent
good fellows
and
eminent comedians
David C.
Montgomery
and
Fred A. Stone
whose clever
personations of
the
Tin Woodman
and the
Scarecrow
have delighted
thousands of
children
throughout the land,
this book is
gratefully dedicated
by
THE AUTHOR

LIST OF CHAPTERS

Tip Manufactures a Pumpkinhead

In the Country of the Gillikins, which is at the North of the Land of Oz, lived a youth called Tip. There was more to his name than that, for old Mombi often declared that his whole name was Tippetarius; but no one was expected to say such a long word when "Tip" would do just as well.

This boy remembered nothing of his parents, for he had been brought when quite young to be reared by the old woman known as Mombi, whose reputation, I am sorry to say, was none of the best. For the Gillikin people had reason to suspect her of indulging in magical arts, and therefore hesitated to associate with her.

Mombi was not exactly a Witch, because the Good Witch who ruled that part of the Land of Oz had forbidden any other Witch to exist in her dominions. So Tip's guardian, however much she might aspire to working magic, realized it was unlawful to be more than a Sorceress, or at most a Wizardess.

Tip was made to carry wood from the forest, that the old woman might boil her pot. He also worked in the corn-fields, hoeing and husking; and he fed the pigs and milked the four-horned cow that was Mombi's especial pride.

But you must not suppose he worked all the time, for he felt that would be bad for him. When sent to the forest Tip often climbed trees for birds' eggs or amused himself chasing the fleet white rabbits or fishing in the brooks with bent pins. Then he would hastily gather his armful of wood and carry it home. And when he was supposed to be working in the corn-fields, and the tall stalks hid him from Mombi's view, Tip would often dig in the gopher holes, or— if the mood seized him—lie upon his back between the rows of corn and take a nap. So, by taking care not to exhaust his strength, he grew as strong and rugged as a boy may be.

Mombi's curious magic often frightened her neighbors, and they treated her shyly, yet respectfully, because of her weird powers. But Tip frankly hated her, and took no pains to hide his feelings. Indeed, he sometimes showed less respect for the old woman than he should have done, considering she was his guardian.

There were pumpkins in Mombi's corn-fields, lying golden red among the rows of green stalks; and these had been planted and carefully tended that the four-horned cow might eat of them in the winter time. But one day, after the corn had all been cut and stacked, and Tip was carrying the pumpkins to the stable, he took a notion to make a "Jack Lantern" and try to give the old woman a fright with it.

So he selected a fine, big pumpkin—one with a lustrous, orange-red color—and began carving it. With the point of his knife he made two round eyes, a three-cornered nose, and a mouth shaped like a new moon. The face, when completed, could not have been considered strictly beautiful; but it wore a smile so big and broad, and was so jolly in expression, that even Tip laughed as he looked admiringly at his work.

The child had no playmates, so he did not know that boys often dig out the inside of a "pumpkin-jack," and in the space thus made put a lighted candle to render the face more startling; but he conceived an idea of his own that promised to be quite as effective. He decided to manufacture the form of a man, who would wear this pumpkin head, and to stand it in a place where old Mombi would meet it face to face.

"And then," said Tip to himself, with a laugh, "she'll squeal louder than the brown pig does when I pull her tail, and shiver with fright worse than I did last year when I had the ague!"

He had plenty of time to accomplish this task, for Mombi had gone to a village—to buy groceries, she said—and it was a journey of at least two days.

So he took his axe to the forest, and selected some stout, straight saplings, which he cut down and trimmed of all their twigs and leaves. From these he would make the arms, and legs, and feet of his man. For the body he stripped a sheet of thick bark from around a big tree, and with much labor fashioned it into a cylinder of about the right size, pinning the edges together with wooden pegs. Then, whistling happily as he worked, he carefully jointed the limbs and fastened them to the body with pegs whittled into shape with his knife.

By the time this feat had been accomplished it began to grow dark, and Tip remembered he must milk the cow and feed the pigs. So he picked up his wooden man and carried it back to the house with him.

During the evening, by the light of the fire in the kitchen, Tip carefully rounded all the edges of the joints and smoothed the rough places in a neat and workmanlike manner. Then he stood the

figure up against the wall and admired it. It seemed remarkably tall, even for a full-grown man; but that was a good point in a small boy's eyes, and Tip did not object at all to the size of his creation.

Next morning, when he looked at his work again, Tip saw he had forgotten to give the dummy a neck, by means of which he might fasten the pumpkin head to the body. So he went again to the forest, which was not far away, and chopped from a tree several pieces of wood with which to complete his work. When he returned he fastened a cross-piece to the upper end of the body, making a hole through the center to hold upright the neck. The bit of wood which formed this neck was also sharpened at the upper end, and when all was ready Tip put on the pumpkin head, pressing it well down onto the neck, and found that it fitted very well. The head could be turned to one side or the other, as he pleased, and the hinges of the arms and legs allowed him to place the dummy in any position he desired.

"Now, that," declared Tip, proudly, "is really a very fine man, and it ought to frighten several screeches out of old Mombi! But it would be much more lifelike if it were properly dressed."

To find clothing seemed no easy task; but Tip boldly ransacked the great chest in which Mombi kept all her keepsakes and treasures, and at the very bottom he discovered some purple trousers, a red shirt and a pink vest which was dotted with white spots. These he carried away to his man and succeeded, although the garments did not fit very well, in dressing the creature in a jaunty fashion. Some knit stockings belonging to Mombi and a much worn pair of his own shoes completed the man's apparel, and Tip was so delighted that he danced up and down and laughed aloud in boyish ecstacy.

"I must give him a name!" he cried. "So good a man as this must surely have a name. I believe," he added, after a moment's thought, "I will name the fellow 'Jack Pumpkinhead'!"

The Marvelous Powder of Life

After considering the matter carefully, Tip decided that the best place to locate Jack would be at the bend in the road, a little way from the house. So he started to carry his man there, but found him heavy and rather awkward to handle. After dragging the creature a short distance Tip stood him on his feet, and by first bending the joints of one leg, and then those of the other,—at the same time pushing from behind,—the boy managed to induce Jack to walk to the bend in the road. It was not accomplished without a few tumbles, and Tip really worked harder than he ever had in the fields or forest; but a love of mischief urged him on, and it pleased him to test the cleverness of his workmanship.

"Jack's all right, and works fine!" he said to himself, panting with the unusual exertion. But just then he discovered the man's left arm had fallen off in the journey; so he went back to find it, and afterward, by whittling a new and stouter pin for the shoulder-joint, he repaired the injury so successfully that the arm was stronger than before. Tip also noticed that Jack's pumpkin head had twisted around until it faced his back; but this was easily remedied. When, at last, the man was set up facing the turn in the path where old Mombi was to appear, he looked natural enough to be a fair imitation of a Gillikin farmer,—and unnatural enough to startle anyone that came on him unawares.

As it was yet too early in the day to expect the old woman to return home, Tip went down into the valley below the farm-house and began to gather nuts from the trees that grew there.

However, old Mombi returned earlier than usual. She had met a crooked wizard who resided in a lonely cave in the mountains, and had traded several important secrets of magic with him. Having in this way secured three new recipes, four magical powders and a selection of herbs of wonderful power and potency, she hobbled home as fast as she could, in order to test her new sorceries.

So intent was Mombi on the treasures she had gained that when she turned the bend in the road and caught a glimpse of the man, she merely nodded and said:

"Good evening, sir."

But, a moment after, noting that the person did not move or reply, she cast a shrewd glance into his face and discovered his pumpkin head—elaborately carved by Tip's jack-knife.

"Heh!" ejaculated Mombi, giving a sort of grunt; "that rascally boy has been playing tricks again! Very good! ve—ry *good*! I'll beat him black-and-blue for trying to scare me in this fashion!"

Angrily she raised her stick to smash in the grinning pumpkin head of the dummy; but a sudden thought made her pause, the uplifted stick left motionless in the air.

"Why, here is a good chance to try my new powder!" said she, eagerly. "And then I can tell whether that crooked wizard has fairly traded secrets, or whether he has fooled me as wickedly as I fooled him."

So she set down her basket and began fumbling in it for one of the precious powders she had obtained.

While Mombi was thus occupied Tip strolled back, with his pockets full of nuts, and discovered the old woman standing beside his man and apparently not the least bit frightened by it.

At first he was greatly disappointed; but the next moment he became curious to know what Mombi was going to do. So he hid be-

"OLD MOMBI DANCED AROUND HIM"

hind a hedge, where he could see without being seen, and prepared to watch.

After some search the woman drew from her basket an old pepper-box, upon the faded label of which the wizard had written with a lead-pencil: "Powder of Life."

"Ah—here it is!" she cried, joyfully. "And now let us see if it is potent. The stingy wizard didn't give me much of it, but I guess there's enough for two or three doses."

Tip was much surprised when he overheard this speech. Then he saw old Mombi raise her arm and sprinkle the powder from the box over the pumpkin head of his man Jack. She did this in the same way one would pepper a baked potato, and the powder sifted down from Jack's head and scattered over the red shirt and pink waistcoat and purple trousers Tip had dressed him in, and a portion even fell upon the patched and worn shoes.

Then, putting the pepper-box back into the basket, Mombi lifted her left hand, with its little finger pointed upward, and said:

"Weaugh!"

Then she lifted her right hand, with the thumb pointed upward, and said:

"Teaugh!"

Then she lifted both hands, with all the fingers and thumbs spread out, and cried:

"Peaugh!"

Jack Pumpkinhead stepped back a pace, at this, and said in a reproachful voice:

"Don't yell like that! Do you think I'm deaf?"

Old Mombi danced around him, frantic with delight.

"He lives!" she screamed: "he lives! he lives!"

Then she threw her stick into the air and caught it as it came down; and she hugged herself with both arms, and tried to do a step of a jig; and all the time she repeated, rapturously:

"He lives!—he lives!—he lives!"

Now you may well suppose that Tip observed all this with amazement.

At first he was so frightened and horrified that he wanted to run away, but his legs trembled and shook so badly that he couldn't. Then it struck him as a very funny thing for Jack to come to life, especially as the expression on his pumpkin face was so droll and comical it excited laughter on the instant. So, recovering from his first fear, Tip began to laugh; and the merry peals reached old Mombi's ears and made her hobble quickly to the hedge, where she seized Tip's collar and dragged him back to where she had left her basket and the pumpkin-headed man.

"You naughty, sneaking, wicked boy!" she exclaimed, furiously; "I'll teach you to spy out my secrets and to make fun of me!"

"I wasn't making fun of you," protested Tip. "I was laughing at old Pumpkinhead! Look at him! Isn't he a picture, though?"

"I hope you are not reflecting on my personal appearance," said Jack; and it was so funny to hear his grave voice, while his face continued to wear its jolly smile, that Tip again burst into a peal of laughter.

Even Mombi was not without a curious interest in the man her magic had brought to life; for, after staring at him intently, she presently asked:

"What do you know?"

"Well, that is hard to tell," replied Jack. "For although I feel that I know a tremendous lot, I am not yet aware how much there is in the world to find out about. It will take me a little time to discover whether I am very wise or very foolish."

"To be sure," said Mombi, thoughtfully.

"But what are you going to do with him, now he is alive?" asked Tip, wondering.

"I must think it over," answered Mombi. "But we must get home at once, for it is growing dark. Help the Pumpkinhead to walk."

"Never mind me," said Jack; "I can walk as well as you can. Haven't I got legs and feet, and aren't they jointed?"

"Are they?" asked the woman, turning to Tip.

"Of course they are; I made 'em myself," returned the boy, with pride.

So they started for the house; but when they reached the farm yard old Mombi led the pumpkin man to the cow stable and shut

OLD MOMBI PUTS JACK IN THE STABLE.

him up in an empty stall, fastening the door securely on the outside.

"I've got to attend to you, first," she said, nodding her head at Tip.

Hearing this, the boy became uneasy; for he knew Mombi had a bad and revengeful heart, and would not hesitate to do any evil thing.

They entered the house. It was a round, dome-shaped structure, as are nearly all the farm-houses in the Land of Oz.

Mombi bade the boy light a candle, while she put her basket in a cupboard and hung her cloak on a peg. Tip obeyed quickly, for he was afraid of her.

After the candle had been lighted Mombi ordered him to build a fire in the hearth, and while Tip was thus engaged the old woman ate her supper. When the flames began to crackle the boy came to her and asked a share of the bread and cheese; but Mombi refused him.

"I'm hungry!" said Tip, in a sulky tone.

"You won't be hungry long," replied Mombi, with a grim look.

The boy didn't like this speech, for it sounded like a threat; but he happened to remember he had nuts in his pocket, so he cracked some of those and ate them while the woman rose, shook the crumbs from her apron, and hung above the fire a small black kettle.

Then she measured out equal parts of milk and vinegar and poured them into the kettle. Next she produced several packets of herbs and powders and began adding a portion of each to the contents of the kettle. Occasionally she would draw near the candle and read from a yellow paper the recipe of the mess she was concocting.

As Tip watched her his uneasiness increased.

"What is that for?" he asked.

"For you," returned Mombi, briefly.

Tip wriggled around upon his stool and stared awhile at the kettle, which was beginning to bubble. Then he would glance at the stern and wrinkled features of the witch and wish he were any place but in that dim and smoky kitchen, where even the shadows cast by the candle upon the wall were enough to give one the horrors. So an hour passed away, during which the silence was only broken by the bubbling of the pot and the hissing of the flames.

Finally, Tip spoke again.

"Have I got to drink that stuff?" he asked, nodding toward the pot.

"Yes," said Mombi.

"What'll it do to me?" asked Tip.

"If it's properly made," replied Mombi, "it will change or transform you into a marble statue."

Tip groaned, and wiped the perspiration from his forehead with his sleeve.

"I don't want to be a marble statue!" he protested.

"That doesn't matter; I want you to be one," said the old woman, looking at him severely.

"What use'll I be then?" asked Tip. "There won't be any one to work for you."

"I'll make the Pumpkinhead work for me," said Mombi.

Again Tip groaned.

"Why don't you change me into a goat, or a chicken?" he asked, anxiously. "You can't do anything with a marble statue."

"Oh, yes; I can," returned Mombi. "I'm going to plant a flower garden, next Spring, and I'll put you in the middle of it, for an ornament. I wonder I haven't thought of that before; you've been a bother to me for years."

At this terrible speech Tip felt the beads of perspiration starting all over his body; but he sat still and shivered and looked anxiously at the kettle.

"Perhaps it won't work," he muttered, in a voice that sounded weak and discouraged.

"Oh, I think it will," answered Mombi, cheerfully. "I seldom make a mistake."

Again there was a period of silence—a silence so long and gloomy that when Mombi finally lifted the kettle from the fire it was close to midnight.

"You cannot drink it until it has become quite cold," announced the old witch—for in spite of the law she had acknowledged prac-

"I DON'T WANT TO BE A MARBLE STATUE."

tising witchcraft. "We must both go to bed now, and at daybreak I will call you and at once complete your transformation into a marble statue."

With this she hobbled into her room, bearing the steaming kettle with her, and Tip heard her close and lock the door.

The boy did not go to bed, as he had been commanded to do, but still sat glaring at the embers of the dying fire.

The Flight of the Fugitives

Tip reflected.

"It's a hard thing, to be a marble statue," he thought, rebelliously, "and I'm not going to stand it. For years I've been a bother to her, she says; so she's going to get rid of me. Well, there's an easier way than to become a statue. No boy could have any fun forever standing in the middle of a flower garden! I'll run away, that's what I'll do—and I may as well go before she makes me drink that nasty stuff in the kettle."

He waited until the snores of the old witch announced she was fast asleep, and then he arose softly and went to the cupboard to find something to eat.

"No use starting on a journey without food," he decided, searching upon the narrow shelves.

He found some crusts of bread; but he had to look into Mombi's basket to find the cheese she had brought from the village. While turning over the contents of the basket he came upon the pepper-box which contained the "Powder of Life."

"I may as well take this with me," he thought, "or Mombi'll be using it to make more mischief with." So he put the box in his pocket, together with the bread and cheese.

Then he cautiously left the house and latched the door behind him. Outside both moon and stars shone brightly, and the night seemed peaceful and inviting after the close and ill-smelling kitchen.

"I'll be glad to get away," said Tip, softly; "for I never did like that old woman. I wonder how I ever came to live with her."

He was walking slowly toward the road when a thought made him pause.

"I don't like to leave Jack Pumpkinhead to the tender mercies of old Mombi," he muttered. "And Jack belongs to me, for I made him—even if the old witch did bring him to life."

He retraced his steps to the cow-stable and opened the door of the stall where the pumpkin-headed man had been left.

Jack was standing in the middle of the stall, and by the moonlight Tip could see he was smiling just as jovially as ever.

"Come on!" said the boy, beckoning.

"Where to?" asked Jack.

"You'll know as soon as I do," answered Tip, smiling sympathetically into the pumpkin face. "All we've got to do now is to tramp."

"Very well," returned Jack, and walked awkwardly out of the stable and into the moonlight.

Tip turned toward the road and the man followed him. Jack walked with a sort of limp, and occasionally one of the joints of his legs would turn backward, instead of frontwise, almost causing him to tumble. But the Pumpkinhead was quick to notice this, and began to take more pains to step carefully; so that he met with few accidents.

Tip led him along the path without stopping an instant. They could not go very fast, but they walked steadily; and by the time the moon sank away and the sun peeped over the hills they had travelled so great a distance that the boy had no reason to fear pursuit from the old witch. Moreover, he had turned first into one path, and then into another, so that should anyone follow them it would prove very difficult to guess which way they had gone, or where to seek them.

Fairly satisfied that he had escaped—for a time, at least—being turned into a marble statue, the boy stopped his companion and seated himself upon a rock by the roadside.

"TIP LED HIM ALONG THE PATH."

"Let's have some breakfast," he said.

Jack Pumpkinhead watched Tip curiously, but refused to join in the repast.

"I don't seem to be made the same way you are," he said.

"I know you are not," returned Tip; "for I made you."

"Oh! Did you?" asked Jack.

"Certainly. And put you together. And carved your eyes and nose and ears and mouth," said Tip, proudly. "And dressed you."

Jack looked at his body and limbs critically.

"It strikes me you made a very good job of it," he remarked.

"Just so-so," replied Tip, modestly; for he began to see certain defects in the construction of his man. "If I'd known we were going to travel together I might have been a little more particular."

"Why, then," said the Pumpkinhead, in a tone that expressed surprise, "you must be my creator—my parent—my father!"

"Or your inventor," replied the boy with a laugh. "Yes, my son; I really believe I am!"

"Then I owe you obedience," continued the man, "and you owe me—support."

"That's it, exactly," declared Tip, jumping up. "So let us be off."

"Where are we going?" asked Jack, when they had resumed their journey.

"I'm not exactly sure," said the boy; "but I believe we are headed South, and that will bring us, sooner or later, to the Emerald City."

"What city is that?" enquired the Pumpkinhead.

"Why, it's the center of the Land of Oz, and the biggest town in all the country. I've never been there, myself, but I've heard all about its history. It was built by a mighty and wonderful Wizard named Oz, and everything there is of a green color—just as everything in this Country of the Gillikins is of a purple color."

"Is everything here purple?" asked Jack.

"Of course it is. Can't you see?" returned the boy.

"I believe I must be color-blind," said the Pumpkinhead, after staring about him.

"Well, the grass is purple, and the trees are purple, and the houses and fences are purple," explained Tip. "Even the mud in the roads is purple. But in the Emerald City everything is green that is purple here. And in the Country of the Munchkins, over at the East, everything is blue; and in the South country of the Quadlings everything is red; and in the West country of the Winkies, where the Tin Woodman rules, everything is yellow."

"Oh!" said Jack. Then, after a pause, he asked: "Did you say a Tin Woodman rules the Winkies?"

"Yes; he was one of those who helped Dorothy to destroy the Wicked Witch of the West, and the Winkies were so grateful that they invited him to become their ruler,—just as the people of the Emerald City invited the Scarecrow to rule them."

"Dear me!" said Jack. "I'm getting confused with all this history. Who is the Scarecrow?"

"Another friend of Dorothy's," replied Tip.

"And who is Dorothy?"

"She was a girl that came here from Kansas, a place in the big, outside World. She got blown to the Land of Oz by a cyclone, and while she was here the Scarecrow and the Tin Woodman accompanied her on her travels."

"And where is she now?" inquired the Pumpkinhead.

"Glinda the Good, who rules the Quadlings, sent her home again," said the boy.

"Oh. And what became of the Scare-crow?"

"I told you. He rules the Emerald City," answered Tip.

"I thought you said it was ruled by a wonderful Wiz-ard," objected Jack, seeming more and more confused.

"Well, so I did. Now, pay attention,

and I'll explain it," said Tip, speaking slowly and looking the smiling Pumpkinhead squarely in the eye. "Dorothy went to the Emerald City to ask the Wizard to send her back to Kansas; and the Scarecrow and the Tin Woodman went with her. But the Wizard couldn't send her back, because he wasn't so much of a Wizard as he might have been. And then they got angry at the Wizard, and threatened to expose him; so the Wizard made a big balloon and escaped in it, and no one has ever seen him since."

"Now, that is very interesting history," said Jack, well pleased; "and I understand it perfectly—all but the explanation."

"I'm glad you do," responded Tip. "After the Wizard was gone, the people of the Emerald City made His Majesty, the Scarecrow, their King; and I have heard that he became a very popular ruler."

"Are we going to see this queer King?" asked Jack, with interest.

"I think we may as well," replied the boy; "unless you have something better to do."

"Oh, no, dear father," said the Pumpkinhead. "I am quite willing to go wherever you please."

Tip Makes an Experiment in Magic

The boy, small and rather delicate in appearance, seemed somewhat embarrassed at being called "father" by the tall, awkward, pumpkin-headed man; but to deny the relationship would involve another long and tedious explanation; so he changed the subject by asking, abruptly:

"Are you tired?"

"Of course not!" replied the other. "But," he continued, after a pause, "it is quite certain I shall wear out my wooden joints if I keep on walking."

Tip reflected, as they journeyed on, that this was true. He began to regret that he had not constructed the wooden limbs more carefully and substantially. Yet how could he ever have guessed that the man he had made merely to scare old Mombi with would be brought to life by means of a magical powder contained in an old pepper-box?

So he ceased to reproach himself, and began to think how he might yet remedy the deficiencies of Jack's weak joints.

While thus engaged they came to the edge of a wood, and the boy sat down to rest upon an old saw-horse that some wood-cutter had left there.

"Why don't you sit down?" he asked the Pumpkinhead.

"Won't it strain my joints?" inquired the other.

"Of course not. It'll rest them," declared the boy.

So Jack tried to sit down; but as soon as he bent his joints farther than usual they gave way altogether, and he came clattering to the ground with such a crash that Tip feared he was entirely ruined.

He rushed to the man, lifted him to his feet, straightened his arms and legs, and felt of his head to see if by chance it had become cracked. But Jack seemed to be in pretty good shape, after all, and Tip said to him:

"I guess you'd better remain standing, hereafter. It seems the safest way."

"Very well, dear father; just as you say," replied the smiling Jack, who had been in no wise confused by his tumble.

Tip sat down again. Presently the Pumpkinhead asked:

"What is that thing you are sitting on?"

"Oh, this is a horse," replied the boy, carelessly.

"What is a horse?" demanded Jack.

"A horse? Why, there are two kinds of horses," returned Tip, slightly puzzled how to explain. "One kind of horse is alive, and has four legs and a head and a tail. And people ride upon its back."

"I understand," said Jack, cheerfully. "That's the kind of horse you are now sitting on."

"No, it isn't," answered Tip, promptly.

"Why not? That one has four legs, and a head, and a tail."

Tip looked at the saw-horse more carefully, and found that the Pumpkinhead was right. The body had been formed from a tree-trunk, and a branch had been left sticking up at one end that looked very much like a tail. In the other end were two big knots that resembled eyes, and a place had been chopped away that might easily be mistaken for the horse's mouth. As for the legs, they were four

THE MAGICAL POWDER OF LIFE

straight limbs cut from trees and stuck fast into the body, being spread wide apart so that the saw-horse would stand firmly when a log was laid across it to be sawed.

"This thing resembles a real horse more than I imagined," said Tip, trying to explain. "But a real horse is alive, and trots and prances and eats oats, while this is nothing more than a dead horse, made of wood, and used to saw logs upon."

"If it were alive, wouldn't it trot, and prance, and eat oats?" inquired the Pumpkinhead.

"It would trot and prance, perhaps; but it wouldn't eat oats," replied the boy, laughing at the idea. "And of course it can't ever be alive, because it is made of wood."

"So am I," answered the man.

Tip looked at him in surprise.

"Why, so you are!" he exclaimed. "And the magic powder that brought you to life is here in my pocket."

He brought out the pepper-box, and eyed it curiously.

"I wonder," said he, musingly, "if it would bring the saw-horse to life."

"If it would," returned Jack, calmly—for nothing seemed to surprise him—"I could ride on its back, and that would save my joints from wearing out."

"I'll try it!" cried the boy, jumping up. "But I wonder if I can remember the words old Mombi said, and the way she held her hands up."

He thought it over for a minute, and as he had watched carefully from the hedge every motion of the old witch, and listened to her words, he believed he could repeat exactly what she had said and done.

So he began by sprinkling some of the magic Powder of Life from the pepper-box upon the body of the saw-horse. Then he lifted his left hand, with the little finger pointing upward, and said: "Weaugh!"

"What does that mean, dear father?" asked Jack, curiously.

"I don't know," answered Tip. Then he lifted his right hand, with the thumb pointing upward, and said: "Teaugh!"

"What's that, dear father?" inquired Jack.

"It means you must keep quiet!" replied the boy, provoked at being interrupted at so important a moment.

"How fast I am learning!" remarked the Pumpkinhead, with his eternal smile.

Tip now lifted both hands above his head, with all the fingers and thumbs spread out, and cried in a loud voice: "Peaugh!"

Immediately the saw-horse moved, stretched its legs, yawned with its chopped-out mouth, and shook a few grains of the powder off its back. The rest of the powder seemed to have vanished into the body of the horse.

"Good!" called Jack, while the boy looked on in astonishment. "You are a very clever sorcerer, dear father!"

The Awakening of the Saw-Horse

The Saw-Horse, finding himself alive, seemed even more astonished than Tip. He rolled his knotty eyes from side to side, taking a first wondering view of the world in which he had now so important an existence. Then he tried to look at himself; but he had, indeed, no neck to turn; so that in the endeavor to see his body he kept circling around and around, without catching even a glimpse of it. His legs were stiff and awkward, for there were no knee-joints in them; so that presently he bumped against Jack Pumpkinhead and sent that personage tumbling upon the moss that lined the roadside.

Tip became alarmed at this accident, as well as at the persistence of the Saw-Horse in prancing around in a circle; so he called out:

"Whoa! Whoa, there!"

The Saw-Horse paid no attention whatever to this command, and the next instant brought one of his wooden legs down upon Tip's foot so forcibly that the boy danced away in pain to a safer distance, from where he again yelled:

"Whoa! Whoa, I say!"

Jack had now managed to raise himself to a sitting position, and he looked at the Saw-Horse with much interest.

"I don't believe the animal can hear you," he remarked.

"I shout loud enough, don't I?" answered Tip, angrily.

"Yes; but the horse has no ears," said the smiling Pumpkinhead.

"Sure enough!" exclaimed Tip, noting the fact for the first time. "How, then, am I going to stop him?"

But at that instant the Saw-Horse stopped himself, having concluded it was impossible to see his own body. He saw Tip, however, and came close to the boy to observe him more fully.

It was really comical to see the creature walk; for it moved the legs on its right side together, and those on its left side together, as a pacing horse does; and that made its body rock sidewise, like a cradle.

Tip patted it upon the head, and said "Good boy! Good boy!" in a coaxing tone; and the Saw-Horse pranced away to examine with its bulging eyes the form of Jack Pumpkinhead.

"I must find a halter for him," said Tip; and having made a search in his pocket he produced a roll of strong cord. Unwinding this, he approached the Saw-Horse and tied the cord around its neck, afterward fastening the other end to a large tree. The Saw-Horse, not understanding the action, stepped backward and snapped the string easily; but it made no attempt to run away.

"He's stronger than I thought," said the boy, "and rather obstinate, too."

"Why don't you make him some ears?" asked Jack. "Then you can tell him what to do."

"That's a splendid idea!" said Tip. "How did you happen to think of it?"

"Why, I didn't think of it," answered the Pumpkinhead; "I didn't need to, for it's the simplest and easiest thing to do."

So Tip got out his knife and fashioned some ears out of the bark of a small tree.

"I mustn't make them too big," he said, as he whittled, "or our horse would become a donkey."

"How is that?" inquired Jack, from the roadside.

"Why, a horse has bigger ears than a man; and a donkey has bigger ears than a horse," explained Tip.

"Then, if my ears were longer, would I be a horse?" asked Jack.

"My friend, said Tip, gravely, "you'll never be anything but a Pumpkinhead, no matter how big your ears are."

"Oh," returned Jack, nodding; "I think I understand."

"If you do, you're a wonder," remarked the boy; "but there's no harm in *thinking* you understand. I guess these ears are ready now. Will you hold the horse while I stick them on?"

"Certainly, if you'll help me up," said Jack.

So Tip raised him to his feet, and the Pumpkinhead went to the horse and held its head while the boy bored two holes in it with his knife-blade and inserted the ears.

"They make him look very handsome," said Jack, admiringly.

But those words, spoken close to the Saw-Horse, and being the first sounds he had ever heard, so startled the animal that he made a bound forward and tumbled Tip on one side and Jack on the other. Then he continued to rush forward as if frightened by the clatter of his own foot-steps.

"Whoa!" shouted Tip, picking himself up; "whoa! you idiot—whoa!"

The Saw-Horse would probably have paid no attention to this, but just then it stepped a leg into a gopher-hole and stumbled head-over-heels to the ground, where it lay upon its back, frantically waving its four legs in the air.

Tip ran up to it.

"You're a nice sort of a horse, I must say!" he exclaimed. "Why didn't you stop when I yelled 'whoa'?"

"Does 'whoa' mean to stop?" asked the Saw-Horse, in a surprised voice, as it rolled its eyes upward to look at the boy.

"Of course it does," answered Tip.

"And a hole in the ground means to stop, also, doesn't it?" continued the horse.

"To be sure; unless you step over it," said Tip.

"What a strange place this is," the creature exclaimed, as if amazed. "What am I doing here, anyway?"

"DO KEEP THOSE LEGS STILL."

"Why, I've brought you to life," answered the boy; "but it won't hurt you any, if you mind me and do as I tell you."

"Then I will do as you tell me," replied the Saw-Horse, humbly. "But what happened to me, a moment ago? I don't seem to be just right, someway."

"You're upside down," explained Tip. "But just keep those legs still a minute and I'll set you right side up again."

"How many sides have I?" asked the creature, wonderingly.

"Several," said Tip, briefly. "But do keep those legs still."

The Saw-Horse now became quiet, and held its legs rigid; so that Tip, after several efforts, was able to roll him over and set him upright.

"Ah, I seem all right now," said the queer animal, with a sigh.

"One of your ears is broken," Tip announced, after a careful examination. "I'll have to make a new one."

Then he led the Saw-Horse back to where Jack was vainly struggling to regain his feet, and after assisting the Pumpkinhead to stand upright Tip whittled out a new ear and fastened it to the horse's head.

"Now," said he, addressing his steed, "pay attention to what I'm going to tell you. 'Whoa!' means to stop; 'Get-Up!' means to walk forward; 'Trot!' means to go as fast as you can. Understand?"

"I believe I do," returned the horse.

"Very good. We are all going on a journey to the Emerald City, to see His Majesty, the Scarecrow; and Jack Pumpkinhead is going to ride on your back, so he won't wear out his joints."

"I don't mind," said the Saw-Horse. "Anything that suits you suits me."

Then Tip assisted Jack to get upon the horse.

"Hold on tight," he cautioned, "or you may fall off and crack your pumpkin head."

"That would be horrible!" said Jack, with a shudder. "What shall I hold on to?"

"Why, hold on to his ears," replied Tip, after a moment's hesitation.

"Don't do that!" remonstrated the Saw-Horse; "for then I can't hear."

That seemed reasonable, so Tip tried to think of something else.

"I'll fix it!" said he, at length. He went into the wood and cut a short length of limb from a young, stout tree. One end of this he sharpened to a point, and then he dug a hole in the back of the Saw-Horse, just behind its head. Next he brought a piece of rock from the road and hammered the post firmly into the animal's back.

"Stop! Stop!" shouted the horse; "you're jarring me terribly."

"Does it hurt?" asked the boy.

"Not exactly hurt," answered the animal; "but it makes me quite nervous to be jarred."

"Well, it's all over now," said Tip, encouragingly. "Now, Jack, be sure to hold fast to this post, and then you can't fall off and get smashed."

So Jack held on tight, and Tip said to the horse:

"Get-up."

The obedient creature at once walked forward, rocking from side to side as he raised his feet from the ground.

Tip walked beside the Saw-Horse, quite content with this addition to their party. Presently he began to whistle.

"What does that sound mean?" asked the horse.

"Don't pay any attention to it," said Tip. "I'm just whistling, and that only means I'm pretty well satisfied."

"I'd whistle myself, if I could push my lips together," remarked Jack. "I fear, dear father, that in some respects I am sadly lacking."

After journeying on for some distance the narrow path they were following turned into a broad roadway, paved with yellow brick. By the side of the road Tip noticed a sign-post that read:

"NINE MILES TO THE EMERALD CITY."

But it was now growing dark, so he decided to camp for the night by the roadside and to resume the journey next morning by day-break. He led the Saw-Horse to a grassy mound upon which grew several bushy trees, and carefully assisted the Pumpkinhead to alight.

"DOES IT HURT?" ASKED THE BOY.

"I think I'll lay you upon the ground, overnight," said the boy. "You will be safer that way."

"How about me?" asked the Saw-Horse.

"It won't hurt you to stand," replied Tip; "and, as you can't sleep, you may as well watch out and see that no one comes near to disturb us."

Then the boy stretched himself upon the grass beside the Pumpkinhead, and being greatly wearied by the journey was soon fast asleep.

Jack Pumpkinhead's Ride to the Emerald City

At daybreak Tip was awakened by the Pumpkinhead. He rubbed the sleep from his eyes, bathed in a little brook, and then ate a portion of his bread and cheese. Having thus prepared for a new day the boy said:

"Let us start at once. Nine miles is quite a distance, but we ought to reach the Emerald City by noon if no accidents happen."

So the Pumpkinhead was again perched upon the back of the Saw-Horse and the journey was resumed.

Tip noticed that the purple tint of the grass and trees had now faded to a dull lavender, and before long this lavender appeared to take on a greenish tinge that gradually brightened as they drew nearer to the great City where the Scarecrow ruled.

The little party had traveled but a short two miles upon their way when the road of yellow brick was parted by a broad and swift river. Tip was puzzled how to cross over; but after a time he discovered a man in a ferry-boat approaching from the other side of the stream.

When the man reached the bank Tip asked:

"Will you row us to the other side?"

"Yes, if you have money," returned the ferryman, whose face looked cross and disagreeable.

"But I have no money," said Tip.

"None at all?" inquired the man.

"None at all," answered the boy.

"Then I'll not break my back rowing you over," said the ferryman, decidedly.

"What a nice man!" remarked the Pumpkinhead, smilingly.

The ferryman stared at him, but made no reply. Tip was trying to think, for it was a great disappointment to him to find his journey so suddenly brought to an end.

"I must certainly get to the Emerald City," he said to the boatman; "but how can I cross the river if you do not take me?"

The man laughed, and it was not a nice laugh.

"That wooden horse will float," said he; "and you can ride him across. As for the pumpkin-headed loon who accompanies you, let him sink or swim—it won't matter greatly which."

"Don't worry about me," said Jack, smiling pleasantly upon the crabbed ferryman; "I'm sure I ought to float beautifully."

Tip thought the experiment was worth making, and the Saw-Horse, who did not know what danger meant, offered no objections whatever. So the boy led it down into the water and climbed upon its back. Jack also waded in up to his knees and grasped the tail of the horse so that he might keep his pumpkin head above the water.

"Now," said Tip, instructing the Saw-Horse, "if you wiggle your legs you will probably swim; and if you swim we shall probably reach the other side."

The Saw-Horse at once began to wiggle its legs, which acted as oars and moved the adventurers slowly across the river to the opposite side. So successful was the trip that presently they were climbing, wet and dripping, up the grassy bank.

Tip's trouser-legs and shoes were thoroughly soaked; but the Saw-Horse had floated so perfectly that from his knees up the boy was entirely dry. As for the Pumpkinhead, every stitch of his gorgeous clothing dripped water.

"The sun will soon dry us," said Tip; "and, anyhow, we are now safely across, in spite of the ferryman, and can continue our journey."

"I didn't mind swimming, at all," remarked the horse.

"Nor did I," added Jack.

They soon regained the road of yellow brick, which proved to be a continuation of the road they had left on the other side, and then Tip once more mounted the Pumpkinhead upon the back of the Saw-Horse.

"If you ride fast," said he, "the wind will help to dry your clothing. I will hold on to the horse's tail and run after you. In this way we all will become dry in a very short time."

"Then the horse must step lively," said Jack.

"I'll do my best," returned the Saw-Horse, cheerfully.

Tip grasped the end of the branch that served as tail to the Saw-Horse, and called loudly: "Get-up!"

The horse started at a good pace, and Tip followed behind. Then he decided they could go faster, so he shouted: "Trot!"

Now, the Saw-Horse remembered that this word was the command to go as fast as he could; so he began rocking along the road at a tremendous pace, and Tip had hard work—running faster than he ever had before in his life—to keep his feet.

Soon he was out of breath, and although he wanted to call "Whoa!" to the horse, he found he could not get the word out of his throat. Then the end of the tail he was clutching, being nothing more than a dead branch, suddenly broke away, and the next minute the boy was rolling in the dust of the road, while the horse and its pumpkin-headed rider dashed on and quickly disappeared in the distance.

By the time Tip had picked himself up and cleared the dust from his throat so he could say "Whoa!" there was no further need of saying it, for the horse was long since out of sight.

So he did the only sensible thing he could do. He sat down and took a good rest, and afterward began walking along the road.

"Some time I will surely overtake them," he reflected; "for the road will end at the gates of the Emerald City, and they can go no further than that."

Meantime Jack was holding fast to the post and the Saw-Horse was tearing along the road like a racer. Neither of them knew Tip was left behind, for the Pumpkinhead did not look around and the Saw-Horse couldn't.

As he rode, Jack noticed that the grass and trees had become a bright emerald-green in color, so he guessed they were nearing the Emerald City even before the tall spires and domes came into sight.

At length a high wall of green stone, studded thick with emeralds, loomed up before them; and fearing the Saw-Horse would not know enough to stop and so might smash them both against this wall, Jack ventured to cry "Whoa!" as loud as he could.

So suddenly did the horse obey that had it not been for his post Jack would have been pitched off head foremost, and his beautiful face ruined.

"That was a fast ride, dear father!" he exclaimed; and then, hearing no reply, he turned around and discovered for the first time that Tip was not there.

This apparent desertion puzzled the Pumpkinhead, and made him uneasy. And while he was wondering what had become of the boy, and what he ought to do next under such trying circumstances, the gateway in the green wall opened and a man came out.

This man was short and round, with a fat face that seemed remarkably good-natured. He was clothed all in green and wore a high, peaked green hat upon his head and green spectacles over his eyes. Bowing before the Pumpkinhead he said:

"I am the Guardian of the Gates of the Emerald City. May I inquire who you are, and what is your business?"

"My name is Jack Pumpkinhead," returned the other, smilingly; "but as to my business, I haven't the least idea in the world what it is."

The Guardian of the Gates looked surprised, and shook his head as if dissatisfied with the reply.

"What are you, a man or a pumpkin?" he asked, politely.

"Both, if you please," answered Jack.

"And this wooden horse—is it alive?" questioned the Guardian.

The horse rolled one knotty eye upward and winked at Jack. Then it gave a prance and brought one leg down on the Guardian's toes.

"Ouch!" cried the man; "I'm sorry I asked that question. But the answer is most convincing. Have you any errand, sir, in the Emerald City?"

"It seems to me that I have," replied the Pumpkinhead, seriously; "but I cannot think what it is. My father knows all about it, but he is not here."

"This is a strange affair—very strange!" declared the Guardian. "But you seem harmless. Folks do not smile so delightfully when they mean mischief."

"As for that," said Jack, "I cannot help my smile, for it is carved on my face with a jack-knife."

"Well, come with me into my room," resumed the Guardian, "and I will see what can be done for you."

So Jack rode the Saw-Horse through the gateway into a little room built into the wall. The Guardian pulled a bell-cord, and presently a very tall soldier—clothed in a green uniform—entered from the opposite door. This soldier carried a long green gun over his shoulder and had lovely green whiskers that fell quite to his knees. The Guardian at once addressed him, saying:

"Here is a strange gentleman who doesn't know why he has come to the Emerald City, or what he wants. Tell me, what shall we do with him?"

The Soldier with the Green Whiskers looked at Jack with much care and curiosity. Finally he shook his head so positively that little waves rippled down his whiskers, and then he said:

"I must take him to His Majesty, the Scarecrow."

"But what will His Majesty, the Scarecrow, do with him?" asked the Guardian of the Gates.

"That is His Majesty's business," returned the soldier. "I have troubles enough of my own. All outside troubles must be turned over to His Majesty. So put the spectacles on this fellow, and I'll take him to the royal palace."

So the Guardian opened a big box of spectacles and tried to fit a pair to Jack's great round eyes.

"I haven't a pair in stock that will really cover those eyes up," said the little man, with a sigh; "and your head is so big that I shall be obliged to tie the spectacles on."

"But why need I wear spectacles?" asked Jack.

"It's the fashion here," said the Soldier, "and they will keep you from being blinded by the glitter and glare of the gorgeous Emerald City."

"Oh!" exclaimed Jack. "Tie them on, by all means. I don't wish to be blinded."

"Nor I!" broke in the Saw-Horse; so a pair of green spectacles was quickly fastened over the bulging knots that served it for eyes.

Then the Soldier with the Green Whiskers led them through the inner gate and they at once found themselves in the main street of the magnificent Emerald City.

Sparkling green gems ornamented the fronts of the beautiful houses and the towers and turrets were all faced with emeralds. Even the green marble pavement glittered with precious stones, and it was indeed a grand and marvelous sight to one who beheld it for the first time.

However, the Pumpkinhead and the Saw-Horse, knowing nothing of wealth and beauty, paid little attention to the wonderful sights they saw through their green spectacles. They calmly followed after the green soldier and scarcely noticed the crowds of green people who stared at them in surprise. When a green dog ran out and barked at them the Saw-Horse promptly kicked at it with its wooden leg and sent the little animal howling into one of the houses; but nothing more serious than this happened to interrupt their progress to the royal palace.

The Pumpkinhead wanted to ride up the green marble steps and straight into the Scarecrow's presence; but the soldier would not permit that. So Jack dismounted, with much difficulty, and a servant led the Saw-Horse around to the rear while the Soldier with the Green Whiskers escorted the Pumpkinhead into the palace, by the front entrance.

The stranger was left in a handsomely furnished waiting room while the soldier went to announce him. It so happened that at this hour His Majesty was at leisure and greatly bored for want of something to do, so he ordered his visitor to be shown at once into his throne room.

Jack felt no fear or embarrassment at meeting the ruler of this magnificent city, for he was entirely ignorant of all worldly customs. But when he entered the room and saw for the first time His Majesty the Scarecrow seated upon his glittering throne, he stopped short in amazement.

His majesty the Scarecrow

I suppose every reader of this book knows what a scarecrow is; but Jack Pumpkinhead, never having seen such a creation, was more surprised at meeting the remarkable King of the Emerald City than by any other one experience of his brief life.

His Majesty the Scarecrow was dressed in a suit of faded blue clothes, and his head was merely a small sack stuffed with straw, upon which eyes, ears, a nose and a mouth had been rudely painted to represent a face. The clothes were also stuffed with straw, and that so unevenly or carelessly that His Majesty's legs and arms seemed more bumpy than was necessary. Upon his hands were gloves with long fingers, and these were padded with cotton. Wisps of straw stuck out from the monarch's coat and also from his neck and boot-tops. Upon his head he wore a heavy golden crown set thick with sparkling jewels, and the weight of this crown caused his brow to sag in wrinkles, giving a thoughtful expression to the painted face. Indeed, the crown alone betokened majesty; in all else the Scarecrow King was but a simple scarecrow—flimsy, awkward, and unsubstantial.

But if the strange appearance of His Majesty the Scarecrow seemed startling to Jack, no less wonderful was the form of the

Pumpkinhead to the Scarecrow. The purple trousers and pink waistcoat and red shirt hung loosely over the wooden joints Tip had manufactured, and the carved face on the pumpkin grinned perpetually, as if its wearer considered life the jolliest thing imaginable.

At first, indeed, His Majesty thought his queer visitor was laughing at him, and was inclined to resent such a liberty; but it was not without reason that the Scarecrow had attained the reputation of being the wisest personage in the Land of Oz. He made a more careful examination of his visitor, and soon discovered that Jack's features were carved into a smile and that he could not look grave if he wished to.

The King was the first to speak. After regarding Jack for some minutes he said, in a tone of wonder:

"Where on earth did you come from, and how do you happen to be alive?"

"I beg Your Majesty's pardon," returned the Pumpkinhead; "but I do not understand you."

"What don't you understand?" asked the Scarecrow.

"Why, I don't understand your language. You see, I came from the Country of the Gillikins, so that I am a foreigner."

"Ah, to be sure!" exclaimed the Scarecrow. "I myself speak the language of the Munchkins, which is also the language of the Emerald City. But you, I suppose, speak the language of the Pumpkinheads?"

"Exactly so, Your Majesty," replied the other, bowing; "so it will be impossible for us to understand one another."

"That is unfortunate, certainly," said the Scarecrow, thoughtfully. "We must have an interpreter."

"What is an interpreter?" asked Jack.

"A person who understands both my language and your own. When I say anything, the interpreter can tell you what I mean; and when you say anything the interpreter can tell me what *you* mean. For the interpreter can speak both languages as well as understand them."

"That is certainly clever," said Jack, greatly pleased at finding so simple a way out of the difficulty.

So the Scarecrow commanded the Soldier with the Green Whiskers to search among his people until he found one who understood the language of the Gillikins as well as the language of the Emerald City, and to bring that person to him at once.

When the Soldier had departed the Scarecrow said:

"Won't you take a chair while we are waiting?"

"Your Majesty forgets that I cannot understand you," replied the Pumpkinhead. "If you wish me to sit down you must make a sign for me to do so."

The Scarecrow came down from his throne and rolled an armchair to a position behind the Pumpkinhead. Then he gave Jack a sudden push that sent him sprawling upon the cushions in so awkward a fashion that he doubled up like a jack-knife, and had hard work to untangle himself.

"Did you understand that sign?" asked His Majesty, politely.

"Perfectly," declared Jack, reaching up his arms to turn his head to the front, the pumpkin having twisted around upon the stick that supported it.

"You seem hastily made," remarked the Scarecrow, watching Jack's efforts to straighten himself.

"Not more so than Your Majesty," was the frank reply.

"There is this difference between us," said the Scarecrow, "that whereas I will bend, but not break, you will break, but not bend."

At this moment the soldier returned leading a young girl by the hand. She seemed very sweet and modest, having a pretty face and beautiful green eyes and hair. A dainty green silk skirt reached to her knees, showing silk stockings embroidered with pea-pods, and green satin slippers with bunches of lettuce for decorations instead of bows or buckles. Upon her silken waist clover leaves were embroidered, and she wore a jaunty little jacket trimmed with sparkling emeralds of a uniform size.

"Why, it's little Jellia Jamb!" exclaimed the Scarecrow, as the green maiden bowed her pretty head before him. "Do you understand the language of the Gillikins, my dear?"

"Yes, Your Majesty," she answered, "for I was born in the North Country."

"Then you shall be our interpreter," said the Scarecrow, "and ex-

"HE GAVE JACK A SUDDEN PUSH."

plain to this Pumpkinhead all that I say, and also explain to me all that *he* says. Is this arrangement satisfactory?" he asked, turning toward his guest.

"Very satisfactory indeed," was the reply.

"Then ask him, to begin with," resumed the Scarecrow, turning to Jellia, "what brought him to the Emerald City."

But instead of this the girl, who had been staring at Jack, said to him:

"You are certainly a wonderful creature. Who made you?"

"A boy named Tip," answered Jack.

"What does he say?" inquired the Scarecrow. "My ears must have deceived me. What did he say?"

"He says that Your Majesty's brains seem to have come loose," replied the girl, demurely.

The Scarecrow moved uneasily upon his throne, and felt of his head with his left hand.

"What a fine thing it is to understand two different languages," he said, with a perplexed sigh. "Ask him, my dear, if he has any objection to being put in jail for insulting the ruler of the Emerald City."

"I didn't insult you!" protested Jack, indignantly.

"Tut—tut!" cautioned the Scarecrow; "wait until Jellia translates my speech. What have we got an interpreter for, if you break out in this rash way?"

"All right, I'll wait," replied the Pumpkinhead, in a surly tone—although his face smiled as genially as ever. "Translate the speech, young woman."

"His Majesty inquires if you are hungry," said Jellia.

"Oh, not at all!" answered Jack, more pleasantly. "For it is impossible for me to eat."

"It's the same way with me," remarked the Scarecrow. "What did he say, Jellia, my dear?"

"He asked if you were aware that one of your eyes is painted larger than the other," said the girl, mischievously.

"Don't you believe her, Your Majesty," cried Jack.

"Oh, I don't," answered the Scarecrow, calmly. Then, casting a sharp look at the girl, he asked:

"Are you quite certain you understand the languages of both the Gillikins and the Munchkins?"

"Quite certain, Your Majesty," said Jellia Jamb, trying hard not to laugh in the face of royalty.

"Then how is it that I seem to understand them myself?" inquired the Scarecrow.

"Because they are one and the same!" declared the girl, now laughing merrily. "Does not Your Majesty know that in all the Land of Oz but one language is spoken?"

"Is it indeed so?" cried the Scarecrow, much relieved to hear this; "then I might easily have been my own interpreter!"

"It was all my fault, Your Majesty," said Jack, looking rather foolish, "I thought we must surely speak different languages, since we came from different countries."

"This should be a warning to you never to think," returned the Scarecrow, severely. "For unless one can think wisely it is better to remain a dummy—which you most certainly are."

"I am!—I surely am!" agreed the Pumpkinhead.

"It seems to me," continued the Scarecrow, more mildly, "that your manufacturer spoiled some good pies to create an indifferent man."

"I assure Your Majesty that I did not ask to be created," answered Jack.

"Ah! It was the same in my case," said the King, pleasantly. "And so, as we differ from all ordinary people, let us become friends."

"With all my heart!" exclaimed Jack.

"What! Have you a heart?" asked the Scarecrow, surprised.

"No; that was only imaginative—I might say, a figure of speech," said the other.

"Well, your most prominent figure seems to be a figure of wood; so I must beg you to restrain an imagination which, having no brains, you have no right to exercise," suggested the Scarecrow, warningly.

"To be sure!" said Jack, without in the least comprehending.

His Majesty then dismissed Jellia Jamb and the Soldier with the Green Whiskers, and when they were gone he took his new friend by the arm and led him into the courtyard to play a game of quoits.

Gen. Jinjur's Army of Revolt

Tip was so anxious to rejoin his man Jack and the Saw-Horse that he walked a full half the distance to the Emerald City without stopping to rest. Then he discovered that he was hungry and the crackers and cheese he had provided for the journey had all been eaten.

While wondering what he should do in this emergency he came upon a girl sitting by the roadside. She wore a costume that struck the boy as being remarkably brilliant: her silken waist being of emerald green and her skirt of four distinct colors—blue in front, yellow at the left side, red at the back and purple at the right side. Fastening the waist in front were four buttons—the top one blue, the next yellow, a third red and the last purple.

The splendor of this dress was almost barbaric; so Tip was fully justified in staring at the gown for some moments before his eyes were attracted by the pretty face above it. Yes, the face was pretty enough, he decided; but it wore an expression of discontent coupled to a shade of defiance or audacity.

While the boy stared the girl looked upon him calmly. A lunch basket stood beside her, and she held a dainty sandwich in one hand and a hard-boiled egg in the other, eating with an evident appetite that aroused Tip's sympathy.

He was just about to ask a share of the luncheon when the girl stood up and brushed the crumbs from her lap.

"There!" said she; "it is time for me to go. Carry that basket for me and help yourself to its contents if you are hungry."

Tip seized the basket eagerly and began to eat, following for a time the strange girl without bothering to ask questions. She walked along before him with swift strides, and there was about her an air of decision and importance that led him to suspect she was some great personage.

Finally, when he had satisfied his hunger, he ran up beside her and tried to keep pace with her swift footsteps—a very difficult feat, for she was much taller than he, and evidently in a hurry.

"Thank you very much for the sandwiches," said Tip, as he trotted along. "May I ask your name?"

"I am General Jinjur," was the brief reply.

"Oh!" said the boy, surprised. "What sort of a General?"

"I command the Army of Revolt in this war," answered the General, with unnecessary sharpness.

"Oh!" he again exclaimed. "I didn't know there was a war."

"You were not supposed to know it," she returned, "for we have kept it a secret; and considering that our Army is composed entirely of girls," she added, with some pride, "it is surely a remarkable thing that our Revolt is not yet discovered."

"It is, indeed," acknowledged Tip. "But where is your Army?"

"About a mile from here," said General Jinjur. "The forces have assembled from all parts of the Land of Oz, at my express command. For this is the day we are to conquer His Majesty the Scarecrow, and wrest from him the throne. The Army of Revolt only awaits my coming to march upon the Emerald City."

"Well!" declared Tip, drawing a long breath, "this is certainly a surprising thing! May I ask why you wish to conquer His Majesty the Scarecrow?"

"Because the Emerald City has been ruled by men long enough, for one reason," said the girl. "Moreover, the City glitters with beautiful gems, which might far better be used for rings, bracelets and necklaces; and there is enough money in the King's treasury to buy every girl in our Army a dozen new gowns. So we intend to conquer the City and run the government to suit ourselves."

Jinjur spoke these words with an eagerness and decision that proved she was in earnest.

"But war is a terrible thing," said Tip, thoughtfully.

"This war will be pleasant," replied the girl, cheerfully.

"Many of you will be slain!" continued the boy, in an awed voice.

"Oh, no," said Jinjur. "What man would oppose a girl, or dare to harm her? And there is not an ugly face in my entire Army."

Tip laughed.

"Perhaps you are right," said he. "But the Guardian of the Gate is considered a faithful Guardian, and the King's Army will not let the City be conquered without a struggle."

"The Army is old and feeble," replied General Jinjur, scornfully. "His strength has all been used to grow whiskers, and his wife has such a temper that she has already pulled more than half of them out by the roots. When the Wonderful Wizard reigned the Soldier with the Green Whiskers was a very good Royal Army, for people feared the Wizard. But no one is afraid of the Scarecrow, so his Royal Army don't count for much in time of war."

After this conversation they proceeded some distance in silence, and before long reached a large clearing in the forest where fully four hundred young women were assembled. These were laughing and talking together as gaily as if they had gathered for a picnic instead of a war of conquest.

They were divided into four companies, and Tip noticed that all were dressed in costumes similar to that worn by General Jinjur. The only real difference was that while those girls from the Munchkin country had the blue strip in front of their skirts, those from the country of the Quadlings had the red strip in front; and those from the country of the Winkies had the yellow strip in front, and the Gillikin girls wore the purple strip in front. All had green waists, representing the Emerald City they intended to conquer, and the top button on each waist indicated by its color which country the wearer came from. The uniforms were jaunty and becoming, and quite effective when massed together.

Tip thought this strange Army bore no weapons whatever; but in this he was wrong. For each girl had stuck through the knot of her back hair two long, glittering knitting-needles.

General Jinjur immediately mounted the stump of a tree and addressed her army.

"Friends, fellow-citizens, and girls!" she said; "we are about to begin our great Revolt against the men of Oz! We march

to conquer the Emerald City—to dethrone the Scarecrow King—
to acquire thousands of gorgeous gems—to rifle the royal treasury—and to obtain power over our former oppressors!"

"Hurrah!" said those who had listened; but Tip thought most of
the Army was too much engaged in chattering to pay attention to
the words of the General.

The command to march was now given, and the girls formed
themselves into four bands, or companies, and set off with eager
strides toward the Emerald City.

The boy followed after them, carrying several baskets and wraps
and packages which various members of the Army of Revolt had
placed in his care. It was not long before they came to the green
granite walls of the City and halted before the gateway.

The Guardian of the Gate at once came out and looked at them curiously, as if a circus had come to town. He carried a bunch of keys swung round his neck by a golden chain; his hands were thrust carelessly into his pockets, and he seemed to have no idea at all that the City was threatened by rebels. Speaking pleasantly to the girls, he said:

"Good morning, my dears! What can I do for you?"

"Surrender instantly!" answered General Jinjur, standing before him and frowning as terribly as her pretty face would allow her to.

"Surrender!" echoed the man, astounded. "Why, it's impossible. It's against the law! I never heard of such a thing in my life."

"Still, you must surrender!" exclaimed the General, fiercely. "We are revolting!"

"You don't look it," said the Guardian, gazing from one to another, admiringly.

"But we are!" cried Jinjur, stamping her foot, impatiently; "and we mean to conquer the Emerald City!"

"Good gracious!" returned the surprised Guardian of the Gates; "what a nonsensical idea! Go home to your mothers, my good girls, and milk the cows and bake the bread. Don't you know it's a dangerous thing to conquer a city?"

"We are not afraid!" responded the General; and she looked so determined that it made the Guardian uneasy.

So he rang the bell for the Soldier with the Green Whiskers, and

GENERAL JINJUR AND HER ARMY CAPTURE THE CITY.

the next minute was sorry he had done so. For immediately he was surrounded by a crowd of girls who drew the knitting-needles from their hair and began jabbing them at the Guardian with the sharp points dangerously near his fat cheeks and blinking eyes.

The poor man howled loudly for mercy and made no resistance when Jinjur drew the bunch of keys from around his neck.

Followed by her Army the General now rushed to the gateway, where she was confronted by the Royal Army of Oz—which was the other name for the Soldier with the Green Whiskers.

"Halt!" he cried, and pointed his long gun full in the face of the leader.

Some of the girls screamed and ran back, but General Jinjur bravely stood her ground and said, reproachfully:

"Why, how now? Would you shoot a poor, defenceless girl?"

"No," replied the soldier; "for my gun isn't loaded."

"Not loaded?"

"No; for fear of accidents. And I've forgotten where I hid the powder and shot to load it with. But if you'll wait a short time I'll try to hunt them up."

"Don't trouble yourself," said Jinjur, cheerfully. Then she turned to her Army and cried:

"Girls, the gun isn't loaded!"

"Hooray," shrieked the rebels, delighted at this good news, and they proceeded to rush upon the Soldier with the Green Whiskers in such a crowd that it was a wonder they didn't stick the knitting-needles into one another.

But the Royal Army of Oz was too much afraid of women to meet the onslaught. He simply turned about and ran with all his might through the gate and toward the royal palace, while General Jinjur and her mob flocked into the unprotected City.

In this way was the Emerald City captured without a drop of blood being spilled. The Army of Revolt had become an Army of Conquerors!

The Scarecrow Plans an escape

Tip slipped away from the girls and followed swiftly after the Soldier with the Green Whiskers. The invading army entered the City more slowly, for they stopped to dig emeralds out of the walls and paving-stones with the points of their knitting-needles. So the Soldier and the boy reached the palace before the news had spread that the City was conquered.

The Scarecrow and Jack Pumpkinhead were still playing at quoits in the courtyard when the game was interrupted by the abrupt entrance of the Royal Army of Oz, who came flying in without his hat or gun, his clothes in sad disarray and his long beard floating a yard behind him as he ran.

"Tally one for me," said the Scarecrow, calmly. "What's wrong, my man?" he added, addressing the Soldier.

"Oh! Your Majesty—Your Majesty! The City is conquered!" gasped the Royal Army, who was all out of breath.

"This is quite sudden," said the Scarecrow. "But please go and bar all the doors and windows of the palace, while I show this Pumpkinhead how to throw a quoit."

The Soldier hastened to do this, while Tip, who had arrived at his heels, remained in the courtyard to look at the Scarecrow with wondering eyes.

His Majesty continued to throw the quoits as coolly as if no danger threatened his throne, but the Pumpkinhead, having caught sight of Tip, ambled toward the boy as fast as his wooden legs would go.

"Good afternoon, noble parent!" he cried, delightedly. "I'm glad to see you are here. That terrible Saw-Horse ran away with me."

"I suspected it," said Tip. "Did you get hurt? Are you cracked at all?"

"No, I arrived safely," answered Jack, "and His Majesty has been very kind indeed to me."

At this moment the Soldier with the Green Whiskers returned, and the Scarecrow asked:

"By the way, who has conquered me?"

"A regiment of girls, gathered from the four corners of the Land of Oz," replied the Soldier, still pale with fear.

"But where was my Standing Army at the time?" inquired His Majesty, looking at the Soldier, gravely.

"Your Standing Army was running," answered the fellow, honestly; "for no man could face the terrible weapons of the invaders."

"Well," said the Scarecrow, after a moment's thought, "I don't mind much the loss of my throne, for it's a tiresome job to rule over the Emerald City. And this crown is so heavy that it makes my head ache. But I hope the Conquerors have no intention of injuring me, just because I happen to be the King."

"I heard them say," remarked Tip, with some hesitation, "that they intend to make a rag carpet of your outside and stuff their sofa-cushions with your inside."

"Then I am really in danger," declared His Majesty, positively, "and it will be wise for me to consider a means to escape."

"Where can you go?" asked Jack Pumpkinhead.

"Why, to my friend the Tin Woodman, who rules over the Winkies, and calls himself their Emperor," was the answer. "I am sure he will protect me."

Tip was looking out of the window.

"The palace is surrounded by the enemy," said he. "It is too late to escape. They would soon tear you to pieces."

The Scarecrow sighed.

"In an emergency," he announced, "it is always a good thing to pause and reflect. Please excuse me while I pause and reflect."

"But we also are in danger," said the Pumpkinhead, anxiously. "If any of these girls understand cooking, my end is not far off!"

"Nonsense!" exclaimed the Scarecrow; "they're too busy to cook, even if they know how!"

"But should I remain here a prisoner for any length of time," protested Jack, "I'm liable to spoil."

"Ah! then you would not be fit to associate with," returned the Scarecrow. "The matter is more serious than I suspected."

"You," said the Pumpkinhead, gloomily, "are liable to live for many years. My life is necessarily short. So I must take advantage of the few days that remain to me."

"There, there! Don't worry," answered the Scarecrow, soothingly; "if you'll keep quiet long enough for me to think, I'll try to find some way for us all to escape."

So the others waited in patient silence while the Scarecrow walked to a corner and stood with his face to the wall for a good five minutes. At the end of that time he faced them with a more cheerful expression upon his painted face.

"Where is the Saw-Horse you rode here?" he asked the Pumpkinhead.

"Why, I said he was a jewel, and so your man locked him up in the royal treasury," said Jack.

"It was the only place I could think of, Your Majesty," added the Soldier, fearing he had made a blunder.

"It pleases me very much," said the Scarecrow. "Has the animal been fed?"

"Oh, yes; I gave him a heaping peck of sawdust."

"Excellent!" cried the Scarecrow. "Bring the horse here at once."

The Soldier hastened away, and presently they heard the clattering of the horse's wooden legs upon the pavement as he was led into the courtyard.

His Majesty regarded the steed critically.

"He doesn't seem especially graceful," he remarked, musingly; "but I suppose he can run?"

"He can, indeed," said Tip, gazing upon the Saw-Horse admiringly.

"Then, bearing us upon his back, he must make a dash through the ranks of the rebels and carry us to my friend the Tin Woodman," announced the Scarecrow.

"He can't carry four!" objected Tip.

"No, but he may be induced to carry three," said His Majesty. "I shall therefore leave my Royal Army behind. For, from the ease with which he was conquered, I have little confidence in his powers."

"Still, he can run," declared Tip, laughing.

"I expected this blow," said the Soldier, sulkily; "but I can bear it. I shall disguise myself by cutting off my lovely green whiskers. And, after all, it is no more dangerous to face those reckless girls than to ride this fiery, untamed wooden horse!"

"Perhaps you are right," observed His Majesty. "But, for my part, not being a soldier, I am fond of danger. Now, my boy, you must mount first. And please sit as close to the horse's neck as possible."

Tip climbed quickly to his place, and the Soldier and the Scarecrow managed to hoist the Pumpkinhead to a seat just behind him. There remained so little space for the King that he was liable to fall off as soon as the horse started.

"WE WILL MAKE A DASH TO LIBERTY OR TO DEATH."

"Fetch a clothesline," said the King to his Army, "and tie us all together. Then if one falls off we will all fall off."

And while the Soldier was gone for the clothesline His Majesty continued, "It is well for me to be careful, for my very existence is in danger."

"I have to be as careful as you do," said Jack.

"Not exactly," replied the Scarecrow; "for if anything happened to me, that would be the end of me. But if anything happened to you, they could use you for seed."

The Soldier now returned with a long line and tied all three firmly together, also lashing them to the body of the Saw-Horse; so there seemed little danger of their tumbling off.

"Now throw open the gates," commanded the Scarecrow, "and we will make a dash to liberty or to death."

The courtyard in which they were standing was located in the center of the great palace, which surrounded it on all sides. But in one place a passage led to an outer gateway, which the Soldier had barred by order of his sovereign. It was through this gateway His Majesty proposed to escape, and the Royal Army now led the Saw-Horse along the passage and unbarred the gate, which swung backward with a loud crash.

"Now," said Tip to the horse, "you must save us all. Run as fast as you can for the gate of the City, and don't let anything stop you."

"All right!" answered the Saw-Horse, gruffly, and dashed away so suddenly that Tip had to gasp for breath and hold firmly to the post he had driven into the creature's neck.

Several of the girls, who stood outside guarding the palace, were knocked over by the Saw-Horse's mad rush. Others ran screaming out of the way, and only one or two jabbed their knitting-needles frantically at the escaping prisoners. Tip got one small prick in his left arm, which smarted for an hour afterward; but the needles had no effect upon the Scarecrow or Jack Pumpkinhead, who never even suspected they were being prodded.

As for the Saw-Horse, he made a wonderful record, upsetting a fruit cart, overturning several meek looking men, and finally bowl-

THE WOODEN STEED GAVE ONE FINAL LEAP.

ing over the new Guardian of the Gate—a fussy little fat woman appointed by General Jinjur.

Nor did the impetuous charger stop then. Once outside the walls of the Emerald City he dashed along the road to the West with fast and violent leaps that shook the breath out of the boy and filled the Scarecrow with wonder.

Jack had ridden at this mad rate once before, so he devoted every effort to holding, with both hands, his pumpkin head upon its stick, enduring meantime the dreadful jolting with the courage of a philosopher.

"Slow him up! Slow him up!" shouted the Scarecrow. "My straw is all shaking down into my legs."

But Tip had no breath to speak, so the Saw-Horse continued his wild career unchecked and with unabated speed.

Presently they came to the banks of a wide river, and without a pause the wooden steed gave one final leap and launched them all in mid-air.

A second later they were rolling, splashing and bobbing about in the water, the horse struggling frantically to find a rest for its feet and its riders being first plunged beneath the rapid current and then floating upon the surface like corks.

The Journey to the Tin Woodman

Tip was well soaked and dripping water from every angle of his body; but he managed to lean forward and shout in the ear of the Saw-Horse:

"Keep still, you fool! Keep still!"

The horse at once ceased struggling and floated calmly upon the surface, its wooden body being as buoyant as a raft.

"What does that word 'fool' mean?" enquired the horse.

"It is a term of reproach," answered Tip, somewhat ashamed of the expression. "I only use it when I am angry."

"Then it pleases me to be able to call you a fool, in return," said the horse. "For I did not make the river, nor put it in our way; so only a term of reproach is fit for one who becomes angry with me for falling into the water."

"That is quite evident," replied Tip; "so I will acknowledge myself in the wrong." Then he called out to the Pumpkinhead: "Are you all right, Jack?"

There was no reply. So the boy called to the King: "Are you all right, Your Majesty?"

The Scarecrow groaned.

"I'm all wrong, somehow," he said, in a weak voice. "How very wet this water is!"

Tip was bound so tightly by the cord that he could not turn his head to look at his companions; so he said to the Saw-Horse:

"Paddle with your legs toward the shore."

The horse obeyed, and although their progress was slow they finally reached the opposite river bank at a place where it was low enough to enable the creature to scramble upon dry land.

With some difficulty the boy managed to get his knife out of his pocket and cut the cords that bound the riders to one another and to the wooden horse. He heard the Scarecrow fall to the ground with a mushy sound, and then he himself quickly dismounted and looked at his friend Jack.

The wooden body, with its gorgeous clothing, still sat upright upon the horse's back; but the pumpkin head was gone, and only the sharpened stick that served for a neck was visible. As for the Scarecrow, the straw in his body had shaken down with the jolting and packed itself into his legs and the lower part of his body—which appeared very plump and round while his upper half seemed like an empty sack. Upon his head the Scarecrow still wore the heavy crown, which had been sewed on to prevent his losing it; but the head was now so damp and limp that the weight of the gold and jewels sagged forward and crushed the painted face into a mass of wrinkles that made him look exactly like a Japanese pug dog.

Tip would have laughed—had he not been so anxious about his man Jack. But the Scarecrow, however damaged, was all there, while the pumpkin head that was so necessary to Jack's existence was missing; so the boy seized a long pole that fortunately lay near at hand and anxiously turned again toward the river.

Far out upon the waters he sighted the golden hue of the pumpkin, which gently bobbed up and down with the motion of the waves. At that moment it was quite out of Tip's reach, but after a time it floated nearer and still nearer until the boy was able to reach it with his pole and draw it to the shore. Then he brought it to the top of the bank, carefully wiped the water from its pumpkin face

TIP RESCUES JACK'S PUMPKIN HEAD.

with his handkerchief, and ran with it to Jack and replaced the head upon the man's neck.

"Dear me!" were Jack's first words. "What a dreadful experience! I wonder if water is liable to spoil pumpkins?"

Tip did not think a reply was necessary, for he knew that the Scarecrow also stood in need of his help. So he carefully removed the straw from the King's body and legs, and spread it out in the sun to dry. The wet clothing he hung over the body of the Saw-Horse.

"If water spoils pumpkins," observed Jack, with a deep sigh, "then my days are numbered."

"I've never noticed that water spoils pumpkins," returned Tip; "unless the water happens to be boiling. If your head isn't cracked, my friend, you must be in fairly good condition."

"Oh, my head isn't cracked in the least," declared Jack, more cheerfully.

"Then don't worry," retorted the boy. "Care once killed a cat."

"Then," said Jack, seriously, "I am very glad indeed that I am not a cat."

The sun was fast drying their clothing, and Tip stirred up His Majesty's straw so that the warm rays might absorb the moisture and make it as crisp and dry as ever. When this had been accomplished he stuffed the Scarecrow into symmetrical shape and smoothed out his face so that he wore his usual gay and charming expression.

"Thank you very much," said the monarch, brightly, as he walked about and found himself to be well balanced. "There are several distinct advantages in being a Scarecrow. For if one has friends near at hand to repair damages, nothing very serious can happen to you."

"I wonder if hot sunshine is liable to crack pumpkins," said Jack, with an anxious ring in his voice.

"Not at all—not at all!" replied the Scarecrow, gaily. "All you need fear, my boy, is old age. When your golden youth has decayed we shall quickly part company—but you needn't look forward to it; we'll discover the fact ourselves, and notify you. But come! Let us

TIP STUFFS THE SCARECROW WITH DRY STRAW.

resume our journey. I am anxious to greet my friend the Tin Wood-man."

So they remounted the Saw-Horse, Tip holding to the post, the Pumpkinhead clinging to Tip, and the Scarecrow with both arms around the wooden form of Jack.

"Go slowly, for now there is no danger of pursuit," said Tip to his steed.

"All right!" responded the creature, in a voice rather gruff.

"Aren't you a little hoarse?" asked the Pumpkinhead, politely.

The Saw-Horse gave an angry prance and rolled one knotty eye backward toward Tip.

"See here," he growled, "can't you protect me from insult?"

"To be sure!" answered Tip, soothingly. "I am sure Jack meant no harm. And it will not do for us to quarrel, you know; we must all remain good friends."

"I'll have nothing more to do with that Pumpkinhead," declared the Saw-Horse, viciously; "he loses his head too easily to suit me."

There seemed no fitting reply to this speech, so for a time they rode along in silence.

After a while the Scarecrow remarked:

"This reminds me of old times. It was upon this grassy knoll that I once saved Dorothy from the Stinging Bees of the Wicked Witch of the West."

"Do Stinging Bees injure pumpkins?" asked Jack, glancing around fearfully.

"They are all dead, so it doesn't matter," replied the Scarecrow. "And here is where Nick Chopper destroyed the Wicked Witch's Grey Wolves."

"Who was Nick Chopper?" asked Tip.

"That is the name of my friend the Tin Woodman," answered His Majesty. "And here is where the Winged Monkeys captured and bound us, and flew away with little Dorothy," he continued, after they had traveled a little way farther.

"Do Winged Monkeys ever eat pumpkins?" asked Jack, with a shiver of fear.

"I do not know; but you have little cause to worry, for the Winged Monkeys are now the slaves of Glinda the Good, who owns the Golden Cap that commands their services," said the Scarecrow, reflectively.

Then the stuffed monarch became lost in thought, recalling the days of past adventures. And the Saw-Horse rocked and rolled over the flower-strewn fields and carried its riders swiftly upon their way.

Twilight fell, bye and bye, and then the dark shadows of night. So Tip stopped the horse and they all proceeded to dismount.

"I'm tired out," said the boy, yawning wearily; "and the grass is soft and cool. Let us lie down here and sleep until morning."

"I can't sleep," said Jack.

"I never do," said the Scarecrow.

"I do not even know what sleep is," said the Saw-Horse.

"Still, we must have consideration for this poor boy, who is made of flesh and blood and bone, and gets tired," suggested the Scarecrow, in his usual thoughtful manner. "I remember it was the same way with little Dorothy. We always had to sit through the night while she slept."

"I'm sorry," said Tip, meekly, "but I can't help it. And I'm dreadfully hungry, too!"

"Here is a new danger!" remarked Jack, gloomily. "I hope you are not fond of eating pumpkins."

"Not unless they're stewed and made into pies," answered the boy, laughing. "So have no fears of me, friend Jack."

"What a coward that Pumpkinhead is!" said the Saw-Horse, scornfully.

"You might be a coward yourself, if you knew you were liable to spoil!" retorted Jack, angrily.

"There!—there!" interrupted the Scarecrow; "don't let us quarrel. We all have our weaknesses, dear friends; so we must strive to be considerate of one another. And since this poor boy is hungry and has nothing whatever to eat, let us all remain quiet and allow him to sleep; for it is said that in sleep a mortal may forget even hunger."

"Thank you!" exclaimed Tip, gratefully. "Your Majesty is fully as good as you are wise—and that is saying a good deal!"

He then stretched himself upon the grass and, using the stuffed form of the Scarecrow for a pillow, was presently fast asleep.

A Nickel-Plated Emperor

Tip awoke soon after dawn, but the Scarecrow had already risen and plucked, with his clumsy fingers, a double-handful of ripe berries from some bushes near by. These the boy ate greedily, finding them an ample breakfast, and afterward the little party resumed its journey.

After an hour's ride they reached the summit of a hill from whence they espied the City of the Winkies and noted the tall domes of the Emperor's palace rising from the clusters of more modest dwellings.

The Scarecrow became greatly animated at this sight, and exclaimed:

"How delighted I shall be to see my old friend the Tin Woodman again! I hope that he rules his people more successfully than I have ruled mine!"

"Is the Tin Woodman the Emperor of the Winkies?" asked the horse.

"Yes, indeed. They invited him to rule over them soon after the Wicked Witch was destroyed; and as Nick Chopper has the best heart in all the world I am sure he has proved an excellent and able emperor."

"I thought that 'Emperor' was the title of a person who rules an empire," said Tip, "and the Country of the Winkies is only a King-dom."

"Don't mention that to the Tin Woodman!" exclaimed the Scare-crow, earnestly. "You would hurt his feelings terribly. He is a proud man, as he has every reason to be, and it pleases him to be termed Emperor rather than King."

"I'm sure it makes no difference to me," replied the boy.

The Saw-Horse now ambled forward at a pace so fast that its riders had hard work to stick upon its back; so there was little fur-ther conversation until they drew up beside the palace steps.

An aged Winkie, dressed in a uniform of silver cloth, came for-ward to assist them to alight. Said the Scarecrow to this personage:

"Show us at once to your master, the Emperor."

The man looked from one to another of the party in an embar-rassed way, and finally answered:

"I fear I must ask you to wait for a time. The Emperor is not re-ceiving this morning."

"How is that?" enquired the Scarecrow, anxiously. "I hope noth-ing has happened to him."

"Oh, no; nothing serious," returned the man. "But this is His Majesty's day for being polished, and just now his august presence is thickly smeared with putz-pomade."

"Oh, I see!" cried the Scarecrow, greatly reassured. "My friend was ever inclined to be a dandy, and I suppose he is now more proud than ever of his personal appearance."

"He is, indeed," said the man, with a polite bow. "Our mighty Emperor has lately caused himself to be nickel-plated."

"Good Gracious!" the Scarecrow exclaimed at hearing this. "If his wit bears the same polish, how sparkling it must be! But show us in—I'm sure the Emperor will receive us, even in his present state."

"The Emperor's state is always magnificent," said the man. "But I will venture to tell him of your arrival, and will receive his com-mands concerning you."

So the party followed the servant into a splendid ante-room, and the Saw-Horse ambled awkwardly after them, having no knowl-edge that a horse might be expected to remain outside.

CAUGHT THE SCARECROW IN A CLOSE AND
LOVING EMBRACE.

The travelers were at first somewhat awed by their surroundings, and even the Scarecrow seemed impressed as he examined the rich hangings of silver cloth caught up into knots and fastened with tiny silver axes. Upon a handsome center-table stood a large silver oil-can, richly engraved with scenes from the past adventures of the Tin Woodman, Dorothy, the Cowardly Lion and the Scarecrow: the lines of the engraving being traced upon the silver in yellow gold. On the walls hung several portraits, that of the Scarecrow seeming to be the most prominent and carefully executed, while a large painting of the famous Wizard of Oz, in the act of presenting the Tin Woodman with a heart, covered almost one entire end of the room.

While the visitors gazed at these things in silent admiration they suddenly heard a loud voice in the next room exclaim:

"Well! well! well! What a great surprise!"

And then the door burst open and Nick Chopper rushed into their midst and caught the Scarecrow in a close and loving embrace that creased him into many folds and wrinkles.

"My dear old friend! My noble comrade!" cried the Tin Woodman, joyfully; "how delighted I am to meet you once again!"

And then he released the Scarecrow and held him at arms' length while he surveyed the beloved, painted features.

But, alas! the face of the Scarecrow and many portions of his body bore great blotches of putz-pomade; for the Tin Woodman, in his eagerness to welcome his friend, had quite forgotten the condition of his toilet and had rubbed the thick coating of paste from his own body to that of his comrade.

"Dear me!" said the Scarecrow, dolefully. "What a mess I'm in!"

"Never mind, my friend," returned the Tin Woodman, "I'll send you to my Imperial Laundry, and you'll come out as good as new."

"Won't I be mangled?" asked the Scarecrow.

"No, indeed!" was the reply. "But tell me, how came Your Majesty here? and who are your companions?"

The Scarecrow, with great politeness, introduced Tip and Jack Pumpkinhead, and the latter personage seemed to interest the Tin Woodman greatly.

"You are not very substantial, I must admit," said the Emperor; "but you are certainly unusual, and therefore worthy to become a member of our select society."

"I thank Your Majesty," said Jack, humbly.

"I hope you are enjoying good health?" continued the Woodman.

"At present, yes," replied the Pumpkinhead, with a sigh; "but I am in constant terror of the day when I shall spoil."

"Nonsense!" said the Emperor—but in a kindly, sympathetic tone. "Do not, I beg of you, dampen today's sun with the showers of tomorrow. For before your head has time to spoil you can have it canned, and in that way it may be preserved indefinitely."

Tip, during this conversation, was looking at the Woodman with undisguised amazement, and noticed that the celebrated Emperor of the Winkies was composed entirely of pieces of tin, neatly soldered and riveted together into the form of a man. He rattled and clanked a little, as he moved, but in the main he seemed to be most cleverly constructed, and his appearance was only marred by the thick coating of polishing-paste that covered him from head to foot.

The boy's intent gaze caused the Tin Woodman to remember that he was not in the most presentable condition, so he begged his friends to excuse him while he retired to his private apartment and allowed his servants to polish him. This was accomplished in a short time, and when the Emperor returned his nickel-plated body shone so magnificently that the Scarecrow heartily congratulated him on his improved appearance.

"That nickel-plate was, I confess, a happy thought," said Nick; "and it was the more necessary because I had become somewhat scratched during my adventurous experiences. You will observe this engraved star upon my left breast. It not only indicates where my excellent heart lies, but covers very neatly the patch made by the Wonderful Wizard when he placed that valued organ in my breast with his own skillful hands."

"Is your heart, then, a hand-organ?" asked the Pumpkinhead, curiously.

"By no means," responded the Emperor, with dignity. "It is, I am convinced, a strictly orthodox heart, although somewhat larger and warmer than most people possess."

Then he turned to the Scarecrow and asked:

"Are your subjects happy and contented, my dear friend?"

"I cannot say," was the reply; "for the girls of Oz have risen in revolt and driven me out of the Emerald City."

"Great Goodness!" cried the Tin Woodman. "What a calamity! They surely do not complain of your wise and gracious rule?"

"No; but they say it is a poor rule that don't work both ways," answered the Scarecrow; "and these females are also of the opinion that men have ruled the land long enough. So they have captured my city, robbed the treasury of all its jewels, and are running things to suit themselves."

"Dear me! What an extraordinary idea!" cried the Emperor, who was both shocked and surprised.

"And I heard some of them say," said Tip, "that they intend to march here and capture the castle and city of the Tin Woodman."

"Ah! we must not give them time to do that," said the Emperor, quickly; "we will go at once and recapture the Emerald City and place the Scarecrow again upon his throne."

RENOVATING HIS MAJESTY, THE SCARECROW.

"I was sure you would help me," remarked the Scarecrow in a pleased voice. "How large an army can you assemble?"

"We do not need an army," replied the Woodman. "We four, with the aid of my gleaming axe, are enough to strike terror into the hearts of the rebels."

"We five," corrected the Pumpkinhead.

"Five?" repeated the Tin Woodman.

"Yes; the Saw-Horse is brave and fearless," answered Jack, forgetting his recent quarrel with the quadruped.

The Tin Woodman looked around him in a puzzled way, for the Saw-Horse had until now remained quietly standing in a corner, where the Emperor had not noticed him. Tip immediately called the odd-looking creature to them, and it approached so awkwardly that it nearly upset the beautiful center-table and the engraved oil-can.

"I begin to think," remarked the Tin Woodman as he looked earnestly at the Saw-Horse, "that wonders will never cease! How came this creature alive?"

"I did it with a magic powder," modestly asserted the boy; "and the Saw-Horse has been very useful to us."

"He enabled us to escape the rebels," added the Scarecrow.

"Then we must surely accept him as a comrade," declared the Emperor. "A live Saw-Horse is a distinct novelty, and should prove an interesting study. Does he know anything?"

"Well, I cannot claim any great experience in life," the Saw-Horse answered for himself; "but I seem to learn very quickly, and often it occurs to me that I know more than any of those around me."

"Perhaps you do," said the Emperor; "for experience does not always mean wisdom. But time is precious just now, so let us quickly make preparations to start upon our journey."

The Emperor called his Lord High Chancellor and instructed him how to run the kingdom during his absence. Meanwhile the Scarecrow was taken apart and the painted sack that served him for a head was carefully laundered and restuffed with the brains originally given him by the great Wizard. His clothes were also cleaned and pressed by the Imperial tailors, and his crown polished and again sewed upon his head, for the Tin Woodman insisted he should not renounce this badge of royalty. The Scarecrow now presented a very respectable appearance, and although in no way addicted to vanity he was quite pleased with himself and strutted a trifle as he walked. While this was being done Tip mended the wooden limbs of Jack Pumpkinhead and made them stronger than before, and the Saw-Horse was also inspected to see if he was in good working order.

Then bright and early the next morning they set out upon the return journey to the Emerald City, the Tin Woodman bearing upon his shoulder a gleaming axe and leading the way, while the Pumpkinhead rode upon the Saw-Horse and Tip and the Scarecrow walked upon either side to make sure that he didn't fall off or become damaged.

Mr. H.M.Woggle-Bug, T.E.

Now, General Jinjur—who, you will remember, commanded the Army of Revolt—was rendered very uneasy by the escape of the Scarecrow from the Emerald City. She feared, and with good reason, that if His Majesty and the Tin Woodman joined forces, it would mean danger to her and her entire army; for the people of Oz had not yet forgotten the deeds of these famous heroes, who had passed successfully through so many startling adventures.

So Jinjur sent post-haste for old Mombi, the witch, and promised her large rewards if she would come to the assistance of the rebel army.

Mombi was furious at the trick Tip had played upon her, as well as at his escape and the theft of the precious Powder of Life; so she needed no urging to induce her to travel to the Emerald City to assist Jinjur in defeating the Scarecrow and the Tin Woodman, who had made Tip one of their friends.

Mombi had no sooner arrived at the royal palace than she discovered, by means of her secret magic, that the adventurers were starting upon their journey to the Emerald City; so she retired to a small room high up in a tower and locked herself in while she practised such arts as she could command to prevent the return of the Scarecrow and his companions.

That was why the Tin Woodman presently stopped and said:

"Something very curious has happened. I ought to know by heart every step of this journey, and yet I fear we have already lost our way."

"That is quite impossible!" protested the Scarecrow. "Why do you think, my dear friend, that we have gone astray?"

"Why, here before us is a great field of sunflowers—and I never saw this field before in all my life."

At these words they all looked around, only to find that they were indeed surrounded by a field of tall stalks, every stalk bearing at its top a gigantic sunflower. And not only were these flowers almost blinding in their vivid hues of red and gold, but each one whirled around upon its stalk like a miniature wind-mill, completely dazzling the vision of the beholders and so mystifying them that they knew not which way to turn.

"It's witchcraft!" exclaimed Tip.

While they paused, hesitating and wondering, the Tin Woodman uttered a cry of impatience and advanced with swinging axe to cut down the stalks before him. But now the sunflowers suddenly stopped their rapid whirling, and the travelers plainly saw a girl's face appear in the center of each flower. These lovely faces looked upon the astonished band with mocking smiles, and then burst into a chorus of merry laughter at the dismay their appearance caused.

"Stop! stop!" cried Tip, seizing the Woodman's arm; "they're alive! they're girls!"

At that moment the flowers began whirling again, and the faces faded away and were lost in the rapid revolutions.

The Tin Woodman dropped his axe and sat down upon the ground.

"It would be heartless to chop down those pretty creatures," said he, despondently; "and yet I do not know how else we can proceed upon our way."

"They looked to me strangely like the faces of the Army of Revolt," mused the Scarecrow. "But I cannot conceive how the girls could have followed us here so quickly."

"I believe it's magic," said Tip, positively, "and that someone is playing a trick upon us. I've known old Mombi to do things like that before. Probably it's nothing more than an illusion, and there are no sunflowers here at all."

"Then let us shut our eyes and walk forward," suggested the Woodman.

"Excuse me," replied the Scarecrow. "My eyes are not painted to shut. Because you happen to have tin eyelids, you must not imagine we are all built in the same way."

"And the eyes of the Saw-Horse are knot eyes," said Jack, leaning forward to examine them.

"Nevertheless, you must ride quickly forward," commanded Tip, "and we will follow after you and so try to escape. My eyes are already so dazzled that I can scarcely see."

So the Pumpkinhead rode boldly forward, and Tip grasped the stub tail of the Saw-Horse and followed with closed eyes. The Scarecrow and the Tin Woodman brought up the rear, and before they had gone many yards a joyful shout from Jack announced that the way was clear before them.

Then all paused to look backward, but not a trace of the field of sunflowers remained.

More cheerfully, now, they proceeded upon their journey; but old Mombi had so changed the appearance of the landscape that they would surely have been lost had not the Scarecrow wisely concluded to take their direction from the sun. For no witch-craft could change the course of the sun, and it was therefore a safe guide.

However, other difficulties lay before them. The Saw-Horse stepped into a rabbit hole and fell to the ground. The Pumpkin-head was pitched high into the air, and his history would probably have ended at that exact moment had not the Tin Woodman skill-fully caught the pumpkin as it descended and saved it from injury.

Tip soon had it fitted to the neck again and replaced Jack upon his feet. But the Saw-Horse did not escape so easily. For when his leg was pulled from the rabbit hole it was found to be broken short

THE TIN WOODMAN SKILLFULLY CAUGHT THE PUMPKIN

off, and must be replaced or repaired before he could go a step farther.

"This is quite serious," said the Tin Woodman. "If there were
trees near by I might soon manufacture another leg for this animal;
but I cannot see even a shrub for miles around."

"And there are neither fences nor houses in this part of the land
of Oz," added the Scarecrow, disconsolately.

"Then what shall we do?" enquired the boy.

"I suppose I must start my brains working," replied His Majesty
the Scarecrow; "for experience has taught me that I can do anything if I but take time to think it out."

"Let us all think," said Tip; "and perhaps we shall find a way to
repair the Saw-Horse."

So they sat in a row upon the grass and began to think, while the
Saw-Horse occupied itself by gazing curiously upon its broken
limb.

"Does it hurt?" asked the Tin Woodman, in a soft, sympathetic
voice.

"Not in the least," returned the Saw-Horse; "but my pride is injured to find that my anatomy is so brittle."

For a time the little group remained in silent thought. Presently
the Tin Woodman raised his head and looked over the fields.

"What sort of creature is that which approaches us?" he asked,
wonderingly.

The others followed his gaze, and discovered coming toward
them the most extraordinary object they had ever beheld. It advanced quickly and noiselessly over the soft grass and in a few
minutes stood before the adventurers and regarded them with an
astonishment equal to their own.

The Scarecrow was calm under all circumstances.

"Good morning!" he said, politely.

The stranger removed his hat with a flourish, bowed very low,
and then responded:

"Good morning, one and all. I hope you are, as an aggregation,
enjoying excellent health. Permit me to present my card."

With this courteous speech it extended a card toward the Scarecrow, who accepted it, turned it over and over, and then handed it with a shake of his head to Tip.

The boy read aloud:

"MR. H. M. WOGGLE-BUG, T. E."

"Dear me!" ejaculated the Pumpkinhead, staring somewhat intently.

"How very peculiar!" said the Tin Woodman.

Tip's eyes were round and wondering, and the Saw-Horse uttered a sigh and turned away its head.

"Are you really a Woggle-Bug?" enquired the Scarecrow.

"Most certainly, my dear sir!" answered the stranger, briskly. "Is not my name upon the card?"

"It is," said the Scarecrow. "But may I ask what 'H. M.' stands for?"

" 'H. M.' means Highly Magnified," returned the Woggle-Bug, proudly.

"Oh, I see." The Scarecrow viewed the stranger critically. "And are you, in truth, highly magnified?"

"Sir," said the Woggle-Bug, "I take you for a gentleman of judgment and discernment. Does it not occur to you that I am several thousand times greater than any Woggle-Bug you ever saw before? Therefore it is plainly evident that I am Highly Magnified, and there is no good reason why you should doubt the fact."

"Pardon me," returned the Scarecrow. "My brains are slightly mixed since I was last laundered. Would it be improper for me to ask, also, what the 'T. E.' at the end of your name stands for?"

"Those letters express my degree," answered the Woggle-Bug,

with a condescending smile. "To be more explicit, the initials mean that I am Thoroughly Educated."

"Oh!" said the Scarecrow, much relieved.

Tip had not yet taken his eyes off this wonderful personage. What he saw was a great, round, bug-like body supported upon two slender legs which ended in delicate feet—the toes curling upward. The body of the Woggle-Bug was rather flat, and judging from what could be seen of it was of a glistening dark brown color upon the back, while the front was striped with alternate bands of light brown and white, blending together at the edges. Its arms were fully as slender as its legs, and upon a rather long neck was perched its head—not unlike the head of a man, except that its nose ended in a curling antenna, or "feeler," and its ears from the upper points bore antennæ that decorated the sides of its head like two miniature, curling pig tails. It must be admitted that the round, black eyes were rather bulging in appearance; but the expression upon the Woggle-Bug's face was by no means unpleasant.

For dress the insect wore a dark-blue swallow-tail coat with a yellow silk lining and a flower in the button-hole; a vest of white duck that stretched tightly across the wide body; knickerbockers of fawn-colored plush, fastened at the knees with gilt buckles; and, perched upon its small head, was jauntily set a tall silk hat.

Standing upright before our amazed friends the Woggle-Bug appeared to be fully as tall as the Tin Woodman; and surely no bug in all the Land of Oz had ever before attained so enormous a size.

"I confess," said the Scarecrow, "that your abrupt appearance has caused me surprise, and no doubt has startled my companions. I hope, however, that this circumstance will not distress you. We shall probably get used to you in time."

"Do not apologize, I beg of you!" returned the Woggle-Bug, earnestly. "It affords me great pleasure to surprise people; for surely I cannot be classed with ordinary insects and am entitled to both curiosity and admiration from those I meet."

"You are, indeed," agreed His Majesty.

"If you will permit me to seat myself in your august company," continued the stranger, "I will gladly relate my history, so that you will be better able to comprehend my unusual—may I say remarkable?—appearance."

"You may say what you please," answered the Tin Woodman, briefly.

So the Woggle-Bug sat down upon the grass, facing the little group of wanderers, and told them the following story:

A Highly Magnified History

"It is but honest that I should acknowledge at the beginning of my recital that I was born an ordinary Woggle-Bug," began the creature, in a frank and friendly tone. "Knowing no better, I used my arms as well as my legs for walking, and crawled under the edges of stones or hid among the roots of grasses with no thought beyond finding a few insects smaller than myself to feed upon.

"The chill nights rendered me stiff and motionless, for I wore no clothing, but each morning the warm rays of the sun gave me new life and restored me to activity. A horrible existence is this, but you must remember it is the regularly ordained existence of Woggle-Bugs, as well as of many other tiny creatures that inhabit the earth.

"But Destiny had singled me out, humble though I was, for a grander fate! One day I crawled near to a country school-house, and my curiosity being excited by the monotonous hum of the students within, I made bold to enter and creep along a crack between two boards until I reached the far end, where, in front of a hearth of glowing embers, sat the master at his desk.

"No one noticed so small a creature as a Woggle-Bug, and when I found that the hearth was even warmer and more comfortable than the sunshine, I resolved to establish my future home beside it. So I found a charming nest between two bricks and hid myself therein for many, many months.

"Professor Nowitall is, doubtless, the most famous scholar in the Land of Oz, and after a few days I began to listen to the lectures and discourses he gave his pupils. Not one of them was more attentive than the humble, unnoticed Woggle-Bug, and I acquired in this way a fund of knowledge that I will myself confess is simply marvelous. That is why I place 'T. E.'—Thoroughly Educated—upon my cards; for my greatest pride lies in the fact that the world cannot produce another Woggle-Bug with a tenth part of my own culture and erudition."

"I do not blame you," said the Scarecrow. "Education is a thing to be proud of. I'm educated myself. The mess of brains given me by the Great Wizard is considered by my friends to be unexcelled."

"Nevertheless," interrupted the Tin Woodman, "a good heart is, I believe, much more desirable than education or brains."

"To me," said the Saw-Horse, "a good leg is more desirable than either."

"Could seeds be considered in the light of brains?" enquired the Pumpkinhead, abruptly.

"Keep quiet!" commanded Tip, sternly.

"Very well, dear father," answered the obedient Jack.

The Woggle-Bug listened patiently—even respectfully—to these remarks, and then resumed his story.

"I must have lived fully three years in that secluded school-house hearth," said he, "drinking thirstily of the ever-flowing fount of limpid knowledge before me."

"Quite poetical," commented the Scarecrow, nodding his head approvingly.

"But one day," continued the Bug, "a marvelous circumstance occurred that altered my very existence and brought me to my present pinnacle of greatness. The Professor discovered me in the act of crawling across the hearth, and before I could escape he had caught me between his thumb and forefinger.

" 'My dear children,' said he, 'I have captured a Woggle-Bug— a very rare and interesting specimen. Do any of you know what a Woggle-Bug is?'

" 'No!' yelled the scholars, in chorus.

" 'Then,' said the Professor, 'I will get out my famous magnifying-glass and throw the insect upon a screen in a highly-magnified condition, that you may all study carefully its peculiar construction and become acquainted with its habits and manner of life.'

"He then brought from a cupboard a most curious instrument, and before I could realize what had happened I found myself thrown upon a screen in a highly-magnified state—even as you now behold me.

"The students stood up on their stools and craned their heads forward to get a better view of me, and two little girls jumped upon the sill of an open window where they could see more plainly.

" 'Behold!' cried the Professor, in a loud voice, 'this highly-magnified Woggle-Bug; one of the most curious insects in existence!'

"Being Thoroughly Educated, and knowing what is required of a cultured gentleman, at this juncture I stood upright and, placing my hand upon my bosom, made a very polite bow. My action, being unexpected, must have startled them, for one of the little girls perched upon the window-sill gave a scream and fell backward out the window, drawing her companion with her as she disappeared.

"The Professor uttered a cry of horror and rushed away through the door to see if the poor children were injured by the fall. The scholars followed after him in a wild mob, and I was left alone in the school-room, still in a Highly-Magnified state and free to do as I pleased.

"It immediately occurred to me that this was a good opportunity to escape. I was proud of my great size, and realized that now I could safely travel anywhere in the world, while my superior culture would make me a fit associate for the most learned person I might chance to meet.

"So, while the Professor picked the little girls—who were more frightened than hurt—off the ground, and the pupils clustered

"THE STUDENTS STOOD UP ON THEIR STOOLS."

around him closely grouped, I calmly walked out of the school-house, turned a corner, and escaped unnoticed to a grove of trees that stood near."

"Wonderful!" exclaimed the Pumpkinhead, admiringly.

"It was, indeed," agreed the Woggle-Bug. "I have never ceased to congratulate myself for escaping while I was Highly Magnified; for even my excessive knowledge would have proved of little use to me had I remained a tiny, insignificant insect."

"I didn't know before," said Tip, looking at the Woggle-Bug with a puzzled expression, "that insects wore clothes."

"Nor do they, in their natural state," returned the stranger. "But in the course of my wanderings I had the good fortune to save the ninth life of a tailor—tailors having, like cats, nine lives, as you probably know. The fellow was exceedingly grateful, for had he lost that ninth life it would have been the end of him; so he begged permission to furnish me with the stylish costume I now wear. It fits very nicely, does it not?" and the Woggle-Bug stood up and turned himself around slowly, that all might examine his person.

"He must have been a good tailor," said the Scarecrow, somewhat enviously.

"He was a good-hearted tailor, at any rate," observed Nick Chopper.

"But where were you going, when you met us?" Tip asked the Woggle-Bug.

"Nowhere in particular," was the reply, "although it is my intention soon to visit the Emerald City and arrange to give a course of lectures to select audiences on the 'Advantages of Magnification.'"

"We are bound for the Emerald City now," said the Tin Woodman;

"so, if it pleases you to do so, you are welcome to travel in our company."

The Woggle-Bug bowed with profound grace.

"It will give me great pleasure," said he, "to accept your kind invitation; for nowhere in the Land of Oz could I hope to meet with so congenial a company."

"That is true," acknowledged the Pumpkinhead. "We are quite as congenial as flies and honey."

"But—pardon me if I seem inquisitive—are you not all rather—ahem!—rather unusual?" asked the Woggle-Bug, looking from one to another with unconcealed interest.

"Not more so than yourself," answered the Scarecrow. "Everything in life is unusual until you get accustomed to it."

"What rare philosophy!" exclaimed the Woggle-Bug, admiringly.

"Yes; my brains are working well today," admitted the Scarecrow, an accent of pride in his voice.

"Then, if you are sufficiently rested and refreshed, let us bend our steps toward the Emerald City," suggested the magnified one.

"We can't," said Tip. "The Saw-Horse has broken a leg, so he can't bend his steps. And there is no wood around to make him a new limb from. And we can't leave the horse behind because the Pumpkinhead is so stiff in his joints that he has to ride."

"How very unfortunate!" cried the Woggle-Bug. Then he looked the party over carefully and said:

"If the Pumpkinhead is to ride, why not use one of his legs to make a leg for the horse that carries him? I judge that both are made of wood."

"Now, that is what I call real cleverness," said the Scarecrow, approvingly. "I wonder my brains did not think of that long ago! Get to work, my dear Nick, and fit the Pumpkinhead's leg to the Saw-Horse."

Jack was not especially pleased with this idea; but he submitted to having his left leg amputated by the Tin Woodman and whittled down to fit the left leg of the Saw-Horse. Nor was the Saw-Horse especially pleased with the operation, either; for he growled a good deal about being "butchered," as he called it, and afterward declared that the new leg was a disgrace to a respectable Saw-Horse.

"I beg you to be more careful in your speech," said the Pumpkinhead, sharply. "Remember, if you please, that it is my leg you are abusing."

"I cannot forget it," retorted the Saw-Horse, "for it is quite as flimsy as the rest of your person."

"Flimsy! me flimsy!" cried Jack, in a rage. "How dare you call me flimsy?"

"Because you are built as absurdly as a jumping-jack," sneered the horse, rolling his knotty eyes in a vicious manner. "Even your head won't stay straight, and you never can tell whether you are looking backwards or forward!"

"Friends, I entreat you not to quarrel!" pleaded the Tin Woodman, anxiously. "As a matter of fact, we are none of us above criticism; so let us bear with each other's faults."

"An excellent suggestion," said the Woggle-Bug, approvingly. "You must have an excellent heart, my metallic friend."

"I have," returned Nick, well pleased. "My heart is quite the best part of me. But now let us start upon our journey."

They perched the one-legged Pumpkinhead upon the Saw-Horse, and tied him to his seat with cords, so that he could not possibly fall off.

And then, following the lead of the Scarecrow, they all advanced in the direction of the Emerald City.

Old Mombi indulges in Witchcraft

They soon discovered that the Saw-Horse limped, for his new leg was a trifle too long. So they were obliged to halt while the Tin Woodman chopped it down with his axe, after which the wooden steed paced along more comfortably. But the Saw-Horse was not entirely satisfied, even yet.

"It was a shame that I broke my other leg!" it growled.

"On the contrary," airily remarked the Woggle-Bug, who was walking alongside, "you should consider the accident most fortunate. For a horse is never of much use until he has been broken."

"I beg your pardon," said Tip, rather provoked, for he felt a warm interest in both the Saw-Horse and his man Jack; "but permit me to say that your joke is a poor one, and as old as it is poor."

"Still, it is a joke," declared the Woggle-Bug, firmly, "and a joke derived from a play upon words is considered among educated people to be eminently proper."

"What does that mean?" enquired the Pumpkinhead, stupidly.

"It means, my dear friend," explained the Woggle-Bug, "that our language contains many words having a double meaning; and that to pronounce a joke that allows both meanings of a certain word, proves the joker a person of culture and refinement, who has, moreover, a thorough command of the language."

"I don't believe that," said Tip, plainly; "anybody can make a pun."

"Not so," rejoined the Woggle-Bug, stiffly. "It requires education of a high order. Are you educated, young sir?"

"Not especially," admitted Tip.

"Then you cannot judge the matter. I myself am Thoroughly Educated, and I say that puns display genius. For instance, were I to ride upon this Saw-Horse, he would not only be an animal—he would become an equipage. For he would then be a horse-and-buggy."

At this the Scarecrow gave a gasp and the Tin Woodman stopped short and looked reproachfully at the Woggle-Bug. At the same time the Saw-Horse loudly snorted his derision; and even the Pumpkinhead put up his hand to hide the smile which, because it was carved upon his face, he could not change to a frown.

But the Woggle-Bug strutted along as if he had made some brilliant remark, and the Scarecrow was obliged to say:

"I have heard, my dear friend, that a person can become over-educated; and although I have a high respect for brains, no matter how they may be arranged or classified, I begin to suspect that yours are slightly tangled. In any event, I must beg you to restrain your superior education while in our society."

"We are not very particular," added the Tin Woodman; "and we are exceedingly kind hearted. But if your superior culture gets leaky again—" He did not complete the sentence, but he twirled his gleaming axe so carelessly that the Woggle-Bug looked frightened, and shrank away to a safe distance.

The others marched on in silence, and the Highly-Magnified one, after a period of deep thought, said in an humble voice:

"I will endeavor to restrain myself."

"That is all we can expect," returned the Scarecrow, pleasantly; and good nature being thus happily restored to the party, they proceeded upon their way.

When they again stopped to allow Tip to rest—the boy being the only one that seemed to tire—the Tin Woodman noticed many small, round holes in the grassy meadow.

"This must be a village of the Field Mice," he said to the Scarecrow. "I wonder if my old friend, the Queen of the Mice, is in this neighborhood."

"If she is, she may be of great service to us," answered the Scarecrow, who was impressed by a sudden thought. "See if you can call her, my dear Nick."

So the Tin Woodman blew a shrill note upon a silver whistle that hung around his neck, and presently a tiny grey mouse popped from a near-by hole and advanced fearlessly toward them. For the Tin Woodman had once saved her life, and the Queen of the Field Mice knew he was to be trusted.

"Good day, Your Majesty," said Nick, politely addressing the mouse; "I trust you are enjoying good health?"

"Thank you, I am quite well," answered the Queen, demurely, as she sat up and displayed the tiny golden crown upon her head. "Can I do anything to assist my old friends?"

"You can, indeed," replied the Scarecrow, eagerly. "Let me, I intreat you, take a dozen of your subjects with me to the Emerald City."

"Will they be injured in any way?" asked the Queen, doubtfully.

"I think not," replied the Scarecrow. "I will carry them hidden in the straw which stuffs my body, and when I give them the signal by unbuttoning my jacket, they have only to rush out and scamper home again as fast as they can. By doing this they will assist me to regain my throne, which the Army of Revolt has taken from me."

"In that case," said the Queen, "I will not refuse your request. Whenever you are ready, I will call twelve of my most intelligent subjects."

"I am ready now," returned the Scarecrow. Then he lay flat upon the ground and unbuttoned his jacket, displaying the mass of straw with which he was stuffed.

The Queen uttered a little piping call, and in an instant a dozen pretty field mice had emerged from their holes and stood before their ruler, awaiting her orders.

What the Queen said to them none of our travelers could understand, for it was in the mouse language; but the field mice obeyed without hesitation, running one after the other to the Scarecrow and hiding themselves in the straw of his breast.

When all of the twelve mice had thus concealed themselves, the Scarecrow buttoned his jacket securely and then arose and thanked the Queen for her kindness.

"One thing more you might do to serve us," suggested the Tin Woodman; "and that is to run ahead and show us the way to the Emerald City. For some enemy is evidently trying to prevent us from reaching it."

"I will do that gladly," returned the Queen. "Are you ready?"

The Tin Woodman looked at Tip.

"I'm rested," said the boy. "Let us start."

Then they resumed their journey, the little grey Queen of the Field Mice running swiftly ahead and then pausing until the travelers drew near, when away she would dart again.

Without this unerring guide the Scarecrow and his comrades might never have gained the Emerald City; for many were the obstacles thrown in their way by the arts of old Mombi. Yet not one of the obstacles really existed—all were cleverly contrived deceptions. For when they came to the banks of a rushing river that threatened to bar their way the little Queen kept steadily on, passing through the seeming flood in safety; and our travelers followed her without encountering a single drop of water.

Again, a high wall of granite towered high above their heads and opposed their advance. But the grey Field Mouse walked straight through it, and the others did the same, the wall melting into mist as they passed it.

Afterward, when they had stopped for a moment to allow Tip to rest, they saw forty roads branching off from their feet in forty different directions; and soon these forty roads began whirling around like a mighty wheel, first in one direction and then in the other, completely bewildering their vision.

But the Queen called for them to follow her and darted off in a straight line; and when they had gone a few paces the whirling pathways vanished and were seen no more.

Mombi's last trick was most fearful of all. She sent a sheet of crackling flame rushing over the meadow to consume them; and for the first time the Scarecrow became afraid and turned to fly.

"If that fire reaches me I will be gone in no time!" said he, trembling until his straw rattled. "It's the most dangerous thing I ever encountered."

"I'm off, too!" cried the Saw-Horse, turning and prancing with agitation; "for my wood is so dry it would burn like kindlings."

"Is fire dangerous to pumpkins?" asked Jack, fearfully.

"You'll be baked like a tart—and so will I!" answered the Woggle-Bug, getting down on all fours so he could run the faster.

But the Tin Woodman, having no fear of fire, averted the stampede by a few sensible words.

"Look at the Field Mouse!" he shouted. "The fire does not burn her in the least. In fact, it is no fire at all, but only a deception."

Indeed, to watch the little Queen march calmly through the advancing flames restored courage to every member of the party, and they followed her without being even scorched.

"This is surely a most extraordinary adventure," said the Woggle-Bug, who was greatly amazed; "for it upsets all the Natural Laws that I heard Professor Nowitall teach in the school-house."

"Of course it does," said the Scarecrow, wisely. "All magic is unnatural, and for that reason is to be feared and avoided. But I see before us the gates of the Emerald City, so I imagine we have now overcome all the magical obstacles that seemed to oppose us."

Indeed, the walls of the City were plainly visible, and the Queen of the Field Mice, who had guided them so faithfully, came near to bid them good-bye.

"We are very grateful to Your Majesty for your kind assistance," said the Tin Woodman, bowing before the pretty creature.

"I am always pleased to be of service to my friends," answered the Queen, and in a flash she had darted away upon her journey home.

The Prisoners of the Queen

Approaching the gateway of the Emerald City the travelers found it guarded by two girls of the Army of Revolt, who opposed their entrance by drawing the knitting-needles from their hair and threatening to prod the first that came near.

But the Tin Woodman was not afraid.

"At the worst they can but scratch my beautiful nickel-plate," he said. "But there will be no 'worst,' for I think I can manage to frighten these absurd soldiers very easily. Follow me closely, all of you!"

Then, swinging his axe in a great circle to right and left before him, he advanced upon the gate, and the others followed him without hesitation.

The girls, who had expected no resistance whatever, were terrified by the sweep of the glittering axe and fled screaming into the city; so that our travelers passed the gates in safety and marched down the green marble pavement of the wide street toward the royal palace.

"At this rate we will soon have Your Majesty upon the throne again," said the Tin Woodman, laughing at his easy conquest of the guards.

"Thank you, friend Nick," returned the Scarecrow, gratefully. "Nothing can resist your kind heart and your sharp axe."

As they passed the rows of houses they saw through the open doors that men were sweeping and dusting and washing dishes, while the women sat around in groups, gossiping and laughing.

"What has happened?" the Scarecrow asked a sad-looking man with a bushy beard, who wore an apron and was wheeling a baby-carriage along the sidewalk.

"Why, we've had a revolution, Your Majesty—as you ought to know very well," replied the man; "and since you went away the women have been running things to suit themselves. I'm glad you have decided to come back and restore order, for doing housework and minding the children is wearing out the strength of every man in the Emerald City."

"Hm!" said the Scarecrow, thoughtfully. "If it is such hard work as you say, how did the women manage it so easily?"

"I really do not know," replied the man, with a deep sigh. "Perhaps the women are made of cast-iron."

No movement was made, as they passed along the street, to oppose their progress. Several of the women stopped their gossip long enough to cast curious looks upon our friends, but immediately they would turn away with a laugh or a sneer and resume their chatter. And when they met with several girls belonging to the Army of Revolt, those soldiers, instead of being alarmed or appearing surprised, merely stepped out of the way and allowed them to advance without protest.

This action rendered the Scarecrow uneasy.

"I'm afraid we are walking into a trap," said he.

"Nonsense!" returned Nick Chopper, confidently; "the silly creatures are conquered already!"

But the Scarecrow shook his head in a way that expressed doubt, and Tip said:

"It's too easy, altogether. Look out for trouble ahead."

"I will," returned His Majesty.

Unopposed they reached the royal palace and marched up the marble steps, which had once been thickly encrusted with emeralds but were now filled with tiny holes where the jewels had been ruth-

"IT'S TOO EASY, ALTOGETHER."

lessly torn from their settings by the Army of Revolt. And so far not a rebel barred their way.

Through the arched hallways and into the magnificent throne room marched the Tin Woodman and his followers, and here, when the green silken curtains fell behind them, they saw a curious sight.

Seated within the glittering throne was General Jinjur, with the Scarecrow's second-best crown upon her head, and the royal sceptre in her right hand. A box of caramels, from which she was eating, rested in her lap, and the girl seemed entirely at ease in her royal surroundings.

The Scarecrow stepped forward and confronted her, while the Tin Woodman leaned upon his axe and the others formed a half-circle back of His Majesty's person.

"How dare you sit in my throne?" demanded the Scarecrow, sternly eyeing the intruder. "Don't you know you are guilty of treason, and that there is a law against treason?"

"The throne belongs to whoever is able to take it," answered Jinjur, as she slowly ate another caramel. "I have taken it, as you see; so just now I am the Queen, and all who oppose me are guilty of treason, and must be punished by the law you have just mentioned."

This view of the case puzzled the Scarecrow.

"How is it, friend Nick?" he asked, turning to the Tin Woodman.

"Why, when it comes to Law, I have nothing to say," answered that personage; "for laws were never meant to be understood, and it is foolish to make the attempt."

"Then what shall we do?" asked the Scarecrow, in dismay.

"Why don't you marry the Queen? And then you can both rule," suggested the Woggle-Bug.

Jinjur glared at the insect fiercely.

"Why don't you send her back to her mother, where she belongs?" asked Jack Pumpkinhead.

Jinjur frowned.

"Why don't you shut her up in a closet until she behaves herself, and promises to be good?" enquired Tip. Jinjur's lip curled scornfully.

"Or give her a good shaking!" added the Saw-Horse.

"No," said the Tin Woodman, "we must treat the poor girl with gentleness. Let us give her all the jewels she can carry, and send her away happy and contented."

At this Queen Jinjur laughed aloud, and the next minute clapped her pretty hands together thrice, as if for a signal.

"You are very absurd creatures," said she; "but I am tired of your nonsense and have no time to bother with you longer."

While the monarch and his friends listened in amazement to this impudent speech, a startling thing happened. The Tin Woodman's axe was snatched from his grasp by some person behind him, and he found himself disarmed and helpless. At the same instant a shout of laughter rang in the ears of the devoted band, and turning to see whence this came they found themselves surrounded by the Army of Revolt, the girls bearing in either hand their glistening knitting-needles. The entire throne room seemed to be filled with the rebels, and the Scarecrow and his comrades realized that they were prisoners.

"You see how foolish it is to oppose a woman's wit," said Jinjur, gaily; "and this event only proves that I am more fit to rule the Emerald City than a Scarecrow. I bear you no ill will, I assure you; but lest you should prove troublesome to me in the future I shall order you all to be destroyed. That is, all except the boy, who belongs to old Mombi and must be restored to her keeping. The rest of you are not human, and therefore it will not be wicked to demolish you. The Saw-Horse and the Pumpkinhead's body I will have chopped up for kindling-wood; and the pumpkin shall be made into tarts. The Scarecrow will do nicely to start a bonfire, and the tin man can be cut into small pieces and fed to the goats. As for this immense Woggle-Bug—"

"Highly Magnified, if you please!" interrupted the insect.

"I think I will ask the cook to make green-turtle soup of you," continued the Queen, reflectively.

The Woggle-Bug shuddered.

"Or, if that won't do, we might use you for a Hungarian goulash, stewed and highly spiced," she added, cruelly.

This programme of extermination was so terrible that the prisoners looked upon one another in a panic of fear. The Scarecrow alone did not give way to despair. He stood quietly before the Queen and his brow was wrinkled in deep thought as he strove to find some means to escape.

While thus engaged he felt the straw within his breast move gently. At once his expression changed from sadness to joy, and raising his hand he quickly unbuttoned the front of his jacket.

This action did not pass unnoticed by the crowd of girls clustering about him, but none of them suspected what he was doing until a tiny grey mouse leaped from his bosom to the floor and scampered away between the feet of the Army of Revolt. Another mouse

quickly followed; then another and another, in rapid succession. And suddenly such a scream of terror went up from the Army that it might easily have filled the stoutest heart with consternation. The flight that ensued turned to a stampede, and the stampede to a panic.

For while the startled mice rushed wildly about the room the Scarecrow had only time to note a whirl of skirts and a twinkling of feet as the girls disappeared from the palace—pushing and crowding one another in their mad efforts to escape.

The Queen, at the first alarm, stood up on the cushions of the throne and began to dance frantically upon her tiptoes. Then a mouse ran up the cushions, and with a terrified leap poor Jinjur shot clear over the head of the Scarecrow and escaped through an archway—never pausing in her wild career until she had reached the city gates.

So, in less time than I can explain, the throne room was deserted by all save the Scarecrow and his friends, and the Woggle-Bug heaved a deep sigh of relief as he exclaimed:

"Thank goodness, we are saved!"

"For a time, yes," answered the Tin Woodman. "But the enemy will soon return, I fear."

"Let us bar all the entrances to the palace!" said the Scarecrow. "Then we shall have time to think what is best to be done."

So all except Jack Pumpkinhead, who was still tied fast to the Saw-Horse, ran to the various entrances of the royal palace and closed the heavy doors, bolting and locking them securely. Then, knowing that the Army of Revolt could not batter down the barriers in several days, the adventurers gathered once more in the throne room for a council of war.

The Scarecrow
Takes Time to Think

"It seems to me," began the Scarecrow, when all were again assembled in the throne room, "that the girl Jinjur is quite right in claiming to be Queen. And if she is right, then I am wrong, and we have no business to be occupying her palace."

"But you were the King until she came," said the Woggle-Bug, strutting up and down with his hands in his pockets; "so it appears to me that she is the interloper instead of you."

"Especially as we have just conquered her and put her to flight," added the Pumpkinhead, as he raised his hands to turn his face toward the Scarecrow.

"Have we really conquered her?" asked the Scarecrow, quietly. "Look out of the window, and tell me what you see."

Tip ran to the window and looked out.

"The palace is surrounded by a double row of girl soldiers," he announced.

"I thought so," returned the Scarecrow. "We are as truly their prisoners as we were before the mice frightened them from the palace."

"My friend is right," said Nick Chopper, who had been polishing his breast with a bit of chamois-leather. "Jinjur is still the Queen, and we are her prisoners."

"But I hope she cannot get at us," exclaimed the Pumpkinhead, with a shiver of fear. "She threatened to make tarts of me, you know."

"Don't worry," said the Tin Woodman. "It cannot matter greatly. If you stay shut up here you will spoil in time, anyway. A good tart is far more admirable than a decayed intellect."

"Very true," agreed the Scarecrow.

"Oh, dear!" moaned Jack; "what an unhappy lot is mine! Why, dear father, did you not make me out of tin—or even out of straw—so that I would keep indefinitely."

"Shucks!" returned Tip, indignantly. "You ought to be glad that I made you at all." Then he added, reflectively, "Everything has to come to an end, some time."

"But I beg to remind you," broke in the Woggle-Bug, who had a distressed look in his bulging, round eyes, "that this terrible Queen Jinjur suggested making a goulash of me—Me! the only Highly Magnified and Thoroughly Educated Woggle-Bug in the wide, wide world!"

"I think it was a brilliant idea," remarked the Scarecrow, approvingly.

"Don't you imagine he would make a better soup?" asked the Tin Woodman, turning toward his friend.

"Well, perhaps," acknowledged the Scarecrow.

The Woggle-Bug groaned.

"I can see, in my mind's eye," said he, mournfully, "the goats eating small pieces of my dear comrade, the Tin Woodman, while my soup is being cooked on a bonfire built of the Saw-Horse and Jack Pumpkinhead's body, and Queen Jinjur watches me boil while she feeds the flames with my friend the Scarecrow!"

This morbid picture cast a gloom over the entire party, making them restless and anxious.

"It can't happen for some time," said the Tin Woodman, trying to speak cheerfully; "for we shall be able to keep Jinjur out of the palace until she manages to break down the doors."

"And in the meantime I am liable to starve to death, and so is the Woggle-Bug," announced Tip.

"As for me," said the Woggle-Bug, "I think that I could live for some time on Jack Pumpkinhead. Not that I prefer pumpkins for food; but I believe they are somewhat nutritious, and Jack's head is large and plump."

"How heartless!" exclaimed the Tin Woodman, greatly shocked. "Are we cannibals, let me ask? Or are we faithful friends?"

"I see very clearly that we cannot stay shut up in this palace," said the Scarecrow, with decision. "So let us end this mournful talk and try to discover a means to escape."

At this suggestion they all gathered eagerly around the throne, wherein was seated the Scarecrow, and as Tip sat down upon a stool there fell from his pocket a pepper-box, which rolled upon the floor.

"What is this?" asked Nick Chopper, picking up the box.

"Be careful!" cried the boy. "That's my Powder of Life. Don't spill it, for it is nearly gone."

"And what is the Powder of Life?" enquired the Scarecrow, as Tip replaced the box carefully in his pocket.

"It's some magical stuff old Mombi got from a crooked sorcerer," explained the boy. "She brought Jack to life with it, and afterward I used it to bring the Saw-Horse to life. I guess it will make anything live that is sprinkled with it; but there's only about one dose left."

"Then it is very precious," said the Tin Woodman.

"Indeed it is," agreed the Scarecrow. "It may prove our best

means of escape from our difficulties. I believe I will think for a few minutes; so I will thank you, friend Tip, to get out your knife and rip this heavy crown from my forehead."

Tip soon cut the stitches that had fastened the crown to the Scarecrow's head, and the former monarch of the Emerald City removed it with a sigh of relief and hung it on a peg beside the throne.

"That is my last memento of royalty,"

said he; "and I'm glad to get rid of it. The former King of this City, who was named Pastoria, lost the crown to the Wonderful Wizard, who passed it on to me. Now the girl Jinjur claims it, and I sincerely hope it will not give her a headache."

"A kindly thought, which I greatly admire," said the Tin Woodman, nodding approvingly.

"And now I will indulge in a quiet think," continued the Scarecrow, lying back in the throne.

The others remained as silent and still as possible, so as not to disturb him; for all had great confidence in the extraordinary brains of the Scarecrow.

And, after what seemed a very long time indeed to the anxious watchers, the thinker sat up, looked upon his friends with his most whimsical expression, and said:

"My brains work beautifully today. I'm quite proud of them. Now, listen! If we attempt to escape through the doors of the palace we shall surely be captured. And, as we can't escape through the ground, there is only one other thing to be done. We must escape through the air!"

He paused to note the effect of these words; but all his hearers seemed puzzled and unconvinced.

"The Wonderful Wizard escaped in a balloon," he continued. "We don't know how to make a balloon, of course; but any sort of thing that can fly through the air can carry us easily. So I suggest that my friend the Tin Woodman, who is a skillful mechanic, shall build some sort of a machine, with good strong wings, to carry us; and our friend Tip can then bring the Thing to life with his magical powder."

"Bravo!" cried Nick Chopper.

"What splendid brains!" murmured Jack.

"Really quite clever!" said the Educated Woggle-Bug.

"I believe it can be done," declared Tip; "that is, if the Tin Woodman is equal to making the Thing."

"I'll do my best," said Nick, cheerily; "and, as a matter of fact, I do not often fail in what I attempt. But the Thing will have to be built on the roof of the palace, so it can rise comfortably into the air."

"To be sure," said the Scarecrow.

"Then let us search through the palace," continued the Tin Woodman, "and carry all the material we can find to the roof, where I will begin my work."

"First, however," said the Pumpkinhead, "I beg you will release me from this horse, and make me another leg to walk with. For in my present condition I am of no use to myself or to anyone else."

So the Tin Woodman knocked a mahogany center-table to pieces with his axe and fitted one of the legs, which was beautifully carved, on to the body of Jack Pumpkinhead, who was very proud of the acquisition.

"It seems strange," said he, as he watched the Tin Woodman work, "that my left leg should be the most elegant and substantial part of me."

"That proves you are unusual," returned the Scarecrow; "and I am convinced that the only people worthy of consideration in this world are the unusual ones. For the common folks are like the leaves of a tree, and live and die unnoticed."

"Spoken like a philosopher!" cried the Woggle-Bug, as he assisted the Tin Woodman to set Jack upon his feet.

"How do you feel now?" asked Tip, watching the Pumpkinhead stump around to try his new leg.

"As good as new," answered Jack, joyfully, "and quite ready to assist you all to escape."

"Then let us get to work," said the Scarecrow, in a business-like tone.

So, glad to be doing anything that might lead to the end of their captivity, the friends separated to wander over the palace in search of fitting material to use in the construction of their aerial machine.

The Astonishing Flight of the Gump

When the adventurers reassembled upon the roof it was found that a remarkably queer assortment of articles had been selected by the various members of the party. No one seemed to have a very clear idea of what was required, but all had brought something.

The Woggle-Bug had taken from its position over the mantle-piece in the great hallway the head of a Gump, which was adorned with wide-spreading antlers; and this, with great care and greater difficulty, the insect had carried up the stairs to the roof. This Gump resembled an Elk's head, only the nose turned upward in a saucy manner and there were whiskers upon its chin, like those of a billy-goat. Why the Woggle-Bug selected this article he could not have explained, except that it had aroused his curiosity.

Tip, with the aid of the Saw-Horse, had brought a large, upholstered sofa to the roof. It was an old-fashioned piece of furniture, with high back and ends, and it was so heavy that even by resting the greatest weight upon the back of the Saw-Horse, the boy found himself out of breath when at last the clumsy sofa was dumped upon the roof.

The Pumpkinhead had brought a broom, which was the first

thing he saw. The Scarecrow arrived with a coil of clothes-lines and ropes which he had taken from the courtyard, and in his trip up the stairs he had become so entangled in the loose ends of the ropes that both he and his burden tumbled in a heap upon the roof and might have rolled off if Tip had not rescued him.

The Tin Woodman appeared last. He also had been to the court-yard, where he had cut four great, spreading leaves from a huge palm-tree that was the pride of all the inhabitants of the Emerald City.

"My dear Nick!" exclaimed the Scarecrow, seeing what his friend had done; "you have been guilty of the greatest crime any person can commit in the Emerald City. If I remember rightly, the penalty for chopping leaves from the royal palm-tree is to be killed seven times and afterward imprisoned for life."

"It cannot be helped now," answered the Tin Woodman, throwing down the big leaves upon the roof. "But it may be one more reason why it is necessary for us to escape. And now let us see what you have found for me to work with."

Many were the doubtful looks cast upon the heap of miscellaneous material that now cluttered the roof, and finally the Scarecrow shook his head and remarked:

"Well, if friend Nick can manufacture, from this mess of rubbish, a Thing that will fly through the air and carry us to safety, then I will acknowledge him to be a better mechanic than I suspected."

But the Tin Woodman seemed at first by no means sure of his powers, and only after polishing his forehead vigorously with the chamois-leather did he resolve to undertake the task.

"The first thing required for the machine," said he, "is a body big enough to carry the entire party. This sofa is the biggest thing we have, and might be used for a body. But, should the machine ever tip sideways, we would all slide off and fall to the ground."

"Why not use two sofas?" asked Tip. "There's another one just like this down stairs."

"That is a very sensible suggestion," exclaimed the Tin Wood-man. "You must fetch the other sofa at once."

So Tip and the Saw-Horse managed, with much labor, to get the

ALL BROUGHT SOMETHING TO THE ROOF.

second sofa to the roof; and when the two were placed together, edge to edge, the backs and ends formed a protecting rampart all around the seats.

"Excellent!" cried the Scarecrow. "We can ride within this snug nest quite at our ease."

The two sofas were now bound firmly together with ropes and clothes-lines, and then Nick Chopper fastened the Gump's head to one end.

"That will show which is the front end of the Thing," said he, greatly pleased with the idea. "And, really, if you examine it critically, the Gump looks very well as a figure-head. These great palm-leaves, for which I have endangered my life seven times, must serve us as wings."

"Are they strong enough?" asked the boy.

"They are as strong as anything we can get," answered the Woodman; "and although they are not in proportion to the Thing's body, we are not in a position to be very particular."

So he fastened the palm-leaves to the sofas, two on each side.

Said the Woggle-Bug, with considerable admiration:

"The Thing is now complete, and only needs to be brought to life."

"Stop a moment!" exclaimed Jack. "Are you not going to use my broom?"

"What for?" asked the Scarecrow.

"Why, it can be fastened to the back end for a tail," answered the Pumpkinhead. "Surely you would not call the Thing complete without a tail."

"Hm!" said the Tin Woodman; "I do not see the use of a tail. We are not trying to copy a beast, or a fish, or a bird. All we ask of the Thing is to carry us through the air."

"Perhaps, after the Thing is brought to life, it can use a tail to steer with," suggested the Scarecrow. "For if it flies through the air it will not be unlike a bird, and I've noticed that all birds have tails, which they use for a rudder while flying."

"Very well," answered Nick, "the broom shall be used for a tail," and he fastened it firmly to the back end of the sofa body.

Tip took the pepper-box from his pocket.

"The Thing looks very big," said he, anxiously; "and I am not sure there is enough powder left to bring all of it to life. But I'll make it go as far as possible."

"Put most on the wings," said Nick Chopper; "for they must be made as strong as possible."

"And don't forget the head!" exclaimed the Woggle-Bug.

"Or the tail!" added Jack Pumpkinhead.

"Do be quiet," said Tip, nervously; "you must give me a chance to work the magic charm in the proper manner."

Very carefully he began sprinkling the Thing with the precious powder. Each of the four wings was first lightly covered with a layer; then the sofas were sprinkled, and the broom given a slight coating.

"The head! The head! Don't, I beg of you, forget the head!" cried the Woggle-Bug, excitedly.

"There's only a little of the powder left," announced Tip, looking within the box. "And it seems to me it is more important to bring the legs of the sofas to life than the head."

"Not so," decided the Scarecrow. "Every thing must have a head to direct it; and since this creature is to fly, and not walk, it is really unimportant whether its legs are alive or not."

So Tip abided by this decision and sprinkled the Gump's head with the remainder of the powder.

"Now," said he, "keep silence while I work the charm!"

Having heard old Mombi pronounce the magic words, and having also succeeded in bringing the Saw-

Horse to life, Tip did not hesitate an instant in speaking the three cabalistic words, each accompanied by the peculiar gesture of the hands.

It was a grave and impressive ceremony.

As he finished the incantation the Thing shuddered throughout its huge bulk, the Gump gave the screeching cry that is familiar to those animals, and then the four wings began flopping furiously.

Tip managed to grasp a chimney, else he would have been blown off the roof by the terrible breeze raised by the wings. The Scarecrow, being light in weight, was caught up bodily and borne through the air until Tip luckily seized him by one leg and held him fast. The Woggle-Bug lay flat upon the roof and so escaped harm, and the Tin Woodman, whose weight of tin anchored him firmly, threw both arms around Jack Pumpkinhead and managed to save him. The Saw-Horse toppled over upon his back and lay with his legs waving helplessly above him.

And now, while all were struggling to recover themselves, the Thing rose slowly from the roof and mounted into the air.

"Here! Come back!" cried Tip, in a frightened voice, as he clung to the chimney with one hand and the Scarecrow with the other. "Come back at once, I command you!"

It was now that the wisdom of the Scarecrow, in bringing the head of the Thing to life instead of the legs, was proved beyond a doubt. For the Gump, already high in the air, turned its head at Tip's command and gradually circled around until it could view the roof of the palace.

"Come back!" shouted the boy, again.

And the Gump obeyed, slowly and gracefully waving its four wings in the air until the Thing had settled once more upon the roof and become still.

In the Jackdaws' Nest

"This," said the Gump, in a squeaky voice not at all proportioned to the size of its great body, "is the most novel experience I ever heard of. The last thing I remember distinctly is walking through the forest and hearing a loud noise. Something probably killed me then, and it certainly ought to have been the end of me. Yet here I am, alive again, with four monstrous wings and a body which I venture to say would make any respectable animal or fowl weep with shame to own. What does it all mean? Am I a Gump, or am I a juggernaut?" The creature, as it spoke, wiggled its chin whiskers in a very comical manner.

"You're just a Thing," answered Tip, "with a Gump's head on it. And we have made you and brought you to life so that you may carry us through the air wherever we wish to go."

"Very good!" said the Thing. "As I am not a Gump, I cannot have a Gump's pride or independent spirit. So I may as well become your servant as anything else. My only satisfaction is that I do not seem to have a very strong constitution, and am not likely to live long in a state of slavery."

"Don't say that, I beg of you!" cried the Tin Woodman, whose excellent heart was strongly affected by this sad speech. "Are you not feeling well today?"

"Oh, as for that," returned the Gump, "it is my first day of existence; so I cannot judge whether I am feeling well or ill." And it waved its broom tail to and fro in a pensive manner.

"Come, come!" said the Scarecrow, kindly; "do try to be more cheerful and take life as you find it. We shall be kind masters, and will strive to render your existence as pleasant as possible. Are you willing to carry us through the air wherever we wish to go?"

"Certainly," answered the Gump. "I greatly prefer to navigate the air. For should I travel on the earth and meet with one of my own species, my embarrassment would be something awful!"

"I can appreciate that," said the Tin Woodman, sympathetically.

"And yet," continued the Thing, "when I carefully look you over, my masters, none of you seems to be constructed much more artistically than I am."

"Appearances are deceitful," said the Woggle-Bug, earnestly. "I am both Highly Magnified and Thoroughly Educated."

"Indeed!" murmured the Gump, indifferently.

"And my brains are considered remarkably rare specimens," added the Scarecrow, proudly.

"How strange!" remarked the Gump.

"Although I am of tin," said the Woodman, "I own a heart altogether the warmest and most admirable in the whole world."

"I'm delighted to hear it," replied the Gump, with a slight cough.

"My smile," said Jack Pumpkinhead, "is worthy your best attention. It is always the same."

"*Semper idem,*" explained the Woggle-Bug, pompously; and the Gump turned to stare at him.

"And I," declared the Saw-Horse, filling in an awkward pause, "am only remarkable because I can't help it."

"I am proud, indeed, to meet with such exceptional masters," said the Gump, in a careless tone. "If I could but secure so complete an introduction to myself, I would be more than satisfied."

"That will come in time," remarked the Scarecrow. "To 'Know Thyself' is considered quite an accomplishment, which it has taken us, who are your elders, months to perfect. But now," he added, turning to the others, "let us get aboard and start upon our journey."

"Where shall we go?" asked Tip, as he clambered to a seat on the sofas and assisted the Pumpkinhead to follow him.

"In the South Country rules a very delightful Queen called Glinda the Good, who I am sure will gladly receive us," said the Scarecrow, getting into the Thing clumsily. "Let us go to her and ask her advice."

"That is cleverly thought of," declared Nick Chopper, giving the Woggle-Bug a boost and then toppling the Saw-Horse into the rear end of the cushioned seats. "I know Glinda the Good, and believe she will prove a friend indeed."

"Are we all ready?" asked the boy.

"Yes," announced the Tin Woodman, seating himself beside the Scarecrow.

"Then," said Tip, addressing the Gump, "be kind enough to fly with us to the Southward; and do not go higher than to escape the houses and trees, for it makes me dizzy to be up so far."

"All right," answered the Gump, briefly.

It flopped its four huge wings and rose slowly into the air; and then, while our little band of adventurers clung to the backs and sides of the sofas for support, the Gump turned toward the South and soared swiftly and majestically away.

"The scenic effect, from this altitude, is marvelous," commented the educated Woggle-Bug, as they rode along.

"Never mind the scenery," said the Scarecrow. "Hold on tight, or you may get a tumble. The Thing seems to rock badly."

"It will be dark soon," said Tip, observing that the sun was low on the horizon. "Perhaps we should have waited until morning. I wonder if the Gump can fly in the night."

"I've been wondering that myself," returned the Gump, quietly. "You see, this is a new experience to me. I used to have legs that carried me swiftly over the ground. But now my legs feel as if they were asleep."

"They are," said Tip. "We didn't bring 'em to life."

"You're expected to fly," explained the Scarecrow; "not to walk."

"We can walk ourselves," said the Woggle-Bug.

"I begin to understand what is required of me," remarked the Gump; "so I will do my best to please you," and he flew on for a time in silence.

Presently Jack Pumpkinhead became uneasy.

"I wonder if riding through the air is liable to spoil pumpkins," he said.

"Not unless you carelessly drop your head over the side," answered the Woggle-Bug. "In that event your head would no longer be a pumpkin, for it would become a squash."

"Have I not asked you to restrain these unfeeling jokes?" demanded Tip, looking at the Woggle-Bug with a severe expression.

"You have; and I've restrained a good many of them," replied the insect. "But there are opportunities for so many excellent puns in our language that, to an educated person like myself, the temptation to express them is almost irresistible."

"People with more or less education discovered those puns centuries ago," said Tip.

"Are you sure?" asked the Woggle-Bug, with a startled look.

"Of course I am," answered the boy. "An educated Woggle-Bug may be a new thing; but a Woggle-Bug education is as old as the hills, judging from the display you make of it."

The insect seemed much impressed by this remark, and for a time maintained a meek silence.

The Scarecrow, in shifting his seat, saw upon the cushions the pepper-box which Tip had cast aside, and began to examine it.

"Throw it overboard," said the boy; "it's quite empty now, and there's no use keeping it."

"Is it really empty?" asked the Scarecrow, looking curiously into the box.

"Of course it is," answered Tip. "I shook out every grain of the powder."

"Then the box has two bottoms," announced the Scarecrow; "for the bottom on the inside is fully an inch away from the bottom on the outside."

"Let me see," said the Tin Woodman, taking the box from his

friend. "Yes," he declared, after looking it over, "the thing certainly has a false bottom. Now, I wonder what that is for?"

"Can't you get it apart, and find out?" enquired Tip, now quite interested in the mystery.

"Why, yes; the lower bottom unscrews," said the Tin Woodman. "My fingers are rather stiff; please see if you can open it."

He handed the pepper-box to Tip, who had no difficulty in unscrewing the bottom. And in the cavity below were three silver pills, with a carefully folded paper lying underneath them.

This paper the boy proceeded to unfold, taking care not to spill the pills, and found several lines clearly written in red ink.

"Read it aloud," said the Scarecrow; so Tip read as follows:

"DR. NIKIDIK'S CELEBRATED WISHING PILLS.

"*Directions for Use:* Swallow one pill; count seventeen by twos; then make a Wish.—The Wish will immediately be granted.
CAUTION: Keep in a Dry and Dark Place."

"Why, this is a very valuable discovery!" cried the Scarecrow.

"It is, indeed," replied Tip, gravely. "These pills may be of great use to us. I wonder if old Mombi knew they were in the bottom of the pepper-box. I remember hearing her say that she got the Powder of Life from this same Nikidik."

"He must be a powerful Sorcerer!" exclaimed the Tin Woodman; "and since the powder proved a success we ought to have confidence in the pills."

"But how," asked the Scarecrow, "can anyone count seventeen by twos? Seventeen is an odd number."

"That is true," replied Tip, greatly disappointed. "No one can possibly count seventeen by twos."

"Then the pills are of no use to us," wailed the Pumpkinhead; "and this fact overwhelms me with grief. For I had intended wishing that my head would never spoil."

"Nonsense!" said the Scarecrow, sharply. "If we could use the pills at all we would make far better wishes than that."

"I do not see how anything could be better," protested poor Jack. "If you were liable to spoil at any time you could understand my anxiety."

"For my part," said the Tin Woodman, "I sympathize with you in every respect. But since we cannot count seventeen by twos, sympathy is all you are liable to get."

By this time it had become quite dark, and the voyagers found above them a cloudy sky, through which the rays of the moon could not penetrate.

The Gump flew steadily on, and for some reason the huge sofa-body rocked more and more dizzily every hour.

The Woggle-Bug declared he was sea-sick; and Tip was also pale and somewhat distressed. But the others clung to the backs of the sofas and did not seem to mind the motion as long as they were not tipped out.

Darker and darker grew the night, and on and on sped the Gump through the black heavens. The travelers could not even see one another, and an oppressive silence settled down upon them.

After a long time Tip, who had been thinking deeply, spoke.

"How are we to know when we come to the palace of Glinda the Good?" he asked.

"It's a long way to Glinda's palace," answered the Woodman; "I've traveled it."

"But how are we to know how fast the Gump is flying?" persisted the boy. "We cannot see a single thing down on the earth, and before morning we may be far beyond the place we want to reach."

"That is all true enough," the Scarecrow replied, a little uneasily. "But I do not see how we can stop just now; for we might alight in a river, or on the top of a steeple; and that would be a great disaster."

So they permitted the Gump to fly on, with regular flops of its great wings, and waited patiently for morning.

Then Tip's fears were proven to be well founded; for with the first streaks of grey dawn they looked over the sides of the sofas and discovered rolling plains dotted with queer villages, where the houses, instead of being dome-shaped—as they all are in the Land of Oz—had slanting roofs that rose to a peak in the center. Odd looking animals were also moving about upon the open plains, and the country was unfamiliar to both the Tin Woodman and the Scarecrow, who had formerly visited Glinda the Good's domain and knew it well.

"We are lost!" said the Scarecrow, dolefully. "The Gump must have carried us entirely out of the Land of Oz and over the sandy deserts and into the terrible outside world that Dorothy told us about."

"We must get back," exclaimed the Tin Woodman, earnestly; "we must get back as soon as possible!"

"Turn around!" cried Tip to the Gump; "turn as quickly as you can!"

"If I do I shall upset," answered the Gump. "I'm not at all used to flying, and the best plan would be for me to alight in some place, and then I can turn around and take a fresh start."

Just then, however, there seemed to be no stopping-place that would answer their purpose. They flew over a village so big that the Woggle-Bug declared it was a city; and then they came to a range of high mountains with many deep gorges and steep cliffs showing plainly.

"Now is our chance to stop," said the boy, finding they were very close to the mountain tops. Then he turned to the Gump and commanded: "Stop at the first level place you see!"

"Very well," answered the Gump, and settled down upon a table of rock that stood between two cliffs.

But not being experienced in such matters, the Gump did not judge his speed correctly; and instead of coming to a stop upon the flat rock he missed it by half the width of his body, breaking off both his right wings against the sharp edge of the rock and then tumbling over and over down the cliff.

Our friends held on to the sofas as long as they could, but when the Gump caught on a projecting rock the Thing stopped suddenly—bottom side up—and all were immediately dumped out.

By good fortune they fell only a few feet; for underneath them was a monster nest, built by a colony of Jackdaws in a hollow ledge of rock; so none of them—not even the Pumpkinhead—was in-

ALL WERE IMMEDIATELY DUMPED OUT.

jured by the fall. For Jack found his precious head resting on the soft breast of the Scarecrow, which made an excellent cushion; and Tip fell on a mass of leaves and papers, which saved him from injury. The Woggle-Bug had bumped his round head against the Saw-Horse, but without causing him more than a moment's inconvenience.

The Tin Woodman was at first much alarmed; but finding he had escaped without even a scratch upon his beautiful nickel-plate he at once regained his accustomed cheerfulness and turned to address his comrades.

"Our journey has ended rather suddenly," said he, "and we cannot justly blame our friend the Gump for our accident, because he did the best he could under the circumstances. But how we are ever to escape from this nest I must leave to someone with better brains than I possess."

Here he gazed at the Scarecrow, who crawled to the edge of the nest and looked over. Below them was a sheer precipice several hundred feet in depth. Above them was a smooth cliff unbroken save by the point of rock where the wrecked body of the Gump still hung suspended from the end of one of the sofas. There really seemed to be no means of escape, and as they realized their helpless plight the little band of adventurers gave way to their bewilderment.

"This is a worse prison than the palace," sadly remarked the Woggle-Bug.

"I wish we had stayed there," moaned Jack. "I'm afraid the mountain air isn't good for pumpkins."

"It won't be when the Jackdaws come back," growled the Saw-Horse, which lay waving its legs in a vain endeavor to get upon its feet again. "Jackdaws are especially fond of pumpkins."

"Do you think the birds will come here?" asked Jack, much distressed.

"Of course they will," said Tip; "for this is their nest. And there must be hundreds of them," he continued, "for see what a lot of things they have brought here!"

Indeed, the nest was half filled with a most curious collection of

TURNED UP A BEAUTIFUL DIAMOND NECKLACE.

small articles for which the birds could have no use, but which the thieving Jackdaws had stolen during many years from the homes of men. And as the nest was safely hidden where no human being could reach it, this lost property would never be recovered.

The Woggle-Bug, searching among the rubbish—for the Jackdaws stole useless things as well as valuable ones—turned up with his foot a beautiful diamond necklace. This was so greatly admired by the Tin Woodman that the Woggle-Bug presented it to him with a graceful speech, after which the Woodman hung it around his neck with much pride, rejoicing exceedingly when the big diamonds glittered in the sun's rays.

But now they heard a great jabbering and flopping of wings, and as the sound grew nearer to them Tip exclaimed:

"The Jackdaws are coming! And if they find us here they will surely kill us in their anger."

"I was afraid of this!" moaned the Pumpkinhead. "My time has come!"

"And mine, also!" said the Woggle-Bug; "for Jackdaws are the greatest enemies of my race."

The others were not at all afraid; but the Scarecrow at once decided to save those of the party who were liable to be injured by the angry birds. So he commanded Tip to take off Jack's head and lie down with it in the bottom of the nest, and when this was done he ordered the Woggle-Bug to lie beside Tip. Nick Chopper, who knew from past experience just what to do, then took the Scarecrow to pieces—(all except his head)—and scattered the straw over Tip and the Woggle-Bug, completely covering their bodies.

Hardly had this been accomplished when the flock of Jackdaws reached them. Perceiving the intruders in their nest the birds flew down upon them with screams of rage.

Dr. Nikidik's Famous Wishing Pills

The Tin Woodman was usually a peaceful man, but when occasion required he could fight as fiercely as a Roman gladiator. So, when the Jackdaws nearly knocked him down in their rush of wings, and their sharp beaks and claws threatened to damage his brilliant plating, the Woodman picked up his axe and made it whirl swiftly around his head.

But although many were beaten off in this way, the birds were so numerous and so brave that they continued the attack as furiously as before. Some of them pecked at the eyes of the Gump, which hung over the nest in a helpless condition; but the Gump's eyes were of glass and could not be injured. Others of the Jackdaws rushed at the Saw-Horse; but that animal, being still upon his back, kicked out so viciously with his wooden legs that he beat off as many assailants as did the Woodman's axe.

Finding themselves thus opposed, the birds fell upon the Scarecrow's straw, which lay at the center of the nest, covering Tip and the Woggle-Bug and Jack's pumpkin head, and began tearing it away and flying off with it, only to let it drop, straw by straw into the great gulf beneath.

The Scarecrow's head, noting with dismay this wanton destruction of his interior, cried to the Tin Woodman to save him; and that good friend responded with renewed energy. His axe fairly flashed among the Jackdaws, and fortunately the Gump began wildly waving the two wings remaining on the left side of its body. The flutter of these great wings filled the Jackdaws with terror, and when the Gump by its exertions freed itself from the peg of rock on which it hung, and sank flopping into the nest, the alarm of the birds knew no bounds and they fled screaming over the mountains.

When the last foe had disappeared, Tip crawled from under the sofas and assisted the Woggle-Bug to follow him.

"We are saved!" shouted the boy, delightedly.

"We are, indeed!" responded the Educated Insect, fairly hugging the stiff head of the Gump in his joy; "and we owe it all to the flopping of the Thing and the good axe of the Woodman!"

"If I am saved, get me out of here!" called Jack, whose head was still beneath the sofas; and Tip managed to roll the pumpkin out and place it upon its neck again. He also set the Saw-Horse upright, and said to it:

"We owe you many thanks for the gallant fight you made."

"I really think we have escaped very nicely," remarked the Tin Woodman, in a tone of pride.

"Not so!" exclaimed a hollow voice.

At this they all turned in surprise to look at the Scarecrow's head, which lay at the back of the nest.

"I am completely ruined!" declared the Scarecrow, as he noted their astonishment. "For where is the straw that stuffs my body?"

The awful question startled them all. They gazed around the nest with horror, for not a vestige of straw remained. The Jackdaws had stolen it to the last wisp and flung it all into the chasm that yawned for hundreds of feet beneath the nest.

"My poor, poor friend!" said the Tin Woodman, taking up the Scarecrow's head and caressing it tenderly; "whoever could imagine you would come to this untimely end?"

"I did it to save my friends," returned the head; "and I am glad that I perished in so noble and unselfish a manner."

"But why are you all so despondent?" inquired the Woggle-Bug. "The Scarecrow's clothing is still safe."

"Yes," answered the Tin Woodman; "but our friend's clothes are useless without stuffing."

"Why not stuff him with money?" asked Tip.

"Money!" they all cried, in an amazed chorus.

"To be sure," said the boy. "In the bottom of the nest are thousands of dollar bills—and two-dollar bills— and five-dollar bills—and tens, and twenties, and fifties. There are enough of them to stuff a dozen Scarecrows. Why not use the money?"

The Tin Woodman began to turn over the rubbish with the handle of his axe; and, sure enough, what they had first thought only worthless papers were found to be all bills of various denominations, which the mischievous Jackdaws had for years been engaged in stealing from the villages and cities they visited.

There was an immense fortune lying in that inaccessible nest; and Tip's suggestion was, with the Scarecrow's consent, quickly acted upon.

They selected all the newest and cleanest bills and assorted them into various piles. The Scarecrow's left leg and boot were stuffed with five-dollar bills; his right leg was stuffed with ten-dollar bills, and his body so closely filled with fifties, one-hundreds and one-thousands that he could scarcely button his jacket with comfort.

"You are now," said the Woggle-Bug, impressively, when the task had been completed, "the most valuable member of our party; and as you are among faithful friends there is little danger of your being spent."

"Thank you," returned the Scarecrow, gratefully. "I feel like a new man; and although at
first glance I might be mistaken for a
Safety Deposit Vault, I beg you to remember that my brains are still composed of the same old material. And
these are the possessions that have
always made me a person to
be depended upon in an
emergency."

"Well, the emergency
is here," observed Tip;
"and unless your brains
help us out of it we shall
be compelled to pass the
remainder of our lives in
this nest."

"How about these wishing
pills?" enquired the Scarecrow, taking the
box from his jacket pocket. "Can't we use them to escape?"

"Not unless we can count seventeen by twos," answered the Tin
Woodman. "But our friend the Woggle-Bug claims to be highly educated, so he ought easily to figure out how that can be done."

"It isn't a question of education," returned the Insect; "it's
merely a question of mathematics. I've seen the Professor work lots
of sums on the blackboard, and he claimed anything could be done
with x's and y's and a's, and such things, by mixing them up with
plenty of plusses and minuses and equals, and so forth. But he never
said anything, so far as I can remember, about counting up to the
odd number of seventeen by the even numbers of twos."

"Stop! stop!" cried the Pumpkinhead. "You're making my head
ache."

"And mine," added the Scarecrow. "Your mathematics seem to
me very like a bottle of mixed pickles—the more you fish for what
you want the less chance you have of getting it. I am certain that if
the thing can be accomplished at all, it is in a very simple manner."

"Yes," said Tip; "old Mombi couldn't use x's and minuses, for she never went to school."

"Why not start counting at a half of one?" asked the Saw-Horse, abruptly. "Then anyone can count up to seventeen by twos very easily."

They looked at each other in surprise, for the Saw-Horse was considered the most stupid of the entire party.

"You make me quite ashamed of myself," said the Scarecrow, bowing low to the Saw-Horse.

"Nevertheless, the creature is right," declared the Woggle-Bug; "for twice one-half is one, and if you get to one it is easy to count from one up to seventeen by twos."

"I wonder I didn't think of that myself," said the Pumpkinhead.

"I don't," returned the Scarecrow. "You're no wiser than the rest of us, are you? But let us make a wish at once. Who will swallow the first pill?"

"Suppose you do it," suggested Tip.

"I can't," said the Scarecrow.

"Why not? You've a mouth, haven't you?" asked the boy.

"Yes; but my mouth is painted on, and there's no swallow connected with it," answered the Scarecrow. "In fact," he continued, looking from one to another critically, "I believe the boy and the Woggle-Bug are the only ones in our party that are able to swallow."

Observing the truth of this remark, Tip said:

"Then I will undertake to make the first wish. Give me one of the Silver Pills."

This the Scarecrow tried to do; but his padded gloves were too clumsy to clutch so small an object, and he held the box toward the boy while Tip selected one of the pills and swallowed it.

"Count!" cried the Scarecrow.

"One-half, one, three, five, seven, nine, eleven, thirteen, fifteen, seventeen!" counted Tip.

"Now wish!" said the Tin Woodman anxiously.

But just then the boy began to suffer such fearful pains that he became alarmed.

"The pill has poisoned me!" he gasped; "O—h! O-o-o-o-o! Ouch! Murder! Fire! O-o-h!" and here he rolled upon the bottom of the nest in such contortions that he frightened them all.

"What can we do for you? Speak, I beg!" entreated the Tin Woodman, tears of sympathy running down his nickel cheeks.

"I—I don't know!" answered Tip. "O—h! I wish I'd never swallowed that pill!"

Then at once the pain stopped, and the boy rose to his feet again and found the Scarecrow looking with amazement at the end of the pepper-box.

"What's happened?" asked the boy, a little ashamed of his recent exhibition.

"Why, the three pills are in the box again!" said the Scarecrow.

"Of course they are," the Woggle-Bug declared. "Didn't Tip wish that he'd never swallowed one of them? Well, the wish came true, and he *didn't* swallow one of them. So of course they are all three in the box."

"That may be; but the pill gave me a dreadful pain, just the same," said the boy.

"Impossible!" declared the Woggle-Bug. "If you have never swallowed it, the pill can not have given you a pain. And as your wish, being granted, proves you did not swallow the pill, it is also plain that you suffered no pain."

"Then it was a splendid imitation of a pain," retorted Tip, angrily. "Suppose you try the next pill yourself. We've wasted one wish already."

"Oh, no, we haven't!" protested the Scarecrow. "Here are still three pills in the box, and each pill is good for a wish."

"Now you're making *my* head ache," said Tip. "I can't understand the thing at all. But I won't take another pill, I promise you!" and with this remark he retired sulkily to the back of the nest.

"Well," said the Woggle-Bug, "it remains for me to save us in my most Highly Magnified and Thoroughly Educated manner; for I seem to be the only one able and willing to make a wish. Let me have one of the pills."

He swallowed it without hesitation, and they all stood admiring his courage while the Insect counted seventeen by twos in the same way that Tip had done. And for some reason—perhaps because Woggle-Bugs have stronger stomachs than boys—the silver pellet caused it no pain whatever.

"I wish the Gump's broken wings mended, and as good as new!" said the Woggle-Bug, in a slow, impressive voice.

All turned to look at the Thing, and so quickly had the wish been granted that the Gump lay before them in perfect repair, and as well able to fly through the air as when it had first been brought to life on the roof of the palace.

The Scarecrow Appeals to Glinda the Good

"Hooray!" shouted the Scarecrow, gaily. "We can now leave this miserable Jackdaws' nest whenever we please."

"But it is nearly dark," said the Tin Woodman; "and unless we wait until morning to make our flight we may get into more trouble. I don't like these night trips, for one never knows what will happen."

So it was decided to wait until daylight, and the adventurers amused themselves in the twilight by searching the Jackdaws' nest for treasures.

The Woggle-Bug found two handsome bracelets of wrought gold, which fitted his slender arms very well. The Scarecrow took a fancy for rings, of which there were many in the nest. Before long he had fitted a ring to each finger of his padded gloves, and not being content with that display he added one more to each thumb. As he carefully chose those rings set with sparkling stones, such as rubies, amethysts and sapphires, the Scarecrow's hands now presented a most brilliant appearance.

"This nest would be a picnic for Queen Jinjur," said he, musingly; "for as nearly as I can make out she and her girls conquered me merely to rob my city of its emeralds."

The Tin Woodman was content with his diamond necklace and refused to accept any additional decorations; but Tip secured a fine gold watch, which was attached to a heavy fob, and placed it in his pocket with much pride. He also pinned several jeweled brooches to Jack Pumpkinhead's red waistcoat, and attached a lorgnette, by means of a fine chain, to the neck of the Saw-Horse.

"It's very pretty," said the creature, regarding the lorgnette approvingly; "but what is it for?"

None of them could answer that question, however; so the Saw-Horse decided it was some rare decoration and became very fond of it.

That none of the party might be slighted, they ended by placing several large seal rings upon the points of the Gump's antlers, although that odd personage seemed by no means gratified by the attention.

Darkness soon fell upon them, and Tip and the Woggle-Bug went to sleep while the others sat down to wait patiently for the day.

Next morning they had cause to congratulate themselves upon the useful condition of the Gump; for with daylight a great flock of Jackdaws approached to engage in one more battle for the possession of the nest.

But our adventurers did not wait for the assault. They tumbled into the cushioned seats of the sofas as quickly as possible, and Tip gave the word to the Gump to start.

At once it rose into the air, the great wings flopping strongly and with regular motions, and in a few moments they were so far from the nest that the chattering Jackdaws took possession without any attempt at pursuit.

The Thing flew due North, going in the same direction from whence it had come. At least, that was the Scarecrow's opinion, and the others agreed that the Scarecrow was the best judge of direction. After passing over several cities and villages the Gump carried them high above a broad plain where houses became more and more scattered until they disappeared altogether. Next came the wide, sandy desert separating the rest of the world from the Land of Oz, and before noon they saw the dome-shaped houses that proved they were once more within the borders of their native land.

"But the houses and fences are blue," said the Tin Woodman, "and that indicates we are in the land of the Munchkins, and therefore a long distance from Glinda the Good."

"What shall we do?" asked the boy, turning to their guide.

"I don't know," replied the Scarecrow, frankly. "If we were at the Emerald City we could then move directly southward, and so reach our destination. But we dare not go to the Emerald City, and the Gump is probably carrying us further in the wrong direction with every flop of its wings."

"Then the Woggle-Bug must swallow another pill," said Tip, decidedly, "and wish us headed in the right direction."

"Very well," returned the Highly Magnified one; "I'm willing."

But when the Scarecrow searched in his pocket for the pepperbox containing the two silver Wishing Pills, it was not to be found. Filled with anxiety, the voyagers hunted throughout every inch of the Thing for the precious box; but it had disappeared entirely.

And still the Gump flew onward, carrying them they knew not where.

"I must have left the pepper-box in the Jackdaws' nest," said the Scarecrow, at length.

"It is a great misfortune," the Tin Woodman declared. "But we are no worse off than before we discovered the Wishing Pills."

"We are better off," replied Tip; "for the one pill we used has enabled us to escape from that horrible nest."

"Yet the loss of the other two is serious, and I deserve a good scolding for my carelessness," the Scarecrow rejoined, penitently. "For in such an unusual party as this accidents are liable to happen any moment, and even now we may be approaching a new danger."

No one dared contradict this, and a dismal silence ensued.

The Gump flew steadily on.

Suddenly Tip uttered an exclamation of surprise.

"We must have reached the South Country," he cried, "for below us everything is red!"

Immediately they all leaned over the backs of the sofas to look—

all except Jack, who was too careful of his pumpkin head to risk its slipping off his neck. Sure enough; the red houses and fences and trees indicated they were within the domain of Glinda the Good; and presently, as they glided rapidly on, the Tin Woodman recognized the roads and buildings they passed, and altered slightly the flight of the Gump so that they might reach the palace of the celebrated Sorceress.

"Good!" cried the Scarecrow, delightedly. "We do not need the lost Wishing Pills now, for we have arrived at our destination."

Gradually the Thing sank lower and nearer to the ground until at length it came to rest within the beautiful gardens of Glinda, settling upon a velvety green lawn close by a fountain which sent sprays of flashing gems, instead of water, high into the air, whence they fell with a soft, tinkling sound into the carved marble basin placed to receive them.

Everything was very gorgeous in Glinda's gardens, and while our voyagers gazed about with admiring eyes a company of soldiers silently appeared and surrounded them. But these soldiers of the great Sorceress were entirely different from those of Jinjur's Army of Revolt, although they were likewise girls. For Glinda's soldiers wore neat uniforms and bore swords and spears; and they marched with a skill and precision that proved them well trained in the arts of war.

The Captain commanding this troop—which was Glinda's private Body Guard—recognized the Scarecrow and the Tin Woodman at once, and greeted them with respectful salutations.

"Good day!" said the Scarecrow, gallantly removing his hat, while the Woodman gave a soldierly salute; "we have come to request an audience with your fair Ruler."

"Glinda is now within her palace, awaiting you," returned the Captain; "for she saw you coming long before you arrived."

"That is strange!" said Tip, wondering.

"Not at all," answered the Scarecrow; "for Glinda the Good is a mighty Sorceress, and nothing that goes on in the Land of Oz escapes her notice. I suppose she knows why we came as well as we do ourselves."

"Then what was the use of our coming?" asked Jack, stupidly.

"To prove you are a Pumpkinhead!" retorted the Scarecrow. "But, if the Sorceress expects us, we must not keep her waiting."

So they all clambered out of the sofas and followed the Captain toward the palace—even the Saw-Horse taking his place in the queer procession.

Upon her throne of finely wrought gold sat Glinda, and she could scarcely repress a smile as her peculiar visitors entered and bowed before her. Both the Scarecrow and the Tin Woodman she knew and liked; but the awkward Pumpkinhead and Highly Magnified Woggle-Bug were creatures she had never seen before, and they seemed even more curious than the others. As for the Saw-Horse, he looked to be nothing more than an animated chunk of wood; and he bowed so stiffly that his head bumped against the floor, causing a ripple of laughter among the soldiers, in which Glinda frankly joined.

"I beg to announce to Your Glorious Highness," began the Scarecrow, in a solemn voice, "that my Emerald City has been overrun by a crowd of impudent girls with knitting-needles, who have enslaved all the men, robbed the streets and public buildings of all their emerald jewels, and usurped my throne."

"I know it," said Glinda.

"They also threatened to destroy me, as well as all the good friends and allies you see before you," continued the Scarecrow; "and had we not managed to escape their clutches our days would long since have ended."

"I know it," repeated Glinda.

"Therefore I have come to beg your assistance," resumed the Scarecrow, "for I believe you are always glad to succor the unfortunate and oppressed."

"That is true," replied the Sorceress, slowly. "But the Emerald City is now ruled by General Jinjur, who has caused herself to be proclaimed Queen. What right have I to oppose her?"

"Why, she stole the throne from me," said the Scarecrow.

"And how came you to possess the throne?" asked Glinda.

"I got it from the Wizard of Oz, and by the choice of the people," returned the Scarecrow, uneasy at such questioning.

"And where did the Wizard get it?" she continued, gravely.

"I am told he took it from Pastoria, the former King," said the Scarecrow, becoming confused under the intent look of the Sorceress.

"Then," declared Glinda, "the throne of the Emerald City belongs neither to you nor to Jinjur, but to this Pastoria from whom the Wizard usurped it."

"That is true," acknowledged the Scarecrow, humbly; "but Pastoria is now dead and gone, and some one must rule in his place."

"Pastoria had a daughter, who is the rightful heir to the throne of the Emerald City. Did you know that?" questioned the Sorceress.

"No," replied the Scarecrow. "But if the girl still lives I will not stand in her way. It will satisfy me as well to have Jinjur turned out, as an impostor, as to regain the throne myself. In fact, it isn't much fun to be King, especially if one has good brains. I have known for some time that I am fitted to occupy a far more exalted position. But where is this girl who owns the throne, and what is her name?"

"Her name is Ozma," answered Glinda. "But where she is I have tried in vain to discover. For the Wizard of Oz, when he stole the throne from Ozma's father, hid the girl in some secret place; and by means of a magical trick with which I am not familiar he also managed to prevent her being discovered—even by so experienced a Sorceress as myself."

"That is strange," interrupted the Woggle-Bug, pompously. "I have been informed that the Wonderful Wizard of Oz was nothing more than a humbug!"

"Nonsense!" exclaimed the Scarecrow, much provoked by this speech. "Didn't he give me a wonderful set of brains?"

"There's no humbug about my heart," announced the Tin Woodman, glaring indignantly at the Woggle-Bug.

"Perhaps I was misinformed," stammered the Insect, shrinking back; "I never knew the Wizard personally."

"Well, we did," retorted the Scarecrow, "and he was a very great Wizard, I assure you. It is true he was guilty of some slight impostures, but unless he was a great Wizard how—let me ask—could he have hidden this girl Ozma so securely that no one can find her?"

"I—I give it up!" replied the Woggle-Bug, meekly.

"That is the most sensible speech you've made," said the Tin Woodman.

"I must really make another effort to discover where this girl is hidden," resumed the Sorceress, thoughtfully. "I have in my library a book in which is inscribed every action of the Wizard while he was in our Land of Oz—or, at least, every action that could be observed by my spies. This book I will read carefully tonight, and try to single out the acts that may guide us in discovering the lost Ozma. In the meantime, pray amuse yourselves in my palace and command my servants as if they were your own. I will grant you another audience tomorrow."

With this gracious speech Glinda dismissed the adventurers, and they wandered away through the beautiful gardens, where they passed several hours enjoying all the delightful things with which the Queen of the Southland had surrounded her royal palace.

On the following morning they again appeared before Glinda, who said to them:

"I have searched carefully through the records of the Wizard's actions, and among them I can find but three that appear to have been suspicious. He ate beans with a knife, made three secret visits to old Mombi, and limped slightly on his left foot."

"Ah! that last is certainly suspicious!" exclaimed the Pumpkinhead.

"Not necessarily," said the Scarecrow; "he may have had corns. Now, it seems to me his eating beans with a knife is more suspicious."

"Perhaps it is a polite custom in Omaha, from which great country the Wizard originally came," suggested the Tin Woodman.

"It may be," admitted the Scarecrow.

"But why," asked Glinda, "did he make three secret visits to old Mombi?"

"Ah! Why, indeed!" echoed the Woggle-Bug, impressively.

"We know that the Wizard taught the old woman many of his tricks of magic," continued Glinda; "and this he would not have done had she not assisted him in some way. So we may suspect with good reason that Mombi aided him to hide the girl Ozma, who was the real heir to the throne of the Emerald City, and a constant danger to the usurper. For, if the people knew that she lived, they would quickly make her their Queen and restore her to her rightful position."

"An able argument!" cried the Scarecrow. "I have no doubt that Mombi was mixed up in this wicked business. But how does that knowledge help us?"

"We must find Mombi," replied Glinda, "and force her to tell where the girl is hidden."

"Mombi is now with Queen Jinjur, in the Emerald City," said Tip. "It was she who threw so many obstacles in our pathway, and made Jinjur threaten to destroy my friends and give me back into the old witch's power."

"Then," decided Glinda, "I will march with my army to the Emerald City, and take Mombi prisoner. After that we can, perhaps, force her to tell the truth about Ozma."

"She is a terrible old woman!" remarked Tip, with a shudder at the thought of Mombi's black kettle; "and obstinate, too."

"I am quite obstinate myself," returned the Sorceress, with a sweet smile; "so I do not fear Mombi in the least. Today I will make all necessary preparations, and we will march upon the Emerald City at daybreak tomorrow."

The Tin-Woodman Plucks a Rose

The Army of Glinda the Good looked very grand and imposing when it assembled at daybreak before the palace gates. The uniforms of the girl soldiers were pretty and of gay colors, and their silver-tipped spears were bright and glistening, the long shafts being inlaid with mother-of-pearl. All the officers wore sharp, gleaming swords, and shields edged with peacock-feathers; and it really seemed that no foe could by any possibility defeat such a brilliant army.

The Sorceress rode in a beautiful palanquin which was like the body of a coach, having doors and windows with silken curtains; but instead of wheels, which a coach has, the palanquin rested upon two long, horizontal bars, which were borne upon the shoulders of twelve servants.

The Scarecrow and his comrades decided to ride in the Gump, in order to keep up with the swift march of the army; so, as soon as Glinda had started and her soldiers had marched away to the inspiring strains of music played by the royal band, our friends climbed into the sofas and followed. The Gump flew along slowly at a point directly over the palanquin in which rode the Sorceress.

"Be careful," said the Tin Woodman to the Scarecrow, who was leaning far over the side to look at the army below. "You might fall."

"It wouldn't matter," remarked the educated Woggle-Bug; "he can't get broke so long as he is stuffed with money."

"Didn't I ask you—" began Tip, in a reproachful voice.

"You did!" said the Woggle-Bug, promptly. "And I beg your pardon. I will really try to restrain myself."

"You'd better," declared the boy. "That is, if you wish to travel in our company."

"Ah! I couldn't bear to part with you now," murmured the Insect, feelingly; so Tip let the subject drop.

The army moved steadily on, but night had fallen before they came to the walls of the Emerald City. By the dim light of the new moon, however, Glinda's forces silently surrounded the city and pitched their tents of scarlet silk upon the greensward. The tent of the Sorceress was larger than the others, and was composed of pure white silk, with scarlet banners flying above it. A tent was also pitched for the Scarecrow's party; and when these preparations had been made, with military precision and quickness, the army retired to rest.

Great was the amazement of Queen Jinjur next morning when her soldiers came running to inform her of the vast army surrounding them. She at once climbed to a high tower of the royal palace and saw banners waving in every direction and the great white tent of Glinda standing directly before the gates.

"We are surely lost!" cried Jinjur, in despair; "for how can our knitting-needles avail against the long spears and terrible swords of our foes?"

"The best thing we can do," said one of the girls, "is to surrender as quickly as possible, before we get hurt."

"Not so," returned Jinjur, more bravely. "The enemy is still outside the walls, so we must try to gain time by engaging them in parley. Go you with a flag of truce to Glinda and ask her why she has dared to invade my dominions, and what are her demands."

So the girl passed through the gates, bearing a white flag to show she was on a mission of peace, and came to Glinda's tent.

"Tell your Queen," said the Sorceress to the girl, "that she must deliver up to me old Mombi, to be my prisoner. If this is done I will not molest her farther."

Now when this message was delivered to the Queen it filled her with dismay, for Mombi was her chief counsellor, and Jinjur was terribly afraid of the old hag. But she sent for Mombi, and told her what Glinda had said.

"I see trouble ahead for all of us," muttered the old witch, after glancing into a magic mirror she carried in her pocket. "But we may even yet escape by deceiving this Sorceress, clever as she thinks herself."

"Don't you think it will be safer for me to deliver you into her hands?" asked Jinjur, nervously.

"If you do, it will cost you the throne of the Emerald City!" answered the witch, positively. "But, if you will let me have my own way, I can save us both very easily."

"Then do as you please," replied Jinjur, "for it is so aristocratic to be a Queen that I do not wish to be obliged to return home again, to make beds and wash dishes for my mother."

So Mombi called Jellia Jamb to her, and performed a certain magical rite with which she was familiar. As a result of the enchantment Jellia took on the form and features of Mombi, while the old witch grew to resemble the girl so closely that it seemed impossible anyone could guess the deception.

"Now," said old Mombi to the Queen, "let your soldiers deliver up this girl to Glinda. She will think she has the real Mombi in her power, and so will return immediately to her own country in the South."

Therefore Jellia, hobbling along like an aged woman, was led from the city gates and taken before Glinda.

"Here is the person you demanded," said one of the guards, "and our Queen now begs you will go away, as you promised, and leave us in peace."

"That I will surely do," replied Glinda, much pleased; "if this is really the person she seems to be."

"It is certainly old Mombi," said the guard, who believed she was speaking the truth; and then Jinjur's soldiers returned within the city's gates.

The Sorceress quickly summoned the Scarecrow and his friends to her tent, and began to question the supposed Mombi about the lost girl Ozma. But Jellia knew nothing at all of this affair, and presently she grew so nervous under the questioning that she gave way and began to weep, to Glinda's great astonishment.

"Here is some foolish trickery!" said the Sorceress, her eyes flashing with anger. "This is not Mombi at all, but some other person who has been made to resemble her! Tell me," she demanded, turning to the trembling girl, "what is your name?"

This Jellia dared not tell, having been threatened with death by the witch if she confessed the fraud. But Glinda, sweet and fair though she was, understood magic better than any other person in the Land of Oz. So, by uttering a few potent words and making a peculiar gesture, she quickly transformed the girl into her proper shape, while at the same time old Mombi, far away in Jinjur's palace, suddenly resumed her own crooked form and evil features.

"Why, it's Jellia Jamb!" cried the Scarecrow, recognizing in the girl one of his old friends.

"It's our interpreter!" said the Pumpkinhead, smiling pleasantly.

Then Jellia was forced to tell of the trick Mombi had played, and she also begged Glinda's protection, which the Sorceress readily granted. But Glinda was now really angry, and sent word to Jinjur that the fraud was discovered and she must deliver up the real Mombi or suffer terrible consequences. Jinjur was prepared for this message, for the witch well understood, when her natural form was thrust upon her, that Glinda had discovered her trickery. But the wicked old creature had already thought up a new deception, and had made Jinjur promise to carry it out. So the Queen said to Glinda's messenger:

"Tell your mistress that I cannot find Mombi anywhere; but that

Glinda is welcome to enter the city and search herself for the old woman. She may also bring her friends with her, if she likes; but if she does not find Mombi by sundown, the Sorceress must promise to go away peaceably and bother us no more."

Glinda agreed to these terms, well knowing that Mombi was somewhere within the city walls. So Jinjur caused the gates to be thrown open, and Glinda marched in at the head of a company of soldiers, followed by the Scarecrow and the Tin Woodman, while Jack Pumpkinhead rode astride the Saw-Horse, and the Educated, Highly Magnified Woggle-Bug sauntered behind in a dignified manner. Tip walked by the side of the Sorceress, for Glinda had conceived a great liking for the boy.

Of course old Mombi had no intention of being found by Glinda; so, while her enemies were marching up the street, the witch transformed herself into a red rose growing upon a bush in the garden of the palace. It was a clever idea, and a trick Glinda did not suspect; so several precious hours were spent in a vain search for Mombi.

As sundown approached the Sorceress realized she had been defeated by the superior cunning of the aged witch; so she gave the command to her people to march out of the city and back to their tents.

The Scarecrow and his comrades happened to be searching in the garden of the palace just then, and they turned with disappointment to obey Glinda's command. But before they left the garden the Tin Woodman, who was fond of flowers, chanced to espy a big red rose growing upon a bush; so he plucked the flower and fastened it securely in the tin button-hole of his tin bosom.

As he did this he fancied he heard a low moan proceed from the rose; but he paid no attention to the sound, and Mombi was thus carried out of the city and into Glinda's camp without anyone having a suspicion that they had succeeded in their quest.

The Transformation of Old Mombi

The Witch was at first frightened at finding herself captured by the enemy; but soon she decided that she was exactly as safe in the Tin Woodman's button-hole as growing upon the bush. For no one knew the rose and Mombi to be one, and now that she was without the gates of the City her chances of escaping altogether from Glinda were much improved.

"But there is no hurry," thought Mombi. "I will wait awhile and enjoy the humiliation of this Sorceress when she finds I have out-witted her."

So throughout the night the rose lay quietly on the Woodman's bosom, and in the morning, when Glinda summoned our friends to a consultation, Nick Chopper carried his pretty flower with him to the white silk tent.

"For some reason," said Glinda, "we have failed to find this cunning old Mombi; so I fear our expedition will prove a failure. And for that I am sorry, because without our assistance little Ozma will never be rescued and restored to her rightful position as Queen of the Emerald City."

"Do not let us give up so easily," said the Pumpkinhead. "Let us do something else."

"Something else must really be done," replied Glinda, with a smile; "yet I cannot understand how I have been defeated so easily by an old Witch who knows far less of magic than I do myself."

"While we are on the ground I believe it would be wise for us to conquer the Emerald City for Princess Ozma, and find the girl afterward," said the Scarecrow. "And while the girl remains hidden I will gladly rule in her place, for I understand the business of ruling much better than Jinjur does."

"But I have promised not to molest Jinjur," objected Glinda.

"Suppose you all return with me to my Kingdom—or Empire, rather," said the Tin Woodman, politely including the entire party in a royal wave of his arm. "It will give me great pleasure to entertain you in my castle, where there is room enough and to spare. And if any of you wish to be nickel-plated, my valet will do it free of all expense."

While the Woodman was speaking Glinda's eyes had been noting the rose in his button-hole, and now she imagined she saw the big red leaves of the flower tremble slightly. This quickly aroused her suspicions, and in a moment more the Sorceress had decided that the seeming rose was nothing else than a transformation of old Mombi. At the same instant Mombi knew she was discovered and must quickly plan an escape, and as transformations were easy to her she immediately took the form of a Shadow and glided along the wall of the tent toward the entrance, thinking thus to disappear.

But Glinda had not only equal cunning, but far more experience than the Witch. So the Sorceress reached the opening of the tent before the Shadow, and with a wave of her hand closed the entrance so securely that Mombi could not find a crack big enough to creep through. The Scarecrow and his friends were greatly surprised at Glinda's actions; for none of them had noted the Shadow. But the Sorceress said to them:

"Remain perfectly quiet, all of you! For the old Witch is even now with us in this tent, and I hope to capture her."

These words so alarmed Mombi that she quickly transformed herself from a shadow to a Black Ant, in which shape she crawled along the ground, seeking a crack or crevice in which to hide her tiny body.

Fortunately, the ground where the tent had been pitched, being just before the city gates, was hard and smooth; and while the Ant still crawled about, Glinda discovered it and ran quickly forward to effect its capture. But, just as her hand was descending, the Witch, now fairly frantic with fear, made her last transformation, and in the form of a huge Griffin sprang through the wall of the tent—tearing the silk asunder in her rush—and in a moment had darted away with the speed of a whirlwind.

Glinda did not hesitate to follow. She sprang upon the back of the Saw-Horse and cried:

"Now you shall prove that you have a right to be alive! Run—run—run!"

The Saw-Horse ran. Like a flash he followed the Griffin, his wooden legs moving so fast that they twinkled like the rays of a star. Before our friends could recover from their surprise both the Griffin and the Saw-Horse had dashed out of sight.

"Come! Let us follow!" cried the Scarecrow.

They ran to the place where the Gump was lying and quickly tumbled aboard.

"Fly!" commanded Tip, eagerly.

"Where to?" asked the Gump, in its calm voice.

"I don't know," returned Tip, who was very nervous at the delay;

"but if you will mount into the air I think we can discover which way Glinda has gone."

"Very well," returned the Gump, quietly; and it spread its great wings and mounted high into the air.

Far away, across the meadows, they could now see two tiny specks, speeding one after the other; and they knew these specks must be the Griffin and the Saw-Horse. So Tip called the Gump's attention to them and bade the creature try to overtake the Witch and the Sorceress. But, swift as was the Gump's flight, the pursued and pursuer moved more swiftly yet, and within a few moments were blotted out against the dim horizon.

"Let us continue to follow them, nevertheless," said the Scarecrow; "for the Land of Oz is of small extent, and sooner or later they must both come to a halt."

Old Mombi had thought herself very wise to choose the form of a Griffin, for its legs were exceedingly fleet and its strength more enduring than that of other animals. But she had not reckoned on the untiring energy of the Saw-Horse, whose wooden limbs could run for days without slacking their speed. Therefore, after an hour's hard running, the Griffin's breath began to fail, and it panted and gasped painfully, and moved more slowly than before. Then it reached the edge of the desert and began racing across the deep sands. But its tired feet sank far into the sand, and in a few minutes the Griffin fell forward, completely exhausted, and lay still upon the desert waste.

Glinda came up a moment later, riding the still vigorous Saw-Horse; and having unwound a slender golden thread from her girdle the Sorceress threw it over the head of the panting and helpless Griffin, and so destroyed the magical power of Mombi's transformation.

For the animal, with one fierce shudder, disappeared from view, while in its place was discovered the form of the old Witch, glaring savagely at the serene and beautiful face of the Sorceress.

Princess Ozma of Oz

"You are my prisoner, and it is useless for you to struggle any longer," said Glinda, in her soft, sweet voice. "Lie still a moment, and rest yourself, and then I will carry you back to my tent."

"Why do you seek me?" asked Mombi, still scarce able to speak plainly for lack of breath. "What have I done to you, to be so persecuted?"

"You have done nothing to me," answered the gentle Sorceress; "but I suspect you have been guilty of several wicked actions; and if I find it is true that you have so abused your knowledge of magic, I intend to punish you severely."

"I defy you!" croaked the old hag. "You dare not harm me!"

Just then the Gump flew up to them and alighted upon the desert sands beside Glinda. Our friends were delighted to find that Mombi had finally been captured, and after a hurried consultation it was decided they should all return to the camp in the Gump. So the Saw-Horse was tossed aboard, and then Glinda, still holding an end of the golden thread that was around Mombi's neck, forced her prisoner to climb into the sofas. The others now followed, and Tip gave the word to the Gump to return.

The journey was made in safety, Mombi sitting in her place with a grim and sullen air; for the old hag was absolutely helpless so long as the magical thread encircled her throat. The army hailed Glinda's return with loud cheers, and the party of friends soon gathered again in the royal tent, which had been neatly repaired during their absence.

"Now," said the Sorceress to Mombi, "I want you to tell us why the Wonderful Wizard of Oz paid you three visits, and what became of the child, Ozma, which so curiously disappeared."

The Witch looked at Glinda defiantly, but said not a word.

"Answer me!" cried the Sorceress.

But still Mombi remained silent.

"Perhaps she doesn't know," remarked Jack.

"I beg you will keep quiet," said Tip. "You might spoil everything with your foolishness."

"Very well, dear father!" returned the Pumpkinhead, meekly.

"How glad I am to be a Woggle-Bug!" murmured the Highly Magnified Insect, softly. "No one can expect wisdom to flow from a pumpkin."

"Well," said the Scarecrow, "what shall we do to make Mombi speak? Unless she tells us what we wish to know her capture will do us no good at all."

"Suppose we try kindness," suggested the Tin Woodman. "I've heard that anyone can be conquered with kindness, no matter how ugly they may be."

At this the Witch turned to glare upon him so horribly that the Tin Woodman shrank back abashed.

Glinda had been carefully considering what to do, and now she turned to Mombi and said:

"You will gain nothing, I assure you, by thus defying us. For I am determined to learn the truth about the girl Ozma, and unless you tell me all that you know, I will certainly put you to death."

"Oh, no! Don't do that!" exclaimed the Tin Woodman. "It would be an awful thing to kill anyone—even old Mombi!"

"But it is merely a threat," returned Glinda. "I shall not put Mombi to death, because she will prefer to tell me the truth."

"Oh, I see!" said the tin man, much relieved.

"Suppose I tell you all that you wish to know," said Mombi,

speaking so suddenly that she startled them all. "What will you do with me then?"

"In that case," replied Glinda, "I shall merely ask you to drink a powerful draught which will cause you to forget all the magic you have ever learned."

"Then I would become a helpless old woman!"

"But you would be alive," suggested the Pumpkinhead, consolingly.

"Do try to keep silent!" said Tip, nervously.

"I'll try," responded Jack; "but you will admit that it's a good thing to be alive."

"Especially if one happens to be Thoroughly Educated," added the Woggle-Bug, nodding approval.

"You may make your choice," Glinda said to old Mombi, "between death if you remain silent, and the loss of your magical powers if you tell me the truth. But I think you will prefer to live."

Mombi cast an uneasy glance at the Sorceress, and saw that she was in earnest, and not to be trifled with. So she replied, slowly:

"I will answer your questions."

"That is what I expected," said Glinda, pleasantly. "You have chosen wisely, I assure you."

She then motioned to one of her Captains, who brought her a beautiful golden casket. From this the Sorceress drew an immense white pearl, attached to a slender chain which she placed around her neck in such a way that the pearl rested upon her bosom, directly over her heart.

"Now," said she, "I will ask my first question: Why did the Wizard pay you three visits?"

"Because I would not come to him," answered Mombi.

"That is no answer," said Glinda, sternly. "Tell me the truth."

"Well," returned Mombi, with downcast eyes, "he visited me to learn the way I make tea-biscuits."

"Look up!" commanded the Sorceress.

Mombi obeyed.

"What is the color of my pearl?" demanded Glinda.

"Why—it is black!" replied the old Witch, in a tone of wonder.

"Then you have told me a falsehood!" cried Glinda, angrily. "Only when the truth is spoken will my magic pearl remain a pure white in color."

Mombi now saw how useless it was to try to deceive the Sorceress; so she said, meanwhile scowling at her defeat:

"The Wizard brought to me the girl Ozma, who was then no more than a baby, and begged me to conceal the child."

"That is what I thought," declared Glinda, calmly. "What did he give you for thus serving him?"

"He taught me all the magical tricks he knew. Some were good tricks, and some were only frauds; but I have remained faithful to my promise."

"What did you do with the girl?" asked Glinda; and at this question everyone bent forward and listened eagerly for the reply.

"I enchanted her," answered Mombi.

"In what way?"

"I transformed her into—into—"

"Into what?" demanded Glinda, as the Witch hesitated.

"Into a boy!" said Mombi, in a low tone.

"A boy!" echoed every voice; and then, because they knew that this old woman had reared Tip from childhood, all eyes were turned to where the boy stood.

"Yes," said the old Witch, nodding her head; "that is the Princess Ozma—the child brought to me by the Wizard who stole her father's throne. That is the rightful ruler of the Emerald City!" and she pointed her long bony finger straight at the boy.

"I!" cried Tip, in amazement. "Why, I'm no Princess Ozma—I'm not a girl!"

Glinda smiled, and going to Tip she took his small brown hand within her dainty white one.

"You are not a girl just now," said she, gently, "because Mombi transformed you into a boy. But you were born a girl, and also a Princess; so you must resume your proper form, that you may become Queen of the Emerald City."

"Oh, let Jinjur be the Queen!" exclaimed Tip, ready to cry. "I want to stay a boy, and travel with the Scarecrow and the Tin

MOMBI POINTED HER LONG,
BONY FINGER AT THE BOY.

Woodman, and the Woggle-Bug, and Jack—yes! and my friend the Saw-Horse—and the Gump! I don't want to be a girl!"

"Never mind, old chap," said the Tin Woodman, soothingly; "it don't hurt to be a girl, I'm told; and we will all remain your faithful friends just the same. And, to be honest with you, I've always considered girls nicer than boys."

"They're just as nice, anyway," added the Scarecrow, patting Tip affectionately upon the head.

"And they are equally good students," proclaimed the Woggle-Bug. "I should like to become your tutor, when you are transformed into a girl again."

"But—see here!" said Jack Pumpkinhead, with a gasp: "if you become a girl, you can't be my dear father any more!"

"No," answered Tip, laughing in spite of his anxiety; "and I shall not be sorry to escape the relationship." Then he added, hesitatingly, as he turned to Glinda: "I might try it for awhile,—just to see how it seems, you know. But if I don't like being a girl you must promise to change me into a boy again."

"Really," said the Sorceress, "that is beyond my magic. I never deal in transformations, for they are not honest, and no respectable sorceress likes to make things appear to be what they are not. Only unscrupulous witches use the art, and therefore I must ask Mombi to effect your release from her charm, and restore you to your proper form. It will be the last opportunity she will have to practice magic."

Now that the truth about Princess Ozma had been discovered, Mombi did not care what became of Tip; but she feared Glinda's anger, and the boy generously promised to provide for Mombi in her old age if he became the ruler of the Emerald City. So the Witch consented to effect the transformation, and preparations for the event were at once made.

Glinda ordered her own royal couch to be placed in the center of the tent. It was piled high with cushions covered with rose-colored silk, and from a golden railing above hung many folds of pink gossamer, completely concealing the interior of the couch.

The first act of the Witch was to make the boy drink a potion which quickly sent him into a deep and dreamless sleep. Then the Tin Woodman and the Woggle-Bug bore him gently to the couch, placed him upon the soft cushions, and drew the gossamer hangings to shut him from all earthly view.

The Witch squatted upon the ground and kindled a tiny fire of dried herbs, which she drew from her bosom. When the blaze shot up and burned clearly old Mombi scattered a handful of magical powder over the fire, which straightway gave off a rich violet vapor, filling all the tent with its fragrance and forcing the Saw-Horse to sneeze—although he had been warned to keep quiet.

Then, while the others watched her curiously, the hag chanted a rhythmical verse in words which no one understood, and bent her lean body seven times back and forth over the fire. And now the incantation seemed complete, for the Witch stood upright and cried the one word "Yeowa!" in a loud voice.

MOMBI AT HER MAGICAL INCANTATIONS.

The vapor floated away; the atmo-
sphere became clear again; a whiff
of fresh air filled the tent, and the
pink curtains of the couch trembled slightly, as if stirred from
within.

Glinda walked to the can-
opy and parted the silken
hangings. Then she bent over
the cushions, reached out her
hand, and from the couch
arose the form of a young girl,
fresh and beautiful as a May
morning. Her eyes sparkled as
two diamonds, and her lips were
tinted like a tourmaline. All adown
her back floated tresses of ruddy gold, with
a slender jeweled circlet confining them at the brow. Her robes of
silken gauze floated around her like a cloud, and dainty satin slippers shod her feet.

At this exquisite vision Tip's old comrades stared in wonder for
the space of a full minute, and then every head bent low in honest
admiration of the lovely Princess Ozma. The girl herself cast one
look into Glinda's bright face, which glowed with pleasure and satisfaction, and then turned upon the others. Speaking the words
with sweet diffidence, she said:

"I hope none of you will care less for me than you did before. I'm
just the same Tip, you know; only—only—"

"Only you're different!" said the Pumpkinhead; and everyone
thought it was the wisest speech he had ever made.

The Riches of Content

When the wonderful tidings reached the ears of Queen Jinjur—how Mombi the Witch had been captured; how she had confessed her crime to Glinda; and how the long-lost Princess Ozma had been discovered in no less a personage than the boy Tip—she wept real tears of grief and despair.

"To think," she moaned, "that after having ruled as Queen, and lived in a palace, I must go back to scrubbing floors and churning butter again! It is too horrible to think of! I will never consent!"

So when her soldiers, who spent most of their time making fudge in the palace kitchens, counseled Jinjur to resist, she listened to their foolish prattle and sent a sharp defiance to Glinda the Good and the Princess Ozma. The result was a declaration of war, and the very next day Glinda marched upon the Emerald City with pennants flying and bands playing, and a forest of shining spears sparkling brightly beneath the sun's rays.

But when it came to the walls this brave assembly made a sudden halt; for Jinjur had closed and barred every gateway, and the walls of the Emerald City were built high and thick with many blocks of green marble. Finding her advance thus baffled, Glinda bent her brows in deep thought, while the Woggle-Bug said, in his most positive tone:

"We must lay siege to the city, and starve it into submission. It is the only thing we can do."

"Not so," answered the Scarecrow. "We still have the Gump, and the Gump can still fly."

The Sorceress turned quickly at this speech, and her face now wore a bright smile.

"You are right," she exclaimed, "and certainly have reason to be proud of your brains. Let us go to the Gump at once!"

So they passed through the ranks of the army until they came to the place, near the Scarecrow's tent, where the Gump lay. Glinda and Princess Ozma mounted first, and sat upon the sofas. Then the Scarecrow and his friends climbed aboard, and still there was room for a Captain and three soldiers, which Glinda considered sufficient for a guard.

Now, at a word from the Princess, the queer Thing they had called the Gump flopped its palm-leaf wings and rose into the air, carrying the party of adventurers high above the walls. They hovered over the palace, and soon perceived Jinjur reclining in a hammock in the courtyard, where she was comfortably reading a novel with a green cover and eating green chocolates, confident that the walls would protect her from her enemies. Obeying a quick command, the Gump alighted safely in this very courtyard, and before Jinjur had time to do more than scream, the Captain and three soldiers leaped out and made the former Queen a prisoner, locking strong chains upon both her wrists.

That act really ended the war; for the Army of Revolt submitted as soon as they knew Jinjur to be a captive, and the Captain marched in safety through the streets and up to the gates of the city, which she threw wide open. Then the bands played their most stirring music while Glinda's army marched into the city, and heralds proclaimed the conquest of the audacious Jinjur and the accession of the beautiful Princess Ozma to the throne of her royal ancestors.

At once the men of the Emerald City cast off their aprons. And it is said that the women were so tired eating of their husbands' cooking that they all hailed the conquest of Jinjur with joy. Certain it is that, rushing one and all to the kitchens of their houses, the good wives prepared so delicious a feast for the weary men that harmony was immediately restored in every family.

Ozma's first act was to oblige the Army of Revolt to return to her every emerald or other gem stolen from the public streets and buildings; and so great was the number of precious stones picked from their settings by these vain girls, that every one of the royal jewelers worked steadily for more than a month to replace them in their settings.

Meantime the Army of Revolt was disbanded and the girls sent home to their mothers. On promise of good behavior Jinjur was likewise released.

Ozma made the loveliest Queen the Emerald City had ever known; and, although she was so young and inexperienced, she ruled her people with wisdom and justice. For Glinda gave her good advice on all occasions; and the Woggle-Bug, who was appointed to the important post of Public Educator, was quite helpful to Ozma when her royal duties grew perplexing.

The girl, in her gratitude to the Gump for its services, offered the creature any reward it might name.

"Then," replied the Gump, "please take me to pieces. I did not wish to be brought to life, and I am greatly ashamed of my conglomerate personality. Once I was a monarch of the forest, as my antlers fully prove; but now, in my present upholstered condition of servitude, I am compelled to fly through the air—my legs being of no use to me whatever. Therefore I beg to be dispersed."

So Ozma ordered the Gump taken apart. The antlered head was again hung over the mantle-piece in the hall, and the sofas were untied and placed in the reception parlors. The broom tail resumed its accustomed duties in the kitchen, and finally, the Scarecrow replaced all the clothes-lines and ropes on the pegs from which he had taken them on the eventful day when the Thing was constructed.

You might think that was the end of the Gump; and so it was, as a flying-machine. But the head over the mantle-piece continued to talk whenever it took a notion to do so, and it frequently startled, with its abrupt questions, the people who waited in the hall for an audience with the Queen.

The Saw-Horse, being Ozma's personal property, was tenderly

cared for; and often she rode the queer creature along the streets of the Emerald City. She had its wooden legs shod with gold, to keep them from wearing out, and the tinkle of these golden shoes upon the pavement always filled the Queen's subjects with awe as they thought upon this evidence of her magical powers.

"The Wonderful Wizard was never so wonderful as Queen Ozma," the people said to one another, in whispers; "for he claimed to do many things he could not do; whereas our new Queen does many things no one would ever expect her to accomplish."

Jack Pumpkinhead remained with Ozma to the end of his days; and he did not spoil as soon as he had feared, although he always remained as stupid as ever. The Woggle-Bug tried to teach him several arts and sciences; but Jack was so poor a student that any attempt to educate him was soon abandoned.

After Glinda's army had marched back home, and peace was restored to the Emerald City, the Tin Woodman announced his intention to return to his own Kingdom of the Winkies.

"It isn't a very big Kingdom," said he to Ozma, "but for that very reason it is easier to rule; and I have called myself an Emperor because I am an Absolute Monarch, and no one interferes in any way with my conduct of public or personal affairs. When I get home I shall have a new coat of nickel-plate; for I have become somewhat marred and scratched lately; and then I shall be glad to have you pay me a visit."

"Thank you," replied Ozma. "Some day I may accept the invitation. But what is to become of the Scarecrow?"

"I shall return with my friend the Tin Woodman," said the stuffed one, seriously. "We have decided never to be parted in the future."

"And I have made the Scarecrow my Royal Treasurer," explained the Tin Woodman. "For it has occurred to me that it is a good thing to have a Royal Treasurer who is made of money. What do you think?"

"I think," said the little Queen, smiling, "that your friend must be the richest man in all the world."

"I am," returned the Scarecrow; "but not on account of my money. For I consider brains far superior to money, in every way. You may have noticed that if one has money without brains, he can not use it to advantage; but if one has brains without money, they will enable him to live comfortably to the end of his days."

"At the same time," declared the Tin Woodman, "you must acknowledge that a good heart is a thing that brains can not create, and that money can not buy. Perhaps, after all, it is I who am the richest man in all the world."

"You are both rich, my friends," said Ozma, gently; "and your riches are the only riches worth having—the riches of content!"

The End

Ozma

OZMA OF OZ

A Record of Her Adventures with Dorothy Gale of
Kansas, the Yellow Hen, the Scarecrow, the Tin
Woodman, Tiktok, the Cowardly Lion and
the Hungry Tiger; Besides Other Good
People too Numerous to Mention
Faithfully Recorded Herein

BY

L. FRANK BAUM

THE AUTHOR OF THE WIZARD OF OZ,
THE LAND OF OZ, ETC.

ILLUSTRATED BY

JOHN R. NEILL

———

CHICAGO:
THE REILLY & BRITTON CO.
PUBLISHERS

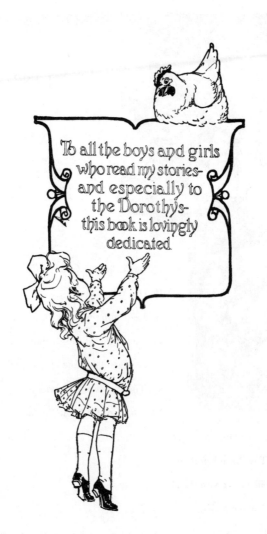

To all the boys and girls
who read my stories-
and especially to
the Dorothys-
this book is lovingly
dedicated.

LIST

OF

CHAPTERS

LIST

OF

CHAPTERS

AUTHOR'S NOTE

My friends the children are responsible for this new "Oz Book," as they were for the last one, which was called *The Land of Oz*. Their sweet little letters plead to know "more about Dorothy"; and they ask: "What became of the Cowardly Lion?" and "What did Ozma do afterward?"—meaning, of course, after she became the Ruler of Oz. And some of them suggest plots to me, saying: "Please have Dorothy go to the Land of Oz again"; or, "Why don't you make Ozma and Dorothy meet, and have a good time together?" Indeed, could I do all that my little friends ask, I would be obliged to write dozens of books to satisfy their demands. And I wish I could, for I enjoy writing these stories just as much as the children say they enjoy reading them.

Well, here is "more about Dorothy," and about our old friends the Scarecrow and the Tin Woodman, and about the Cowardly Lion, and Ozma, and all the rest of them; and here, likewise, is a good deal about some new folks that are queer and unusual. One little friend, who read this story before it was printed, said to me: "Billina is *real Ozzy*, Mr. Baum, and so are Tiktok and the Hungry Tiger."

If this judgment is unbiased and correct, and the little folks find this new story "real Ozzy," I shall be very glad indeed that I wrote it. But perhaps I shall get some more of those very welcome letters from my readers, telling me just how they like "Ozma of Oz." I hope so, anyway.

L. FRANK BAUM.

MACATAWA, 1907.

The Girl in the Chicken Coop

The wind blew hard and joggled the water of the ocean, sending ripples across its surface. Then the wind pushed the edges of the ripples until they became waves, and shoved the waves around until they became billows. The billows rolled dreadfully high: higher even than the tops of houses. Some of them, indeed, rolled as high as the tops of tall trees, and seemed like mountains; and the gulfs between the great billows were like deep valleys.

All this mad dashing and splashing of the waters of the big ocean, which the mischievous wind caused without any good reason whatever, resulted in a terrible storm, and a storm on the ocean is liable to cut many queer pranks and do a lot of damage.

At the time the wind began to blow, a ship was sailing far out upon the waters. When the waves began to tumble and toss and to grow bigger and bigger the ship rolled up and down, and tipped sidewise—first one way and then the other—and was jostled around so roughly that even the sailor-men had to hold fast to the ropes and railings to keep themselves from being swept away by the wind or pitched headlong into the sea.

And the clouds were so thick in the sky that the sunlight couldn't get through them; so that the day grew dark as night, which added to the terrors of the storm.

The Captain of the ship was not afraid, because he had seen storms before, and had sailed his ship through them in safety; but he knew that his passengers would be in danger if they tried to stay on deck, so he put them all into the cabin and told them to stay there until after the storm was over, and to keep brave hearts and not be scared, and all would be well with them.

Now, among these passengers was a little Kansas girl named Dorothy Gale, who was going with her Uncle Henry to Australia, to visit some relatives they had never before seen. Uncle Henry, you must know, was not very well, because he had been working so hard on his Kansas farm that his health had given way and left him weak and nervous. So he left Aunt Em at home to watch after the hired men and to take care of the farm, while he traveled far away to Australia to visit his cousins and have a good rest.

Dorothy was eager to go with him on this journey, and Uncle Henry thought she would be good company and help cheer him up; so he decided to take her along. The little girl was quite an experienced traveller, for she had once been carried by a cyclone as far away from home as the marvelous Land of Oz, and she had met with a good many adventures in that strange country before she managed to get back to Kansas again. So she wasn't easily frightened, whatever happened, and when the wind began to howl and whistle, and the waves began to tumble and toss, our little girl didn't mind the uproar the least bit.

"Of course we'll have to stay in the cabin," she said to Uncle Henry and the other passengers, "and keep as quiet as possible until the storm is over. For the Captain says if we go on deck we may be blown overboard."

No one wanted to risk such an accident as that, you may be sure; so all the passengers stayed huddled up in the dark cabin, listening to the shrieking of the storm and the creaking of the masts and rigging and trying to keep from bumping into one another when the ship tipped sidewise.

Dorothy had almost fallen asleep when she was aroused with a start to find that Uncle Henry was missing. She couldn't imagine where he had gone, and as he was not very strong she began to worry about him, and to fear he might have been careless enough to go on deck. In that case he would be in great danger unless he instantly came down again.

The fact was that Uncle Henry had gone to lie down in his little sleeping-berth, but Dorothy did not know that. She only remembered that Aunt Em had cautioned her to take good care of her uncle, so at once she decided to go on deck and find him, in spite of the fact that the tempest was now worse than ever, and the ship was plunging in a really dreadful manner. Indeed, the little girl found it was as much as she could do to mount the stairs to the deck, and as soon as she got there the wind struck her so fiercely that it almost tore away the skirts of her dress. Yet Dorothy felt a sort of joyous excitement in defying the storm, and while she held fast to the railing she peered around through the gloom and thought she saw the dim form of a man clinging to a mast not far away from her. This might be her uncle, so she called as loudly as she could:

"Uncle Henry! Uncle Henry!"

But the wind screeched and howled so madly that she scarce heard her own voice, and the man certainly failed to hear her, for he did not move.

Dorothy decided she must go to him; so she made a dash forward, during a lull in the storm, to where a big square chicken-coop had been lashed to the deck with ropes. She reached this place in safety, but no sooner had she seized fast hold of the slats of the big box in which the chickens were kept than the wind, as if enraged because the little girl dared to resist its power, suddenly redoubled its fury. With a scream like that of an angry giant it tore away the ropes that held the coop and lifted it high into the air, with Dorothy still clinging to the slats. Around and over it whirled, this way and that, and a few moments later the chicken-coop dropped far away into the sea, where the big waves caught it and slid it up-hill to a foaming crest and then down-hill into a deep valley, as if it were nothing more than a plaything to keep them amused.

"UNCLE HENRY! UNCLE HENRY!" CALLED DOROTHY

Dorothy had a good ducking, you may be sure, but she didn't loose her presence of mind even for a second. She kept tight hold of the stout slats and as soon as she could get the water out of her eyes she saw that the wind had ripped the cover from the coop, and the poor chickens were fluttering away in every direction, being blown by the wind until they looked like feather dusters without handles. The bottom of the coop was made of thick boards, so Dorothy found she was clinging to a sort of raft, with sides of slats, which readily bore up her weight. After coughing the water out of her throat and getting her breath again, she managed to climb over the slats and stand upon the firm wooden bottom of the coop, which supported her easily enough.

"Why, I've got a ship of my own!" she thought, more amused than frightened at her sudden change of condition; and then, as the coop climbed up to the top of a big wave, she looked eagerly around for the ship from which she had been blown.

It was far, far away, by this time. Perhaps no one on board had yet missed her, or knew of her strange adventure. Down into a valley between the waves the coop swept her, and when she climbed another crest the ship looked like a toy boat, it was such a long way off. Soon it had entirely disappeared in the gloom, and then Dorothy gave a sigh of regret at parting with Uncle Henry and began to wonder what was going to happen to her next.

Just now she was tossing on the bosom of a big ocean, with nothing to keep her afloat but a miserable wooden hen-coop that had a plank bottom and slatted sides, through which the water constantly splashed and wetted her through to the skin! And there was nothing to eat when she became hungry—as she was sure to do before long—and no fresh water to drink and no dry clothes to put on.

"Well, I declare!" she exclaimed, with a laugh. "You're in a pretty fix, Dorothy Gale, I can tell you! and I haven't the least idea how you're going to get out of it!"

As if to add to her troubles the night was now creeping on, and the gray clouds overhead changed to inky blackness. But the wind, as if satisfied at last with its mischievous pranks, stopped blowing this ocean and hurried away to another part of the world to blow

DOROTHY AFLOAT IN THE HEN-COOP

something else; so that the waves, not being joggled any more, began to quiet down and behave themselves.

It was lucky for Dorothy, I think, that the storm subsided; otherwise, brave though she was, I fear she might have perished. Many children, in her place, would have wept and given way to despair; but because Dorothy had encountered so many adventures and come safely through them it did not occur to her at this time to be especially afraid. She was wet and uncomfortable, it is true; but, after sighing that one sigh I told you of, she managed to recall some of her customary cheerfulness and decided to patiently await whatever her fate might be.

By and by the black clouds rolled away and showed a blue sky overhead, with a silver moon shining sweetly in the middle of it and little stars winking merrily at Dorothy when she looked their way. The coop did not toss around any more, but rode the waves more gently—almost like a cradle rocking—so that the floor upon which Dorothy stood was no longer swept by water coming through the slats. Seeing this, and being quite exhausted by the excitement of the past few hours, the little girl decided that sleep would be the best thing to restore her strength and the easiest way in which she could pass the time. The floor was damp and she was herself wringing wet, but fortunately this was a warm climate and she did not feel at all cold.

So she sat down in a corner of the coop, leaned her back against the slats, nodded at the friendly stars before she closed her eyes, and was asleep in half a minute.

The Yellow Hen

strange noise awoke Dorothy, who opened her eyes to find that day had dawned and the sun was shining brightly in a clear sky. She had been dreaming that she was back in Kansas again, and playing in the old barn-yard with the calves and pigs and chickens all around her; and at first, as she rubbed the sleep from her eyes, she really imagined she was there.

"Kut-kut-kut, ka-daw-kut! Kut-kut-kut, ka-daw-kut!"

Ah; here again was the strange noise that had awakened her. Surely it was a hen cackling! But her wide-open eyes first saw, through the slats of the coop, the blue waves of the ocean, now calm and placid, and her thoughts flew back to the past night, so full of danger and discomfort. Also she began to remember that she was a waif of the storm, adrift upon a treacherous and unknown sea.

"Kut-kut-kut, ka-daw-w-w—kut!"

"What's that?" cried Dorothy, starting to her feet.

"Why, I've just laid an egg, that's all," replied a small, but sharp and distinct voice, and looking around her the little girl discovered a yellow hen squatting in the opposite corner of the coop.

"Dear me!" she exclaimed, in surprise; "have *you* been here all night, too?"

"Of course," answered the hen, fluttering her wings and yawning. "When the coop blew away from the ship I clung fast to this corner, with claws and beak, for I knew if I fell into the water I'd surely be drowned. Indeed, I nearly drowned, as it was, with all that water washing over me. I never was so wet before in my life!"

"Yes," agreed Dorothy, "it was pretty wet, for a time, I know. But do you feel comfor'ble now?"

"Not very. The sun has helped to dry my feathers, as it has your dress, and I feel better since I laid my morning egg. But what's to become of us, I should like to know, afloat on this big pond?"

"I'd like to know that, too," said Dorothy. "But, tell me; how does it happen that you are able to talk? I thought hens could only cluck and cackle."

"Why, as for that," answered the yellow hen thoughtfully, "I've clucked and cackled all my life, and never spoken a word before this morning, that I can remember. But when you asked a question, a minute ago, it seemed the most natural thing in the world to answer you. So I spoke, and I seem to keep on speaking, just as you and other human beings do. Strange, isn't it?"

"Very," replied Dorothy. "If we were in the Land of Oz, I wouldn't think it so queer, because many of the animals can talk in that fairy country. But out here in the ocean must be a good long way from Oz."

"How is my grammar?" asked the yellow hen, anxiously. "Do I speak quite properly, in your judgment?"

"Yes," said Dorothy, "you do very well, for a beginner."

"I'm glad to know that," continued the yellow hen, in a confidential tone; "because, if one is going to talk, it's best to talk correctly. The red rooster has often said that my cluck and my cackle were quite perfect; and now it's a comfort to know I am talking properly."

"I'm beginning to get hungry," remarked Dorothy. "It's breakfast time; but there's no breakfast."

"You may have my egg," said the yellow hen. "I don't care for it, you know."

"Don't you want to hatch it?" asked the little girl, in surprise.

"No, indeed; I never care to hatch eggs unless I've a nice snug nest, in some quiet place, with a baker's dozen of eggs under me. That's thirteen, you know, and it's a lucky number for hens. So you may as well eat this egg."

"Oh, I couldn't *poss'bly* eat it, unless it was cooked," exclaimed Dorothy. "But I'm much obliged for your kindness, just the same."

"Don't mention it, my dear," answered the hen, calmly, and began pruning her feathers.

For a moment Dorothy stood looking out over the wide sea. She was still thinking of the egg, though; so presently she asked:

"Why do you lay eggs, when you don't expect to hatch them?"

"It's a habit I have," replied the yellow hen. "It has always been my pride to lay a fresh egg every morning, except when I'm moulting. I never feel like having my morning cackle till the egg is properly laid, and without the chance to cackle I would not be happy."

"It's strange," said the girl, reflectively; "but as I'm not a hen I can't be 'spected to understand that."

"Certainly not, my dear."

Then Dorothy fell silent again. The yellow hen was some company, and a bit of comfort, too; but it was dreadfully lonely out on the big ocean, nevertheless.

After a time the hen flew up and perched upon the topmost slat of the coop, which was a little above Dorothy's head when she was sitting upon the bottom, as she had been doing for some moments past.

"Why, we are not far from land!" exclaimed the hen.

"Where? Where is it?" cried Dorothy, jumping up in great excitement.

"Over there a little way," answered the hen, nodding her head in a certain direction. "We seem to to be drifting toward it, so that before noon we ought to find ourselves upon dry land again."

"I shall like that!" said Dorothy, with a little sigh, for her feet and legs were still wetted now and then by the sea-water that came through the open slats.

"So shall I," answered her companion. "There is nothing in the world so miserable as a wet hen."

The land, which they seemed to be rapidly approaching, since it

THE YELLOW HEN

grew more distinct every minute, was quite beautiful as viewed by the little girl in the floating hen-coop. Next to the water was a broad beach of white sand and gravel, and farther back were several rocky hills, while beyond these appeared a strip of green trees that marked the edge of a forest. But there were no houses to be seen, nor any sign of people who might inhabit this unknown land.

"I hope we shall find something to eat," said Dorothy, looking eagerly at the pretty beach toward which they drifted. "It's long past breakfast time, now."

"I'm a trifle hungry, myself," declared the yellow hen.

"Why don't you eat the egg?" asked the child. "You don't need to have your food cooked, as I do."

"Do you take me for a cannibal?" cried the hen, indignantly. "I do not know what I have said or done that leads you to insult me!"

"I beg your pardon, I'm sure Mrs.—Mrs.—by the way, may I inquire your name, ma'am?" asked the little girl.

"My name is Bill," said the yellow hen, somewhat gruffly.

"Bill! Why, that's a boy's name."

"What difference does that make?"

"You're a lady hen, aren't you?"

"Of course. But when I was first hatched out no one could tell whether I was going to be a hen or a rooster; so the little boy at the farm where I was born called me Bill, and made a pet of me because I was the only yellow chicken in the whole brood. When I grew up, and he found that I didn't crow and fight, as all the roosters do, he did not think to change my name, and every creature in the barnyard, as well as the people in the house, knew me as 'Bill.' So Bill I've always been called, and Bill is my name."

"But it's all wrong, you know," declared Dorothy, earnestly; "and, if you don't mind, I shall call you 'Billina.' Putting the 'eena' on the end makes it a girl's name, you see."

"Oh, I don't mind it in the least," returned the yellow hen. "It doesn't matter at all what you call me, so long as I know the name means *me*."

"Very well, Billina. *My* name is Dorothy Gale—just Dorothy to my friends and Miss Gale to strangers. You may call me Dorothy, if you like. We're getting very near the shore. Do you suppose it is too deep for me to wade the rest of the way?"

"Wait a few minutes longer. The sunshine is warm and pleasant, and we are in no hurry."

"But my feet are all wet and soggy," said the girl. "My dress is dry enough, but I won't feel real comfor'ble till I get my feet dried."

She waited, however, as the hen advised, and before long the big wooden coop grated gently on the sandy beach and the dangerous voyage was over.

It did not take the castaways long to reach the shore, you may be sure. The yellow hen flew to the sands at once, but Dorothy had to climb over the high slats. Still, for a country girl, that was not much of a feat, and as soon as she was safe ashore Dorothy drew off her wet shoes and stockings and spread them upon the sun-warmed beach to dry.

Then she sat down and watched Billina, who was pick-pecking away with her sharp bill in the sand and gravel, which she scratched up and turned over with her strong claws.

"What are you doing?" asked Dorothy.

"Getting my breakfast, of course," murmured the hen, busily pecking away.

"What do you find?" inquired the girl, curiously.

"Oh, some fat red ants, and some sand-bugs, and once in a while a tiny crab. They are very sweet and nice, I assure you."

"How dreadful!" exclaimed Dorothy, in a shocked voice.

"What is dreadful?" asked the hen, lifting her head to gaze with one bright eye at her companion.

"Why, eating live things, and horrid bugs, and crawly ants. You ought to be *'shamed* of yourself!"

"Goodness me!" returned the hen, in a puzzled tone; "how queer you are, Dorothy! Live things are much fresher and more wholesome than dead ones, and you humans eat all sorts of dead creatures."

"We don't!" said Dorothy.

"You do, indeed," answered Billina. "You eat lambs and sheep and cows and pigs and even chickens."

"HOW DREADFUL!" EXCLAIMED DOROTHY

"But we cook 'em," said Dorothy, triumphantly.

"What difference does that make?"

"A good deal," said the girl, in a graver tone. "I can't just 'splain the diff'rence, but it's there. And, anyhow, we never eat such dreadful things as *bugs*."

"But you eat the chickens that eat the bugs," retorted the yellow hen, with an odd cackle. "So you are just as bad as we chickens are."

This made Dorothy thoughtful. What Billina said was true enough, and it almost took away her appetite for breakfast. As for the yellow hen, she continued to peck away at the sand busily, and seemed quite contented with her bill-of-fare.

Finally, down near the water's edge, Billina stuck her bill deep into the sand, and then drew back and shivered.

"Ow!" she cried. "I struck metal, that time, and it nearly broke my beak."

"It prob'bly was a rock," said Dorothy, carelessly.

"Nonsense. I know a rock from metal, I guess," said the hen. "There's a different feel to it."

"But there couldn't be any metal on this wild, deserted seashore," persisted the girl. "Where's the place? I'll dig it up, and prove to you I'm right."

Billina showed her the place where she had "stubbed her bill," as she expressed it, and Dorothy dug away the sand until she felt something hard. Then, thrusting in her hand, she pulled the thing out, and discovered it to be a large sized golden key—rather old, but still bright and of perfect shape.

"What did I tell you?" cried the hen, with a cackle of triumph. "Can I tell metal when I bump into it, or is the thing a rock?"

"It's metal, sure enough," answered the child, gazing thoughtfully at the curious thing she had found. "I think it is pure gold, and it must have lain hidden in the sand for a long time. How do you suppose it came there, Billina? And what do you suppose this mysterious key unlocks?"

"I can't say," replied the hen. "You ought to know more about locks and keys than I do."

Dorothy glanced around. There was no sign of any house in that part of the country, and she reasoned that every key must fit a lock and every lock must have a purpose. Perhaps the key had been lost by somebody who lived far away, but had wandered on this very shore.

Musing on these things the girl put the key in the pocket of her dress and then slowly drew on her shoes and stockings, which the sun had fully dried.

"I b'lieve, Billina," she said, "I'll have a look 'round, and see if I can find some breakfast."

Letters in the Sand

Walking

a little way back from the water's
edge, toward the grove of trees,
Dorothy came to a flat stretch of
white sand that seemed to have queer
signs marked upon its surface, just as
one would write upon sand with a stick.

"What does it say?" she asked the yellow
hen, who trotted along beside her in a rather
dignified fashion.

"How should I know?" returned the hen. "I
cannot read."

"Oh! Can't you?"

"Certainly not; I've never been to school, you
know."

"Well, I have," admitted Dorothy; "but the letters are
big and far apart, and it's hard to spell out the words."

But she looked at each letter carefully, and finally discovered
that these words were written in the sand:

"BEWARE THE WHEELERS!"

"That's rather strange," declared the hen, when Dorothy had
read aloud the words. "What do you suppose the Wheelers are?"

"Folks that wheel, I guess. They must have wheelbarrows, or
baby-cabs or hand-carts," said Dorothy.

"Perhaps they're automobiles," suggested the yellow hen. "There is no need to beware of baby-cabs and wheelbarrows; but automobiles are dangerous things. Several of my friends have been run over by them."

"It can't be auto'biles," replied the girl, "for this is a new, wild country, without even trolley-cars or tel'phones. The people here haven't been discovered yet, I'm sure; that is, if there *are* any people. So I don't b'lieve there *can* be any auto'biles, Billina."

"Perhaps not," admitted the yellow hen. "Where are you going now?"

"Over to those trees, to see if I can find some fruit or nuts," answered Dorothy.

She tramped across the sand, skirting the foot of one of the little rocky hills that stood near, and soon reached the edge of the forest.

At first she was greatly disappointed, because the nearer trees were all punita, or cotton-wood or eucalyptus, and bore no fruit or nuts at all. But, bye and bye, when she was almost in despair, the little girl came upon two trees that promised to furnish her with plenty of food.

One was quite full of square paper boxes, which grew in clusters on all the limbs, and upon the biggest and ripest boxes the word "Lunch" could be read, in neat raised letters. This tree seemed to bear all the year around, for there were lunch-box blossoms on some of the branches, and on others tiny little lunch-boxes that were as yet quite green, and evidently not fit to eat until they had grown bigger.

The leaves of this tree were all paper napkins, and it presented a very pleasing appearance to the hungry little girl.

But the tree next to the lunch-box tree was even more wonderful, for it bore quantities of tin dinner-pails, which were so full and heavy that the stout branches bent underneath their weight. Some were small and dark-brown in color; those larger were of a dull tin color; but the really ripe ones were pails of bright tin that shone and glistened beautifully in the rays of sunshine that touched them.

Dorothy was delighted, and even the yellow hen acknowledged that she was surprised.

THE LITTLE GIRL PICKED ONE OF THE LUNCH-BOXES

The little girl stood on tip-toe and picked one of the nicest and biggest lunch-boxes, and then she sat down upon the ground and eagerly opened it. Inside she found, nicely wrapped in white papers, a ham sandwich, a piece of sponge-cake, a pickle, a slice of new cheese, and an apple. Each thing had a separate stem, and so had to be picked off the side of the box; but Dorothy found them all to be delicious, and she ate every bit of luncheon in the box before she had finished.

"A lunch isn't zactly breakfast," she said to Billina, who sat beside her curiously watching. "But when one is hungry one can eat even supper in the morning, and not complain."

"I hope your lunch-box was perfectly ripe," observed the yellow hen, in an anxious tone. "So much sickness is caused by eating green things."

"Oh, I'm sure it was ripe," declared Dorothy, "all, that is, 'cept the pickle, and a pickle just *has* to be green, Billina. But everything tasted perfectly splendid, and I'd rather have it than a church picnic. And now I think I'll pick a dinner-pail, to have when I get hungry again, and then we'll start out and 'splore the country, and see where we are."

"Haven't you any idea what country this is?" inquired Billina.

"None at all. But listen: I'm quite sure it's a fairy country, or such things as lunch-boxes and dinner-pails wouldn't be growing upon trees. Besides, Billina, being a hen, you wouldn't be able to talk in any civ'lized country, like Kansas, where no fairies live at all."

"Perhaps we're in the Land of Oz," said the hen, thoughtfully.

"No, that can't be," answered the little girl; "because I've been to the Land of Oz, and it's all surrounded by a horrid desert that no one can cross."

"Then how did you get away from there again?" asked Billina.

"I had a pair of silver shoes, that carried me through the air; but I lost them," said Dorothy.

"Ah, indeed," remarked the yellow hen, in a tone of unbelief.

"Anyhow," resumed the girl, "there is no sea-shore near the Land of Oz, so this must surely be some other fairy country."

While she was speaking she selected a bright and pretty dinner-pail that seemed to have a stout handle, and picked it from its branch. Then, accompanied by the yellow hen, she walked out of the shadow of the trees toward the sea-shore.

They were part way across the sands when Billina suddenly cried, in a voice of terror:

"What's that?"

Dorothy turned quickly around, and saw coming out of a path that led from between the trees the most peculiar person her eyes had ever beheld.

It had the form of a man, except that it walked, or rather rolled, upon all fours, and its legs were the same length as its arms, giving them the appearance of the four legs of a beast. Yet it was no beast that Dorothy had discovered, for the person was clothed most gorgeously in embroidered garments of many colors, and wore a straw hat perched jauntily upon the side of its head. But it differed from human beings in this respect, that instead of hands and feet there grew at the end of its arms and legs round wheels, and by means of these wheels it rolled very swiftly over the level ground. Afterward Dorothy found that these odd wheels were of the same hard substance that our finger-nails and toe-nails are composed of, and she also learned that creatures of this strange race were born in this queer fashion. But when our little girl first caught sight of the first individual of a race that was destined to cause her a lot of trouble, she had an idea that the brilliantly-clothed personage was on roller-skates, which were attached to his hands as well as to his feet.

"Run!" screamed the yellow hen, fluttering away in great fright. "It's a Wheeler!"

"A Wheeler?" exclaimed Dorothy. "What can that be?"

"Don't you remember the warning in the sand: 'Beware the Wheelers'? Run, I tell you—run!"

So Dorothy ran, and the Wheeler gave a sharp, wild cry and came after her in full chase.

Looking over her shoulder as she ran, the girl now saw a great procession of Wheelers emerging from the forest—dozens and dozens of them—all clad in splendid, tight-fitting garments and all rolling swiftly toward her and uttering their wild, strange cries.

"They're sure to catch us!" panted the girl, who was still carrying the heavy dinner-pail she had picked. "I can't run much farther, Billina."

"Climb up this hill,—quick!" said the hen; and Dorothy found she was very near to the heap of loose and jagged rocks they had passed on their way to the forest. The yellow hen was even now fluttering among the rocks, and Dorothy followed as best she could, half climbing and half tumbling up the rough and rugged steep.

She was none too soon, for the foremost Wheeler reached the hill a moment after her; but while the girl scrambled up the rocks the creature stopped short with howls of rage and disappointment.

Dorothy now heard the yellow hen laughing, in her cackling, henny way.

"Don't hurry, my dear," cried Billina. "They can't follow us among these rocks, so we're safe enough now."

Dorothy stopped at once and sat down upon a broad boulder, for she was all out of breath.

The rest of the Wheelers had now reached the foot of the hill, but it was evident that their wheels would not roll upon the rough and jagged rocks, and therefore they were helpless to follow Dorothy and the hen to where they had taken refuge. But they cir-

"IT'S A WHEELER!"

cled all around the little hill, so the child and Billina were fast prisoners and could not come down without being captured.

Then the creatures shook their front wheels at Dorothy in a threatening manner, and it seemed they were able to speak as well as to make their dreadful outcries, for several of them shouted:

"We'll get you in time, never fear! And when we do get you, we'll tear you into little bits!"

"Why are you so cruel to me?" asked Dorothy. "I'm a stranger in your country, and have done you no harm."

"No harm!" cried one who seemed to be their leader. "Did you not pick our lunch-boxes and dinner-pails? Have you not a stolen dinner-pail still in your hand?"

"I only picked one of each," she answered. "I was hungry, and I didn't know the trees were yours."

"That is no excuse," retorted the leader, who was clothed in a most gorgeous suit. "It is the law here that whoever picks a dinner-pail without our permission must die immediately."

"Don't you believe him," said Billina. "I'm sure the trees do not belong to these awful creatures. They are fit for any mischief, and it's my opinion they would try to kill us just the same if you hadn't picked a dinner-pail."

"I think so, too," agreed Dorothy. "But what shall we do now?"

"Stay where we are," advised the yellow hen. "We are safe from the Wheelers until we starve to death, anyhow; and before that time comes a good many things can happen."

Tiktok *the* Machine Man

After an hour or so most of the band of Wheelers rolled back into the forest, leaving only three of their number to guard the hill. These curled themselves up like big dogs and pretended to go to sleep on the sands; but neither Dorothy nor Billina were fooled by this trick, so they remained in security among the rocks and paid no attention to their cunning enemies.

Finally the hen, fluttering over the mound, exclaimed: "Why, here's a path!"

So Dorothy at once clambered to where Billina sat, and there, sure enough, was a smooth path cut between the rocks. It seemed to wind around the mound from top to bottom, like a cork-screw, twisting here and there between the rough boulders but always remaining level and easy to walk upon.

Indeed, Dorothy wondered at first why the Wheelers did not roll up this path; but when she followed it to the foot of the mound she found that several big pieces of rock had been placed directly across the end of the way, thus preventing any one outside from seeing it and also preventing the Wheelers from using it to climb up the mound.

Then Dorothy walked back up the path, and followed it until she came to the very top of the hill, where a solitary round rock stood that was bigger than any of the others surrounding it. The path came to an end just beside this great rock, and for a moment it puzzled the girl to know why the path had been made at all. But the hen, who had been gravely following her around and was now perched upon a point of rock behind Dorothy, suddenly remarked:

"It looks something like a door, doesn't it?"

"What looks like a door?" enquired the child.

"Why, that crack in the rock, just facing you," replied Billina, whose little round eyes were very sharp and seemed to see everything. "It runs up one side and down the other, and across the top and the bottom."

"What does?"

"Why, the crack. So I think it must be a door of rock, although I do not see any hinges."

"Oh, yes," said Dorothy, now observing for the first time the crack in the rock. "And isn't this a key-hole, Billina?" pointing to a round, deep hole at one side of the door.

"Of course. If we only had the key, now, we could unlock it and see what is there," replied the yellow hen. "May be it's a treasure chamber full of diamonds and rubies, or heaps of shining gold, or—"

"That reminds me," said Dorothy, "of the golden key I picked up on the shore. Do you think that it would fit this key-hole, Billina?"

"Try it and see," suggested the hen.

So Dorothy searched in the pocket of her dress and found the golden key. And when she had put it into the hole of the rock, and turned it, a sudden sharp snap was heard; then, with a solemn creak that made the shivers run down the child's back, the face of the rock fell outward, like a door on hinges, and revealed a small dark chamber just inside.

"Good gracious!" cried Dorothy, shrinking back as far as the narrow path would let her.

For, standing within the narrow chamber of rock, was the form of a man—or, at least, it seemed like a man, in the dim light. He was only about as tall as Dorothy herself, and his body was round as a ball and made out of burnished copper. Also his head and limbs were copper, and these were jointed or hinged to his body in a peculiar way, with metal caps over the joints, like the armor worn by knights in days of old. He stood perfectly still, and where the light struck upon his form it glittered as if made of pure gold.

"Don't be frightened," called Billina, from her perch. "It isn't alive."

"I see it isn't," replied the girl, drawing a long breath.

"It is only made out of copper, like the old kettle in the barn-yard at home," continued the hen, turning her head first to one side and then to the other, so that both her little round eyes could examine the object.

"Once," said Dorothy, "I knew a man made out of tin, who was a woodman named Nick Chopper. But he was as alive as we are,

"THIS COPPER MAN IS NOT ALIVE AT ALL"

'cause he was born a real man, and got his tin body a little at a time—first a leg and then a finger and then an ear—for the reason that he had so many accidents with his axe, and cut himself up in a very careless manner."

"Oh," said the hen, with a sniff, as if she did not believe the story.

"But this copper man," continued Dorothy, looking at it with big eyes, "is not alive at all, and I wonder what it was made for, and why it was locked up in this queer place."

"That is a mystery," remarked the hen, twisting her head to arrange her wing-feathers with her bill.

Dorothy stepped inside the little room to get a back view of the copper man, and in this way discovered a printed card that hung between his shoulders, it being suspended from a small copper peg at the back of his neck. She unfastened this card and returned to the path, where the light was better, and sat herself down upon a slab of rock to read the printing.

"What does it say?" asked the hen, curiously.

Dorothy read the card aloud, spelling out the big words with some difficulty; and this is what she read:

SMITH & TINKER'S
Patent Double-Action, Extra-Responsive,
Thought-Creating, Perfect-Talking
MECHANICAL MAN
Fitted with our Special Clock-Work Attachment.
Thinks, Speaks, Acts, and Does Everything but Live.
Manufactured only at our Works at Evna, Land of Ev.
All infringements will be promptly Prosecuted according to Law.

"How queer!" said the yellow hen. "Do you think that is all true, my dear?"

"I don't know," answered Dorothy, who had more to read. "Listen to this, Billina:"

DIRECTIONS FOR USING:

For THINKING:—Wind the Clock-Work Man under his left arm,
(marked No. 1.)

For SPEAKING:—Wind the Clock-Work Man under his right arm,
(marked No. 2.)

For WALKING and ACTION:—Wind Clock-Work in the middle of his
back, (marked No. 3.)

N. B.—This Mechanism is guaranteed to work perfectly for a thousand years.

"Well, I declare!" gasped the yellow hen, in amazement; "if the copper man can do half of these things he is a very wonderful machine. But I suppose it is all humbug, like so many other patented articles."

"We might wind him up," suggested Dorothy, "and see what he'll do."

"Where is the key to the clock-work?" asked Billina.

"Hanging on the peg where I found the card."

"Then," said the hen, "let us try him, and find out if he will go. He is warranted for a thousand years, it seems; but we do not know how long he has been standing inside this rock."

Dorothy had already taken the clock key from the peg.

"Which shall I wind up first?" she asked, looking again at the directions on the card.

"Number One, I should think," returned Billina. "That makes him think, doesn't it?"

"Yes," said Dorothy, and wound up Number One, under the left arm.

"He doesn't seem any different," remarked the hen, critically.

"Why, of course not; he is only thinking, now," said Dorothy.

"I wonder what he is thinking about."

"I'll wind up his talk, and then perhaps he can tell us," said the girl.

So she wound up Number Two, and immediately the clock-work man said, without moving any part of his body except his lips:

"Good morn-ing, lit-tle girl. Good morn-ing, Mrs. Hen."

DOROTHY WOUND UP NUMBER ONE

The words sounded a little hoarse and creakey, and they were uttered all in the same tone, without any change of expression whatever; but both Dorothy and Billina understood them perfectly.

"Good morning, sir," they answered, politely.

"Thank you for res-cu-ing me," continued the machine, in the same monotonous voice, which seemed to be worked by a bellows inside of him, like the little toy lambs and cats the children squeeze so that they will make a noise.

"Don't mention it," answered Dorothy. And then, being very curious, she asked: "How did you come to be locked up in this place?"

"It is a long sto-ry," replied the copper man; "but I will tell it to you brief-ly. I was pur-chased from Smith & Tin-ker, my man-u-fac-tur-ers, by a cru-el King of Ev, named Ev-ol-do, who used to beat all his serv-ants un-til they died. How-ev-er, he was not a-ble to kill me, be-cause I was not a-live, and one must first live in or-der to die. So that all his beat-ing did me no harm, and mere-ly kept my cop-per bod-y well pol-ished.

"This cru-el king had a love-ly wife and ten beau-ti-ful chil-dren—five boys and five girls—but in a fit of an-ger he sold them all to the Nome King, who by means of his mag-ic arts changed them all in-to oth-er forms and put them in his un-der-ground pal-ace to or-na-ment the rooms.

"Af-ter-ward the King of Ev re-gret-ted his wick-ed ac-tion, and tried to get his wife and chil-dren a-way from the Nome King, but with-out a-vail. So, in de-spair, he locked me up in this rock, threw the key in-to the o-cean, and then jumped in af-ter it and was drowned."

"How very dreadful!" exclaimed Dorothy.

"It is, in-deed," said the machine. "When I found my-self im-pris-oned I shout-ed for help un-til my voice ran down; and then I walked back and forth in this lit-tle room un-til my ac-tion ran down; and then I stood still and thought un-til my thoughts ran down. Af-ter that I re-mem-ber noth-ing un-til you wound me up a-gain."

"It's a very wonderful story," said Dorothy, "and proves that the Land of Ev is really a fairy land, as I thought it was."

"Of course it is," answered the copper man. "I do not sup-pose such a per-fect ma-chine as I am could be made in an-y place but a fair-y land."

"I've never seen one in Kansas," said Dorothy.

"But where did you get the key to un-lock this door?" asked the clock-work voice.

"I found it on the shore, where it was prob'ly washed up by the waves," she answered. "And now, sir, if you don't mind, I'll wind up your action."

"That will please me ve-ry much," said the machine.

So she wound up Number Three, and at once the copper man in a somewhat stiff and jerky fashion walked out of the rocky cavern, took off his copper hat and bowed politely, and then kneeled before Dorothy. Said he:

"From this time forth I am your o-be-di-ent ser-vant. What-ev-er you com-mand, that I will do will-ing-ly—if you keep me wound up."

"What is your name?" she asked.

"Tik-tok," he replied. "My for-mer mas-ter gave me that name be-cause my clock-work al-ways ticks when it is wound up."

"I can hear it now," said the yellow hen.

"So can I," said Dorothy. And then she added, with some anxiety: "You don't strike, do you?"

THE COPPER MAN WALKED OUT OF THE ROCKY CAVERN

"No," answered Tiktok; "and there is no a-larm con-nec-ted with my ma-chin-er-y. I can tell the time, though, by speak-ing, and as I nev-er sleep I can wak-en you at an-y hour you wish to get up in the morn-ing."

"That's nice," said the little girl; "only I never wish to get up in the morning."

"You can sleep until I lay my egg," said the yellow hen. "Then, when I cackle, Tiktok will know it is time to waken you."

"Do you lay your egg very early?" asked Dorothy.

"About eight o'clock," said Billina. "And everybody ought to be up by that time, I'm sure."

Dorothy Opens the Dinner Pail

"Now Tiktok," said Dorothy, "the first thing to be done is to find a way for us to escape from these rocks. The Wheelers are down below, you know, and threaten to kill us."

"There is no rea-son to be a-fraid of the Wheel-ers," said Tiktok, the words coming more slowly than before.

"Why not?" she asked.

"Be-cause they are ag-g-g—gr-gr-r-r-"

He gave a sort of gurgle and stopped short, waving his hands frantically until suddenly he became motionless, with one arm in the air and the other held stiffly before him with all the copper fingers of the hand spread out like a fan.

"Dear me!" said Dorothy, in a frightened tone. "What can the matter be?"

"He's run down, I suppose," said the hen, calmly. "You couldn't have wound him up very tight."

"I didn't know how much to wind him," replied the girl; "but I'll try to do better next time."

She ran around the copper man to take the key from the peg at the back of his neck, but it was not there.

"It's gone!" cried Dorothy, in dismay.

"What's gone?" asked Billina.

"The key."

"It probably fell off when he made that low bow to you," returned the hen. "Look around, and see if you cannot find it again."

Dorothy looked, and the hen helped her, and by and by the girl discovered the clock-key, which had fallen into a crack of the rock.

At once she wound up Tiktok's voice, taking care to give the key as many turns as it would go around. She found this quite a task, as you may imagine if you have ever tried to wind a clock, but the machine man's first words were to assure Dorothy that he would now run for at least twenty-four hours.

"You did not wind me much, at first," he calmly said, "and I told you that long sto-ry a-bout King Ev-ol-do; so it is no won-der that I ran down."

She next rewound the action clock-work, and then Billina advised her to carry the key to Tiktok in her pocket, so it would not get lost again.

"And now," said Dorothy, when all this was accomplished, "tell me what you were going to say about the Wheelers."

"Why, they are noth-ing to be fright-en'd at," said the machine. "They try to make folks be-lieve that they are ver-y ter-ri-ble, but as a mat-ter of fact the Wheel-ers are harm-less e-nough to an-y one that dares to fight them. They might try to hurt a lit-tle girl like you, per-haps, be-cause they are ver-y mis-chiev-ous. But if I had a club they would run a-way as soon as they saw me."

"Haven't you a club?" asked Dorothy.

"No," said Tiktok.

"And you won't find such a thing among these rocks, either," declared the yellow hen.

"Then what shall we do?" asked the girl.

"Wind up my think-works tight-ly, and I will try to think of some oth-er plan," said Tiktok.

So Dorothy rewound his thought machinery, and while he was thinking she decided to eat her dinner. Billina was already pecking away at the cracks in the rocks, to find something to eat, so Dorothy sat down and opened her tin dinner-pail.

In the cover she found a small tank that was full of very nice lemonade. It was covered by a cup, which might also, when removed, be used to drink the lemonade from. Within the pail were three slices of turkey, two slices of cold tongue, some lobster salad, four slices of bread and butter, a small custard pie, an orange and nine large strawberries, and some nuts and raisins. Singularly enough, the nuts in this dinner-pail grew already cracked, so that Dorothy had no trouble in picking out their meats to eat.

She spread the feast upon the rock beside her and began her dinner, first offering some of it to Tiktok, who declined because, as he said, he was merely a machine. Afterward she offered to share with Billina, but the hen murmured something about "dead things" and said she preferred her bugs and ants.

"Do the lunch-box trees and the dinner-pail trees belong to the

Wheelers?" the child asked Tiktok, while engaged in eating her meal.

"Of course not," he answered. "They be-long to the roy-al fam-il-y of Ev, on-ly of course there is no roy-al fam-il-y just now be-cause King Ev-ol-do jumped in-to the sea and his wife and ten chil-dren have been trans-formed by the Nome King. So there is no one to rule the Land of Ev, that I can think of. Per-haps it is for this rea-son that the Wheel-ers claim the trees for their own, and pick the lunch-eons and din-ners to eat them-selves. But they be-long to the King, and you will find the roy-al "E" stamped up-on the bot-tom of ev-er-y din-ner-pail."

Dorothy turned the pail over, and at once discovered the royal mark upon it, as Tiktok had said.

"Are the Wheelers the only folks living in the Land of Ev?" en-quired the girl.

"No; they on-ly in-hab-it a small por-tion of it just back of the woods," replied the machine. "But they have al-ways been mis-chiev-ous and im-per-ti-nent, and my old mas-ter, King Ev-ol-do, used to car-ry a whip with him, when he walked out, to keep the crea-tures in or-der. When I was first made the Wheel-ers tried to run o-ver me, and butt me with their heads; but they soon found I was built of too sol-id a ma-ter-i-al for them to in-jure."

"You seem very durable," said Dorothy. "Who made you?"

"The firm of Smith & Tin-ker, in the town of Ev-na, where the roy-al pal-ace stands," answered Tiktok.

"Did they make many of you?" asked the child.

"No; I am the on-ly au-to-mat-ic me-chan-i-cal man they ev-er com-plet-ed," he replied. "They were ver-y won-der-ful in-ven-tors, were my mak-ers, and quite ar-tis-tic in all they did."

"I am sure of that," said Dorothy. "Do they live in the town of Evna now?"

"They are both gone," replied the machine. "Mr. Smith was an art-ist, as well as an in-vent-or, and he paint-ed a pic-ture of a riv-er which was so nat-ur-al that, as he was reach-ing a-cross it to paint some flow-ers on the op-po-site bank, he fell in-to the wa-ter and was drowned."

DOROTHY OPENED HER TIN DINNER-PAIL

"Oh, I'm sorry for that!" exclaimed the little girl.

"Mis-ter Tin-ker," continued Tiktok, "made a lad-der so tall that he could rest the end of it a-gainst the moon, while he stood on the high-est rung and picked the lit-tle stars to set in the points of the king's crown. But when he got to the moon Mis-ter Tin-ker found it such a love-ly place that he de-cid-ed to live there, so he pulled up the lad-der af-ter him and we have nev-er seen him since."

"He must have been a great loss to this country," said Dorothy, who was by this time eating her custard pie.

"He was," acknowledged Tiktok. "Also he is a great loss to me. For if I should get out of or-der I do not know of an-y one a-ble to re-pair me, be-cause I am so com-pli-cat-ed. You have no i-de-a how full of ma-chin-er-y I am."

"I can imagine it," said Dorothy, readily.

"And now," continued the machine, "I must stop talk-ing and be-gin think-ing a-gain of a way to es-cape from this rock." So he turned half way around, in order to think without being disturbed.

"The best thinker I ever knew," said Dorothy to the yellow hen, "was a scarecrow."

"Nonsense!" snapped Billina.

"It is true," declared Dorothy. "I met him in the Land of Oz, and he travelled with me to the city of the great Wizard of Oz, so as to get some brains, for his head was only stuffed with straw. But it seemed to me that he thought just as well before he got his brains as he did afterward."

"Do you expect me to believe all that rubbish about the Land of Oz?" enquired Billina, who seemed a little cross—perhaps because bugs were scarce.

"What rubbish?" asked the child, who was now finishing her nuts and raisins.

"Why, your impossible stories about animals that can talk, and a tin woodman who is alive, and a scarecrow who can think."

"They are all there," said Dorothy, "for I have seen them."

"I don't believe it!" cried the hen, with a toss of her head.

"That's 'cause you're so ign'rant," replied the girl, who was a lit-tle offended at her friend Billina's speech.

MISTER TINKER VISITS THE MOON

"In the Land of Oz," remarked Tiktok, turning toward them, "an-y-thing is pos-si-ble. For it is a won-der-ful fair-y coun-try."

"There, Billina! what did I say?" cried Dorothy. And then she turned to the machine and asked in an eager tone: "Do you know the Land of Oz, Tiktok?"

"No; but I have heard a-bout it," said the copper man. "For it is on-ly sep-a-ra-ted from this Land of Ev by a broad des-ert."

Dorothy clapped her hands together delightedly.

"I'm glad of that!" she exclaimed. "It makes me quite happy to be so near my old friends. The scarecrow I told you of, Billina, is the king of the Land of Oz."

"Par-don me. He is not the king now," said Tiktok.

"He was when I left there," declared Dorothy.

"I know," said Tiktok, "but there was a rev-o-lu-tion in the Land of Oz, and the Scare-crow was de-posed by a sol-dier wo-man named Gen-er-al Jin-jur. And then Jin-jur was de-posed by a lit-tle girl named Oz-ma, who was the right-ful heir to the throne and now rules the land un-der the ti-tle of Oz-ma of Oz."

"That is news to me," said Dorothy, thoughtfully. "But I s'pose lots of things have happened since I left the Land of Oz. I wonder what has become of the Scarecrow, and of the Tin Woodman, and the Cowardly Lion. And I wonder who this girl Ozma is, for I never heard of her before."

But Tiktok did not reply to this. He had turned around again to resume his thinking.

Dorothy packed the rest of the food back into the pail, so as not to be wasteful of good things, and the yellow hen forgot her dignity far enough to pick up all of the scattered crumbs, which she ate rather greedily, although she had so lately pretended to despise the things that Dorothy preferred as food.

By this time Tiktok approached them with his stiff bow.

"Be kind e-nough to fol-low me," he said, "and I will lead you a-way from here to the town of Ev-na, where you will be more com-for-ta-ble, and al-so I will pro-tect you from the Wheel-ers."

"All right," answered Dorothy, promptly. "I'm ready!"

The Heads of Langwidere

They

walked slowly down the path between the rocks, Tiktok going first, Dorothy following him, and the yellow hen trotting along last of all.

At the foot of the path the copper man leaned down and tossed aside with ease the rocks that cumbered the way. Then he turned to Dorothy and said:

"Let me car-ry your din-ner-pail."

She placed it in his right hand at once, and the copper fingers closed firmly over the stout handle.

Then the little procession marched out upon the level sands.

As soon as the three Wheelers who were guarding the mound saw them, they began to shout their wild cries and rolled swiftly toward the little group, as if to capture them or bar their way. But when the foremost had approached near enough, Tiktok swung the tin dinner-pail and struck the Wheeler a sharp blow over its head with the queer weapon. Perhaps it did not hurt very much, but it made a great noise, and the Wheeler uttered a howl and tumbled over upon its side. The next minute it scrambled to its wheels and rolled away as fast as it could go, screeching with fear at the same time.

"I told you they were harm-less," began Tiktok; but before he could say more another Wheeler was upon them. Crack! went the dinner-pail against its head, knocking its straw hat a dozen feet away; and that was enough for this Wheeler, also. It rolled away after the first one, and the third did not wait to be pounded with the pail, but joined its fellows as quickly as its wheels would whirl.

The yellow hen gave a cackle of delight, and flying to a perch upon Tiktok's shoulder, she said:

"Bravely done, my copper friend! and wisely thought of, too. Now we are free from those ugly creatures."

But just then a large band of Wheelers rolled from the forest, and relying upon their numbers to conquer, they advanced fiercely upon Tiktok. Dorothy grabbed Billina in her arms and held her tight, and the machine embraced the form of the little girl with his left arm, the better to protect her. Then the Wheelers were upon them.

Rattlety, bang! bang! went the dinner-pail in every direction, and it made so much clatter bumping against the heads of the Wheelers that they were much more frightened than hurt and fled in a great panic. All, that is, except their leader. This Wheeler had stumbled against another and fallen flat upon his back, and before he could get his wheels under him to rise again, Tiktok had fastened his copper fingers into the neck of the gorgeous jacket of his foe and held him fast.

"Tell your peo-ple to go a-way," commanded the machine.

The leader of the Wheelers hesitated to give this order, so Tiktok shook him as a terrier dog does a rat, until the Wheeler's teeth rattled together with a noise like hailstones on a window pane. Then, as soon as the creature could get its breath, it shouted to the others to roll away, which they immediately did.

"Now," said Tiktok, "you shall come with us and tell me what I want to know."

"You'll be sorry for treating me in this way," whined the Wheeler. "I'm a terribly fierce person."

"As for that," answered Tiktok, "I am only a ma-chine, and can-not feel sor-row or joy, no mat-ter what hap-pens. But you are wrong to think your-self ter-ri-ble or fierce."

"Why so?" asked the Wheeler.

"Be-cause no one else thinks as you do. Your wheels make you help-less to in-jure an-y one. For you have no fists and can not scratch or e-ven pull hair. Nor have you an-y feet to kick with. All you can do is to yell and shout, and that does not hurt an-y one at all."

The Wheeler burst into a flood of tears, to Dorothy's great sur-prise.

"Now I and my people are ruined forever!" he sobbed; "for you have discovered our secret. Being so helpless, our only hope is to make people afraid of us, by pretending we are very fierce and ter-rible, and writing in the sand warnings to Beware the Wheelers. Until now we have frightened everyone, but since you have discov-ered our weakness our enemies will fall upon us and make us very miserable and unhappy."

"Oh, no," exclaimed Dorothy, who was sorry to see this beauti-fully dressed Wheeler so miserable; "Tiktok will keep your secret,

ON THE WAY TO THE ROYAL PALACE OF EV

and so will Billina and I. Only, you must promise not to try to frighten children any more, if they come near to you."

"I won't—indeed I won't!" promised the Wheeler, ceasing to cry and becoming more cheerful. "I'm not really bad, you know; but we have to pretend to be terrible in order to prevent others from attacking us."

"That is not ex-act-ly true," said Tiktok, starting to walk toward the path through the forest, and still holding fast to his prisoner, who rolled slowly along beside him. "You and your peo-ple are full of mis-chief, and like to both-er those who fear you. And you are of-ten im-pu-dent and dis-a-gree-a-ble, too. But if you will try to cure those faults I will not tell any one how help-less you are."

"I'll try, of course," replied the Wheeler, eagerly. "And thank you, Mr. Tiktok, for your kindness."

"I am on-ly a ma-chine," said Tiktok. "I can not be kind an-y more than I can be sor-ry or glad. I can on-ly do what I am wound up to do."

"Are you wound up to keep my secret?" asked the Wheeler, anxiously.

"Yes; if you be-have your-self. But tell me: who rules the Land of Ev now?" asked the machine.

"There is no ruler," was the answer, "because every member of the royal family is imprisoned by the Nome King. But the Princess Langwidere, who is a niece of our late King Evoldo, lives in a part of the royal palace and takes as much money out of the royal treasury as she can spend. The Princess Langwidere is not exactly a ruler, you see, because she doesn't rule; but she is the nearest approach to a ruler we have at present."

"I do not re-mem-ber her," said Tiktok. "What does she look like?"

"That I cannot say," replied the Wheeler, "although I have seen her twenty times. For the Princess Langwidere is a different person every time I see her, and the only way her subjects can recognize her at all is by means of a beautiful ruby key which she always wears on a chain attached to her left wrist. When we see the key we know we are beholding the Princess."

"That is strange," said Dorothy, in astonishment. "Do you mean to say that so many different princesses are one and the same person?"

"Not exactly," answered the Wheeler. "There is, of course, but one princess; but she appears to us in many forms, which are all more or less beautiful."

"She must be a witch," exclaimed the girl.

"I do not think so," declared the Wheeler. "But there is some mystery connected with her, nevertheless. She is a very vain creature, and lives mostly in a room surrounded by mirrors, so that she can admire herself whichever way she looks."

No one answered this speech, because they had just passed out of the forest and their attention was fixed upon the scene before them—a beautiful vale in which were many fruit trees and green fields, with pretty farm-houses scattered here and there and broad, smooth roads that led in every direction.

In the center of this lovely vale, about a mile from where our friends were standing, rose the tall spires of the royal palace, which glittered brightly against their background of blue sky. The palace was surrounded by charming grounds, full of flowers and shrubbery. Several tinkling fountains could be seen, and there were pleasant walks bordered by rows of white marble statuary.

All these details Dorothy was, of course, unable to notice or admire until they had advanced along the road to a position quite near to the palace, and she was still looking at the pretty sights when her little party entered the grounds and approached the big front door of the King's own apartments. To their disappointment they found the door tightly closed. A sign was tacked to the panel which read as follows:

OWNER ABSENT.
Please Knock at the Third Door in the Left Wing.

"Now," said Tiktok to the captive Wheeler, "you must show us the way to the Left Wing."

"Very well," agreed the prisoner, "it is around here at the right."

A SIGN WAS TACKED TO THE PANEL

"How can the Left Wing be at the right?" demanded Dorothy, who feared the Wheeler was fooling them.

"Because there used to be three wings, and two were torn down, so the one on the right is the only one left. It is a trick of the Princess Langwidere to prevent visitors from annoying her."

Then the captive led them around to the wing, after which the machine man, having no further use for the Wheeler, permitted him to depart and rejoin his fellows. He immediately rolled away at a great pace and was soon lost to sight.

Tiktok now counted the doors in the wing and knocked loudly upon the third one.

It was opened by a little maid in a cap trimmed with gay ribbons, who bowed respectfully and asked:

"What do you wish, good people?"

"Are you the Princess Langwidere?" asked Dorothy.

"No, miss; I am her servant," replied the maid.

"May I see the Princess, please?"

"I will tell her you are here, miss, and ask her to grant you an audience," said the maid. "Step in, please, and take a seat in the drawing-room."

So Dorothy walked in, followed closely by the machine. But as the yellow hen tried to enter after them, the little maid cried "Shoo!" and flapped her apron in Billina's face.

"Shoo, yourself!" retorted the hen, drawing back in anger and ruffling up her feathers. "Haven't you any better manners than that?"

"Oh, do you talk?" enquired the maid, evidently surprised.

"Can't you hear me?" snapped Billina. "Drop that apron, and get out of the doorway, so that I may enter with my friends!"

"The Princess won't like it," said the maid, hesitating.

"I don't care whether she likes it or not," replied Billina, and fluttering her wings with a loud noise she flew straight at the maid's face. The little servant at once ducked her head, and the hen reached Dorothy's side in safety.

"Very well," sighed the maid; "if you are all ruined because of this obstinate hen, don't blame me for it. It isn't safe to annoy the Princess Langwidere."

"Tell her we are waiting, if you please," Dorothy requested, with dignity. "Billina is my friend, and must go wherever I go."

Without more words the maid led them to a richly furnished drawing-room, lighted with subdued rainbow tints that came in through beautiful stained-glass windows.

"Remain here," she said. "What names shall I give the Princess?"

"I am Dorothy Gale, of Kansas," replied the child; "and this gentleman is a machine named Tiktok, and the yellow hen is my friend Billina."

The little servant bowed and withdrew, going through several passages and mounting two marble stairways before she came to the apartments occupied by her mistress.

Princess Langwidere's sitting-room was panelled with great mirrors, which reached from the ceiling to the floor; also the ceiling was composed of mirrors, and the floor was of polished silver that reflected every object upon it. So when Langwidere sat in her easy chair and played soft melodies upon her mandolin, her form

"THE PRINCESS WON'T LIKE IT," SAID THE MAID

was mirrored hundreds of times, in walls and ceiling and floor, and whichever way the lady turned her head she could see and admire her own features. This she loved to do, and just as the maid entered she was saying to herself:

"This head with the auburn hair and hazel eyes is quite attractive. I must wear it more often than I have done of late, although it may not be the best of my collection."

"You have company, Your Highness," announced the maid, bowing low.

"Who is it?" asked Langwidere, yawning.

"Dorothy Gale of Kansas, Mr. Tiktok and Billina," answered the maid.

"What a queer lot of names!" murmured the Princess, beginning to be a little interested. "What are they like? Is Dorothy Gale of Kansas pretty?"

"She might be called so," the maid replied.

"And is Mr. Tiktok attractive?" continued the Princess.

"That I cannot say, Your Highness. But he seems very bright. Will Your Gracious Highness see them?"

"Oh, I may as well, Nanda. But I am tired admiring this head, and if my visitor has any claim to beauty I must take care that she does not surpass me. So I will go to my cabinet and change to No. 17, which I think is my best appearance. Don't you?"

"Your No. 17 is exceedingly beautiful," answered Nanda, with another bow.

Again the Princess yawned. Then she said:

"Help me to rise."

So the maid assisted her to gain her feet, although Langwidere was the stronger of the two; and then the Princess slowly walked across the silver floor to her cabinet, leaning heavily at every step upon Nanda's arm.

Now I must explain to you that the Princess Langwidere had thirty heads—as many as there are days in the month. But of course she could only wear one of them at a time, because she had but one neck. These heads were kept in what she called her "cabinet," which was a beautiful dressing-room that lay just between Langwidere's sleeping-chamber and the mirrored sitting-room. Each head was in a separate cupboard lined with velvet. The cupboards ran all around the sides of the dressing-room, and had elaborately carved doors with gold numbers on the outside and jewelled-framed mirrors on the inside of them.

When the Princess got out of her crystal bed in the morning she went to her cabinet, opened one of the velvet-lined cupboards, and took the head it contained from its golden shelf. Then, by the aid of the mirror inside the open door, she put on the head—as neat and straight as could be—and afterward called her maids to robe her for the day. She always wore a simple white costume, that suited all the heads. For, being able to change her face whenever she liked, the Princess had no interest in wearing a variety of gowns, as have other ladies who are compelled to wear the same face constantly.

Of course the thirty heads were in great variety, no two formed alike but all being of exceeding loveliness. There were heads with golden hair, brown hair, rich auburn hair and black hair; but none with gray hair. The heads had eyes of blue, of gray, of hazel, of brown and of black; but there were no red eyes among them, and all were bright and handsome. The noses were Grecian, Roman, retroussé and Oriental, representing all types of beauty; and the mouths were of assorted sizes and shapes, displaying pearly teeth when the heads smiled. As for dimples, they appeared in cheeks and chins, wherever they might be most charming, and one or two heads had freckles upon the faces to contrast the better with the brilliancy of their complexions.

One key unlocked all the velvet cupboards containing these treasures—a curious key carved from a single blood-red ruby—and this was fastened to a strong but slender chain which the Princess wore around her left wrist.

When Nanda had supported Langwidere to a position in front of cupboard No. 17, the Princess unlocked the door with her ruby key and after handing head No. 9, which she had been wearing, to the maid, she took No. 17 from its shelf and fitted it to her neck. It had black hair and dark eyes and a lovely pearl-and-white complexion,

BY THE AID OF THE MIRROR SHE PUT ON THE HEAD

and when Langwidere wore it she knew she was remarkably beautiful in appearance.

There was only one trouble with No. 17; the temper that went with it (and which was hidden somewhere under the glossy black hair) was fiery, harsh and haughty in the extreme, and it often led the Princess to do unpleasant things which she regretted when she came to wear her other heads.

But she did not remember this today, and went to meet her guests in the drawing-room with a feeling of certainty that she would surprise them with her beauty.

However, she was greatly disappointed to find that her visitors were merely a small girl in a gingham dress, a copper man that would only go when wound up, and a yellow hen that was sitting contentedly in Langwidere's best work-basket, where there was a china egg used for darning stockings.*

"Oh!" said Langwidere, slightly lifting the nose of No. 17. "I thought some one of importance had called."

"Then you were right," declared Dorothy. "I'm a good deal of 'portance myself, and when Billina lays an egg she has the proudest cackle you ever heard. As for Tiktok, he's the—"

"Stop—Stop!" commanded the Princess, with an angry flash of her splendid eyes. "How dare you annoy me with your senseless chatter?"

"Why, you horrid thing!" said Dorothy, who was not accustomed to being treated so rudely.

The Princess looked at her more closely.

"Tell me," she resumed, "are you of royal blood?"

"Better than that, ma'am," said Dorothy. "I came from Kansas."

"Huh!" cried the Princess, scornfully. "You are a foolish child, and I cannot allow you to annoy me. Run away, you little goose, and bother some one else."

---

*It may surprise you to learn that a princess ever does such a common thing as darn stockings. But, if you will stop to think, you will realize that a princess is sure to wear holes in her stockings, the same as other people; only it isn't considered quite polite to mention the matter.

Dorothy was so indignant that for a moment she could find no words to reply. But she rose from her chair, and was about to leave the room when the Princess, who had been scanning the girl's face, stopped her by saying, more gently:

"Come nearer to me."

Dorothy obeyed, without a thought of fear, and stood before the Princess while Langwidere examined her face with careful attention.

"You are rather attractive," said the lady, presently. "Not at all beautiful, you understand, but you have a certain style of prettiness that is different from that of any of my thirty heads. So I believe I'll take your head and give you No. 26 for it."

"Well, I b'lieve you won't!" exclaimed Dorothy.

"It will do you no good to refuse," continued the Princess; "for I need your head for my collection, and in the Land of Ev my will is law. I never have cared much for No. 26, and you will find that it is very little worn. Besides, it will do you just as well as the one you're wearing, for all practical purposes."

"I don't know anything about your No. 26, and I don't want to," said Dorothy, firmly. "I'm not used to taking cast-off things, so I'll just keep my own head."

"You refuse?" cried the Princess, with a frown.

"Of course I do," was the reply.

"Then," said Langwidere, "I shall lock you up in a tower until you decide to obey me. Nanda," turning to her maid, "call my army."

Nanda rang a silver bell, and at once a big fat colonel in a bright red uniform entered the room, followed by ten lean soldiers, who all looked sad and discouraged and saluted the Princess in a very melancholy fashion.

"Carry that girl to the North Tower and lock her up!" cried the Princess, pointing to Dorothy.

"To hear is to obey," answered the big red colonel, and caught the child by her arm. But at that moment Tiktok raised his dinner-pail and pounded it so forcibly against the colonel's head that the

"WELL I B'LIEVE YOU WON'T!" EXCLAIMED DOROTHY

big officer sat down upon the floor with a sudden bump, looking both dazed and very much astonished.

"Help!" he shouted, and the ten lean soldiers sprang to assist their leader.

There was great excitement for the next few moments, and Tiktok had knocked down seven of the army, who were sprawling in every direction upon the carpet, when suddenly the machine paused, with the dinner-pail raised for another blow, and remained perfectly motionless.

"My ac-tion has run down," he called to Dorothy. "Wind me up, quick."

She tried to obey, but the big colonel had by this time managed to get upon his feet again, so he grabbed fast hold of the girl and she was helpless to escape.

"This is too bad," said the machine. "I ought to have run six hours lon-ger, at least, but I sup-pose my long walk and my fight with the Wheel-ers made me run down fast-er than us-u-al."

"Well, it can't be helped," said Dorothy, with a sigh.

"Will you exchange heads with me?" demanded the Princess.

"No, indeed!" cried Dorothy.

"Then lock her up," said Langwidere to her soldiers, and they led Dorothy to a high tower at the north of the palace and locked her securely within.

The soldiers afterward tried to lift Tiktok, but they found the machine so solid and heavy that they could not stir it. So they left him standing in the center of the drawing-room.

"People will think I have a new statue," said Langwidere, "so it won't matter in the least, and Nanda can keep him well polished."

"What shall we do with the hen?" asked the colonel, who had just discovered Billina in the work-basket.

"Put her in the chicken house," answered the Princess. "Someday I'll have her fried for breakfast."

"She looks rather tough, Your Highness," said Nanda, doubtfully.

"That is a base slander!" cried Billina, struggling frantically in the colonel's arms. "But the breed of chickens I come from is said to be poison to all princesses."

"Then," remarked Langwidere, "I will not fry the hen, but keep her to lay eggs; and if she doesn't do her duty I'll have her drowned in the horse trough."

Ozma of Oz to the Rescue

Nanda

brought Dorothy bread and water for her supper and she slept upon a hard stone couch with a single pillow and a silken coverlet.

In the morning she leaned out of the window of her prison in the tower to see if there was any way to escape. The room was not so very high up, when compared with our modern buildings, but it was far enough above the trees and farm-houses to give her a good view of the surrounding country.

To the east she saw the forest, with the sands beyond it and the ocean beyond that. There was even a dark speck upon the shore that she thought might be the chicken-coop in which she had arrived at this singular country.

Then she looked to the north, and saw a deep but narrow valley lying between two rocky mountains, and a third mountain that shut off the valley at the further end.

Westward the fertile Land of Ev suddenly ended a little way from the palace, and the girl could see miles and miles of sandy desert that stretched further than her eyes could reach. It was this desert, she thought, with much interest, that alone separated her from the wonderful Land of Oz, and she remembered sorrowfully that she had been told no one had ever been able to cross this dangerous waste but herself. Once a cyclone had carried her across it, and a magical pair of silver shoes had carried her back again. But now she had neither a cyclone nor silver shoes to assist her, and her condition was sad indeed. For she had become the prisoner of a disagreeable princess who insisted that she must exchange her head for another one that she was not used to, and which might not fit her at all.

Really, there seemed no hope of help for her from her old friends in the Land of Oz. Thoughtfully she gazed from her narrow window. On all the desert not a living thing was stirring.

Wait, though! Something surely *was* stirring on the desert—something her eyes had not observed at first. Now it seemed like a cloud; now it seemed like a spot of silver; now it seemed to be a mass of rainbow colors that moved swiftly toward her.

What *could* it be, she wondered?

Then, gradually, but in a brief space of time nevertheless, the vision drew near enough to Dorothy to make out what it was.

A broad green carpet was unrolling itself upon the desert, while advancing across the carpet was a wonderful procession that made the girl open her eyes in amazement as she gazed.

First came a magnificent golden chariot, drawn by a great Lion and an immense Tiger, who stood shoulder to shoulder and trotted along as gracefully as a well-matched team of thoroughbred horses. And standing upright within the chariot was a beautiful girl clothed in flowing robes of silver gauze and wearing a jeweled diadem upon her dainty head. She held in one hand the satin ribbons that guided her astonishing team, and in the other an ivory wand that separated at the top into two prongs, the prongs being tipped by the letters "O" and "Z," made of glistening diamonds set closely together.

The girl seemed neither older nor larger than Dorothy herself, and at once the prisoner in the tower guessed that the lovely driver of the chariot must be that Ozma of Oz of whom she had so lately heard from Tiktok.

THE MAGIC CARPET

Following close behind the chariot Dorothy saw her old friend the Scarecrow, riding calmly astride a wooden Saw-Horse, which pranced and trotted as naturally as any meat horse could have done.

And then came Nick Chopper, the Tin Woodman, with his funnel-shaped cap tipped carelessly over his left ear, his gleaming axe over his right shoulder, and his whole body sparkling as brightly as it had ever done in the old days when first she knew him.

The Tin Woodman was on foot, marching at the head of a company of twenty-seven soldiers, of whom some were lean and some fat, some short and some tall; but all the twenty-seven were dressed in handsome uniforms of various designs and colors, no two being alike in any respect.

Behind the soldiers the green carpet rolled itself up again, so that there was always just enough of it for the procession to walk upon, in order that their feet might not come in contact with the deadly, life-destroying sands of the desert.

Dorothy knew at once it was a magic carpet she beheld, and her heart beat high with hope and joy as she realized she was soon to be rescued and allowed to greet her dearly beloved friends of Oz—the Scarecrow, the Tin Woodman and the Cowardly Lion.

Indeed, the girl felt herself as good as rescued as soon as she recognized those in the procession, for she well knew the courage and loyalty of her old comrades, and also believed that any others who came from their marvelous country would prove to be pleasant and reliable acquaintances.

As soon as the last bit of desert was passed and all the procession, from the beautiful and dainty Ozma to the last soldier, had reached the grassy meadows of the Land of Ev, the magic carpet rolled itself together and entirely disappeared.

Then the chariot driver turned her Lion and Tiger into a broad roadway leading up to the palace, and the others followed, while Dorothy still gazed from her tower window in eager excitement.

They came quite close to the front door of the palace and then halted, the Scarecrow dismounting from his Saw-Horse to approach the sign fastened to the door, that he might read what it said.

Dorothy, just above him, could keep silent no longer.

"Here I am!" she shouted, as loudly as she could. "Here's Dorothy!"

"Dorothy who?" asked the Scarecrow, tipping his head to look upward until he nearly lost his balance and tumbled over backward.

"Dorothy Gale, of course. Your friend from Kansas," she answered.

"Why, hello, Dorothy!" said the Scarecrow. "What in the world are you doing up there?"

"Nothing," she called down, "because there's nothing to do. Save me, my friend—save me!"

"You seem to be quite safe now," replied the Scarecrow.

"But I'm a prisoner. I'm locked in, so that I can't get out," she pleaded.

"That's all right," said the Scarecrow. "You might be worse off, little Dorothy. Just consider the matter. You can't get drowned, or be run over by a Wheeler, or fall out of an apple-tree. Some folks would think they were lucky to be up there."

"Well, I don't," declared the girl, "and I want to get down immed'i'tly and see you and the Tin Woodman and the Cowardly Lion."

"SAVE ME, MY FRIEND – SAVE ME!"

"Very well," said the Scarecrow, nodding. "It shall be just as you say, little friend. Who locked you up?"

"The Princess Langwidere, who is a horrid creature," she answered.

At this Ozma, who had been listening carefully to the conversation, called to Dorothy from her chariot, asking:

"Why did the Princess lock you up, my dear?"

"Because," exclaimed Dorothy, "I wouldn't let her have my head for her collection, and take an old, cast-off head in exchange for it."

"I do not blame you," exclaimed Ozma, promptly. "I will see the Princess at once, and oblige her to liberate you."

"Oh, thank you very, very much!" cried Dorothy, who as soon as she heard the sweet voice of the girlish Ruler of Oz knew that she would soon learn to love her dearly.

Ozma now drove her chariot around to the third door of the wing, upon which the Tin Woodman boldly proceeded to knock.

As soon as the maid opened the door Ozma, bearing in her hand her ivory wand, stepped into the hall and made her way at once to the drawing-room, followed by all her company, except the Lion and the Tiger. And the twenty-seven soldiers made such a noise and a clatter that the little maid Nanda ran away screaming to her mistress, whereupon the Princess Langwidere, roused to great anger by this rude invasion of her palace, came running into the drawing-room without any assistance whatever.

There she stood before the slight and delicate form of the little girl from Oz and cried out;—

"How dare you enter my palace unbidden? Leave this room at once, or I will bind you and all your people in chains, and throw you into my darkest dungeons!"

"What a dangerous lady!" murmured the Scarecrow, in a soft voice.

"She seems a little nervous," replied the Tin Woodman.

But Ozma only smiled at the angry Princess.

"Sit down, please," she said, quietly. "I have traveled a long way to see you, and you must listen to what I have to say."

"WHAT A DANGEROUS LADY!"
MURMURED THE SCARECROW

"Must!" screamed the Princess, her black eyes flashing with fury—for she still wore her No. 17 head. "Must, to *me!*"

"To be sure," said Ozma. "I am Ruler of the Land of Oz, and I am powerful enough to destroy all your kingdom, if I so wish. Yet I did not come here to do harm, but rather to free the royal family of Ev from the thrall of the Nome King, the news having reached me that he is holding the Queen and her children prisoners."

Hearing these words, Langwidere suddenly became quiet.

"I wish you could, indeed, free my aunt and her ten royal children," said she, eagerly. "For if they were restored to their proper forms and station they could rule the Kingdom of Ev themselves, and that would save me a lot of worry and trouble. At present there are at least ten minutes every day that I must devote to affairs of state, and I would like to be able to spend my whole time in admiring my beautiful heads."

"Then we will presently discuss this matter," said Ozma, "and try to find a way to liberate your aunt and cousins. But first you must liberate another prisoner—the little girl you have locked up in your tower."

"Of course," said Langwidere, readily. "I had forgotten all about her. That was yesterday, you know, and a Princess cannot be expected to remember today what she did yesterday. Come with me, and I will release the prisoner at once."

So Ozma followed her, and they passed up the stairs that led to the room in the tower.

While they were gone Ozma's followers remained in the drawing-room, and the Scarecrow was leaning against a form that he had mistaken for a copper statue when a harsh, metallic voice said suddenly in his ear:

"Get off my foot, please. You are scratch-ing my pol-ish."

"Oh, excuse me!" he replied, hastily drawing back. "Are you alive?"

"No," said Tiktok, "I am on-ly a ma-chine. But I can think and speak and act, when I am pro-per-ly wound up. Just now my ac-tion is run down, and Dor-o-thy has the key to it."

"That's all right," replied the Scarecrow. "Dorothy will soon be free, and then she'll attend to your works. But it must be a great misfortune not to be alive. I'm sorry for you."

"Why?" asked Tiktok.

"Because you have no brains, as I have," said the Scarecrow.

"Oh, yes, I have," returned Tiktok. "I am fit-ted with Smith & Tin-ker's Improved Com-bi-na-tion Steel Brains. They are what make me think. What sort of brains are you fit-ted with?"

"I don't know," admitted the Scarecrow. "They were given to me by the great Wizard of Oz, and I didn't get a chance to examine them before he put them in. But they work splendidly and my conscience is very active. Have you a conscience?"

"No," said Tiktok.

"And no heart, I suppose?" added the Tin Woodman, who had been listening with interest to this conversation.

"No," said Tiktok.

"Then," continued the Tin Woodman, "I regret to say that you are greatly inferior to my friend the Scarecrow, and to myself. For we are both alive, and he has brains which do not need to be wound up, while I have an excellent heart that is continually beating in my bosom."

"I con-grat-u-late you," replied Tiktok. "I can-not help be-ing your in-fer-i-or for I am a mere ma-chine. When I am wound up I do my du-ty by go-ing just as my ma-chin-er-y is made to go. You have no i-de-a how full of ma-chin-er-y I am."

"I can guess," said the Scarecrow, looking at the machine man curiously. "Some day I'd like to take you apart and see just how you are made."

"Do not do that, I beg of you," said Tiktok; "for you could not put me to-geth-er a-gain, and my use-ful-ness would be de-stroyed."

"Oh! are you useful?" asked the Scarecrow, surprised.

"Ve-ry," said Tiktok.

"In that case," the Scarecrow kindly promised, "I won't fool with your interior at all. For I am a poor mechanic, and might mix you up."

"Thank you," said Tiktok.

Just then Ozma re-entered the room, leading Dorothy by the hand and followed closely by the Princess Langwidere.

The Hungry Tiger

The first thing Dorothy did was to rush into the embrace of the Scarecrow, whose painted face beamed with delight as he pressed her form to his straw-padded bosom. Then the Tin Woodman embraced her—very gently, for he knew his tin arms might hurt her if he squeezed too roughly.

These greetings having been exchanged, Dorothy took the key to Tiktok from her pocket and wound up the machine man's action, so that he could bow properly when introduced to the rest of the company. While doing this she told them how useful Tiktok had been to her, and both the Scarecrow and the Tin Woodman shook hands with the machine once more and thanked him for protecting their friend.

Then Dorothy asked: "Where is Billina?"

"I don't know," said the Scarecrow. "Who is Billina?"

"She's a yellow hen who is another friend of mine," answered the girl, anxiously. "I wonder what has become of her?"

"She is in the chicken house, in the back yard," said the Princess. "My drawing-room is no place for hens."

Without waiting to hear more Dorothy ran to get Billina, and just outside the door she came upon the Cowardly Lion, still hitched to the chariot beside the great Tiger. The Cowardly Lion had a big bow of blue ribbon fastened to the long hair between his ears, and the Tiger wore a bow of red ribbon on his tail, just in front of the bushy end.

In an instant Dorothy was hugging the huge Lion joyfully.

"I'm *so* glad to see you again!" she cried.

"I am also glad to see you, Dorothy," said the Lion. "We've had some fine adventures together, haven't we?"

"Yes, indeed," she replied. "How are you?"

"As cowardly as ever," the beast answered in a meek voice. "Every little thing scares me and makes my heart beat fast. But let me introduce to you a new friend of mine, the Hungry Tiger."

"Oh! Are you hungry?" she asked, turning to the other beast, who was just then yawning so widely that he displayed two rows of terrible teeth and a mouth big enough to startle anyone.

"Dreadfully hungry," answered the Tiger, snapping his jaws together with a fierce click.

"Then why don't you eat something?" she asked.

"It's no use," said the Tiger sadly. "I've tried that, but I always get hungry again."

"Why, it is the same with me," said Dorothy. "Yet I keep on eating."

"But you eat harmless things, so it doesn't matter," replied the Tiger. "For my part, I'm a savage beast, and have an appetite for all sorts of poor little living creatures, from a chipmonk to fat babies."

"How dreadful!" said Dorothy.

"Isn't it, though?" returned the Hungry Tiger, licking his lips with his long red tongue. "Fat babies! Don't they sound delicious? But I've never eaten any, because my conscience tells me it is wrong. If I had no conscience I would probably eat the babies and then get hungry again, which would mean that I had sacrificed the poor babies for nothing. No; hungry I was born, and hungry I shall die. But I'll not have any cruel deeds on my conscience to be sorry for."

"I think you are a very good tiger," said Dorothy, patting the huge head of the beast.

"In that you are mistaken," was the reply. "I am a good beast, perhaps, but a disgracefully bad tiger. For it is the nature of tigers to be cruel and ferocious, and in refusing to eat harmless living creatures I am acting as no good tiger has ever before acted. That is why I left the forest and joined my friend the Cowardly Lion."

"But the Lion is not really cowardly," said Dorothy. "I have seen him act as bravely as can be."

"All a mistake, my dear," protested the Lion gravely. "To others I may have seemed brave, at times, but I have never been in any danger that I was not afraid."

"Nor I," said Dorothy, truthfully. "But I must go and set free Billina, and then I will see you again."

She ran around to the back yard of the palace and soon found the chicken house, being guided to it by a loud cackling and crowing and a distracting hubbub of sounds such as chickens make when they are excited.

Something seemed to be wrong in the chicken house, and when Dorothy looked through the slats in the door she saw a group of hens and roosters huddled in one corner and watching what appeared to be a whirling ball of feathers. It bounded here and there about the chicken house, and at first Dorothy could not tell what it was, while the screeching of the chickens nearly deafened her.

THE HUNGRY TIGER

But suddenly the bunch of feathers stopped whirling, and then, to her amazement, the girl saw Billina crouching upon the prostrate form of a speckled rooster. For an instant they both remained motionless, and then the yellow hen shook her wings to settle the feathers and walked toward the door with a strut of proud defiance and a cluck of victory, while the speckled rooster limped away to the group of other chickens, trailing his crumpled plumage in the dust as he went.

"Why, Billina!" cried Dorothy, in a shocked voice; "have you been fighting?"

"I really think I have," retorted Billina. "Do you think I'd let that speckled villain of a rooster lord it over *me*, and claim to run this chicken house, as long as I'm able to peck and scratch? Not if my name is Bill!"

"It isn't Bill, it's Billina; and you're talking slang, which is very undig'n'fied," said Dorothy, reprovingly. "Come here, Billina, and I'll let you out; for Ozma of Oz is here, and has set us free."

So the yellow hen came to the door, which Dorothy unlatched for her to pass through, and the other chickens silently watched them from their corner without offering to approach nearer.

The girl lifted her friend in her arms and exclaimed:

"Oh, Billina! how dreadful you look. You've lost a lot of feathers, and one of your eyes is nearly pecked out, and your comb is bleeding!"

"That's nothing," said Billina. "Just look at the speckled rooster! Didn't I do him up brown?"

Dorothy shook her head.

"I don't 'prove of this, at all," she said, carrying Billina away toward the palace. "It isn't a good thing for you to 'sociate with those common chickens. They would soon spoil your good manners, and you wouldn't be respec'able any more."

"I didn't ask to associate with them," replied Billina. "It is that cross old Princess who is to blame. But I was raised in the United States, and I won't allow any one-horse chicken of the Land of Ev to run over me and put on airs, as long as I can lift a claw in self-defense."

"WHY, BILLINA!" CRIED DOROTHY; "HAVE YOU
BEEN FIGHTING?"

"Very well, Billina," said Dorothy. "We won't talk about it any more."

Soon they came to the Cowardly Lion and the Hungry Tiger to whom the girl introduced the yellow hen.

"Glad to meet any friend of Dorothy's," said the Lion, politely. "To judge by your present appearance, you are not a coward, as I am."

"Your present appearance makes my mouth water," said the Tiger, looking at Billina greedily. "My, my! how good you would taste if I could only crunch you between my jaws. But don't worry. You would only appease my appetite for a moment; so it isn't worth while to eat you."

"Thank you," said the hen, nestling closer in Dorothy's arms.

"Besides, it wouldn't be right," continued the Tiger, looking steadily at Billina and clicking his jaws together.

"Of course not," cried Dorothy, hastily. "Billina is my friend, and you mustn't ever eat her under any circ'mstances."

"I'll try to remember that," said the Tiger; "but I'm a little absent-minded, at times."

Then Dorothy carried her pet into the drawing-room of the palace, where Tiktok, being invited to do so by Ozma, had seated himself between the Scarecrow and the Tin Woodman. Opposite to them sat Ozma herself and the Princess Langwidere, and beside them there was a vacant chair for Dorothy.

Around this important group was ranged the Army of Oz, and as Dorothy looked at the handsome uniforms of the Twenty-Seven she said:

"Why, they seem to be all officers."

"They are, all except one," answered the Tin Woodman. "I have in my Army eight Generals, six Colonels, seven Majors and five Captains, besides one private for them to command. I'd like to promote the private, for I believe no private should ever be in public life; and I've also noticed that officers usually fight better and are more reliable than common soldiers. Besides, the officers are more important looking, and lend dignity to our army."

"No doubt you are right," said Dorothy, seating herself beside Ozma.

"And now," announced the girlish Ruler of Oz, "we will hold a solemn conference to decide the best manner of liberating the royal family of this fair Land of Ev from their long imprisonment."

The Royal Family of Ev

The

Tin Woodman was
the first to address the
meeting.

"To begin with," said he,
"word came to our noble and il-
lustrous Ruler, Ozma of Oz, that the
wife and ten children—five boys and five
girls—of the former King of Ev, by name
Evoldo, have been enslaved by the Nome King
and are held prisoners in his underground palace.
Also that there was no one in Ev powerful enough to
release them. Naturally our Ozma wished to undertake
the adventure of liberating the poor prisoners; but for a long
time she could find no way to cross the great desert between the
two countries. Finally she went to a friendly sorceress of our land
named Glinda the Good, who heard the story and at once presented Ozma a magic carpet, which would continually unroll beneath our feet and so make a comfortable path for us to cross the
desert. As soon as she had received the carpet our gracious Ruler
ordered me to assemble our army, which I did. You behold in these
bold warriors the pick of all the finest soldiers of Oz; and, if we are
obliged to fight the Nome King, every officer as well as the private,
will battle fiercely unto death."

Then Tiktok spoke.

"Why should you fight the Nome King?" he asked. "He has done no wrong."

"No wrong!" cried Dorothy. "Isn't it wrong to imprison a queen mother and her ten children?"

"They were sold to the Nome King by King Ev-ol-do," replied Tiktok. "It was the King of Ev who did wrong, and when he re-al-ized what he had done he jumped in-to the sea and drowned him-self."

"This is news to me," said Ozma, thoughtfully. "I had supposed the Nome King was all to blame in the matter. But, in any case, he must be made to liberate the prisoners."

"My uncle Evoldo was a very wicked man," declared the Princess Langwidere. "If he had drowned himself before he sold his family, no one would have cared. But he sold them to the pow-erful Nome King in exchange for a long life, and afterward de-stroyed the life by jumping into the sea."

"Then," said Ozma, "he did not get the long life, and the Nome King must give up the prisoners. Where are they confined?"

"No one knows, exactly," replied the Princess. "For the King, whose name is Roquat of the Rocks, owns a splendid palace under-neath the great mountain which is at the north end of this kingdom, and he has transformed the Queen and her children into ornaments and bric-a-brac with which to decorate his rooms."

"I'd like to know," said Dorothy, "who this Nome King is?"

"I will tell you," replied Ozma. "He is said to be the Ruler of the Underground World, and commands the rocks and all that the rocks contain. Under his rule are many thousands of the Nomes, who are queerly shaped but powerful sprites that labor at the fur-naces and forges of their King, making gold and silver and other metals which they conceal in the crevices of the rocks, so that those living upon the earth's surface can only find them with great diffi-culty. Also they make diamonds and rubies and emeralds, which they hide in the ground; so that the Kingdom of the Nomes is won-derfully rich, and all we have of precious stones and silver and gold is what we take from the earth and rocks where the Nome King has hidden them."

"I understand," said Dorothy, nodding her little head wisely.

"For the reason that we often steal his treasures," continued Ozma, "the Ruler of the Underground World is not fond of those who live upon the earth's surface, and never appears among us. If we wish to see King Roquat of the Rocks, we must visit his own country, where he is all powerful, and therefore it will be a dangerous undertaking."

"But, for the sake of the poor prisoners," said Dorothy, "we ought to do it."

"We shall do it," replied the Scarecrow, "although it requires a lot of courage for me to go near to the furnaces of the Nome King. For I am only stuffed with straw, and a single spark of fire might destroy me entirely."

"The furnaces may also melt my tin," said the Tin Woodman; "but I am going."

"I can't bear heat," remarked the Princess Langwidere, yawning lazily, "so I shall stay at home. But I wish you may have success in your undertaking, for I am heartily tired of ruling this stupid kingdom, and I need more leisure in which to admire my beautiful heads."

"We do not need you," said Ozma. "For, if with the aid of my brave followers I cannot accomplish my purpose, then it would be useless for you to undertake the journey."

"Quite true," sighed the Princess. "So, if you'll excuse me, I will now retire to my cabinet. I've worn this head quite awhile, and I want to change it for another."

When she had left them (and you may be sure no one was sorry to see her go) Ozma said to Tiktok:

"Will you join our party?"

"I am the slave of the girl Dor-oth-y, who res-cued me from pris-on," replied the machine. "Where she goes I will go."

"Oh, I am going with my friends, of course," said Dorothy, quickly. "I wouldn't miss the fun for anything. Will you go, too, Billina?"

"I CAN'T BEAR HEAT," REMARKED LANGWIDERE

"To be sure," said Billina in a careless tone. She was smoothing down the feathers of her back and not paying much attention.

"Heat is just in her line," remarked the Scarecrow. "If she is nicely roasted, she will be better than ever."

"Then," said Ozma, "we will arrange to start for the Kingdom of the Nomes at daybreak tomorrow. And, in the meantime, we will rest and prepare ourselves for the journey."

Although Princess Langwidere did not again appear to her guests, the palace servants waited upon the strangers from Oz and did everything in their power to make the party comfortable. There were many vacant rooms at their disposal, and the brave Army of Twenty-Seven was easily provided for and liberally feasted.

The Cowardly Lion and the Hungry Tiger were unharnessed from the chariot and allowed to roam at will throughout the palace, where they nearly frightened the servants into fits, although they did no harm at all. At one time Dorothy found the little maid Nanda crouching in terror in a corner, with the Hungry Tiger standing before her.

"You certainly look delicious," the beast was saying. "Will you kindly give me permission to eat you?"

"No, no, no!" cried the maid in reply.

"Then," said the Tiger, yawning frightfully, "please to get me about thirty pounds of tenderloin steak, cooked rare, with a peck of boiled potatoes on the side, and five gallons of ice-cream for dessert."

"I—I'll do the best I can!" said Nanda, and she ran away as fast as she could go.

"Are you so very hungry?" asked Dorothy, in wonder.

"You can hardly imagine the size of my appetite," replied the Tiger, sadly. "It seems to fill my whole body, from the end of my throat to the tip of my tail. I am very sure the appetite doesn't fit me, and is too large for the size of my body. Some day, when I meet a dentist with a pair of forceps, I'm going to have it pulled."

"What, your tooth?" asked Dorothy.

"No, my appetite," said the Hungry Tiger.

The little girl spent most of the afternoon talking with the

Scarecrow and the Tin Woodman, who related to her all that had taken place in the Land of Oz since Dorothy had left it. She was much interested in the story of Ozma, who had been, when a baby, stolen by a wicked old witch and transformed into a boy. She did not know that she had ever been a girl until she was restored to her natural form by a kind sorceress. Then it was found that she was the only child of the former Ruler of Oz, and was entitled to rule in his place. Ozma had many adventures, however, before she regained her father's throne, and in these she was accompanied by a pumpkin-headed man, a highly magnified and thoroughly educated Woggle-Bug, and a wonderful saw-horse that had been brought to life by means of a magic powder. The Scarecrow and the Tin Woodman had also assisted her; but the Cowardly Lion, who ruled the great forest as the King of Beasts, knew nothing of Ozma until after she became the reigning Princess of Oz. Then he journeyed to the Emerald City to see her, and on hearing she was about to visit the Land of Ev to set free the royal family of that country, the Cowardly Lion begged to go with her, and brought along his friend, the Hungry Tiger, as well.

Having heard this story, Dorothy related to them her own adventures, and then went out with her friends to find the Saw-Horse, which Ozma had caused to be shod with plates of gold, so that its legs would not wear out.

They came upon the Saw-Horse standing motionless beside the garden gate, but when Dorothy was introduced to him he bowed politely and blinked his eyes, which were knots of wood, and wagged his tail, which was only the branch of a tree.

"What a remarkable thing, to be alive!" exclaimed Dorothy.

"I quite agree with you," replied the Saw-Horse, in a rough but not unpleasant voice. "A creature like me has no business to live, as we all know. But it was the magic powder that did it, so I cannot justly be blamed."

"Of course not," said Dorothy. "And you seem to be of some use, 'cause I noticed the Scarecrow riding upon your back."

"Oh, yes; I'm of use," returned the Saw-Horse; "and I never tire, never have to be fed, or cared for in any way."

DOROTHY RELATED TO THEM HER OWN ADVENTURES

"Are you intel'gent?" asked the girl.

"Not very," said the creature. "It would be foolish to waste intelligence on a common Saw-Horse, when so many professors need it. But I know enough to obey my masters, and to gid-dup, or whoa, when I'm told to. So I'm pretty well satisfied."

That night Dorothy slept in a pleasant little bed-chamber next to that occupied by Ozma of Oz, and Billina perched upon the foot

of the bed and tucked her head under her wing and slept as soundly in that position as did Dorothy upon her soft cushions.

But before daybreak every one was awake and stirring, and soon the adventurers were eating a hasty breakfast in the great dining-room of the palace. Ozma sat at the head of a long table, on a raised platform, with Dorothy on her right hand and the Scarecrow on her left. The Scarecrow did not eat, of course; but Ozma placed him near her so that she might ask his advice about the journey while she ate.

Lower down the table were the twenty-seven warriors of Oz, and at the end of the room the Lion and the Tiger were eating out of a kettle that had been placed upon the floor, while Billina fluttered around to pick up any scraps that might be scattered.

It did not take long to finish the meal, and then the Lion and the Tiger were harnessed to the chariot and the party was ready to start for the Nome King's Palace.

First rode Ozma, with Dorothy beside her in the golden chariot and holding Billina fast in her arms. Then came the Scarecrow on the Saw-Horse, with the Tin Woodman and Tiktok marching side by side just behind him. After these tramped the Army, looking brave and handsome in their splendid uniforms. The generals commanded the colonels and the colonels commanded the majors and the majors commanded the captains and the captains commanded the private, who marched with an air of proud importance because it required so many officers to give him his orders.

And so the magnificent procession left the palace and started along the road just as day was breaking, and by the time the sun came out they had made good progress toward the valley that led to the Nome King's domain.

The Giant with the Hammer

The road led for a time through a pretty farm country, and then past a picnic grove that was very inviting. But the procession continued to steadily advance until Billina cried in an abrupt and commanding manner:

"Wait—wait!"

Ozma stopped her chariot so suddenly that the Scarecrow's Saw-Horse nearly ran into it, and the ranks of the Army tumbled over one another before they could come to a halt. Immediately the yellow hen struggled from Dorothy's arms and flew into a clump of bushes by the roadside.

"What's the matter?" called the Tin Woodman, anxiously.

"Why, Billina wants to lay her egg, that's all," said Dorothy.

"Lay her egg!" repeated the Tin Woodman, in astonishment.

"Yes; she lays one every morning, about this time; and it's quite fresh," said the girl.

"But does your foolish old hen suppose that this entire cavalcade, which is bound on an important adventure, is going to stand still while she lays her egg?" enquired the Tin Woodman, earnestly.

"What else can we do?" asked the girl. "It's a habit of Billina's and she can't break herself of it."

"Then she must hurry up," said the Tin Woodman, impatiently.

"No, no!" exclaimed the Scarecrow. "If she hurries she may lay scrambled eggs."

"That's nonsense," said Dorothy. "But Billina won't be long, I'm sure."

So they stood and waited, although all were restless and anxious to proceed. And by and by the yellow hen came from the bushes saying:

"Kut-kut, kut, ka-daw-kutt! Kut, kut, kut—ka-daw-kut!"

"What is she doing—singing her lay?" asked the Scarecrow.

"For-ward—march!" shouted the Tin Woodman, waving his axe, and the procession started just as Dorothy had once more grabbed Billina in her arms.

"Isn't anyone going to get my egg?" cried the hen, in great excitement.

"I'll get it," said the Scarecrow; and at his command the Saw-Horse pranced into the bushes. The straw man soon found the egg, which he placed in his jacket pocket. The cavalcade, having moved rapidly on, was even then far in advance; but it did not take the

Saw-Horse long to catch up with it, and presently the Scarecrow was riding in his accustomed place behind Ozma's chariot.

"What shall I do with the egg?" he asked Dorothy.

"I do not know," the girl answered. "Perhaps the Hungry Tiger would like it."

"It would not be enough to fill one of my back teeth," remarked the Tiger. "A bushel of them, hard boiled, might take a little of the edge off my appetite; but one egg isn't good for anything at all, that I know of."

"No; it wouldn't even make a sponge cake," said the Scarecrow, thoughtfully. "The Tin Woodman might carry it with his axe and hatch it; but after all I may as well keep it myself for a souvenir." So he left it in his pocket.

They had now reached that part of the valley that lay between the two high mountains which Dorothy had seen from her tower window. At the far end was the third great mountain, which blocked the valley and was the northern edge of the Land of Ev. It was underneath this mountain that the Nome King's palace was said to be; but it would be some time before they reached that place.

The path was becoming rocky and difficult for the wheels of the chariot to pass over, and presently a deep gulf appeared at their feet which was too wide for them to leap. So Ozma took a small square of green cloth from her pocket and threw it upon the ground. At once it became the magic carpet, and unrolled itself far enough for all the cavalcade to walk upon. The chariot now advanced, and the green carpet unrolled before it, crossing the gulf on a level with its banks, so that all passed over in safety.

"That's easy enough," said the Scarecrow. "I wonder what will happen next."

He was not long in making the discovery, for the sides of the mountain came closer together until finally there was but a narrow path between them, along which Ozma and her party were forced to pass in single file.

They now heard a low and deep "thump!—thump!—thump!" which echoed throughout the valley and seemed to grow louder as they advanced. Then, turning a corner of rock, they saw before them a huge form, which towered above the path for more than a hundred feet. The form was that of a gigantic man built out of plates of cast iron, and it stood with one foot on either side of the narrow road and swung over its right shoulder an immense iron mallet, with which it constantly pounded the earth. These resounding blows explained the thumping sounds they had heard, for the mallet was much bigger than a barrel, and where it struck the path between the rocky sides of the mountain it filled all the space through which our travelers would be obliged to pass.

Of course they at once halted, a safe distance away from the terrible iron mallet. The magic carpet would do them no good in this case, for it was only meant to protect them from any dangers upon the ground beneath their feet, and not from dangers that appeared in the air above them.

"Wow!" said the Cowardly Lion, with a shudder. "It makes me dreadfully nervous to see that big hammer pounding so near my head. One blow would crush me into a door-mat."

"The ir-on gi-ant is a fine fel-low," said Tiktok, "and works as stead-i-ly as a clock. He was made for the Nome King by Smith &

Tin-ker, who made me, and his du-ty is to keep folks from find-ing the un-der-ground pal-ace. Is he not a great work of art?"

"Can he think, and speak, as you do?" asked Ozma, regarding the giant with wondering eyes.

"No," replied the machine; "he is on-ly made to pound the road, and has no think-ing or speak-ing at-tach-ment. But he pounds ve-ry well, I think."

"Too well," observed the Scarecrow. "He is keeping us from going farther. Is there no way to stop his machinery?"

"On-ly the Nome King, who has the key, can do that," answered Tiktok.

"Then," said Dorothy, anxiously, "what shall we do?"

"Excuse me for a few minutes," said the Scarecrow, "and I will think it over."

He retired, then, to a position in the rear, where he turned his painted face to the rocks and began to think.

Meantime the giant continued to raise his iron mallet high in the air and to strike the path terrific blows that echoed through the mountains like the roar of a cannon. Each time the mallet lifted,

THE TIGER WENT NEXT

however, there was a moment when the path beneath the monster was free, and perhaps the Scarecrow had noticed this, for when he came back to the others he said:

"The matter is a very simple one, after all. We have but to run under the hammer, one at a time, when it is lifted, and pass to the other side before it falls again."

"It will require quick work, if we escape the blow," said the Tin Woodman, with a shake of his head. "But it really seems the only thing to be done. Who will make the first attempt?"

They looked at one another hesitatingly for a moment. Then the Cowardly Lion, who was trembling like a leaf in the wind, said to them:

"I suppose the head of the procession must go first—and that's me. But I'm terribly afraid of the big hammer!"

"What will become of me?" asked Ozma. "You might rush under the hammer yourself, but the chariot would surely be crushed."

"We must leave the chariot," said the Scarecrow. "But you two girls can ride upon the backs of the Lion and the Tiger."

So this was decided upon, and Ozma, as soon as the Lion was unfastened from the chariot, at once mounted the beast's back and said she was ready.

"Cling fast to his mane," advised Dorothy. "I used to ride him myself, and that's the way I held on."

So Ozma clung fast to the mane, and the Lion crouched in the path and eyed the swinging mallet carefully until he knew just the instant it would begin to rise in the air.

Then, before anyone thought he was ready, he made a sudden leap straight between the iron giant's legs, and before the mallet struck the ground again the Lion and Ozma were safe on the other side.

The Tiger went next. Dorothy sat upon his back and locked her arms around his striped neck, for he had no mane to cling to. He made the leap straight and true as an arrow from a bow, and ere Dorothy realized it she was out of danger and standing by Ozma's side.

Now came the Scarecrow on the Saw-Horse, and while they

made the dash in safety they were within a hair's breadth of being caught by the descending hammer.

Tiktok walked up to the very edge of the spot the hammer struck, and as it was raised for the next blow he calmly stepped forward and escaped its descent. That was an idea for the Tin Woodman to follow, and he also crossed in safety while the great hammer was in the air. But when it came to the twenty-six officers and the private, their knees were so weak that they could not walk a step.

"In battle we are wonderfully courageous," said one of the generals, "and our foes find us very terrible to face. But war is one thing and this is another. When it comes to being pounded upon the head by an iron hammer, and smashed into pancakes, we naturally object."

"Make a run for it," urged the Scarecrow.

"Our knees shake so that we cannot run," answered a captain. "If we should try it we would all certainly be pounded to a jelly."

"Well, well," sighed the Cowardly Lion, "I see, friend Tiger, that we must place ourselves in great danger to rescue this bold army. Come with me, and we will do the best we can."

So, Ozma and Dorothy having already dismounted from their backs, the Lion and the Tiger leaped back again under the awful hammer and returned with two generals clinging to their necks. They repeated this daring passage twelve times, when all the officers had been carried beneath the giant's legs and landed safely on the further side. By that time the beasts were very tired, and panted so hard that their tongues hung out of their great mouths.

"But what is to become of the private?" asked Ozma.

"Oh, leave him there to guard the chariot," said the Lion. "I'm tired out, and won't pass under that mallet again."

The officers at once protested that they must have the private with them, else there would be no one for them to command. But neither the Lion or the Tiger would go after him, and so the Scarecrow sent the Saw-Horse.

Either the wooden horse was careless, or it failed to properly time the descent of the hammer, for the mighty weapon caught it squarely upon its head, and thumped it against the ground so pow-

THE WOODEN HORSE WAS CARELESS

erfully that the private flew off its back high into the air, and landed upon one of the giant's cast-iron arms. Here he clung desperately while the arm rose and fell with each one of the rapid strokes.

The Scarecrow dashed in to rescue his Saw-Horse, and had his left foot smashed by the hammer before he could pull the creature out of danger. They then found that the Saw-Horse had been badly dazed by the blow; for while the hard wooden knot of which his head was formed could not be crushed by the hammer, both his ears were broken off and he would be unable to hear a sound until some new ones were made for him. Also his left knee was cracked, and had to be bound up with a string.

Billina having fluttered under the hammer, it now remained only to rescue the private who was riding upon the iron giant's arm, high in the air.

The Scarecrow lay flat upon the ground and called to the man to jump down upon his body, which was soft because it was stuffed with straw. This the private managed to do, waiting until a time when he was nearest the ground and then letting himself drop upon the Scarecrow. He accomplished the feat without breaking any bones, and the Scarecrow declared he was not injured in the least.

Therefore, the Tin Woodman having by this time fitted new ears to the Saw-Horse, the entire party proceeded upon its way, leaving the giant to pound the path behind them.

The Nome King

By and by, when they drew
near to the mountain that
blocked their path and which
was the furthermost edge of the
Kingdom of Ev, the way grew dark
and gloomy for the reason that the
high peaks on either side shut out the
sunshine. And it was very silent, too, as
there were no birds to sing or squirrels to
chatter, the trees being left far behind them and
only the bare rocks remaining.

Ozma and Dorothy were a little awed by the silence, and all the others were quiet and grave except the Saw-Horse, which, as it trotted along with the Scarecrow upon his back, hummed a queer song, of which this was the chorus:

> "Would a wooden horse in a woodland go?
> Aye, aye! I sigh, he would, although
> Had he not had a wooden head
> He'd mount the mountain top instead."

But no one paid any attention to this because they were now close to the Nome King's dominions, and his splendid underground palace could not be very far away.

Suddenly they heard a shout of jeering laughter, and stopped short. They would have to stop in a minute, anyway, for the huge mountain barred their further progress and the path ran close up to a wall of rock and ended.

"Who was that laughing?" asked Ozma.

There was no reply, but in the gloom they could see strange forms flit across the face of the rock. Whatever the creations might be they seemed very like the rock itself, for they were the color of rocks and their shapes were as rough and rugged as if they had been broken away from the side of the mountain. They kept close to the steep cliff facing our friends, and glided up and down, and this way and that, with a lack of regularity that was quite confusing. And they seemed not to need places to rest their feet, but clung to the surface of the rock as a fly does to a window pane, and were never still for a moment.

"Do not mind them," said Tiktok, as Dorothy shrank back. "They are on-ly the Nomes."

"And what are Nomes?" asked the girl, half frightened.

"They are rock fair-ies, and serve the Nome King," replied the machine. "But they will do us no harm. You must call for the King, be-cause with-out him you can ne-ver find the en-trance to the pal-ace."

"*You* call," said Dorothy to Ozma.

Just then the Nomes laughed again, and the sound was so weird and disheartening that the twenty-six officers commanded the private to "right-about-face!" and they all started to run as fast as they could.

The Tin Woodman at once pursued his army and cried "halt!" and when they had stopped their flight he asked: "Where are you going?"

"I—I find I've forgotten the brush for my whiskers," said a general, trembling with fear. "S-s-so we are g-going back after it!"

"That is impossible," replied the Tin Woodman. "For the giant with the hammer would kill you all if you tried to pass him."

"Oh! I'd forgotten the giant," said the general, turning pale.

ONLY THE MOCKING LAUGHTER REPLIED TO HER

"You seem to forget a good many things," remarked the Tin Woodman. "I hope you won't forget that you are brave men."

"Never!" cried the general, slapping his gold-embroidered chest.

"Never!" cried all the other officers, indignantly slapping their chests.

"For my part," said the private, meekly, "I must obey my officers; so when I am told to run, I run; and when I am told to fight, I fight."

"That is right," agreed the Tin Woodman. "And now you must all come back to Ozma, and obey *her* orders. And if you try to run away again I will have her reduce all the twenty-six officers to privates, and make the private your general."

This terrible threat so frightened them that they at once returned to where Ozma was standing beside the Cowardly Lion.

Then Ozma cried out in a loud voice:

"I demand that the Nome King appear to us!"

There was no reply, except that the shifting Nomes upon the mountain laughed in derision.

"You must not command the Nome King," said Tiktok, "for you do not rule him, as you do your own peo-ple."

So Ozma called again, saying:

"I request the Nome King to appear to us."

Only the mocking laughter replied to her, and the shadowy Nomes continued to flit here and there upon the rocky cliff.

"Try en-treat-y," said Tiktok to Ozma. "If he will not come at your re-quest, then the Nome King may list-en to your plead-ing."

Ozma looked around her proudly.

"Do you wish your ruler to plead with this wicked Nome King?" she asked. "Shall Ozma of Oz humble herself to a creature who lives in an underground kingdom?"

"No!" they all shouted, with big voices; and the Scarecrow added:

"If he will not come, we will dig him out of his hole, like a fox, and conquer his stubbornness. But our sweet little ruler must always maintain her dignity, just as I maintain mine."

"I'm not afraid to plead with him," said Dorothy. "I'm only a little girl from Kansas, and we've got more dignity at home than we know what to do with. *I'll* call the Nome King."

"Do," said the Hungry Tiger; "and if he makes hash of you I'll willingly eat you for breakfast tomorrow morning."

So Dorothy stepped forward and said:

"*Please* Mr. Nome King, come here and see us."

The Nomes started to laugh again; but a low growl came from the mountain, and in a flash they had all vanished from sight and were silent.

Then a door in the rock opened, and a voice cried:

"Enter!"

"Isn't it a trick?" asked the Tin Woodman.

"Never mind," replied Ozma. "We came here to rescue the poor Queen of Ev and her ten children, and we must run some risks to do so."

"The Nome King is hon-est and good na-tured," said Tiktok. "You can trust him to do what is right."

So Ozma led the way, hand in hand with Dorothy, and they passed through the arched doorway of rock and entered a long passage which was lighted by jewels set in the walls and having lamps behind them. There was no one to escort them, or to show them the way, but all the party pressed through the passage until they came to a round, domed cavern that was grandly furnished.

In the center of this room was a throne carved out of a solid boulder of rock, rude and rugged in shape but glittering with great rubies and diamonds and emeralds on every part of its surface. And upon the throne sat the Nome King.

This important monarch of the Underground World was a little fat man clothed in gray-brown garments that were the exact color of the rock throne in which he was seated. His bushy hair and flowing beard were also colored like the rocks, and so was his face. He wore no crown of any sort, and his only ornament was a broad, jewel-studded belt that encircled his fat little body. As for his features, they seemed kindly and good humored, and his eyes were turned merrily upon his visitors as Ozma and Dorothy stood before him with their followers ranged in close order behind them.

"Why, he looks just like Santa Claus—only he isn't the same color!" whispered Dorothy to her friend; but the Nome King heard the speech, and it made him laugh aloud.

> " 'He had a red face and a round little belly
> That shook when he laughed like a bowl full of jelly!' "

quoth the monarch, in a pleasant voice; and they could all see that he really did shake like jelly when he laughed.

Both Ozma and Dorothy were much relieved to find the Nome King so jolly, and a minute later he waved his right hand and the girls each found a cushioned stool at her side.

"Sit down, my dears," said the King, "and tell me why you have come all this way to see me, and what I can do to make you happy."

While they seated themselves the Nome King picked up a pipe, and taking a glowing red coal out of his pocket he placed it in the bowl of the pipe and began puffing out clouds of smoke that curled in rings above his head. Dorothy thought this made the little monarch look more like Santa Claus than ever; but Ozma now began speaking, and every one listened intently to her words.

"Your Majesty," said she, "I am the ruler of the Land of Oz, and I have come here to ask you to release the good Queen of Ev and her ten children, whom you have enchanted and hold as your prisoners."

"Oh, no; you are mistaken about that," replied the King. "They are not my prisoners, but my slaves, whom I purchased from the King of Ev."

"But that was wrong," said Ozma.

"According to the laws of Ev, the king can do no wrong," answered the monarch, eyeing a ring of smoke he had just blown from his mouth; "so that he had a perfect right to sell his family to me in exchange for a long life."

"You cheated him, though," declared Dorothy; "for the King of Ev did not have a long life. He jumped into the sea and was drowned."

"That was not my fault," said the Nome King, crossing his legs and smiling contentedly. "I gave him the long life, all right; but he destroyed it."

"Then how could it be a long life?" asked Dorothy.

"Easily enough," was the reply. "Now suppose, my dear, that I gave you a pretty doll in exchange for a lock of your hair, and that after you had received the doll you smashed it into pieces and destroyed it. Could you say that I had not given you a pretty doll?"

"No," answered Dorothy.

"And could you, in fairness, ask me to return to you the lock of hair, just because you had smashed the doll?"

"No," said Dorothy, again.

"Of course not," the Nome King returned. "Nor will I give up the Queen and her children because the King of Ev destroyed his long life by jumping into the sea. They belong to me and I shall keep them."

"But you are treating them cruelly," said Ozma, who was much distressed by the King's refusal.

"In what way?" he asked.

"By making them your slaves," said she.

"Cruelty," remarked the monarch, puffing out wreathes of smoke and watching them float into the air, "is a thing I can't abide. So, as slaves must work hard, and the Queen of Ev and her children were delicate and tender, I transformed them all into articles of ornament and bric-a-brac and scattered them around the various rooms of my palace. Instead of being obliged to labor, they merely decorate my apartments, and I really think I have treated them with great kindness."

"But what a dreadful fate is theirs!" exclaimed Ozma, earnestly. "And the Kingdom of Ev is in great need of its royal family to govern it. If you will liberate them, and restore them to their proper forms, I will give you ten ornaments to replace each one you lose."

The Nome King looked grave.

"Suppose I refuse?" he asked.

"Then," said Ozma, firmly, "I am here with my friends and my army to conquer your kingdom and oblige you to obey my wishes."

The Nome King laughed until he choked; and he choked until he coughed; and he coughed until his face turned from grayish-brown to bright red. And then he wiped his eyes with a rock-colored handkerchief and grew grave again.

"THEY BELONG TO ME AND I SHALL KEEP THEM"

"You are as brave as you are pretty, my dear," he said to Ozma. "But you have little idea of the extent of the task you have undertaken. Come with me for a moment."

He arose and took Ozma's hand, leading her to a little door at one side of the room. This he opened and they stepped out upon a balcony, from whence they obtained a wonderful view of the Underground World.

A vast cave extended for miles and miles under the mountain, and in every direction were furnaces and forges glowing brightly and Nomes hammering upon precious metals or polishing gleaming jewels. All around the walls of the cave were thousands of doors of silver and gold, built into the solid rock, and these extended in rows far away into the distance, as far as Ozma's eyes could follow them.

While the little maid from Oz gazed wonderingly upon this scene the Nome King uttered a shrill whistle, and at once all the silver and gold doors flew open and solid ranks of Nome soldiers marched out from every one. So great were their numbers that they quickly filled the immense underground cavern and forced the busy workmen to abandon their tasks.

Although this tremendous army consisted of rock-colored Nomes, all squat and fat, they were clothed in glittering armor of polished steel, inlaid with beautiful gems. Upon his brow each wore a brilliant electric light, and they bore sharp spears and swords and battle-axes of solid bronze. It was evident they were perfectly trained, for they stood in straight rows, rank after rank, with their weapons held erect and true, as if awaiting but the word of command to level them upon their foes.

"This," said the Nome King, "is but a small part of my army. No ruler upon Earth has ever dared to fight me, and no ruler ever will, for I am too powerful to oppose."

He whistled again, and at once the martial array filed through the silver and gold doorways and disappeared, after which the workmen again resumed their labors at the furnaces.

Then, sad and discouraged, Ozma of Oz turned to her friends, and the Nome King calmly reseated himself on his rock throne.

"THIS IS BUT A SMALL PART OF MY ARMY"

"It would be foolish for us to fight," the girl said to the Tin Woodman. "For our brave Twenty-Seven would be quickly destroyed. I'm sure I do not know how to act in this emergency."

"Ask the King where his kitchen is," suggested the Tiger. "I'm hungry as a bear."

"I might pounce upon the King and tear him in pieces," remarked the Cowardly Lion.

"Try it," said the monarch, lighting his pipe with another hot coal which he took from his pocket.

The Lion crouched low and tried to spring upon the Nome King; but he hopped only a little way into the air and came down again in the same place, not being able to approach the throne by even an inch.

"It seems to me," said the Scarecrow, thoughtfully, "that our best plan is to wheedle His Majesty into giving up his slaves, since he is too great a magician to oppose."

"This is the most sensible thing any of you have suggested," declared the Nome King. "It is folly to threaten me, but I'm so kind-hearted that I cannot stand coaxing or wheedling. If you really wish to accomplish anything by your journey, my dear Ozma, you must coax me."

"Very well," said Ozma, more cheerfully. "Let us be friends, and talk this over in a friendly manner."

"To be sure," agreed the King, his eyes twinkling merrily.

"I am very anxious," she continued, "to liberate the Queen of Ev and her children who are now ornaments and bric-a-brac in Your Majesty's palace, and to restore them to their people. Tell me, sir, how this may be accomplished."

The King remained thoughtful for a moment, after which he asked:

"Are you willing to take a few chances and risks yourself, in order to set free the people of Ev?"

"Yes, indeed!" answered Ozma, eagerly.

"Then," said the Nome King, "I will make you this offer: You shall go alone and unattended into my palace and examine carefully all that the rooms contain. Then you shall have permission to touch eleven different objects, pronouncing at the time the word 'Ev,' and if any one of them, or more than one, proves to be the transformation of the Queen of Ev or any of her ten children, then they will instantly be restored to their true forms and may leave my palace and my kingdom in your company, without any objection whatever. It is possible for you, in this way, to free the entire eleven; but if you do not guess all the objects correctly, and some of the slaves remain transformed, then each one of your friends and followers may, in turn, enter the palace and have the same privileges I grant you."

"Oh, thank you! thank you for this kind offer!" said Ozma, eagerly.

"I make but one condition," added the Nome King, his eyes twinkling.

"What is it?" she enquired.

"If none of the eleven objects you touch proves to be the transformation of any of the royal family of Ev, then, instead of freeing them, you will yourself become enchanted, and transformed into an article of bric-a-brac or an ornament. This is only fair and just, and is the risk you declared you were willing to take."

The Eleven Guesses

Hearing this condition imposed by the Nome King, Ozma became silent and thoughtful, and all her friends looked at her uneasily.

"Don't you do it!" exclaimed Dorothy. "If you guess wrong, you will be enslaved yourself."

"But I shall have eleven guesses," answered Ozma. "Surely I ought to guess one object in eleven correctly; and, if I do, I shall rescue one of the royal family and be safe myself. Then the rest of you may attempt it, and soon we shall free all those who are enslaved."

"What if we fail?" enquired the Scarecrow. "I'd look nice as a piece of bric-a-brac, wouldn't I?"

"We must not fail!" cried Ozma, courageously. "Having come all this distance to free these poor people, it would be weak and cowardly in us to abandon the adventure. Therefore I will accept the Nome King's offer, and go at once into the royal palace."

"Come along, then, my dear," said the King, climbing down from his throne with some difficulty, because he was so fat; "I'll show you the way."

He approached a wall of the cave and waved his hand. Instantly an opening appeared, through which Ozma, after a smiling farewell to her friends, boldly passed.

She found herself in a splendid hall that was more beautiful and grand than anything she had ever beheld. The ceilings were composed of great arches that rose far above her head, and all the walls and floors were of polished marble exquisitely tinted in many colors. Thick velvet carpets were on the floor and heavy silken draperies covered the arches leading to the various rooms of the palace. The furniture was made of rare old woods richly carved and covered with delicate satins, and the entire palace was lighted by a mysterious rosy glow that seemed to come from no particular place but flooded each apartment with its soft and pleasing radiance.

Ozma passed from one room to another, greatly delighted by all she saw. The lovely palace had no other occupant, for the Nome King had left her at the entrance, which closed behind her, and in all the magnificent rooms there appeared to be no other person.

Upon the mantels, and on many shelves and brackets and tables, were clustered ornaments of every description, seemingly made out of all sorts of metals, glass, china, stones and marbles. There were vases, and figures of men and animals, and graven platters and bowls, and mosaics of precious gems, and many other things. Pictures, too, were on the walls, and the underground palace was quite a museum of rare and curious and costly objects.

After her first hasty examination of the rooms Ozma began to wonder which of all the numerous ornaments they contained were the transformations of the royal family of Ev. There was nothing to guide her, for everything seemed without a spark of life. So she must guess blindly; and for the first time the girl came to realize how dangerous was her task, and how likely she was to lose her own freedom in striving to free others from the bondage of the Nome King. No wonder the cunning monarch laughed good naturedly with his visitors, when he knew how easily they might be entrapped.

But Ozma, having undertaken the venture, would not abandon

OZMA SHUT HER EYES TIGHTLY AND ADVANCED

it. She looked at a silver candelabra that had ten branches, and thought: "This may be the Queen of Ev and her ten children." So she touched it and uttered aloud the word "Ev," as the Nome King had instructed her to do when she guessed. But the candelabra remained as it was before.

Then she wandered into another room and touched a china lamb, thinking it might be one of the children she sought. But again she was unsuccessful. Three guesses; four guesses; five, six, seven, eight, nine and ten she made, and still not one of them was right!

The girl shivered a little and grew pale even under the rosy light; for now but one guess remained, and her own fate depended upon the result.

She resolved not to be hasty, and strolled through all the rooms once more, gazing earnestly upon the various ornaments and trying to decide which she would touch. Finally, in despair, she decided to leave it entirely to chance. She faced the doorway of a room, shut her eyes tightly, and then, thrusting aside the heavy draperies, she advanced blindly with her right arm outstretched before her.

Slowly, softly she crept forward until her hand came in contact with an object upon a small round table. She did not know what it was, but in a low voice she pronounced the word "Ev."

The rooms were quite empty of life after that. The Nome King had gained a new ornament. For upon the edge of the table rested a pretty grasshopper, that seemed to have been formed from a single emerald. It was all that remained of Ozma of Oz.

In the throne room just beyond the palace the Nome King suddenly looked up and smiled.

"Next!" he said, in his pleasant voice.

Dorothy, the Scarecrow, and the Tin Woodman, who had been sitting in anxious silence, each gave a start of dismay and stared into one another's eyes.

"Has she failed?" asked Tiktok.

"So it seems," answered the little monarch, cheerfully. "But that is no reason one of you should not succeed. The next may have twelve guesses, instead of eleven, for there are now twelve persons transformed into ornaments. Well, well! Which of you goes next?"

"I'll go," said Dorothy.

"Not so," replied the Tin Woodman. "As commander of Ozma's army, it is my privilege to follow her and attempt her rescue."

"Away you go, then," said the Scarecrow. "But be careful, old friend."

"I will," promised the Tin Woodman; and then he followed the Nome King to the entrance to the palace and the rock closed behind him.

The Nome King Laughs

In a moment the King returned to his throne and relighted his pipe, and the rest of the little band of adventurers settled themselves for another long wait. They were greatly disheartened by the failure of their girl Ruler, and the knowledge that she was now an ornament in the Nome King's palace—a dreadful, creepy place in spite of all its magnificence. Without their little leader they did not know what to do next, and each one, down to the trembling private of the army, began to fear he would soon be more ornamental than useful.

Suddenly the Nome King began laughing.

"Ha, ha, ha! He, he, he! Ho, ho, ho!"

"What's happened?" asked the Scarecrow.

"Why, your friend, the Tin Woodman, has become the funniest thing you can imagine," replied the King, wiping the tears of merriment from his eyes. "No one would ever believe he could make such an amusing ornament. Next!"

They gazed at each other with sinking hearts. One of the generals began to weep dolefully.

"What are you crying for?" asked the Scarecrow, indignant at such a display of weakness.

"He owed me six weeks back pay," said the general, "and I hate to lose him."

"Then you shall go and find him," declared the Scarecrow.

"Me!" cried the general, greatly alarmed.

"Certainly. It is your duty to follow your commander. March!"

"I won't," said the general. "I'd like to, of course; but I just simply *won't*."

The Scarecrow looked enquiringly at the Nome King.

"Never mind," said the jolly monarch. "If he doesn't care to enter the palace and make his guesses I'll throw him into one of my fiery furnaces."

"I'll go!—of course I'm going," yelled the general, as quick as scat. "Where is the entrance—where is it? Let me go at once!"

So the Nome King escorted him into the palace, and again returned to await the result. What the general did, no one can tell; but it was not long before the King called for the next victim, and a colonel was forced to try his fortune.

Thus, one after another, all of the twenty-six officers filed into the palace and made their guesses—and became ornaments.

Meantime the King ordered refreshments to be served to those waiting, and at his command a rudely shaped Nome entered, bearing a tray. This Nome was not unlike the others that Dorothy had seen, but he wore a heavy gold chain around his neck to show that he was the Chief Steward of the Nome King, and he assumed an air of much importance, and even told His Majesty not to eat too much cake late at night, or he would be ill.

Dorothy, however, was hungry, and she was not afraid of being ill; so she ate several cakes and found them good, and also she drank a cup of excellent coffee made of a richly flavored clay, browned in the furnaces and then ground fine, and found it most refreshing and not at all muddy.

Of all the party which had started upon this adventure, the little Kansas girl was now left alone with the Scarecrow, Tiktok, and the private for counsellors and companions. Of course the Cowardly

Lion and the Hungry Tiger were still there, but they, having also eaten some of the cakes, had gone to sleep at one side of the cave, while upon the other side stood the Saw-Horse, motionless and silent, as became a mere thing of wood. Billina had quietly walked around and picked up the crumbs of cake which had been scattered, and now, as it was long after bed-time, she tried to find some dark place in which to go to sleep.

Presently the hen espied a hollow underneath the King's rocky throne, and crept into it unnoticed. She could still hear the chattering of those around her, but it was almost dark underneath the throne, so that soon she had fallen fast asleep.

"Next!" called the King, and the private, whose turn it was to enter the fatal palace, shook hands with Dorothy and the Scarecrow and bade them a sorrowful good-bye, and passed through the rocky portal.

They waited a long time, for the private was in no hurry to become an ornament and made his guesses very slowly. The Nome King, who seemed to know, by some magical power, all that took place in the beautiful rooms of his palace, grew impatient finally and declared he would sit up no longer.

"I love ornaments," said he, "but I can wait until tomorrow to get more of them; so, as soon as that stupid private is transformed, we will all go to bed and leave the job to be finished in the morning."

"Is it so very late?" asked Dorothy.

"Why, it is after midnight," said the King, "and that strikes me as being late enough. There is neither night nor day in my kingdom, because it is under the earth's surface, where the sun does not shine. But we have to sleep, just the same as the up-stairs people do, and for my part I'm going to bed in a few minutes."

Indeed, it was not long after this that the private made his last guess. Of course he guessed wrongly, and of course he at once became an ornament. So the King was greatly pleased, and clapped his hands to summon his Chief Steward.

"Show these guests to some of the sleeping apartments," he commanded, "and be quick about it, too, for I'm dreadfully sleepy myself."

SOON SHE HAD FALLEN FAST ASLEEP

"You've no business to sit up so late," replied the Steward, gruffly. "You'll be as cross as a griffin tomorrow morning."

His Majesty made no answer to this remark, and the Chief Steward led Dorothy through another doorway into a long hall, from which several plain but comfortable sleeping rooms opened. The little girl was given the first room, and the Scarecrow and Tiktok the next—although they never slept—and the Lion and the Tiger the third. The Saw-Horse hobbled after the Steward into a fourth room, to stand stiffly in the center of it until morning. Each night was rather a bore to the Scarecrow, Tiktok and the Saw-Horse; but they had learned from experience to pass the time patiently and quietly, since all their friends who were made of flesh had to sleep and did not like to be disturbed.

When the Chief Steward had left them alone the Scarecrow remarked, sadly:

"I am in great sorrow over the loss of my old comrade, the Tin Woodman. We have had many dangerous adventures together, and escaped them all, and now it grieves me to know he has become an ornament, and is lost to me forever."

"He was al-ways an or-na-ment to so-ci-e-ty," said Tiktok.

"True; but now the Nome King laughs at him, and calls him the funniest ornament in all the palace. It will hurt my poor friend's pride to be laughed at," continued the Scarecrow, sadly.

"We will make rath-er ab-surd or-na-ments, our-selves, to-mor-row," observed the machine, in his monotonous voice.

Just then Dorothy ran into their room, in a state of great anxiety, crying:

"Where's Billina? Have you seen Billina? Is she here?"

"No," answered the Scarecrow.

"Then what has become of her?" asked the girl.

"Why, I thought she was with you," said the Scarecrow. "Yet I do not remember seeing the yellow hen since she picked up the crumbs of cake."

"We must have left her in the room where the King's throne is," decided Dorothy, and at once she turned and ran down the hall to the door through which they had entered. But it was fast closed and locked on the other side, and the heavy slab of rock proved to be so thick that no sound could pass through it. So Dorothy was forced to return to her chamber.

The Cowardly Lion stuck his head into her room to try to console the girl for the loss of her feathered friend.

"The yellow hen is well able to take care of herself," said he; "so don't worry about her, but try to get all the sleep you can. It has been a long and weary day, and you need rest."

"I'll prob'ly get lots of rest tomorrow, when I become an orn'-ment," said Dorothy, sleepily. But she lay down upon her couch, nevertheless, and in spite of all her worries was soon in the land of dreams.

Dorothy Tries to be Brave

Meantime the Chief Steward had returned to the throne room, where he said to the King:

"You are a fool to waste so much time upon these people."

"What!" cried His Majesty, in so enraged a voice that it awoke Billina, who was asleep under his throne. "How dare you call me a fool?"

"Because I like to speak the truth," said the Steward. "Why didn't you enchant them all at once, instead of allowing them to go one by one into the palace and guess which ornaments are the Queen of Ev and her children?"

"Why, you stupid rascal, it is more fun this way," returned the King, "and it serves to keep me amused for a long time."

"But suppose some of them happen to guess aright," persisted the Steward; "then you would lose your old ornaments and these new ones, too."

"There is no chance of their guessing aright," replied the monarch, with a laugh. "How could they know that the Queen of Ev and her family are all ornaments of a royal purple color?"

"HOW DARE YOU CALL ME A FOOL?"

"But there are no other purple ornaments in the palace," said the Steward.

"There are many other colors, however, and the purple ones are scattered throughout the rooms, and are of many different shapes and sizes. Take my word for it, Steward, they will never think of choosing the purple ornaments."

Billina, squatting under the throne, had listened carefully to all this talk, and now chuckled softly to herself as she heard the King disclose his secret.

"Still, you are acting foolishly by running the chance," continued the Steward, roughly; "and it is still more foolish of you to transform all those people from Oz into green ornaments."

"I did that because they came from the Emerald City," replied the King; "and I had no green ornaments in my collection until now. I think they will look quite pretty, mixed with the others. Don't you?"

The Steward gave an angry grunt.

"Have your own way, since you are the King," he growled. "But if you come to grief through your carelessness, remember that I told you so. If I wore the magic belt which enables you to work all your transformations, and gives you so much other power, I am sure I would make a much wiser and better King than you are."

"Oh, cease your tiresome chatter!" commanded the King, getting angry again. "Because you are my Chief Steward you have an idea you can scold me as much as you please. But the very next time you become impudent, I will send you to work in the furnaces, and get another Nome to fill your place. Now follow me to my chamber, for I am going to bed. And see that I am wakened early tomorrow morning. I want to enjoy the fun of transforming the rest of these people into ornaments."

"What color will you make the Kansas girl?" asked the Steward.

"Gray, I think," said His Majesty.

"And the Scarecrow and the machine man?"

"Oh, they shall be of solid gold, because they are so ugly in real life."

Then the voices died away, and Billina knew that the King and his Steward had left the room. She fixed up some of her tail feathers that were not straight, and then tucked her head under her wing again and went to sleep.

In the morning Dorothy and the Lion and Tiger were given their breakfast in their rooms, and afterward joined the King in his throne room. The Tiger complained bitterly that he was half starved, and begged to go into the palace and become an ornament, so that he would no longer suffer the pangs of hunger.

"Haven't you had your breakfast?" asked the Nome King.

"Oh, I had just a bite," replied the beast. "But what good is a bite, to a hungry tiger?"

"He ate seventeen bowls of porridge, a platter full of fried sausages, eleven loaves of bread and twenty-one mince pies," said the Steward.

"What more do you want?" demanded the King.

"A fat baby. I want a fat baby," said the Hungry Tiger. "A nice, plump, juicy, tender, fat baby. But, of course, if I had one, my conscience would not allow me to eat it. So I'll have to be an ornament and forget my hunger."

"Impossible!" exclaimed the King. "I'll have no clumsy beasts enter my palace, to overturn and break all my pretty nick-nacks. When the rest of your friends are transformed you can return to the upper world, and go about your business."

"As for that, we have no business, when our friends are gone," said the Lion. "So we do not care much what becomes of us."

Dorothy begged to be allowed to go first into the palace, but Tiktok firmly maintained that the slave should face danger before the mistress. The Scarecrow agreed with him in that, so the Nome King opened the door for the machine man, who tramped into the palace to meet his fate. Then His Majesty returned to his throne and puffed his pipe so contentedly that a small cloud of smoke formed above his head.

Bye and bye he said:

"I'm sorry there are so few of you left. Very soon, now, my fun will be over, and then for amusement I shall have nothing to do but admire my new ornaments."

THE NOME KING PUFFED HIS PIPE

"It seems to me," said Dorothy, "that you are not so honest as you pretend to be."

"How's that?" asked the King.

"Why, you made us think it would be easy to guess what ornaments the people of Ev were changed into."

"It *is* easy," declared the monarch, "if one is a good guesser. But it appears that the members of your party are all poor guessers."

"What is Tiktok doing now?" asked the girl, uneasily.

"Nothing," replied the King, with a frown. "He is standing perfectly still, in the middle of a room."

"Oh, I expect he's run down," said Dorothy. "I forgot to wind him up this morning. How many guesses has he made?"

"All that he is allowed except one," answered the King. "Suppose you go in and wind him up, and then you can stay there and make your own guesses."

"All right," said Dorothy.

"It is my turn next," declared the Scarecrow.

"Why, you don't want to go away and leave me all alone, do you?" asked the girl. "Besides, if I go now I can wind up Tiktok, so that he can make his last guess."

"Very well, then," said the Scarecrow, with a sigh. "Run along, little Dorothy, and may good luck go with you!"

So Dorothy, trying to be brave in spite of her fears, passed through the doorway into the gorgeous rooms of the palace. The stillness of the place awed her, at first, and the child drew short breaths, and pressed her hand to her heart, and looked all around with wondering eyes.

Yes, it was a beautiful place; but enchantments lurked in every nook and corner, and she had not yet grown accustomed to the wizardries of these fairy countries, so different from the quiet and sensible common-places of her own native land.

Slowly she passed through several rooms until she came upon Tiktok, standing motionless. It really seemed, then, that she had found a friend in this mysterious palace, so she hastened to wind up the machine man's action and speech and thoughts.

"Thank you, Dor-oth-y," were his first words. "I have now one more guess to make."

"Oh, be very careful, Tiktok; won't you?" cried the girl.

"Yes. But the Nome King has us in his power, and he has set a trap for us. I fear we are all lost," he answered.

"I fear so, too," said Dorothy, sadly.

"If Smith & Tin-ker had giv-en me a guess-ing clock-work at-tach-ment," continued Tiktok, "I might have de-fied the Nome King. But my thoughts are plain and sim-ple, and are not of much use in this case."

"Do the best you can," said Dorothy, encouragingly, "and if you fail I will watch and see what shape you are changed into."

So Tiktok touched a yellow glass vase that had daisies painted on one side, and he spoke at the same time the word "Ev."

In a flash the machine man had disappeared, and although the girl looked quickly in every direction, she could not tell which of the many ornaments the room contained had a moment before been her faithful friend and servant.

So all she could do was to accept the hopeless task set her, and make her guesses and abide by the result.

"It can't hurt very much," she thought, "for I haven't heard any of them scream or cry out—not even the poor officers. Dear me! I wonder if Uncle Henry or Aunt Em will ever know I have become an orn'ment in the Nome King's palace, and must stand forever and ever in one place and look pretty—'cept when I'm moved to be dusted. It isn't the way I thought I'd turn out, at all; but I s'pose it can't be helped."

She walked through all the rooms once more, and examined with care all the objects they contained; but there were so many, they bewildered her, and she decided, after all, as Ozma had done, that it could be only guess work at the best, and that the chances were much against her guessing aright.

Timidly she touched an alabaster bowl and said: "Ev."

"That's one failure, anyhow," she thought. "But how am I to know which thing is enchanted, and which is not?"

Next she touched the image of a purple kitten that stood on the corner of a mantel, and as she pronounced the word "Ev" the kitten disappeared, and a pretty, fair-haired boy stood beside her. At the same time a bell rang somewhere in the distance, and as Dorothy started back, partly in surprise and partly in joy, the little one exclaimed:

"Where am I? And who are you? And what has happened to me?"

"Well, I declare!" said Dorothy. "I've really done it."

"Done what?" asked the boy.

"Saved myself from being an ornament," replied the girl, with a laugh, "and saved you from being forever a purple kitten."

"A purple kitten?" he repeated. "There *is* no such thing."

"I know," she answered. "But there was, a minute ago. Don't you remember standing on a corner of the mantel?"

"Of course not. I am a Prince of Ev, and my name is Evring," the little one announced, proudly. "But my father, the King, sold my mother and all her children to the cruel ruler of the Nomes, and after that I remember nothing at all."

"A purple kitten can't be 'spected to remember, Evring," said Dorothy. "But now you are yourself again, and I'm going to try to save some of your brothers and sisters, and perhaps your mother, as well. So come with me."

She seized the child's hand and eagerly hurried here and there, trying to decide which object to choose next. The third guess was another failure, and so was the fourth and the fifth.

Little Evring could not imagine what she was doing, but he trotted along beside her very willingly, for he liked the new companion he had found.

Dorothy's further quest proved unsuccessful; but after her first disappointment was over, the little girl was filled with joy and thankfulness to think that after all she had been able to save one member of the royal family of Ev, and could restore the little Prince to his sorrowing country. Now she might return to the terrible Nome King in safety, carrying with her the prize she had won in the person of the fair-haired boy.

So she retraced her steps until she found the entrance to the palace, and as she approached, the massive doors of rock opened of their own accord, allowing both Dorothy and Evring to pass the portals and enter the throne room.

Billina Frightens the Nome King

NOW when Dorothy had entered the palace to make her guesses and the Scarecrow was left with the Nome King, the two sat in moody silence for several minutes. Then the monarch exclaimed, in a tone of satisfaction:

"Very good!"

"Who is very good?" asked the Scarecrow.

"The machine man. He won't need to be wound up any more, for he has now become a very neat ornament. Very neat, indeed."

"How about Dorothy?" the Scarecrow enquired.

"Oh, she will begin to guess, pretty soon," said the King, cheerfully. "And then she will join my collection, and it will be your turn."

The good Scarecrow was much distressed by the thought that his little friend was about to suffer the fate of Ozma and the rest of their party; but while he sat in gloomy reverie a shrill voice suddenly cried:

"Kut, kut, kut—ka-daw-kutt! Kut, kut, kut—ka-daw-kutt!"

The Nome King nearly jumped off his seat, he was so startled.

"Good gracious! What's that?" he yelled.

"Why, it's Billina," said the Scarecrow.

"What do you mean by making a noise like that?" shouted the King, angrily, as the yellow hen came from under the throne and strutted proudly about the room.

"I've got a right to cackle, I guess," replied Billina. "I've just laid my egg."

"What! Laid an egg! In my throne room! How dare you do such a thing?" asked the King, in a voice of fury.

"I lay eggs wherever I happen to be," said the hen, ruffling her feathers and then shaking them into place.

"But—thunder-ation! Don't you know that eggs are poison?" roared the King, while his rock-colored eyes stuck out in great terror.

"Poison! well, I declare," said Billina, indignantly. "I'll have you know all my eggs are warranted strictly fresh and up to date. Poison, indeed!"

"You don't understand," retorted the little monarch, nervously. "Eggs belong only to the outside world—to the world on the earth's surface, where you came from. Here, in my underground kingdom, they are rank poison, as I said, and we Nomes can't bear them around."

"Well, you'll have to bear this one around," declared Billina; "for I've laid it."

"Where?" asked the King.

"Under your throne," said the hen.

The King jumped three feet into the air, so anxious was he to get away from the throne.

"Take it away! Take it away at once!" he shouted.

"I can't," said Billina. "I haven't any hands."

"I'll take the egg," said the Scarecrow. "I'm making a collection of Billina's eggs. There's one in my pocket now, that she laid yesterday."

Hearing this, the monarch hastened to put a good distance between himself and the Scarecrow, who was about to reach under the throne for the egg when the hen suddenly cried:

"Stop!"

"What's wrong?" asked the Scarecrow.

"DON'T YOU KNOW THAT EGGS ARE POISON?"

"Don't take the egg unless the King will allow me to enter the palace and guess as the others have done," said Billina.

"Pshaw!" returned the King. "You are only a hen. How could you guess my enchantments?"

"I can try, I suppose," said Billina. "And, if I fail, you will have another ornament."

"A pretty ornament you'd make, wouldn't you?" growled the King. "But you shall have your way. It will properly punish you for daring to lay an egg in my presence. After the Scarecrow is enchanted you shall follow him into the palace. But how will you touch the objects?"

"With my claws," said the hen; "and I can speak the word 'Ev' as plainly as anyone. Also I must have the right to guess the enchantments of my friends, and to release them if I succeed."

"Very well," said the King. "You have my promise."

"Then," said Billina to the Scarecrow, "you may get the egg."

He knelt down and reached underneath the throne and found the egg, which he placed in another pocket of his jacket, fearing that if both eggs were in one pocket they would knock together and get broken.

Just then a bell above the throne rang briskly, and the King gave another nervous jump.

"Well, well!" said he, with a rueful face; "the girl has actually done it."

"Done what?" asked the Scarecrow.

"She has made one guess that is right, and broken one of my neatest enchantments. By ricketty, it's too bad! I never thought she would do it."

"Do I understand that she will now return to us in safety?" enquired the Scarecrow, joyfully wrinkling his painted face into a broad smile.

"Of course," said the King, fretfully pacing up and down the room. "I always keep my promises, no matter how foolish they are. But I shall make an ornament of the yellow hen to replace the one I have just lost."

"Perhaps you will, and perhaps you won't," murmured Billina, calmly. "I may surprise you by guessing right."

"Guessing right?" snapped the King. "How should you guess right, where your betters have failed, you stupid fowl?"

Billina did not care to answer this question, and a moment later the doors flew open and Dorothy entered, leading the little Prince Evring by the hand.

The Scarecrow welcomed the girl with a close embrace, and he would have embraced Evring, too, in his delight. But the little Prince was shy, and shrank away from the painted Scarecrow because he did not yet know his many excellent qualities.

But there was little time for the friends to talk, because the Scarecrow must now enter the palace. Dorothy's success had greatly encouraged him, and they both hoped he would manage to make at least one correct guess.

However, he proved as unfortunate as the others except Dorothy, and although he took a good deal of time to select his objects, not one did the poor Scarecrow guess aright.

So he became a solid gold card-receiver, and the beautiful but terrible palace awaited its next visitor.

"It's all over," remarked the King, with a sigh of satisfaction; "and it has been a very amusing performance, except for the one good guess the Kansas girl made. I am richer by a great many pretty ornaments."

"It is my turn, now," said Billina, briskly.

"Oh, I'd forgotten you," said the King. "But you needn't go if you don't wish to. I will be generous, and let you off."

"No you won't," replied the hen. "I insist upon having my guesses, as you promised."

"BY RICKETTY, IT'S TOO BAD!"

"Then go ahead, you absurd feathered fool!" grumbled the King, and he caused the opening that led to the palace to appear once more.

"Don't go, Billina," said Dorothy, earnestly. "It isn't easy to guess those orn'ments, and only luck saved me from being one myself. Stay with me and we'll go back to the Land of Ev together. I'm sure this little Prince will give us a home."

"Indeed I will," said Evring, with much dignity.

"Don't worry, my dear," cried Billina, with a cluck that was meant for a laugh. "I may not be human, but I'm no fool, if I *am* a chicken."

"Oh, Billina!" said Dorothy, "you haven't been a chicken in a long time. Not since you—you've been—grown up."

"Perhaps that's true," answered Billina, thoughtfully. "But if a Kansas farmer sold me to some one, what would he call me?—a hen or a chicken!"

"You are not a Kansas farmer, Billina," replied the girl, "and you said—"

"Never mind that, Dorothy. I'm going. I won't say good-bye, because I'm coming back. Keep up your courage, for I'll see you a little later."

Then Billina gave several loud "cluck-clucks" that seemed to make the fat little King *more* nervous than ever, and marched through the entrance into the enchanted palace.

"I hope I've seen the last of *that* bird," declared the monarch, seating himself again in his throne and mopping the perspiration from his forehead with his rock-colored handkerchief. "Hens are bothersome enough at their best, but when they can talk they're simply dreadful."

"Billina's my friend," said Dorothy quietly. "She may not always be 'zactly polite; but she *means* well, I'm sure."

Purple, Green and Gold

The yellow hen, stepping high and with an air of vast importance, walked slowly over the rich velvet carpets of the splendid palace, examining everything she met with her sharp little eyes.

Billina had a right to feel important; for she alone shared the Nome King's secret and knew how to tell the objects that were transformations from those that had never been alive. She was very sure that her guesses would be correct, but before she began to make them she was curious to behold all the magnificence of this underground palace, which was perhaps one of the most splendid and beautiful places in any fairyland.

As she went through the rooms she counted the purple ornaments; and although some were small and hidden in queer places, Billina spied them all, and found the entire ten scattered about the various rooms. The green ornaments she did not bother to count, for she thought she could find them all when the time came.

Finally, having made a survey of the entire palace and enjoyed its splendor, the yellow hen returned to one of the rooms where she had noticed a large purple footstool. She placed a claw upon this and said "Ev," and at once the footstool vanished and a lovely lady, tall and slender and most beautifully robed, stood before her.

The lady's eyes were round with astonishment for a moment, for she could not remember her transformation, nor imagine what had restored her to life.

"Good morning, ma'am," said Billina, in her sharp voice. "You're looking quite well, considering your age."

"Who speaks?" demanded the Queen of Ev, drawing herself up proudly.

"Why, my name's Bill, by rights," answered the hen, who was now perched upon the back of a chair; "although Dorothy has put scollops on it and made it Billina. But the name doesn't matter. I've saved you from the Nome King, and you are a slave no longer."

"Then I thank you for the gracious favor," said the Queen, with a graceful courtesy. "But, my children—tell me, I beg of you—where are my children?" and she clasped her hands in anxious entreaty.

"Don't worry," advised Billina, pecking at a tiny bug that was crawling over the chair back. "Just at present they are out of mischief and perfectly safe, for they can't even wiggle."

"What mean you, O kindly stranger?" asked the Queen, striving to repress her anxiety.

"They're enchanted," said Billina, "just as you have been—all, that is, except the little fellow Dorothy picked out. And the chances are that they have been good boys and girls for some time, because they couldn't help it."

"Oh, my poor darlings!" cried the Queen, with a sob of anguish.

"Not at all," returned the hen. "Don't let their condition make you unhappy, ma'am, because I'll soon have them crowding 'round to bother and worry you as naturally as ever. Come with me, if you please, and I'll show you how pretty they look."

She flew down from her perch and walked into the next room, the Queen following. As she passed a low table a small green grasshopper caught her eye, and instantly Billina pounced upon it and snapped it up in her sharp bill. For grasshoppers are a favorite food with hens, and they usually must be caught quickly, before they can hop away. It might easily have been the end of Ozma of Oz, had she been a real grasshopper instead of an emerald one. But

Billina found the grasshopper hard and lifeless, and suspecting it was not good to eat she quickly dropped it instead of letting it slide down her throat.

"I might have known better," she muttered to herself, "for where there is no grass there can be no live grasshoppers. This is probably one of the King's transformations."

A moment later she approached one of the purple ornaments, and while the Queen watched her curiously the hen broke the Nome King's enchantment and a sweet-faced girl, whose golden hair fell in a cloud over her shoulders, stood beside them.

"Evanna!" cried the Queen, "my own Evanna!" and she clasped the girl to her bosom and covered her face with kisses.

"That's all right," said Billina, contentedly. "Am I a good guesser, Mr. Nome King? Well, I guess!"

Then she disenchanted another girl, whom the Queen addressed as Evrose, and afterwards a boy named Evardo, who was older than his brother Evring. Indeed, the yellow hen kept the good Queen exclaiming and embracing for some time, until five Princesses and four Princes, all looking very much alike except for the difference in size, stood in a row beside their happy mother.

The Princesses were named, Evanna, Evrose, Evella, Evirene and Evedna, while the Princes were Evrob, Evington, Evardo and Evroland. Of these Evardo was the eldest and would inherit his father's throne and be crowned King of Ev when he returned to his own country. He was a grave and quiet youth, and would doubtless rule his people wisely and with justice.

Billina, having restored all of the royal family of Ev to their proper forms, now began to select the green ornaments which were the transformations of the people of Oz. She had little trouble in finding these, and before long all the twenty-six officers, as well as the private, were gathered around the yellow hen, joyfully congratulating her upon their release. The thirty-seven people who were now alive in the rooms of the palace knew very well that they owed their freedom to the cleverness of the yellow hen, and they were earnest in thanking her for saving them from the magic of the Nome King.

THE QUEEN OF EV THANKS BILLINA

"Now," said Billina, "I must find Ozma. She is sure to be here, somewhere, and of course she is green, being from Oz. So look around, you stupid soldiers, and help me in my search."

For a while, however, they could discover nothing more that was green. But the Queen, who had kissed all her nine children once more and could now find time to take an interest in what was going on, said to the hen:

"Mayhap, my gentle friend, it is the grasshopper whom you seek."

"Of course it's the grasshopper!" exclaimed Billina. "I declare, I'm nearly as stupid as these brave soldiers. Wait here for me, and I'll go back and get it."

So she went into the room where she had seen the grasshopper, and presently Ozma of Oz, as lovely and dainty as ever, entered and approached the Queen of Ev, greeting her as one high born princess greets another.

"But where are my friends, the Scarecrow and the Tin Woodman?" asked the girl Ruler, when these courtesies had been exchanged.

"I'll hunt them up," replied Billina. "The Scarecrow is solid gold, and so is Tiktok; but I don't exactly know what the Tin Woodman is, because the Nome King said he had been transformed into something funny."

Ozma eagerly assisted the hen in her quest, and soon the Scarecrow and the machine man, being ornaments of shining gold, were discovered and restored to their accustomed forms. But, search as they might, in no place could they find a funny ornament that might be the transformation of the Tin Woodman.

"Only one thing can be done," said Ozma, at last, "and that is to return to the Nome King and oblige him to tell us what has become of our friend."

"Perhaps he won't," suggested Billina.

"He must," returned Ozma, firmly. "The King has not treated us honestly, for under the mask of fairness and good nature he entrapped us all, and we would have been forever enchanted had not our wise and clever friend, the yellow hen, found a way to save us."

"The King is a villain," declared the Scarecrow.

"His laugh is worse than another man's frown," said the private, with a shudder.

"I thought he was hon-est, but I was mis-tak-en," remarked Tiktok. "My thoughts are us-u-al-ly cor-rect, but it is Smith & Tinker's fault if they some-times go wrong or do not work prop-er-ly."

"Smith & Tinker made a very good job of you," said Ozma, kindly. "I do not think they should be blamed if you are not quite perfect."

"Thank you," replied Tiktok.

"Then," said Billina, in her brisk little voice, "let us all go back to the Nome King, and see what he has to say for himself."

So they started for the entrance, Ozma going first, with the Queen and her train of little Princes and Princesses following. Then came Tiktok, and the Scarecrow with Billina perched upon his straw-stuffed shoulder. The twenty-seven officers and the private brought up the rear.

As they reached the hall the doors flew open before them; but then they all stopped and stared into the domed cavern with faces of astonishment and dismay. For the room was filled with the mail-clad warriors of the Nome King, rank after rank standing in orderly array. The electric lights upon their brows gleamed brightly, their battle-axes were poised as if to strike down their foes; yet they remained motionless as statues, awaiting the word of command.

And in the center of this terrible army sat the little King upon his throne of rock. But he neither smiled nor laughed. Instead, his face was distorted with rage, and most dreadful to behold.

The Scarecrow Wins the Fight

After Billina had entered the palace Dorothy and Evring sat down to await the success or failure of her mission, and the Nome King occupied his throne and smoked his long pipe for a while in a cheerful and contented mood.

Then the bell above the throne, which sounded whenever an enchantment was broken, began to ring, and the King gave a start of annoyance and exclaimed, "Rocketty-ricketts!"

When the bell rang a second time the King shouted angrily, "Smudge and blazes!" and at a third ring he screamed in a fury, "Hippikaloric!" which must be a dreadful word because we don't know what it means.

After that the bell went on ringing time after time; but the King was now so violently enraged that he could not utter a word, but hopped out of his throne and all around the room in a mad frenzy, so that he reminded Dorothy of a jumping-jack.

The girl was, for her part, filled with joy at every peal of the bell, for it announced the fact that Billina had transformed one more ornament into a living person. Dorothy was also amazed at Billina's success, for she could not imagine how the yellow hen was able to guess correctly from all the bewildering number of articles clustered in the rooms of the palace. But after she had counted ten, and the bell continued to ring, she knew that not only the royal family of Ev, but Ozma and her followers also, were being restored to their natural forms, and she was so delighted that the antics of the angry King only made her laugh merrily.

Perhaps the little monarch could not be more furious than he was before, but the girl's laughter nearly drove him frantic, and he roared at her like a savage beast. Then, as he found that all his enchantments were likely to be dispelled and his victims every one set free, he suddenly ran to the little door that opened upon the balcony and gave the shrill whistle that summoned his warriors.

At once the army filed out of the gold and silver doors in great numbers, and marched up a winding stairs and into the throne room, led by a stern featured Nome who was their captain. When they had nearly filled the throne room they formed ranks in the big underground cavern below, and then stood still until they were told what to do next.

Dorothy had pressed back to one side of the cavern when the warriors entered, and now she stood holding little Prince Evring's hand while the great Lion crouched upon one side and the enormous Tiger crouched on the other side.

"Seize that girl!" shouted the King to his captain, and a group of warriors sprang forward to obey. But both the Lion and Tiger snarled so fiercely and bared their strong, sharp teeth so threateningly, that the men drew back in alarm.

"Don't mind them!" cried the Nome King; "they cannot leap beyond the places where they now stand."

"But they can bite those who attempt to touch the girl," said the captain.

"I'll fix that," answered the King. "I'll enchant them again, so that they can't open their jaws."

He stepped out of the throne to do this, but just then the Saw-Horse ran up behind him and gave the fat monarch a powerful kick with both his wooden hind legs.

"Ow! Murder! Treason!" yelled the King, who had been hurled

against several of his warriors and was considerably bruised. "Who did that?"

"I did," growled the Saw-Horse, viciously. "You let Dorothy alone, or I'll kick you again."

"We'll see about that," replied the King, and at once he waved his hand toward the Saw-Horse and muttered a magical word. "Aha!" he continued; "*now* let us see you move, you wooden mule!"

But in spite of the magic the Saw-Horse moved; and he moved so quickly toward the King, that the fat little man could not get out of his way. Thump—*bang!* came the wooden heels, right against his round body, and the King flew into the air and fell upon the head of his captain, who let him drop flat upon the ground.

"Well, well!" said the King, sitting up and looking surprised. "Why didn't my magic belt work, I wonder?"

"The creature is made of wood," replied the captain. "Your magic will not work on wood, you know."

"Ah, I'd forgotten that," said the King, getting up and limping to his throne. "Very well, let the girl alone. She can't escape us, anyway."

The warriors, who had been rather confused by these incidents, now formed their ranks again, and the Saw-Horse pranced across the room to Dorothy and took a position beside the Hungry Tiger.

At that moment the doors that led to the palace flew open and the people of Ev and the people of Oz were disclosed to view. They paused, astonished, at sight of the warriors and the angry Nome King, seated in their midst.

"Surrender!" cried the King, in a loud voice. "You are my prisoners."

"Go 'long!" answered Billina, from the Scarecrow's shoulder. "You promised me that if I guessed correctly my friends and I might depart in safety. And you always keep your promises."

"I said you might leave the palace in safety," retorted the King; "and so you may, but you cannot leave my dominions. You are my prisoners, and I will hurl you all into my underground dungeons, where the volcanic fires glow and the molten lava flows in every direction, and the air is hotter than blue blazes."

"That will be the end of me, all right," said the Scarecrow, sorrowfully. "One small blaze, blue or green, is enough to reduce me to an ash-heap."

"Do you surrender?" demanded the King.

Billina whispered something in the Scarecrow's ear that made him smile and put his hands in his jacket pockets.

"No!" returned Ozma, boldly answering the King. Then she said to her army:

"Forward, my brave soldiers, and fight for your Ruler and yourselves, unto death!"

"Pardon me, Most Royal Ozma," replied one of her generals; "but I find that I and my brother officers all suffer from heart disease, and the slightest excitement might kill us. If we fight we may get excited. Would it not be well for us to avoid this grave danger?"

"Soldiers should not have heart disease," said Ozma.

"Private soldiers are not, I believe, afflicted that way," declared another general, twirling his moustache thoughtfully. "If Your Royal Highness desires, we will order our private to attack yonder warriors."

"Do so," replied Ozma.

"For-ward—march!" cried all the generals, with one voice. "For-ward—march!" yelled the colonels. "For-ward—march!" shouted the majors. "For-ward—march!" commanded the captains.

And at that the private leveled his spear and dashed furiously upon the foe.

The captain of the Nomes was so surprised by this sudden onslaught that he forgot to command his warriors to fight, so that the ten men in the first row, who stood in front of the private's spear, fell over like so many toy soldiers. The spear could not go through their steel armor, however, so the warriors scrambled to their feet again, and by that time the private had knocked over another row of them.

Then the captain brought down his battle-axe with such a strong blow that the private's spear was shattered and knocked from his grasp, and he was helpless to fight any longer.

The Nome King had left his throne and pressed through his

"HELP, HELP!" SCREAMED THE KING

warriors to the front ranks, so he could see what was going on; but as he faced Ozma and her friends the Scarecrow, as if aroused to action by the valor of the private, drew one of Billina's eggs from his right jacket pocket and hurled it straight at the little monarch's head.

It struck him squarely in his left eye, where the egg smashed and scattered, as eggs will, and covered his face and hair and beard with its sticky contents.

"Help, help!" screamed the King, clawing with his fingers at the egg, in a struggle to remove it.

"An egg! an egg! Run for your lives!" shouted the captain of the Nomes, in a voice of horror.

And how they *did* run! The warriors fairly tumbled over one another in their efforts to escape the fatal poison of that awful egg, and those who could not rush down the winding stair fell off the balcony into the great cavern beneath, knocking over those who stood below them.

Even while the King was still yelling for help his throne room became emptied of every one of his warriors, and before the monarch had managed to clear the egg away from his left eye the Scarecrow threw the second egg against his right eye, where it smashed and blinded him entirely. The King was unable to flee because he could not see which way to run; so he stood still and howled and shouted and screamed in abject fear.

While this was going on, Billina flew over to Dorothy, and perching herself upon the Lion's back the hen whispered eagerly to the girl:

"Get his belt! Get the Nome King's jeweled belt! It unbuckles in the back. Quick, Dorothy—quick!"

The Fate of the Tin Woodman

Dorothy

obeyed. She ran
at once behind the
Nome King, who was
still trying to free his
eyes from the egg, and in a
twinkling she had unbuckled
his splendid jeweled belt and
carried it away with her to her place
beside the Tiger and Lion, where, because she did not know what
else to do with it, she fastened it around her own slim waist.

Just then the Chief Steward rushed in with a sponge and a bowl
of water, and began mopping away the broken eggs from his master's face. In a few minutes, and while all the party stood looking on,
the King regained the use of his eyes, and the first thing he did was
to glare wickedly upon the Scarecrow and exclaim:

"I'll make you suffer for this, you hay-stuffed dummy! Don't you
know eggs are poison to Nomes?"

"Really," said the Scarecrow, "they *don't* seem to agree with you,
although I wonder why."

"They were strictly fresh and above suspicion," said Billina. "You
ought to be glad to get them."

"I'll transform you all into scorpions!" cried the King, angrily,
and began waving his arms and muttering magic words.

But none of the people became scorpions, so the King stopped and looked at them in surprise.

"What's wrong?" he asked.

"Why, you are not wearing your magic belt," replied the Chief Steward, after looking the King over carefully. "Where is it? What have you done with it?"

The Nome King clapped his hand to his waist, and his rock-colored face turned white as chalk.

"It's gone," he cried, helplessly. "It's gone, and I am ruined!"

Dorothy now stepped forward and said:

"Royal Ozma, and you, Queen of Ev, I welcome you and your people back to the land of the living. Billina has saved you from your troubles, and now we will leave this drea'ful place, and return to Ev as soon as poss'ble."

While the child spoke they could all see that she wore the magic belt, and a great cheer went up from all her friends, which was led by the voices of the Scarecrow and the private. But the Nome King did not join them. He crept back onto his throne like a whipped dog, and lay there bitterly bemoaning his defeat.

"But we have not yet found my faithful follower, the Tin Woodman," said Ozma to Dorothy, "and without him I do not wish to go away."

"Nor I," replied Dorothy, quickly. "Wasn't he in the palace?"

"He must be there," said Billina; "but I had no clew to guide me in guessing the Tin Woodman, so I must have missed him."

"We will go back into the rooms," said Dorothy. "This magic belt, I am sure, will help us to find our dear old friend."

So she re-entered the palace, the doors of which still stood open, and everyone followed her except the Nome King, the Queen of Ev and Prince Evring. The mother had taken the little Prince in her lap and was fondling and kissing him lovingly, for he was her youngest born.

But the others went with Dorothy, and when she came to the middle of the first room the girl waved her hand, as she had seen the King do, and commanded the Tin Woodman, whatever form he might then have, to resume his proper shape. No result followed

DOROTHY AND BILLINA ARGUE WITH THE KING

this attempt, so Dorothy went into another room and repeated it, and so through all the rooms of the palace. Yet the Tin Woodman did not appear to them, nor could they imagine which among the thousands of ornaments was their transformed friend.

Sadly they returned to the throne room, where the King, seeing that they had met with failure, jeered at Dorothy, saying:

"You do not know how to use my belt, so it is of no use to you. Give it back to me and I will let you go free—you and all the people who came with you. As for the royal family of Ev, they are my slaves, and shall remain here."

"I shall keep the belt," said Dorothy.

"But how can you escape, without my consent?" asked the King.

"Easily enough," answered the girl. "All we need to do is to walk out the way that we came in."

"Oh, that's all, is it?" sneered the King. "Well, where is the passage through which you entered this room?"

They all looked around, but could not discover the place, for it had long since been closed. Dorothy, however, would not be dismayed. She waved her hand toward the seemingly solid wall of the cavern and said:

"I command the passage to open!"

Instantly the order was obeyed; the opening appeared and the passage lay plainly before them.

The King was amazed, and all the others overjoyed.

"Why, then, if the belt obeys you, were we unable to discover the Tin Woodman?" asked Ozma.

"I can't imagine," said Dorothy.

"See here, girl," proposed the King, eagerly; "give me the belt, and I will tell you what shape the Tin Woodman was changed into, and then you can easily find him."

Dorothy hesitated, but Billina cried out:

"Don't you do it! If the Nome King gets the belt again he will make every one of us prisoners, for we will be in his power. Only by keeping the belt, Dorothy, will you ever be able to leave this place in safety."

"I think that is true," said the Scarecrow. "But I have another idea, due to my excellent brains. Let Dorothy transform the King into a goose-egg unless he agrees to go into the palace and bring out to us the ornament which is our friend Nick Chopper, the Tin Woodman."

"A goose-egg!" echoed the horrified King. "How dreadful!"

"Well, a goose-egg you will be unless you go and fetch us the ornament we want," declared Billina, with a joyful chuckle.

"You can see for yourself that Dorothy is able to use the magic belt all right," added the Scarecrow.

The Nome King thought it over and finally consented, for he did not want to be a goose-egg. So he went into the palace to get the ornament which was the transformation of the Tin Woodman, and they all awaited his return with considerable impatience, for they were anxious to leave this underground cavern and see the sunshine once more. But when the Nome King came back he brought nothing with him except a puzzled and anxious expression upon his face.

"He's gone!" he said. "The Tin Woodman is nowhere in the palace."

"Are you sure?" asked Ozma, sternly.

"I'm very sure," answered the King, trembling, "for I know just what I transformed him into, and exactly where he stood. But he is not there, and please don't change me into a goose-egg, because I've done the best I could."

They were all silent for a time, and then Dorothy said:

"There is no use punishing the Nome King any more, and I'm 'fraid we'll have to go away without our friend."

"If he is not here, we cannot rescue him," agreed the Scarecrow, sadly. "Poor Nick! I wonder what has become of him."

"And he owed me six weeks back pay!" said one of the generals, wiping the tears from his eyes with his gold-laced coat sleeve.

Very sorrowfully they determined to return to the upper world without their former companion, and so Ozma gave the order to begin the march through the passage.

The army went first, and then the royal family of Ev, and afterward came Dorothy, Ozma, Billina, the Scarecrow and Tiktok.

They left the Nome King scowling at them from his throne, and had no thought of danger until Ozma chanced to look back and saw a large number of the warriors following them in full chase, with their swords and spears and axes raised to strike down the fugitives as soon as they drew near enough.

Evidently the Nome King had made this last attempt to prevent their escaping him; but it did him no good, for when Dorothy saw the danger they were in she stopped and waved her hand and whispered a command to the magic belt.

Instantly the foremost warriors became eggs, which rolled upon the floor of the cavern in such numbers that those behind could not advance without stepping upon them. But, when they saw the eggs, all desire to advance departed from the warriors, and they turned and fled madly into the cavern, and refused to go back again.

Our friends had no farther trouble in reaching the end of the passage, and soon were standing in the outer air upon the gloomy path between the two high mountains. But the way to Ev lay plainly before them, and they fervently hoped that they had seen the last of the Nome King and of his dreadful palace.

The cavalcade was led by Ozma, mounted on the Cowardly Lion, and the Queen of Ev, who rode upon the back of the Tiger. The children of the Queen walked behind her, hand in hand. Dorothy rode the Saw-Horse, while the Scarecrow walked and commanded the army in the absence of the Tin Woodman.

Presently the way began to lighten and more of the sunshine to come in between the two mountains. And before long they heard the "thump! thump! thump!" of the giant's hammer upon the road.

"How may we pass the monstrous man of iron?" asked the Queen, anxious for the safety of her children. But Dorothy solved the problem by a word to the magic belt.

The giant paused, with his hammer held motionless in the air, thus allowing the entire party to pass between his cast-iron legs in safety.

The King of Ev

If there were any shifting, rock-colored Nomes on the mountain side now, they were silent and respectful, for our adventurers were not annoyed, as before, by their impudent laughter. Really the Nomes had nothing to laugh at, since the defeat of their King.

On the other side they found Ozma's golden chariot, standing as they had left it. Soon the Lion and the Tiger were harnessed to the beautiful chariot, in which was enough room for Ozma and the Queen and six of the royal children.

Little Evring preferred to ride with Dorothy upon the Saw-Horse, which had a long back. The Prince had recovered from his shyness and had become very fond of the girl who had rescued him, so they were fast friends and chatted pleasantly together as they rode along. Billina was also perched upon the head of the wooden steed, which seemed not to mind the added weight in the least, and the boy was full of wonder that a hen could talk, and say such sensible things.

When they came to the gulf, Ozma's magic carpet carried them all over in safety; and now they began to pass the trees, in which birds were singing; and the breeze that was wafted to them from the farms of Ev was spicy with flowers and new-mown hay; and the sunshine fell full upon them, to warm them and drive away from their bodies the chill and dampness of the underground kingdom of the Nomes.

"I would be quite content," said the Scarecrow to Tiktok, "were only the Tin Woodman with us. But it breaks my heart to leave him behind."

"He was a fine fel-low," replied Tiktok, "al-though his ma-ter-i-al was not ve-ry du-ra-ble."

"Oh, tin is an excellent material," the Scarecrow hastened to say; "and if anything ever happened to poor Nick Chopper he was always easily soldered. Besides, he did not have to be wound up, and was not liable to get out of order."

"I some-times wish," said Tiktok, "that I was stuffed with straw, as you are. It is hard to be made of cop-per."

"I have no reason to complain of my lot," replied the Scarecrow. "A little fresh straw, now and then, makes me as good as new. But I can never be the polished gentleman that my poor departed friend, the Tin Woodman, was."

You may be sure the royal children of Ev and their Queen mother were delighted at seeing again their beloved country; and when the towers of the palace of Ev came into view they could not forbear cheering at the sight. Little Evring, riding in front of Dorothy, was so overjoyed that he took a curious tin whistle from his pocket and blew a shrill blast that made the Saw-Horse leap and prance in sudden alarm.

"What is that?" asked Billina, who had been obliged to flutter her wings in order to keep her seat upon the head of the frightened Saw-Horse.

"That's my whistle," said Prince Evring, holding it out upon his hand.

It was in the shape of a little fat pig, made of tin and painted green. The whistle was in the tail of the pig.

"Where did you get it?" asked the yellow hen, closely examining the toy with her bright eyes.

"Why, I picked it up in the Nome King's palace, while Dorothy was making her guesses, and I put it in my pocket," answered the little Prince.

Billina laughed; or at least she made the peculiar cackle that served her for a laugh.

"No wonder I couldn't find the Tin Woodman," she said; "and no wonder the magic belt didn't make him appear, or the King couldn't find him, either!"

"What do you mean?" questioned Dorothy.

"Why, the Prince had him in his pocket," cried Billina, cackling again.

"I did not!" protested little Evring. "I only took the whistle."

"Well, then, watch me," returned the hen, and reaching out a claw she touched the whistle and said "Ev."

Swish!

"Good afternoon," said the Tin Woodman, taking off his funnel cap and bowing to Dorothy and the Prince. "I think I must have been asleep for the first time since I was made of tin, for I do not remember our leaving the Nome King."

"You have been enchanted," answered the girl, throwing an arm around her old friend and hugging him tight in her joy. "But it's all right, now."

"I want my whistle!" said the little Prince, beginning to cry.

"Hush!" cautioned Billina. "The whistle is lost, but you may have another when you get home."

The Scarecrow had fairly thrown himself upon the bosom of his old comrade, so surprised and delighted was he to see him again, and Tiktok squeezed the Tin Woodman's hand so earnestly that he dented some of his fingers. Then they had to make way for Ozma to welcome the tin man, and the army caught sight of him and set up a cheer, and everybody was delighted and happy.

"YOUR FUTURE RULER, KING EVARDO FIFTEENTH"

For the Tin Woodman was a great favorite with all who knew him, and his sudden recovery after they had thought he was lost to them forever was indeed a pleasant surprise.

Before long the cavalcade arrived at the royal palace, where a great crowd of people had gathered to welcome their Queen and her ten children. There was much shouting and cheering, and the people threw flowers in their path, and every face wore a happy smile.

They found the Princess Langwidere in her mirrored chamber, where she was admiring one of her handsomest heads—one with rich chestnut hair, dreamy walnut eyes and a shapely hickorynut nose. She was very glad to be relieved of her duties to the people of Ev, and the Queen graciously permitted her to retain her rooms and her cabinet of heads as long as she lived.

Then the Queen took her eldest son out upon a balcony that overlooked the crowd of subjects gathered below, and said to them:

"Here is your future ruler, King Evardo Fifteenth. He is fifteen years of age, has fifteen silver buckles on his jacket and is the fifteenth Evardo to rule the land of Ev."

The people shouted their approval fifteen times, and even the Wheelers, some of whom were present, loudly promised to obey the new King.

So the Queen placed a big crown of gold, set with rubies, upon Evardo's head, and threw an ermine robe over his shoulders, and proclaimed him King; and he bowed gratefully to all his subjects and then went away to see if he could find any cake in the royal pantry.

Ozma of Oz and her people, as well as Dorothy, Tiktok and Billina, were splendidly entertained by the Queen mother, who owed all her happiness to their kind offices; and that evening the yellow hen was publicly presented with a beautiful necklace of pearls and sapphires, as a token of esteem from the new King.

The Emerald City

Dorothy decided to accept Ozma's
invitation to return with her
to the Land of Oz. There was
no greater chance of her getting
home from Ev than from Oz, and
the little girl was anxious to see
once more the country where she had
encountered such wonderful adventures.
By this time Uncle Henry would have
reached Australia in his ship, and had probably given her up for lost; so he couldn't worry
any more than he did if she stayed away from
him a while longer. So she would go to Oz.

They bade good-bye to the people of Ev, and the
King promised Ozma that he would ever be grateful to
her and render the Land of Oz any service that might lie
within his power.

And then they approached the edge of the dangerous
desert, and Ozma threw down the magic carpet, which at once
unrolled far enough for all of them to walk upon it without being
crowded.

Tiktok, claiming to be Dorothy's faithful follower because he
belonged to her, had been permitted to join the party, and before

they started the girl wound up his machinery as far as possible, and the copper man stepped off as briskly as any one of them.

Ozma also invited Billina to visit the Land of Oz, and the yellow hen was glad enough to go where new sights and scenes awaited her.

They began the trip across the desert early in the morning, and as they stopped only long enough for Billina to lay her daily egg, before sunset they espied the green slopes and wooded hills of the beautiful Land of Oz. They entered it in the Munchkin territory, and the King of the Munchkins met them at the border and welcomed Ozma with great respect, being very pleased by her safe return. For Ozma of Oz ruled the King of the Munchkins, the King of the Winkies, the King of the Quadlings and the King of the Gillikins just as those kings ruled their own people; and this supreme ruler of the Land of Oz lived in a great town of her own, called the Emerald City, which was in the exact center of the four kingdoms of the Land of Oz.

The Munchkin King entertained them at his palace that night, and in the morning they set out for the Emerald City, travelling over a road of yellow brick that led straight to the jewel-studded gates. Everywhere the people turned out to greet their beloved Ozma, and to hail joyfully the Scarecrow, the Tin Woodman and the Cowardly Lion, who were popular favorites. Dorothy, too, remembered some of the people, who had befriended her on the occasion of her first visit to Oz, and they were well pleased to see the little Kansas girl again, and showered her with compliments and good wishes.

At one place, where they stopped to refresh themselves, Ozma accepted a bowl of milk from the hands of a pretty dairy-maid. Then she looked at the girl more closely, and exclaimed:

"Why, it's Jinjur—isn't it!"

"Yes, Your Highness," was the reply, as Jinjur dropped a low curtsy. And Dorothy looked wonderingly at this lively appearing person, who had once assembled an army of women and driven the Scarecrow from the throne of the Emerald City, and even fought a battle with the powerful army of Glinda the Sorceress.

"I've married a man who owns nine cows," said Jinjur to Ozma, "and now I am happy and contented and willing to lead a quiet life and mind my own business."

"Where is your husband?" asked Ozma.

"He is in the house, nursing a black eye," replied Jinjur, calmly. "The foolish man would insist upon milking the red cow when I wanted him to milk the white one; but he will know better next time, I am sure."

Then the party moved on again, and after crossing a broad river on a ferry and passing many fine farm-houses that were dome shaped and painted a pretty green color, they came in sight of a large building that was covered with flags and bunting.

"I don't remember that building," said Dorothy. "What is it?"

"That is the College of Art and Athletic Perfection," replied Ozma. "I had it built quite recently, and the Woggle-Bug is its president. It keeps him busy, and the young men who attend the college are no worse off than they were before. You see, in this country are a number of youths who do not like to work, and the college is an excellent place for them."

And now they came in sight of the Emerald City, and the people flocked out to greet their lovely ruler. There were several bands and many officers and officials of the realm, and a crowd of citizens in their holiday attire.

"I PROMOTE YOU TO BE CAPTAIN-GENERAL"

Thus the beautiful Ozma was escorted by a brilliant procession to her royal city, and so great was the cheering that she was obliged to constantly bow to the right and left to acknowledge the greetings of her subjects.

That evening there was a grand reception in the royal palace, attended by the most important persons of Oz, and Jack Pumpkinhead, who was a little over-ripe but still active, read an address congratulating Ozma of Oz upon the success of her generous mission to rescue the royal family of a neighboring kingdom.

Then magnificent gold medals set with precious stones were presented to each of the twenty-six officers; and the Tin Woodman was given a new axe studded with diamonds; and the Scarecrow received a silver jar of complexion powder. Dorothy was presented with a pretty coronet and made a Princess of Oz, and Tiktok received two bracelets set with eight rows of very clear and sparkling emeralds.

Afterward they sat down to a splendid feast, and Ozma put Dorothy at her right and Billina at her left, where the hen sat upon a golden roost and ate from a jeweled platter. Then were placed the Scarecrow, the Tin Woodman and Tiktok, with baskets of lovely flowers before them, because they did not require food. The twenty-six officers were at the lower end of the table, and the Lion and the Tiger also had seats, and were served on golden platters, that held a half a bushel at one time.

The wealthiest and most important citizens of the Emerald City were proud to wait upon these famous adventurers, and they were assisted by a sprightly little maid named Jellia Jamb, whom the Scarecrow pinched upon her rosy cheeks and seemed to know very well.

During the feast Ozma grew thoughtful, and suddenly she asked: "Where is the private?"

"Oh, he is sweeping out the barracks," replied one of the generals, who was busy eating a leg of a turkey. "But I have ordered him a dish of bread and molasses to eat when his work is done."

"Let him be sent for," said the girl ruler.

While they waited for this command to be obeyed, she enquired:

"Have we any other privates in the armies?"

"Oh, yes," replied the Tin Woodman, "I believe there are three, altogether."

The private now entered, saluting his officers and the royal Ozma very respectfully.

"What is your name, my man?" asked the girl.

"Omby Amby," answered the private.

"Then, Omby Amby," said she, "I promote you to be Captain-General of all the armies of my kingdom, and especially to be Commander of my Body Guard at the royal palace."

"It is very expensive to hold so many offices," said the private, hesitating. "I have no money with which to buy uniforms."

"You shall be supplied from the royal treasury," said Ozma.

Then the private was given a seat at the table, where the other officers welcomed him cordially, and the feasting and merriment were resumed.

Suddenly Jellia Jamb exclaimed:

"There is nothing more to eat! The Hungry Tiger has consumed everything!"

"But that is not the worst of it," declared the Tiger, mournfully. "Somewhere or somehow, I've actually lost my appetite!"

Dorothy's Magic Belt

passed several very happy weeks in the Land of Oz as the guest of the royal Ozma, who delighted to please and interest the little Kansas girl. Many new acquaintances were formed and many old ones renewed, and wherever she went Dorothy found herself among friends.

One day, however, as she sat in Ozma's private room, she noticed hanging upon the wall a picture which constantly changed in appearance, at one time showing a meadow and at another time a forest, a lake or a village.

"How curious!" she exclaimed, after watching the shifting scenes for a few moments.

"Yes," said Ozma, "that is really a wonderful invention in magic. If I wish to see any part of the world or any person living, I need only express the wish and it is shown in the picture."

"May I use it?" asked Dorothy, eagerly.

"Of course, my dear."

"Then I'd like to see the old Kansas farm, and Aunt Em," said the girl.

Instantly the well remembered farm-house appeared in the picture, and Aunt Em could be seen quite plainly. She was engaged in washing dishes by the kitchen window and seemed quite well and contented. The hired men and the teams were in the harvest fields behind the house, and the corn and wheat seemed to the child to be in prime condition. On the side porch Dorothy's pet dog, Toto, was lying fast asleep in the sun, and to her surprise old Speckles was running around with a brood of twelve new chickens trailing after her.

"Everything seems all right at home," said Dorothy, with a sigh of relief. "Now I wonder what Uncle Henry is doing."

The scene in the picture at once shifted to Australia, where, in a pleasant room in Sydney, Uncle Henry was seated in an easy chair, solemnly smoking his briar pipe. He looked sad and lonely, and his hair was now quite white and his hands and face thin and wasted.

"Oh!" cried Dorothy, in an anxious voice, "I'm sure Uncle Henry isn't getting any better, and it's because he is worried about me. Ozma, dear, I must go to him at once!"

"How can you?" asked Ozma.

"I don't know," replied Dorothy; "but let us go to Glinda the Good. I'm sure she will help me, and advise me how to get to Uncle Henry."

Ozma readily agreed to this plan and caused the Saw-Horse to be harnessed to a pretty green and pink phaeton, and the two girls rode away to visit the famous sorceress.

Glinda received them graciously, and listened to Dorothy's story with attention.

"I have the magic belt, you know," said the little girl. "If I buckled it around my waist and commanded it to take me to Uncle Henry, wouldn't it do it?"

"I think so," replied Glinda, with a smile.

"And then," continued Dorothy, "if I ever wanted to come back here again, the belt would bring me."

"In that you are wrong," said the sorceress. "The belt has magical powers only while it is in some fairy country, such as the Land of Oz, or the Land of Ev. Indeed, my little friend, were you to wear

"THAT IS A WISE PLAN," REPLIED GLINDA

it and wish yourself in Australia, with your uncle, the wish would doubtless be fulfilled, because it was made in fairyland. But you would not find the magic belt around you when you arrived at your destination."

"What would become of it?" asked the girl.

"It would be lost, as were your silver shoes when you visited Oz before, and no one would ever see it again. It seems too bad to destroy the use of the magic belt in that way, doesn't it?"

"Then," said Dorothy, after a moment's thought, "I will give the magic belt to Ozma, for she can use it in her own country. And she can wish me transported to Uncle Henry without losing the belt."

"That is a wise plan," replied Glinda.

So they rode back to the Emerald City, and on the way it was arranged that every Saturday morning Ozma would look at Dorothy in her magic picture, wherever the little girl might chance to be. And, if she saw Dorothy make a certain signal, then Ozma would know that the little Kansas girl wanted to revisit the Land of Oz, and by means of the Nome King's magic belt would wish that she might instantly return.

This having been agreed upon, Dorothy bade good-bye to all her friends. Tiktok wanted to go to Australia, too; but Dorothy knew that the machine man would never do for a servant in a civilized country, and the chances were that his machinery wouldn't work at all. So she left him in Ozma's care.

Billina, on the contrary, preferred the Land of Oz to any other country, and refused to accompany Dorothy.

"The bugs and ants that I find here are the finest flavored in the world," declared the yellow hen, "and there are plenty of them. So here I shall end my days; and I must say, Dorothy, my dear, that you are very foolish to go back into that stupid, humdrum world again."

"Uncle Henry needs me," said Dorothy, simply; and every one except Billina thought it was right that she should go.

All Dorothy's friends of the Land of Oz—both old and new—gathered in a group in front of the palace to bid her a sorrowful good-bye and to wish her long life and happiness. After much hand shaking, Dorothy kissed Ozma once more, and then handed her the Nome King's magic belt, saying:

"Now, dear Princess, when I wave my handkerchief, please wish me with Uncle Henry. I'm awf'ly sorry to leave you—and the Scarecrow—and the Tin Woodman—and the Cowardly Lion—and Tiktok—and—and everybody—but I do want my Uncle Henry! So good-bye, all of you."

Then the little girl stood on one of the big emeralds which decorated the courtyard, and after looking once again at each of her friends, waved her handkerchief.

✧ ✧ ✧

"No," said Dorothy, "I wasn't drowned at all. And I've come to nurse you and take care of you, Uncle Henry, and you must promise to get well as soon as poss'ble."

Uncle Henry smiled and cuddled his little niece close in his lap.

"I'm better already, my darling," said he.

THE
EMERALD CITY
OF
OZ

TO
HER ROYAL HIGHNESS
CYNTHIA II
OF SYRACUSE;
AND TO EACH AND EVERY ONE
OF THE CHILDREN WHOSE LOYAL
APPRECIATION HAS ENCOURAGED
ME TO WRITE THE OZ BOOKS
THIS VOLUME IS AFFECTIONATELY
DEDICATED.

THE EMERALD
CITY OF OZ

BY

L. FRANK BAUM

AUTHOR OF THE ROAD TO OZ, DOROTHY AND THE WIZARD IN OZ,
THE LAND OF OZ, ETC.

ILLUSTRATED BY

JOHN R. NEILL

—

CHICAGO
THE REILLY & BRITTON CO.
PUBLISHERS

AUTHOR'S NOTE

Perhaps I should admit on the title page that this book is "By L. Frank Baum and his correspondents," for I have used many suggestions conveyed to me in letters from children. Once on a time I really imagined myself "an author of fairy tales," but now I am merely an editor or private secretary for a host of youngsters whose ideas I am requested to weave into the thread of my stories.

These ideas are often clever. They are also logical and interesting. So I have used them whenever I could find an opportunity, and it is but just that I acknowledge my indebtedness to my little friends.

My, what imaginations these children have developed! Sometimes I am fairly astounded by their daring and genius. There will be no lack of fairy-tale authors in the future, I am sure. My readers have told me what to do with Dorothy, and Aunt Em and Uncle Henry, and I have obeyed their mandates. They have also given me a variety of subjects to write about in the future: enough, in fact, to keep me busy for some time. I am very proud of this alliance. Children love these stories because children have helped to create them. My readers know what they want and realize that I try to please them. The result is very satisfactory to the publishers, to me, and (I am quite sure) to the children.

I hope, my dears, it will be a long time before we are obliged to dissolve partnership.

L. FRANK BAUM.

Coronado, 1910

LIST OF CHAPTERS

How THE NOME KING BECAME ANGRY

CHAPTER ONE

The Nome King was in an angry mood, and at such times he was very disagreeable. Every one kept away from him, even his Chief Steward Kaliko.

Therefore the King stormed and raved all by himself, walking up and down in his jewel-studded cavern and getting angrier all the time. Then he remembered that it was no fun being angry unless he had some one to frighten and make miserable, and he rushed to his big gong and made it clatter as loud as he could.

In came the Chief Steward, trying not to show the Nome King how frightened he was.

"Send the Chief Counselor here!" shouted the angry monarch.

Kaliko ran out as fast as his spindle legs could carry his fat round body, and soon the Chief Counselor entered the cavern. The King scowled and said to him:

"I'm in great trouble over the loss of my Magic Belt. Every little while I want to do something magical, and find I can't because the Belt is gone. That makes me angry, and when I'm angry I can't have a good time. Now, what do you advise?"

"Some people," said the Chief Counselor, "enjoy getting angry."

"But not all the time," declared the King. "To be angry once in a while is really good fun, because it makes others so miserable. But to be angry morning, noon and night, as I am, grows monotonous and prevents my gaining any other pleasure in life. Now, what do you advise?"

"Why, if you are angry because you want to do magical things and can't, and if you don't want to get angry at all, my advice is not to want to do magical things."

Hearing this, the King glared at his Counselor with a furious expression and tugged at his own long white whiskers until he pulled them so hard that he yelled with pain.

"You are a fool!" he exclaimed.

"I share that honor with Your Majesty," said the Chief Counselor.

The King roared with rage and stamped his foot.

"Ho, there, my guards!" he cried. "Ho" is a royal way of saying, "Come here." So, when the guards had hoed, the King said to them:

"Take this Chief Counselor and throw him away."

Then the guards took the Chief Counselor, and bound him with chains to prevent his struggling, and threw him away. And the King paced up and down his cavern more angry than before.

Finally he rushed to his big gong and made it clatter like a fire-alarm. Kaliko appeared again, trembling and white with fear.

"Fetch my pipe!" yelled the King.

"Your pipe is already here, Your Majesty," replied Kaliko.

"Then get my tobacco!" roared the King.

"The tobacco is in your pipe, Your Majesty," returned the Steward.

"Then bring a live coal from the furnace!" commanded the King.

"The tobacco is lighted, and Your Majesty is already smoking your pipe," answered the Steward.

"Why, so I am!" said the King, who had forgotten this fact; "but you are very rude to remind me of it."

"I am a lowborn, miserable villain," declared the Chief Steward, humbly.

The Nome King could think of nothing to say next, so he puffed

away at his pipe and paced up and down the room. Finally he remembered how angry he was, and cried out:

"What do you mean, Kaliko, by being so contented when your monarch is unhappy?"

"What makes you unhappy?" asked the Steward.

"I've lost my Magic Belt. A little girl named Dorothy, who was here with Ozma of Oz, stole my Belt and carried it away with her," said the King, grinding his teeth with rage.

"She captured it in a fair fight," Kaliko ventured to say.

"But I want it! I must have it! Half my power is gone with that Belt!" roared the King.

"You will have to go to the Land of Oz to recover it, and Your Majesty can't get to the Land of Oz in any possible way," said the Steward, yawning because he had been on duty ninety-six hours, and was sleepy.

"Why not?" asked the King.

"Because there is a deadly desert all around that fairy country, which no one is able to cross. You know that fact as well as I do, Your Majesty. Never mind the lost Belt. You have plenty of power left, for you rule this underground kingdom like a tyrant, and thousands of Nomes obey your commands. I advise you to drink a glass of melted silver, to quiet your nerves, and then go to bed."

The King grabbed a big ruby and threw it at Kaliko's head. The Steward ducked to escape the heavy jewel, which crashed against the door just over his left ear.

"Get out of my sight! Vanish! Go away—and send General Blug here," screamed the Nome King.

Kaliko hastily withdrew, and the Nome King stamped up and down until the General of his armies appeared.

This Nome was known far and wide as a terrible fighter and a cruel, desperate commander. He had fifty thousand Nome soldiers, all well drilled, who feared nothing but their stern master. Yet General Blug was a trifle uneasy when he arrived and saw how angry the Nome King was.

"Ha! So you're here!" cried the King.

"So I am," said the General.

"March your army at once to the Land of Oz, capture and destroy the Emerald City, and bring back to me my Magic Belt!" roared the King.

"You're crazy," calmly remarked the General.

"What's that? What's that? What's that?" And the Nome King danced around on his pointed toes, he was so enraged.

"You don't know what you're talking about," continued the General, seating himself upon a large cut diamond. "I advise you to stand in a corner and count sixty before you speak again. By that time you may be more sensible."

The King looked around for something to throw at General Blug, but as nothing was handy he began to consider that perhaps the man was right and he had been talking foolishly. So he merely threw himself into his glittering throne and tipped his crown over his ear and curled his feet up under him and glared wickedly at Blug.

"In the first place," said the General, "we cannot march across the deadly desert to the Land of Oz; and, if we could, the Ruler of that country, Princess Ozma, has certain fairy powers that would render my army helpless. Had you not lost your Magic Belt we might have some chance of defeating Ozma; but the Belt is gone."

"I want it!" screamed the King. "I must have it."

"Well, then, let us try in a sensible way to get it," replied the General. "The Belt was captured by a little girl named Dorothy, who lives in Kansas, in the United States of America."

"But she left it in the Emerald City, with Ozma," declared the King.

"How do you know that?" asked the General.

"One of my spies, who is a Blackbird, flew over the desert to the Land of Oz, and saw the Magic Belt in Ozma's palace," replied the King with a groan.

"Now, that gives me an idea," said General Blug, thoughtfully. "There are two ways to get to the Land of Oz without traveling across the sandy desert."

"What are they?" demanded the King, eagerly.

"One way is *over* the desert, through the air; and the other way is *under* the desert, through the earth."

Hearing this the Nome King uttered a yell of joy and leaped from his throne, to resume his wild walk up and down the cavern.

"That's it, Blug!" he shouted. "That's the idea, General! I'm King of the Under World, and my subjects are all miners. I'll make a secret tunnel under the desert to the Land of Oz—yes! right up to the Emerald City—and you will march your armies there and capture the whole country!"

"Softly, softly, Your Majesty. Don't go too fast," warned the General. "My Nomes are good fighters, but they are not strong enough to conquer the Emerald City."

"Are you sure?" asked the King.

"Absolutely certain, Your Majesty."

"Then what am I to do?"

"Give up the idea and mind your own business," advised the General. "You have plenty to do trying to rule your underground kingdom."

"But I want that Magic Belt—and I'm going to have it!" roared the Nome King.

"I'd like to see you get it," replied the General, laughing maliciously.

The King was by this time so exasperated that he picked up his scepter, which had a heavy ball, made from a sapphire, at the end of it, and threw it with all his force at General Blug. The sapphire hit the General upon his forehead and knocked him flat upon the ground, where he lay motionless. Then the King rang his gong and told his guards to drag out the General and throw him away; which they did.

This Nome King was named Roquat the Red, and no one loved

him. He was a bad man and a powerful monarch, and he had resolved to destroy the Land of Oz and its magnificent Emerald City, to enslave Princess Ozma and little Dorothy and all the Oz people, and recover his Magic Belt. This same Belt had once enabled Roquat the Red to carry out many wicked plans; but that was before Ozma and her people marched to the underground cavern and captured it. The Nome King could not forgive Dorothy or Princess Ozma, and he had determined to be revenged upon them.

But they, for their part, did not know they had so dangerous an enemy. Indeed, Ozma and Dorothy had both almost forgotten that such a person as the Nome King yet lived under the mountains of the Land of Ev—which lay just across the deadly desert to the south of the Land of Oz.

An unsuspected enemy is doubly dangerous.

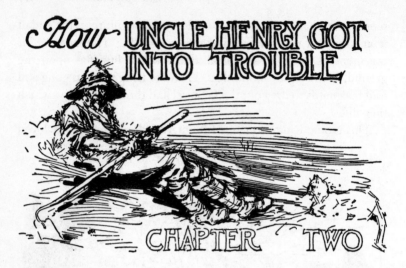

How Uncle Henry Got Into Trouble

CHAPTER TWO

Dorothy Gale lived on a farm in Kansas, with her Aunt Em and her Uncle Henry. It was not a big farm, nor a very good one, because sometimes the rain did not come when the crops needed it, and then everything withered and dried up. Once a cyclone had carried away Uncle Henry's house, so that he was obliged to build another; and as he was a poor man he had to mortgage his farm to get the money to pay for the new house. Then his health became bad and he was too feeble to work. The doctor ordered him to take a sea voyage and he went to Australia and took Dorothy with him. That cost a lot of money, too.

Uncle Henry grew poorer every year, and the crops raised on the farm only bought food for the family. Therefore the mortgage could not be paid. At last the banker who had loaned him the money said that if he did not pay on a certain day, his farm would be taken away from him.

This worried Uncle Henry a good deal, for without the farm he would have no way to earn a living. He was a good man, and worked in the fields as hard as he could; and Aunt Em did all the housework, with Dorothy's help. Yet they did not seem to get along.

This little girl, Dorothy, was like dozens of little girls you know. She was loving and usually sweet-tempered, and had a round rosy face and earnest eyes. Life was a serious thing to Dorothy, and a wonderful thing, too, for she had encountered more strange adventures in her short life than many other girls of her age.

Aunt Em once said she thought the fairies must have marked Dorothy at her birth, because she had wandered into strange places and had always been protected by some unseen power. As for Uncle Henry, he thought his little niece merely a dreamer, as her dead mother had been, for he could not quite believe all the curious stories Dorothy told them of the Land of Oz, which she had several times visited. He did not think that she tried to deceive her uncle and aunt, but he imagined that she had dreamed all of those astonishing adventures, and that the dreams had been so real to her that she had come to believe them true.

Whatever the explanation might be, it was certain that Dorothy had been absent from her Kansas home for several long periods, always disappearing unexpectedly, yet always coming back safe and sound, with amazing tales of where she had been and the unusual people she had met. Her uncle and aunt listened to her stories eagerly and in spite of their doubts began to feel that the little girl had gained a lot of experience and wisdom that were unaccountable in this age, when fairies are supposed no longer to exist.

Most of Dorothy's stories were about the Land of Oz, with its beautiful Emerald City and a lovely girl Ruler named Ozma, who was the most faithful friend of the little Kansas girl. When Dorothy told about the riches of this fairy country Uncle Henry would sigh, for he knew that a single one of the great emeralds that were so common there would pay all his debts and leave his farm free. But Dorothy never brought any jewels home with her, so their poverty became greater every year.

When the banker told Uncle Henry that he must pay the money in thirty days or leave the farm, the poor man was in despair, as he knew he could not possibly get the money. So he told his wife, Aunt Em, of his trouble, and she first cried a little and then said that they must be brave and do the best they could, and go away somewhere and try to earn an honest living. But they were getting old and feeble and she feared that they could not take care of Dorothy as well as they had formerly done. Probably the little girl would also be obliged to go to work.

They did not tell their niece the sad news for several days, not wishing to make her unhappy; but one morning the little girl found Aunt Em softly crying while Uncle Henry tried to comfort her. Then Dorothy asked them to tell her what was the matter.

"We must give up the farm, my dear," replied her uncle, sadly, "and wander away into the world to work for our living."

The girl listened quite seriously, for she had not known before how desperately poor they were.

"We don't mind for ourselves," said her aunt, stroking the little girl's head tenderly; "but we love you as if you were our own child, and we are heart-broken to think that you must also endure poverty, and work for a living before you have grown big and strong."

"What could I do to earn money?" asked Dorothy.

"You might do housework for some one, dear, you are so handy; or perhaps you could be a nurse-maid to little children. I'm sure I don't know exactly what you *can* do to earn money, but if your uncle and I are able to support you we will do it willingly, and send you to school. We fear, though, that we shall have much trouble in earning a living for ourselves. No one wants to employ old people who are broken down in health, as we are."

Dorothy smiled.

"Wouldn't it be funny," she said, "for me to do housework in Kansas, when I'm a Princess in the Land of Oz?"

"A Princess!" they both exclaimed, astonished.

"Yes; Ozma made me a Princess some time ago, and she has often begged me to come and live always in the Emerald City," said the child.

Her uncle and aunt looked at each other in amazement. Then the man said:

"Do you suppose you could manage to return to your fairyland, my dear?"

"Oh, yes," replied Dorothy; "I could do that easily."

"How?" asked Aunt Em.

"Ozma sees me every day at four o'clock, in her Magic Picture. She can see me wherever I am, no matter what I am doing. And at that time, if I make a certain secret sign, she will send for me by means of the Magic Belt, which I once captured from the Nome King. Then, in the wink of an eye, I shall be with Ozma in her palace."

The elder people remained silent for some time after Dorothy had spoken. Finally Aunt Em said, with another sigh of regret:

"If that is the case, Dorothy, perhaps you'd better go and live in the Emerald City. It will break our hearts to lose you from our lives, but you will be so much better off with your fairy friends that it seems wisest and best for you to go."

"I'm not so sure about that," remarked Uncle Henry, shaking his gray head doubtfully. "These things all seem real to Dorothy, I know; but I'm afraid our little girl won't find her fairyland just what she has dreamed it to be. It would make me very unhappy to think that she was wandering among strangers who might be unkind to her."

Dorothy laughed merrily at this speech, and then she became very sober again, for she could see how all this trouble was worrying her aunt and uncle, and knew that unless she found a way to help them their future lives would be quite miserable and unhappy. She knew that she *could* help them. She had thought of a way already. Yet she did not tell them at once what it was, because she must ask Ozma's consent before she would be able to carry out her plans.

So she only said:

"If you will promise not to worry a bit about me, I'll go to the Land of Oz this very afternoon. And I'll make a promise, too; that you shall both see me again before the day comes when you must leave this farm."

"The day isn't far away, now," her uncle sadly replied. "I did not tell you of our trouble until I was obliged to, dear Dorothy, so the evil time is near at hand. But if you are quite sure your fairy friends will give you a home, it will be best for you to go to them, as your aunt says."

That was why Dorothy went to her little room in the attic that afternoon, taking with her a small dog named Toto. The dog had curly black hair and big brown eyes and loved Dorothy very dearly.

The child had kissed her uncle and aunt affectionately before she went upstairs, and now she looked around her little room rather wistfully, gazing at the simple trinkets and worn calico and gingham dresses, as if they were old friends. She was tempted at first to make a bundle of them, yet she knew very well that they would be of no use to her in her future life.

She sat down upon a broken-backed chair—the only one the room contained—and holding Toto in her arms waited patiently until the clock struck four.

Then she made the secret signal that had been agreed upon between her and Ozma.

Uncle Henry and Aunt Em waited downstairs. They were uneasy and a good deal excited, for this is a practical humdrum world, and it seemed to them quite impossible that their little niece could vanish from her home and travel instantly to fairyland.

So they watched the stairs, which seemed to be the only way that Dorothy could get out of the farm-house, and they watched them a long time. They heard the clock strike four, but there was no sound from above.

Half-past four came, and now they were too impatient to wait any longer. Softly they crept up the stairs to the door of the little girl's room.

"Dorothy! Dorothy!" they called.

There was no answer.

They opened the door and looked in.

The room was empty.

How OZMA GRANTED DOROTHY'S REQUEST

CHAPTER THREE

I suppose you have read so much about the magnificent Emerald City that there is little need for me to describe it here. It is the Capital City of the Land of Oz, which is justly considered the most attractive and delightful fairyland in all the world.

The Emerald City is built all of beautiful marbles in which are set a profusion of emeralds, every one exquisitely cut and of very great size. There are other jewels used in the decorations inside the houses and palaces, such as rubies, diamonds, sapphires, amethysts and turquoises. But in the streets and upon the outside of the buildings only emeralds appear, from which circumstance the place is named the Emerald City of Oz. It has nine thousand six hundred and fifty-four buildings, in which lived fifty-seven thousand three hundred and eighteen people, up to the time my story opens.

All the surrounding country, extending to the borders of the desert which enclosed it upon every side, was full of pretty and comfortable farm-houses, in which resided those inhabitants of Oz who preferred country to city life.

Altogether there were more than half a million people in the Land of Oz—although some of them, as you will soon learn, were not made of flesh and blood as we are—and every inhabitant of that favored country was happy and prosperous.

No disease of any sort was ever known among the Ozites, and so no one ever died unless he met with an accident that prevented him from living. This happened very seldom, indeed. There were no poor people in the Land of Oz, because there was no such thing as money, and all property of every sort belonged to the Ruler. The people were her children, and she cared for them. Each person was given freely by his neighbors whatever he required for his use, which is as much as any one may reasonably desire. Some tilled the lands and raised great crops of grain, which was divided equally among the entire population, so that all had enough. There were many tailors and dressmakers and shoemakers and the like, who made things that any who desired them might wear. Likewise there were jewelers who made ornaments for the person, which pleased and beautified the people, and these ornaments also were free to those who asked for them. Each man and woman, no matter what he or she produced for the good of the community, was supplied by the neighbors with food and clothing and a house and furniture and ornaments and games. If by chance the supply ever ran short, more was taken from the great storehouses of the Ruler, which were afterward filled up again when there was more of any article than the people needed.

Every one worked half the time and played half the time, and the people enjoyed the work as much as they did the play, because it is good to be occupied and to have something to do. There were no cruel overseers set to watch them, and no one to rebuke them or to find fault with them. So each one was proud to do all he could for his friends and neighbors, and was glad when they would accept the things he produced.

You will know, by what I have here told you, that the Land of Oz was a remarkable country. I do not suppose such an arrangement would be practical with us, but Dorothy assures me that it works finely with the Oz people.

Oz being a fairy country, the people were, of course, fairy people; but that does not mean that all of them were very unlike the people of our own world. There were all sorts of queer characters among them, but not a single one who was evil, or who possessed a selfish or violent nature. They were peaceful, kind-hearted, loving and merry, and every inhabitant adored the beautiful girl who ruled them, and delighted to obey her every command.

In spite of all I have said in a general way, there were some parts of the Land of Oz not quite so pleasant as the farming country and the Emerald City which was its center. Far away in the South Country there lived in the mountains a band of strange people called Hammer-Heads, because they had no arms and used their flat heads to pound any one who came near them. Their necks were like rubber, so that they could shoot out their heads to quite a distance, and afterward draw them back again to their shoulders. The Hammer-Heads were called the "Wild People," but never harmed any but those who disturbed them in the mountains where they lived.

In some of the dense forests there lived great beasts of every sort; yet these were for the most part harmless and even sociable, and conversed agreeably with those who visited their haunts. The Kalidahs—beasts with bodies like bears and heads like tigers—had once been fierce and bloodthirsty, but even they were now nearly all tamed, although at times one or another of them would get cross and disagreeable.

Not so tame were the Fighting Trees, which had a forest of their own. If any one approached them these curious trees would bend down their branches, twine them around the intruders, and hurl them away.

But these unpleasant things existed only in a few remote parts of the Land of Oz. I suppose every country has some drawbacks, so even this almost perfect fairyland could not be quite perfect. Once there had been wicked witches in the land, too; but now these had all been destroyed; so, as I said, only peace and happiness reigned in Oz.

For some time Ozma has ruled over this fair country, and never was a Ruler more popular or beloved. She is said to be the most beautiful girl the world has ever known, and her heart and mind are as lovely as her person.

Dorothy Gale had several times visited the Emerald City and experienced adventures in the Land of Oz, so that she and Ozma had now become firm friends. The girl Ruler had even made Dorothy a Princess of Oz, and had often implored her to come to Ozma's stately palace and live there always; but Dorothy had been loyal to her Aunt Em and Uncle Henry, who had cared for her since she was a baby, and she had refused to leave them because she knew they would be lonely without her.

However, Dorothy now realized that things were going to be different with her uncle and aunt from this time forth, so after giving the matter deep thought she decided to ask Ozma to grant her a very great favor.

A few seconds after she had made the secret signal in her little bedchamber, the Kansas girl was seated in a lovely room in Ozma's palace in the Emerald City of Oz. When the first loving kisses and embraces had been exchanged, the fair Ruler inquired:

"What is the matter, dear? I know something unpleasant has happened to you, for your face was very sober when I saw it in my Magic Picture. And whenever you signal me to transport you to this safe place, where you are always welcome, I know you are in danger or in trouble."

Dorothy sighed.

"This time, Ozma, it isn't I," she replied. "But it's worse, I guess, for Uncle Henry and Aunt Em are in a heap of trouble, and there seems no way for them to get out of it—anyhow, not while they live in Kansas."

"Tell me about it, Dorothy," said Ozma, with ready sympathy.

"Why, you see Uncle Henry is poor; for the farm in Kansas doesn't 'mount to much, as farms go. So one day Uncle Henry borrowed some money, and wrote a letter saying that if he didn't pay the money back they could take his farm for pay. Course he 'spected to pay by making money from the farm; but he just couldn't. An' so they're going to take the farm, and Uncle Henry and Aunt Em won't have any place to live. They're pretty old to do much hard work, Ozma; so I'll have to work for them, unless—"

Ozma had been thoughtful during the story, but now she smiled and pressed her little friend's hand.

"Unless what, dear?" she asked.

Dorothy hesitated, because her request meant so much to them all.

"Well," said she, "I'd like to live here in the Land of Oz, where you've often 'vited me to live. But I can't, you know, unless Uncle Henry and Aunt Em could live here too."

"Of course not," exclaimed the Ruler of Oz, laughing gaily. "So, in order to get you, little friend, we must invite your uncle and aunt to live in Oz, also."

"Oh, will you, Ozma?" cried Dorothy, clasping her chubby little hands eagerly. "Will you bring them here with the Magic Belt, and give them a nice little farm in the Munchkin Country, or the Winkie Country—or some other place?"

"To be sure," answered Ozma, full of joy at the chance to please her little friend. "I have long been thinking of this very thing, Dorothy dear, and often I have had it in my mind to propose it to you. I am sure your uncle and aunt must be good and worthy people, or you would not love them so much; and for *your* friends, Princess, there is always room in the Land of Oz."

Dorothy was delighted, yet not altogether surprised, for she had clung to the hope that Ozma would be kind enough to grant her request. When, indeed, had her powerful and faithful friend refused her anything?

"But you must not call me 'Princess,' " she said; "for after this I shall live on the little farm with Uncle Henry and Aunt Em, and princesses ought not to live on farms."

"Princess Dorothy will not," replied Ozma, with her sweet smile. "You are going to live in your own rooms in this palace, and be my constant companion."

"But Uncle Henry—" began Dorothy.

"Oh, he is old, and has worked enough in his lifetime," interrupted the girl Ruler; "so we must find a place for your uncle and aunt where they will be comfortable and happy and need not work more than they care to. When shall we transport them here, Dorothy?"

"I promised to go and see them again before they were turned out of the farm-house," answered Dorothy; "so—perhaps next Saturday—"

"But why wait so long?" asked Ozma. "And why make the journey back to Kansas again? Let us surprise them, and bring them here without any warning."

"I'm not sure that they believe in the Land of Oz," said Dorothy, "though I've told 'em 'bout it lots of times."

"They'll believe when they see it," declared Ozma; "and if they are told they are to make a magical journey to our fairyland, it may make them nervous. I think the best way will be to use the Magic Belt without warning them, and when they have arrived you can explain to them whatever they do not understand."

"Perhaps that's best," decided Dorothy. "There isn't much use in their staying at the farm until they are put out, 'cause it's much nicer here."

"Then to-morrow morning they shall come here," said Princess

Ozma. "I will order Jellia Jamb, who is the palace housekeeper, to have rooms all prepared for them, and after breakfast we will get the Magic Belt and by its aid transport your uncle and aunt to the Emerald City."

"Thank you, Ozma!" cried Dorothy, kissing her friend gratefully.

"And now," Ozma proposed, "let us take a walk in the gardens before we dress for dinner. Come, Dorothy dear!"

How THE NOME KING PLANNED REVENGE

CHAPTER FOUR

The reason most people are bad is because they do not try to be good. Now, the Nome King had never tried to be good, so he was very bad indeed. Having decided to conquer the Land of Oz and to destroy the Emerald City and enslave all its people, King Roquat the Red kept planning ways to do this dreadful thing, and the more he planned the more he believed he would be able to accomplish it.

About the time Dorothy went to Ozma the Nome King called his Chief Steward to him and said:

"Kaliko, I think I shall make you the General of my armies."

"I think you won't," replied Kaliko, positively.

"Why not?" inquired the King, reaching for his scepter with the big sapphire.

"Because I'm your Chief Steward, and know nothing of warfare," said Kaliko, preparing to dodge if anything were thrown at him. "I manage all the affairs of your kingdom better than you could yourself, and you'll never find another Steward as good as I am. But there are a hundred Nomes better fitted to command your army, and your Generals get thrown away so often that I have no desire to be one of them."

"Ah, there is some truth in your remarks, Kaliko," remarked the

King, deciding not to throw the scepter. "Summon my army to assemble in the Great Cavern."

Kaliko bowed and retired, and in a few minutes returned to say that the army was assembled. So the King went out upon a balcony that overlooked the Great Cavern, where fifty thousand Nomes, all armed with swords and pikes, stood marshaled in military array.

When they were not required as soldiers all these Nomes were metal workers and miners, and they had hammered so much at the forges and dug so hard with pick and shovel that they had acquired great muscular strength. They were strangely formed creatures, rather round and not very tall. Their toes were curly and their ears broad and flat.

In time of war every Nome left his forge or mine and became part of the great army of King Roquat. The soldiers wore rock-colored uniforms and were excellently drilled.

The King looked upon this tremendous army, which stood silently arrayed before him, and a cruel smile curled the corners of his mouth, for he saw that his legions were very powerful. Then he addressed them from the balcony, saying:

"I have thrown away General Blug, because he did not please me. So I want another General to command this army. Who is next in command?"

"I am," replied Colonel Crinkle, a dapper-looking Nome, as he stepped forward to salute his monarch.

The King looked at him carefully and said:

"I want you to march this army through an underground tunnel, which I am going to bore, to the Emerald City of Oz. When you get there I want you to conquer the Oz people, destroy them and their city, and bring all their gold and silver and precious stones back to my cavern. Also you are to recapture my Magic Belt and return it to me. Will you do this, General Crinkle?"

"No, Your Majesty," replied the Nome; "for it can't be done."

"Oh, indeed!" exclaimed the King. Then he turned to his servants and said: "Please take General Crinkle to the torture chamber. There you will kindly slice him into thin slices. Afterward you may feed him to the seven-headed dogs."

"Anything to oblige Your Majesty," replied the servants, politely, and led the condemned man away.

When they had gone the King addressed the army again.

"Listen!" said he. "The General who is to command my armies must promise to carry out my orders. If he fails he will share the fate of poor Crinkle. Now, then, who will volunteer to lead my hosts to the Emerald City?"

For a time no one moved and all were silent. Then an old Nome with white whiskers so long that they were tied around his waist to prevent their tripping him up, stepped out of the ranks and saluted the King.

"I'd like to ask a few questions, Your Majesty," he said.

"Go ahead," replied the King.

"These Oz people are quite good, are they not?"

"As good as apple pie," said the King.

"And they are happy, I suppose?" continued the old Nome.

"Happy as the day is long," said the King.

"And contented and prosperous?" inquired the Nome.

"Very much so," said the King.

"Well, Your Majesty," remarked he of the white whiskers, "I think I should like to undertake the job, so I'll be your General. I hate good people; I detest happy people; I'm opposed to any one who is contented and prosperous. That is why I am so fond of Your Majesty. Make me your General and I'll promise to conquer and destroy the Oz people. If I fail I'm ready to be sliced thin and fed to the seven-headed dogs."

"Very good! Very good, indeed! That's the way to talk!" cried Roquat the Red, who was greatly pleased. "What is your name, General?"

"I'm called Guph, Your Majesty."

"Well, Guph, come with me to my private cave and we'll talk it over." Then he turned to the army. "Nomes and soldiers," said he, "you are to obey the commands of General Guph until he becomes dog-feed. Any man who fails to obey his new General will be promptly thrown away. You are now dismissed."

Guph went to the King's private cave and sat down upon an

amethyst chair and put his feet on the arm of the King's ruby throne. Then he lighted his pipe and threw the live coal he had taken from his pocket upon the King's left foot and puffed the smoke into the King's eyes and made himself comfortable. For he was a wise old Nome, and he knew that the best way to get along with Roquat the Red was to show that he was not afraid of him.

"I'm ready for the talk, Your Majesty," he said.

The King coughed and looked at his new General fiercely.

"Do you not tremble to take such liberties with your monarch?" he asked.

"Oh, no," said Guph, calmly, and he blew a wreath of smoke that curled around the King's nose and made him sneeze. "You want to conquer the Emerald City, and I'm the only Nome in all your dominions who can conquer it. So you will be very careful not to hurt me until I have carried out your wishes. After that—"

"Well, what then?" inquired the King.

"Then you will be so grateful to me that you won't care to hurt me," replied the General.

"That is a very good argument," said Roquat. "But suppose you fail?"

"Then it's the slicing machine. I agree to that," announced Guph. "But if you do as I tell you there will be no failure. The trouble with you, Roquat, is that you don't think carefully enough. I do. You would go ahead and march through your tunnel into Oz, and get defeated and driven back. I won't. And the reason I won't is because when I march I'll have all my plans made, and a host of allies to assist my Nomes."

"What do you mean by that?" asked the King.

"I'll explain, King Roquat. You're going to attack a fairy country, and a mighty fairy country, too. They haven't much of an army in Oz, but the Princess who rules them has a fairy wand; and the little girl Dorothy has your Magic Belt; and at the North of the Emerald City lives a clever sorceress called Glinda the Good, who commands the spirits of the air. Also I have heard that there is a wonderful Wizard in Ozma's palace, who is so skillful that people used to pay him money in America to see him perform. So you see it will be no easy thing to overcome all this magic."

"We have fifty thousand soldiers!" cried the King, proudly.

"Yes; but they are Nomes," remarked Guph, taking a silk handkerchief from the King's pocket and wiping his own pointed shoes with it. "Nomes are immortals, but they are not strong on magic. When you lost your famous Belt the greater part of your own power was gone from you. Against Ozma you and your Nomes would have no show at all."

Roquat's eyes flashed angrily.

"Then away you go to the slicing machine!" he cried.

"Not yet," said the General, filling his pipe from the King's private tobacco pouch.

"What do you propose to do?" asked the monarch.

"I propose to obtain the power we need," answered Guph. "There are a good many evil creatures who have magic powers sufficient to destroy and conquer the Land of Oz. We will get them on our side, band them all together, and then take Ozma and her people by surprise. It's all very simple and easy when you know how. Alone we should be helpless to injure the Ruler of Oz, but with the aid of the evil powers we can summon we shall easily succeed."

King Roquat was delighted with this idea, for he realized how clever it was.

"Surely, Guph, you are the greatest General I have ever had!" he exclaimed, his eyes sparkling with joy. "You must go at once and make arrangements with the evil powers to assist us, and meantime I'll begin to dig the tunnel."

"I thought you'd agree with me, Roquat," replied the new General. "I'll start this very afternoon to visit the Chief of the Whimsies."

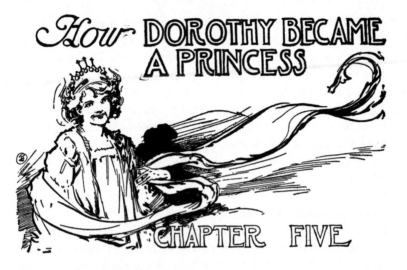

How DOROTHY BECAME A PRINCESS

CHAPTER FIVE

When the people of the Emerald City heard that Dorothy had returned to them every one was eager to see her, for the little girl was a general favorite in the Land of Oz. From time to time some of the folk from the great outside world had found their way into this fairyland, but all except one had been companions of Dorothy and had turned out to be very agreeable people. The exception I speak of was the wonderful Wizard of Oz, a sleight-of-hand performer from Omaha who went up in a balloon and was carried by a current of air to the Emerald City. His queer and puzzling tricks made the people of Oz believe him a great wizard for a time, and he ruled over them until Dorothy arrived on her first visit and showed the Wizard to be a mere humbug. He was a gentle, kindly-hearted little man, and Dorothy grew to like him afterward. When, after an absence, the Wizard returned to the Land of Oz, Ozma received him graciously and gave him a home in a part of the palace.

In addition to the Wizard two other personages from the outside world had been allowed to make their home in the Emerald City. The first was a quaint Shaggy Man, whom Ozma had made the Governor of the Royal Storehouses, and the second a Yellow Hen named Billina, who had a fine house in the gardens back of the palace, where she looked after a large family. Both these had been old comrades of Dorothy, so you see the little girl was quite an important personage in Oz, and the people thought she had brought them good luck, and loved her next best to Ozma. During her several visits this little girl had been the means of destroying two wicked witches who oppressed the people, and she had discovered a live scarecrow who was now one of the most popular personages in all the fairy country. With the Scarecrow's help she had rescued Nick Chopper, a Tin Woodman, who had rusted in a lonely forest, and the tin man was now the Emperor of the Country of the Winkies and much beloved because of his kind heart. No wonder the people thought Dorothy had brought them good luck! Yet, strange as it may seem, she had accomplished all these wonders not because she was a fairy or had any magical powers whatever, but because she was a simple, sweet and true little girl who was honest to herself and to all whom she met. In this world in which we live simplicity and kindness are the only magic wands that work wonders, and in the Land of Oz Dorothy found these same qualities had won for her the love and admiration of the people. Indeed, the little girl had made many warm friends in the fairy country, and the only real grief the Ozites had ever experienced was when Dorothy left them and returned to her Kansas home.

Now she received a joyful welcome, although no one except Ozma knew at first that she had finally come to stay for good and all.

That evening Dorothy had many callers, and among them were such important people as Tiktok, a machine man who thought and spoke and moved by clockwork; her old companion the genial Shaggy Man; Jack Pumpkinhead, whose body was brush-wood and whose head was a ripe pumpkin with a face carved upon it; the Cowardly Lion and the Hungry Tiger, two great beasts from the forest, who served Princess Ozma, and Professor H. M. Woggle-Bug, T. E. This Woggle-Bug was a remarkable creature. He had once been a tiny little bug, crawling around in a school-room, but he was discovered and highly magnified so that he could be seen more plainly, and while in this magnified condition he had escaped. He had always remained big, and he dressed like a dandy and was so full of knowledge and information (which are distinct acquirements), that he had been made a Professor and the head of the Royal College.

Dorothy had a nice visit with these old friends, and also talked a long time with the Wizard, who was little and old and withered and dried up, but as merry and active as a child. Afterward she went to see Billina's fast growing family of chicks.

Toto, Dorothy's little black dog, also met with a cordial reception. Toto was an especial friend of the Shaggy Man, and he knew every one else. Being the only dog in the Land of Oz, he was highly respected by the people, who believed animals entitled to every consideration if they behaved themselves properly.

Dorothy had four lovely rooms in the palace, which were always reserved for her use and were called "Dorothy's rooms." These consisted of a beautiful sitting-room, a dressing-room, a dainty bedchamber and a big marble bathroom. And in these rooms were everything that heart could desire, placed there with loving thoughtfulness by Ozma for her little friend's use. The royal dressmakers had the little girl's measure, so they kept the closets in her dressing-room filled with lovely dresses of every description and suitable for every occasion. No wonder Dorothy had refrained from bringing with her her old calico and gingham dresses! Here everything that was dear to a little girl's heart was supplied in profusion, and nothing so rich and beautiful could ever have been found in the biggest department stores in America. Of course Dorothy enjoyed all these luxuries, and the only reason she had heretofore preferred to live in Kansas was because her uncle and aunt loved her and needed her with them.

Now, however, all was to be changed, and Dorothy was really more delighted to know that her dear relatives were to share in her good fortune and enjoy the delights of the Land of Oz, than she was to possess such luxury for herself.

Next morning, at Ozma's request, Dorothy dressed herself in a pretty sky-blue gown of rich silk, trimmed with real pearls. The buckles of her shoes were set with pearls, too, and more of these priceless gems were on a lovely coronet which she wore upon her forehead.

"For," said her friend Ozma, "from this time forth, my dear, you must assume your rightful rank as a Princess of Oz, and being my chosen companion you must dress in a way befitting the dignity of your position."

Dorothy agreed to this, although she knew that neither gowns nor jewels could make her anything else than the simple, unaffected little girl she had always been.

As soon as they had breakfasted—the girls eating together in Ozma's pretty boudoir—the Ruler of Oz said:

"Now, dear friend, we will use the Magic Belt to transport your uncle and aunt from Kansas to the Emerald City. But I think it would be fitting, in receiving such distinguished guests, for us to sit in my Throne Room."

"Oh, they're not very 'stinguished, Ozma," said Dorothy. "They're just plain people, like me."

"Being your friends and relatives, Princess Dorothy, they are certainly distinguished," replied the Ruler, with a smile.

"They—they won't hardly know what to make of all your splendid furniture and things," protested Dorothy, gravely. "It may scare 'em to see your grand Throne Room, an' p'raps we'd better go into the back yard, Ozma, where the cabbages grow an' the chickens are playing. Then it would seem more natural to Uncle Henry and Aunt Em."

"No; they shall first see me in my Throne Room," replied Ozma, decidedly; and when she spoke in that tone Dorothy knew it was not wise to oppose her, for Ozma was accustomed to having her own way.

So together they went to the Throne Room, an immense domed chamber in the center of the palace. Here stood the royal throne, made of solid gold and encrusted with enough precious stones to stock a dozen jewelry stores in our country.

Ozma, who was wearing the Magic Belt, seated herself in the throne, and Dorothy sat at her feet. In the room were assembled many ladies and gentlemen of the court, clothed in rich apparel and wearing fine jewelry. Two immense animals squatted, one on each side of the throne—the Cowardly Lion and the Hungry Tiger.

In a balcony high up in the dome an orchestra played sweet music, and beneath the dome two electric fountains sent sprays of colored perfumed water shooting up nearly as high as the arched ceiling.

"Are you ready, Dorothy?" asked the Ruler.

"I am," replied Dorothy; "but I don't know whether Aunt Em and Uncle Henry are ready."

"That won't matter," declared Ozma. "The old life can have very little to interest them, and the sooner they begin the new life here the happier they will be. Here they come, my dear!"

As she spoke, there before the throne appeared Uncle Henry and Aunt Em, who for a moment stood motionless, glaring with white and startled faces at the scene that confronted them. If the ladies and gentlemen present had not been so polite I am sure they would have laughed at the two strangers.

Aunt Em had her calico dress skirt "tucked up," and she wore a faded blue-checked apron. Her hair was rather straggly and she had on a pair of Uncle Henry's old slippers. In one hand she held a dish-towel and in the other a cracked earthenware plate, which she had been engaged in wiping when so suddenly transported to the Land of Oz.

Uncle Henry, when the summons came, had been out in the barn "doin' chores." He wore a ragged and much soiled straw hat, a checked shirt without any collar and blue overalls tucked into the tops of his old cowhide boots.

"By gum!" gasped Uncle Henry, looking around as if bewildered.

"Well, I swan!" gurgled Aunt Em, in a hoarse, frightened voice. Then her eyes fell upon Dorothy, and she said: "D-d-d-don't that look like our little girl—our Dorothy, Henry?"

"Hi, there—look out, Em!" exclaimed the old man, as Aunt Em advanced a step; "take care o' the wild beastses, or you're a goner!"

But now Dorothy sprang forward and embraced and kissed her aunt and uncle affectionately, afterward taking their hands in her own.

"Don't be afraid," she said to them. "You are now in the Land of Oz, where you are to live always, and be comfor'ble an' happy. You'll never have to worry over anything again, 'cause there won't be anything to worry about. And you owe it all to the kindness of my friend Princess Ozma."

Here she led them before the throne and continued:

"Your Highness, this is Uncle Henry. And this is Aunt Em. They want to thank you for bringing them here from Kansas."

Aunt Em tried to "slick" her hair, and she hid the dish-towel and dish under her apron while she bowed to the lovely Ozma. Uncle Henry took off his straw hat and held it awkwardly in his hands.

But the Ruler of Oz rose and came from her throne to greet her newly arrived guests, and she smiled as sweetly upon them as if they had been a king and a queen.

"You are very welcome here, where I have brought you for Princess Dorothy's sake," she said, graciously, "and I hope you will be quite happy in your new home." Then she turned to her courtiers, who were silently and gravely regarding the scene, and added: "I present to my people our Princess Dorothy's beloved Uncle Henry and Aunt Em, who will hereafter be subjects of our kingdom. It will please me to have you show them every kindness and honor in your power, and to join me in making them happy and contented."

Hearing this, all those assembled bowed low and respectfully to the old farmer and his wife, who bobbed their own heads in return.

"And now," said Ozma to them, "Dorothy will show you the rooms prepared for you. I hope you will like them, and shall expect you to join me at luncheon."

So Dorothy led her relatives away, and as soon as they were out of the Throne Room and alone in the corridor Aunt Em squeezed Dorothy's hand and said:

"Child, child! How in the world did we ever get here so quick? And is it all real? And are we to stay here, as she says? And what does it all mean, anyhow?"

Dorothy laughed.

"Why didn't you tell us what you were goin' to do?" inquired Uncle Henry, reproachfully. "If I'd known about it I'd'a put on my Sunday clothes."

"I'll 'splain ever'thing as soon as we get to your rooms," promised Dorothy. "You're in great luck, Uncle Henry and Aunt Em; an' so am I! And oh! I'm so happy to have got you here, at last!"

As he walked by the little girl's side Uncle Henry stroked his whiskers thoughtfully.

"'Pears to me, Dorothy, we won't make bang-up fairies," he remarked.

"An' my back hair looks like a fright!" wailed Aunt Em.

"Never mind," returned the little girl, reassuringly. "You won't have anything to do now but to look pretty, Aunt Em; an' Uncle Henry won't have to work till his back aches, that's certain."

"Sure?" they asked, wonderingly, and in the same breath.

"'Course I'm sure," said Dorothy. "You're in the Fairyland of Oz, now; an' what's more, you belong to it!"

How Guph Visited the Whimsies

CHAPTER SIX

The new General of the Nome King's army knew perfectly well that to fail in his plans meant death for him. Yet he was not at all anxious or worried. He hated every one who was good and longed to make all who were happy unhappy. Therefore he had accepted this dangerous position as General quite willingly, feeling sure in his evil mind that he would be able to do a lot of mischief and finally conquer the Land of Oz.

Yet Guph determined to be careful, and to lay his plans well, so as not to fail. He argued that only careless people fail in what they attempt to do.

The mountains underneath which the Nome King's extensive caverns were located lay grouped just north of the Land of Ev, which lay directly across the deadly desert to the east of the Land of Oz. As the mountains were also on the edge of the desert the Nome King found that he had only to tunnel underneath the desert to reach Ozma's dominions. He did not wish his armies to appear above ground in the Country of the Winkies, which was the part of the Land of Oz nearest to King Roquat's own country, as then the people would give the alarm and enable Ozma to fortify the Emerald City and assemble an army. He wanted to take all the Oz people by surprise; so he decided to run the tunnel clear through to the Emerald City, where he and his hosts could break through the ground without warning and conquer the people before they had time to defend themselves.

Roquat the Red began work at once upon his tunnel, setting a thousand miners at the task and building it high and broad enough for his armies to march through it with ease. The Nomes were used to making tunnels, as all the kingdom in which they lived was under ground; so they made rapid progress.

While this work was going on General Guph started out alone to visit the Chief of the Whimsies.

These Whimsies were curious people who lived in a retired country of their own. They had large, strong bodies, but heads so small that they were no bigger than door-knobs. Of course, such tiny heads could not contain any great amount of brains, and the Whimsies were so ashamed of their personal appearance and lack of commonsense that they wore big heads, made of pasteboard, which they fastened over their own little heads. On these pasteboard heads they sewed sheep's wool for hair, and the wool was colored many tints—pink, green and lavender being the favorite colors.

The faces of these false heads were painted in many ridiculous ways, according to the whims of the owners, and these big, burly creatures looked so whimsical and absurd in their queer masks that they were called "Whimsies." They foolishly imagined that no one would suspect the little heads that were inside the imitation ones, not knowing that it is folly to try to appear otherwise than as nature has made us.

The Chief of the Whimsies had as little wisdom as the others, and had been chosen chief merely because none among them was any wiser or more capable of ruling. The Whimsies were evil spirits and could not be killed. They were hated and feared by every one and were known as terrible fighters because they were so strong and muscular and had not sense enough to know when they were defeated.

General Guph thought the Whimsies would be a great help to

the Nomes in the conquest of Oz, for under his leadership they could be induced to fight as long as they could stand up. So he traveled to their country and asked to see the Chief, who lived in a house that had a picture of his grotesque false head painted over the doorway.

The Chief's false head had blue hair, a turned-up nose, and a mouth that stretched half across the face. Big green eyes had been

painted upon it, but in the center of the chin were two small holes made in the pasteboard, so that the Chief could see through them with his own tiny eyes; for when the big head was fastened upon his shoulders the eyes in his own natural head were on a level with the false chin.

Said General Guph to the Chief of the Whimsies:

"We Nomes are going to conquer the Land of Oz and capture our King's Magic Belt, which the Oz people stole from him. Then we are going to plunder and destroy the whole country. And we want the Whimsies to help us."

"Will there be any fighting?" asked the Chief.

"Plenty," replied Guph.

That must have pleased the Chief, for he got up and danced

around the room three times. Then he seated himself again, adjusted his false head, and said:

"We have no quarrel with Ozma of Oz."

"But you Whimsies love to fight, and here is a splendid chance to do so," urged Guph.

"Wait till I sing a song," said the Chief. Then he lay back in his chair and sang a foolish song that did not seem to the General to

mean anything, although he listened carefully. When he had finished, the Chief Whimsie looked at him through the holes in his chin and asked:

"What reward will you give us if we help you?"

The General was prepared for this question, for he had been thinking the matter over on his journey. People often do a good deed without hope of reward, but for an evil deed they always demand payment.

"When we get our Magic Belt," he made reply, "our King, Roquat the Red, will use its power to give every Whimsie a natural head as big and fine as the false head he now wears. Then you will no longer be ashamed because your big strong bodies have such teenty-weenty heads."

"Oh! Will you do that?" asked the Chief, eagerly.

"We surely will," promised the General.

"I'll talk to my people," said the Chief.

So he called a meeting of all the Whimsies and told them of the offer made by the Nomes. The creatures were delighted with the bargain, and at once agreed to fight for the Nome King and help him to conquer Oz.

One Whimsie alone seemed to have a glimmer of sense, for he asked:

"Suppose we fail to capture the Magic Belt? What will happen then, and what good will all our fighting do?"

But they threw him into the river for asking foolish questions, and laughed when the water ruined his pasteboard head before he could swim out again.

So the compact was made and General Guph was delighted with his success in gaining such powerful allies.

But there were other people, too, just as important as the Whimsies, whom the clever old Nome had determined to win to his side.

How AUNT EM CONQUERED THE LION

CHAPTER SEVEN

"These are your rooms," said Dorothy, opening a door.

Aunt Em drew back at sight of the splendid furniture and draperies.

"Ain't there any place to wipe my feet?" she asked.

"You will soon change your slippers for new shoes," replied Dorothy. "Don't be afraid, Aunt Em. Here is where you are to live, so walk right in and make yourself at home."

Aunt Em advanced hesitatingly.

"It beats the Topeka Hotel!" she cried, admiringly. "But this place is too grand for us, child. Can't we have some back room in the attic, that's more in our class?"

"No," said Dorothy. "You've got to live here, 'cause Ozma says so. And all the rooms in this palace are just as fine as these, and some are better. It won't do any good to fuss, Aunt Em. You've got to be swell and high-toned in the Land of Oz, whether you want to or not; so you may as well make up your mind to it."

"It's hard luck," replied her aunt, looking around with an awed expression; "but folks can get used to anything, if they try. Eh, Henry?"

"Why, as to that," said Uncle Henry, slowly, "I b'lieve in takin' what's pervided us, an' askin' no questions. I've traveled some, Em, in my time, and you hain't; an' that makes a difference atween us."

Then Dorothy showed them through the rooms. The first was a handsome sitting-room, with windows opening upon the rose gardens. Then came separate bedrooms for Aunt Em and Uncle Henry, with a fine bathroom between them. Aunt Em had a pretty dressing room, besides, and Dorothy opened the closets and showed several exquisite costumes that had been provided for her aunt by the royal dressmakers, who had worked all night to get them ready. Everything that Aunt Em could possibly need was in the drawers and closets, and her dressing-table was covered with engraved gold toilet articles.

Uncle Henry had nine suits of clothes, cut in the popular Munchkin fashion, with knee-breeches, silk stockings and low shoes with jeweled buckles. The hats to match these costumes had pointed tops and wide brims with small gold bells around the edges. His shirts were of fine linen with frilled bosoms, and his vests were richly embroidered with colored silks.

Uncle Henry decided that he would first take a bath and then dress himself in a blue satin suit that had caught his fancy. He accepted his good fortune with calm composure and refused to have a servant to assist him. But Aunt Em was "all of a flutter," as she said, and it took Dorothy and Jellia Jamb, the housekeeper, and two maids a long time to dress her and do up her hair and get her "rigged like a popinjay," as she quaintly expressed it. She wanted to stop and admire everything that caught her eye, and she sighed continually and declared that such finery was too good for an old country woman, and that she never thought she would have to "put on airs" at her time of life.

Finally she was dressed, and when they went into the sitting-room there was Uncle Henry in his blue satin, walking gravely up and down the room. He had trimmed his beard and mustache and looked very dignified and respectable.

"Tell me, Dorothy," he said; "do all the men here wear duds like these?"

"Yes," she replied; "all 'cept the Scarecrow and the Shaggy Man—and of course the Tin Woodman and Tiktok, who are made of metal. You'll find all the men at Ozma's court dressed just as you are—only perhaps a little finer."

"Henry, you look like a play-actor," announced Aunt Em, looking at her husband critically.

"An' you, Em, look more highfalutin' than a peacock," he replied.

"I guess you're right," she said, regretfully; "but we're helpless victims of high-toned royalty."

Dorothy was much amused.

"Come with me," she said, "and I'll show you 'round the palace."

She took them through the beautiful rooms and introduced them to all the people they chanced to meet. Also she showed them her own pretty rooms, which were not far from their own.

"So it's all true," said Aunt Em, wide-eyed with amazement, "and what Dorothy told us of this fairy country was plain facts instead of dreams! But where are all the strange creatures you used to know here?"

"Yes; where's the Scarecrow?" inquired Uncle Henry.

"Why, he's just now away on a visit to the Tin Woodman, who is Emp'ror of the Winkie Country," answered the little girl. "You'll see him when he comes back, and you're sure to like him."

"And where's the Wonderful Wizard?" asked Aunt Em.

"You'll see him at Ozma's luncheon, for he lives in this palace," was the reply.

"And Jack Pumpkinhead?"

"Oh, he lives a little way out of town, in his own pumpkin field. We'll go there some time and see him, and we'll call on Professor Woggle-Bug, too. The Shaggy Man will be at the luncheon, I guess, and Tiktok. And now I'll take you out to see Billina, who has a house of her own."

So they went into the back yard, and after walking along winding paths some distance through the beautiful gardens they came to an attractive little house where the Yellow Hen sat on the front porch sunning herself.

"Good morning, my dear Mistress," called Billina, fluttering down to meet them. "I was expecting you to call, for I heard you had come back and brought your uncle and aunt with you."

"We're here for good and all, this time, Billina," cried Dorothy, joyfully. "Uncle Henry and Aunt Em belong in Oz now as much as I do!"

"Then they are very lucky people," declared Billina; "for there couldn't be a nicer place to live. But come, my dear; I must show you all my Dorothys. Nine are living and have grown up to be very respectable hens; but one took cold at Ozma's birthday party and died of the pip, and the other two turned out to be horrid roosters, so I had to change their names from Dorothy to Daniel. They all had the letter 'D' engraved upon their gold lockets, you remember, with your picture inside, and 'D' stands for Daniel as well as for Dorothy."

"Did you call both the roosters Daniel?" asked Uncle Henry.

"Yes, indeed. I've nine Dorothys and two Daniels; and the nine Dorothys have eighty-six sons and daughters and over three hundred grandchildren," said Billina, proudly.

"What names do you give 'em all, dear?" inquired the little girl.

"Oh, they are all Dorothys and Daniels, some being Juniors and some Double-Juniors. Dorothy and Daniel are two good names, and I see no object in hunting for others," declared the Yellow Hen. "But just think, Dorothy, what a big chicken family we've grown to be, and our numbers increase nearly every day! Ozma doesn't know what to do with all the eggs we lay, and we are never eaten or harmed in any way, as chickens are in your country. They give us everything to make us contented and happy, and I, my dear, am the acknowledged Queen and Governor of every chicken in Oz, because I'm the eldest and started the whole colony."

"You ought to be very proud, ma'am," said Uncle Henry, who was astonished to hear a hen talk so sensibly.

"Oh, I am," she replied. "I've the loveliest pearl necklace you ever saw. Come in the house and I'll show it to you. And I've nine leg bracelets and a diamond pin for each wing. But I only wear them on state occasions."

They followed the Yellow Hen into the house, which Aunt Em declared was neat as a pin. They could not sit down, because all Billina's chairs were roosting-poles made of silver; so they had to stand while the hen fussily showed them her treasures.

Then they had to go into the back rooms occupied by Billina's nine Dorothys and two Daniels, who were all plump yellow chickens and greeted the visitors very politely. It was easy to see that they were well bred and that Billina had looked after their education.

In the yards were all the children and grandchildren of these eleven elders and they were of all sizes, from well-grown hens to tiny chickens just out of the shell. About fifty fluffy yellow youngsters were at school, being taught good manners and good grammar by a young hen who wore spectacles. They sang in chorus a patriotic song of the Land of Oz, in honor of their visitors, and Aunt Em was much impressed by these talking chickens.

Dorothy wanted to stay and play with the young chickens for awhile, but Uncle Henry and Aunt Em had not seen the palace grounds and gardens yet and were eager to get better acquainted with the marvelous and delightful land in which they were to live.

"I'll stay here, and you can go for a walk," said Dorothy. "You'll be perfec'ly safe anywhere, and may do whatever you want to. When you get tired, go back to the palace and find your rooms, and I'll come to you before luncheon is ready."

So Uncle Henry and Aunt Em started out alone to explore the grounds, and Dorothy knew that they couldn't get lost, because all the palace grounds were enclosed by a high wall of green marble set with emeralds.

It was a rare treat to these simple folk, who had lived in the country all their lives and known little enjoyment of any sort, to wear beautiful clothes and live in a palace and be treated with respect and consideration by all around them. They were very happy indeed as they strolled up the shady walks and looked upon the gorgeous flowers and shrubs, feeling that their new home was more beautiful than any tongue could describe.

Suddenly, as they turned a corner and walked through a gap in a high hedge, they came face to face with an enormous Lion, which crouched upon the green lawn and seemed surprised by their appearance.

They stopped short, Uncle Henry trembling with horror and Aunt Em too terrified to scream. Next moment the poor woman clasped her husband around the neck and cried:

"Save me, Henry, save me!"

"Can't even save myself, Em," he returned, in a husky voice, "for the animile looks as if it could eat both of us, an' lick its chops for more! If I only had a gun—"

"Haven't you, Henry? Haven't you?" she asked anxiously.

"Nary gun, Em. So let's die as brave an' graceful as we can. I knew our luck couldn't last!"

"I won't die. I won't be eaten by a lion!" wailed Aunt Em, glaring upon the huge beast. Then a thought struck her, and she whispered: "Henry, I've heard as savage beastses can be conquered by the human eye. I'll eye that lion out o' countenance an' save our lives."

"Try it, Em," he returned, also in a whisper. "Look at him as you do at me when I'm late to dinner."

Aunt Em turned upon the Lion a determined countenance and a wild dilated eye. She glared at the immense beast steadily, and the

Lion, who had been quietly blinking at them, began to appear uneasy and disturbed.

"Is anything the matter, ma'am?" he asked, in a mild voice.

At this speech from the terrible beast Aunt Em and Uncle Henry both were startled, and then Uncle Henry remembered that this must be the Lion they had seen in Ozma's Throne Room.

"Hold on, Em!" he exclaimed. "Quit the eagle eye conquest an' take courage. I guess this is the same Cowardly Lion Dorothy has told us about."

"Oh, is it?" she asked, much relieved.

"When he spoke, I got the idea; and when he looked so 'shamed like, I was sure of it," Uncle Henry continued.

Aunt Em regarded the animal with new interest.

"Are you the Cowardly Lion?" she inquired. "Are you Dorothy's friend?"

"Yes 'm," answered the Lion, meekly. "Dorothy and I are old chums and are very fond of each other. I'm the King of Beasts, you know, and the Hungry Tiger and I serve Princess Ozma as her body guards."

"To be sure," said Aunt Em, nodding. "But the King of Beasts shouldn't be cowardly."

"I've heard that said before," remarked the Lion, yawning till he showed his two great rows of sharp white teeth; "but that does not keep me from being frightened whenever I go into battle."

"What do you do, run?" asked Uncle Henry.

"No; that would be foolish, for the enemy would run after me," declared the Lion. "So I tremble with fear and pitch in as hard as I can; and so far I have always won my fight."

"Ah, I begin to understand," said Uncle Henry.

"Were you scared when I looked at you just now?" inquired Aunt Em.

"Terribly scared, madam," answered the Lion, "for at first I thought you were going to have a fit. Then I noticed you were trying to overcome me by the power of your eye, and your glance was so fierce and penetrating that I shook with fear."

This greatly pleased the lady, and she said quite cheerfully:

"Well, I won't hurt you, so don't be scared any more. I just wanted to see what the human eye was good for."

"The human eye is a fearful weapon," remarked the Lion, scratching his nose softly with his paw to hide a smile. "Had I not known you were Dorothy's friends I might have torn you both into shreds in order to escape your terrible gaze."

Aunt Em shuddered at hearing this, and Uncle Henry said hastily:

"I'm glad you knew us. Good morning, Mr. Lion; we'll hope to see you again—by and by—some time in the future."

"Good morning," replied the Lion, squatting down upon the lawn again. "You are likely to see a good deal of me, if you live in the Land of Oz."

How THE GRAND GALLIPOOT JOINED THE NOMES

CHAPTER EIGHT

After leaving the Whimsies, Guph continued on his journey and penetrated far into the Northwest. He wanted to get to the Country of the Growleywogs, and in order to do that he must cross the Ripple Land, which was a hard thing to do. For the Ripple Land was a succession of hills and valleys, all very steep and rocky, and they changed places constantly by rippling. While Guph was climbing a hill it sank down under him and became a valley, and while he was descending into a valley it rose up and carried him to the top of a hill. This was very perplexing to the traveler, and a stranger might have thought he could never cross the Ripple Land at all. But Guph knew that if he kept steadily on he would get to the end at last; so he paid no attention to the changing hills and valleys and plodded along as calmly as if walking upon the level ground.

The result of this wise persistence was that the General finally reached firmer soil and, after penetrating a dense forest, came to the Dominion of the Growleywogs.

No sooner had he crossed the border of this domain when two guards seized him and carried him before the Grand Gallipoot of the Growleywogs, who scowled upon him ferociously and asked him why he dared intrude upon his territory.

"I'm the Lord High General of the Invincible Army of the

Nomes, and my name is Guph," was the reply. "All the world trembles when that name is mentioned."

The Growleywogs gave a shout of jeering laughter at this, and one of them caught the Nome in his strong arms and tossed him high into the air. Guph was considerably shaken when he fell upon the hard ground, but he appeared to take no notice of the impertinence and composed himself to speak again to the Grand Gallipoot.

"My master, King Roquat the Red, has sent me here to confer with you. He wishes your assistance to conquer the Land of Oz."

Here the General paused, and the Grand Gallipoot scowled upon him more terribly than ever and said:

"Go on!"

The voice of the Grand Gallipoot was partly a roar and partly a growl. He mumbled his words badly and Guph had to listen carefully in order to understand him.

These Growleywogs were certainly remarkable creatures. They were of gigantic size, yet were all bone and skin and muscle, there being no meat or fat upon their bodies at all. Their powerful muscles lay just underneath their skins, like bunches of tough rope, and the weakest Growleywog was so strong that he could pick up an elephant and toss it seven miles away.

It seems unfortunate that strong people are usually so disagreeable and overbearing that no one cares for them. In fact, to be different from your fellow creatures is always a misfortune. The Growleywogs knew that they were disliked and avoided by every one, so they had become surly and unsociable even among themselves. Guph knew that they hated all people, including the Nomes; but he hoped to win them over, nevertheless, and knew that if he succeeded they would afford him very powerful assistance.

"The Land of Oz is ruled by a namby-pamby girl who is disgustingly kind and good," he continued. "Her people are all happy and contented and have no care or worries whatever."

"Go on!" growled the Grand Gallipoot.

"Once the Nome King enslaved the Royal Family of Ev—another goody-goody lot that we detest," said the General. "But

Ozma interfered, although it was none of her business, and marched her army against us. With her was a Kansas girl named Dorothy, and a Yellow Hen, and they marched directly into the Nome King's cavern. There they liberated our slaves from Ev and stole King Roquat's Magic Belt, which they carried away with them. So now our King is making a tunnel under the deadly desert, so we can march through it to the Emerald City. When we get there we mean to conquer and destroy all the land and recapture the Magic Belt."

Again he paused, and again the Grand Gallipoot growled:

"Go on!"

Guph tried to think what to say next, and a happy thought soon occurred to him.

"We want you to help us in this conquest," he announced, "for we need the mighty aid of the Growleywogs in order to make sure that we shall not be defeated. You are the strongest people in all the world, and you hate good and happy creatures as much as we Nomes do. I am sure it will be a real pleasure to you to tear down the beautiful Emerald City, and in return for your valuable assistance we will allow you to bring back to your country ten thousand people of Oz, to be your slaves."

"Twenty thousand!" growled the Grand Gallipoot.

"All right, we promise you twenty thousand," agreed the General.

The Gallipoot made a signal and at once his attendants picked up General Guph and carried him away to a prison, where the jailor amused himself by sticking pins in the round fat body of the old Nome, to see him jump and hear him yell.

But while this was going on the Grand Gallipoot was talking with his counselors, who were the most important officials of the Growleywogs. When he had stated to them the proposition of the Nome King he said:

"My advice is to offer to help them. Then, when we have conquered the Land of Oz, we will take not only our twenty thousand prisoners but all the gold and jewels we want."

"Let us take the Magic Belt, too," suggested one counselor.

"And rob the Nome King and make him our slave," said another.

"That is a good idea," declared the Grand Gallipoot. "I'd like King Roquat for my own slave. He could black my boots and bring me my porridge every morning while I am in bed."

"There is a famous Scarecrow in Oz. I'll take him for my slave," said a counselor.

"I'll take Tiktok, the machine man," said another.

"Give me the Tin Woodman," said a third.

They went on for some time, dividing up the people and the treasure of Oz in advance of the conquest. For they had no doubt at all that they would be able to destroy Ozma's domain. Were they not the strongest people in all the world?

"The deadly desert has kept us out of Oz before," remarked the Grand Gallipoot, "but now that the Nome King is building a tunnel we shall get into the Emerald City very easily. So let us send the little fat General back to his King with our promise to assist him. We will not say that we intend to conquer the Nomes after we have conquered Oz, but we will do so, just the same."

This plan being agreed upon, they all went home to dinner, leaving General Guph still in prison. The Nome had no idea that he had succeeded in his mission, for finding himself in prison he feared the Growleywogs intended to put him to death.

By this time the jailor had tired of sticking pins in the General, and was amusing himself by carefully pulling the Nome's whiskers out by the roots, one at a time. This enjoyment was interrupted by the Grand Gallipoot sending for the prisoner.

"Wait a few hours," begged the jailor. "I haven't pulled out a quarter of his whiskers yet."

"If you keep the Grand Gallipoot waiting he'll break your back," declared the messenger.

"Perhaps you're right," sighed the jailor. "Take the prisoner away, if you will, but I advise you to kick him at every step he takes. It will be good fun, for he is as soft as a ripe peach."

So Guph was led away to the royal castle, where the Grand Gallipoot told him that the Growleywogs had decided to assist the Nomes in conquering the Land of Oz.

"Whenever you are ready," he added, "send me word and I will march with eighteen thousand of my most powerful warriors to your aid."

Guph was so delighted that he forgot all the smarting caused by the pins and the pulling of whiskers. He did not even complain of the treatment he had received, but thanked the Grand Gallipoot and hurried away upon his journey.

He had now secured the assistance of the Whimsies and the Growleywogs; but his success made him long for still more allies. His own life depended upon his conquering Oz, and he said to himself:

"I'll take no chances. I'll be certain of success. Then, when Oz is destroyed, perhaps I shall be a greater man than old Roquat, and I can throw him away and be King of the Nomes myself. Why not? The Whimsies are stronger than the Nomes, and they are my friends. The Growleywogs are stronger than the Whimsies, and they also are my friends. There are some people still stronger than the Growleywogs, and if I can but induce them to aid me I shall have nothing more to fear."

How THE WOGGLEBUG TAUGHT ATHLETICS

CHAPTER NINE

It did not take Dorothy long to establish herself in her new home, for she knew the people and the manners and customs of the Emerald City just as well as she knew the old Kansas farm.

But Uncle Henry and Aunt Em had some trouble in getting used to the finery and pomp and ceremony of Ozma's palace, and felt uneasy because they were obliged to be "dressed up" all the time. Yet every one was very courteous and kind to them and endeavored to make them happy. Ozma, especially, made much of Dorothy's relatives, for her little friend's sake, and she well knew that the awkwardness and strangeness of their new mode of life would all wear off in time.

The old people were chiefly troubled by the fact that there was no work for them to do.

"Ev'ry day is like Sunday, now," declared Aunt Em, solemnly, "and I can't say I like it. If they'd only let me do up the dishes after meals, or even sweep an' dust my own rooms, I'd be a deal happier. Henry don't know what to do with himself either, and once when he stole out an' fed the chickens Billina scolded him for letting 'em eat between meals. I never knew before what a hardship it is to be rich and have everything you want."

These complaints began to worry Dorothy; so she had a long talk with Ozma upon the subject.

"I see I must find them something to do," said the girlish Ruler of Oz, seriously. "I have been watching your uncle and aunt, and I believe they will be more contented if occupied with some light tasks. While I am considering this matter, Dorothy, you might make a trip with them through the Land of Oz, visiting some of the odd corners and introducing your relatives to some of our curious people."

"Oh, that would be fine!" exclaimed Dorothy, eagerly.

"I will give you an escort befitting your rank as a Princess," continued Ozma; "and you may go to some of the places you have not yet visited yourself, as well as some others that you know. I will mark out a plan of the trip for you and have everything in readiness for you to start tomorrow morning. Take your time, dear, and be gone as long as you wish. By the time you return I shall have found some occupation for Uncle Henry and Aunt Em that will keep them from being restless and dissatisfied."

Dorothy thanked her good friend and kissed the lovely Ruler gratefully. Then she ran to tell the joyful news to her uncle and aunt.

Next morning, after breakfast, everything was found ready for their departure.

The escort included Omby Amby, the Captain-General of Ozma's army, which consisted merely of twenty-seven officers besides the Captain-General. Once Omby Amby had been a private soldier—the only private in the army—but as there was never any fighting to do Ozma saw no need of a private, so she made Omby Amby the highest officer of them all. He was very tall and slim and wore a gay uniform and a fierce mustache. Yet the mustache was the only fierce thing about Omby Amby, whose nature was as gentle as that of a child.

The wonderful Wizard had asked to join the party, and with him came his friend the Shaggy Man, who was shaggy but not ragged, being dressed in fine silks with satin shags and bobtails. The Shaggy Man had shaggy whiskers and hair, but a sweet disposition and a soft, pleasant voice.

There was an open wagon, with three seats for the passengers, and the wagon was drawn by the famous wooden Saw-Horse which had once been brought to life by Ozma by means of a magic powder. The Saw-Horse wore golden shoes to keep his wooden legs from wearing away, and he was strong and swift. As this curious creature was Ozma's own favorite steed, and very popular with all the people of the Emerald City, Dorothy knew that she had been highly favored by being permitted to use the Saw-Horse on her journey.

In the front seat of the wagon sat Dorothy and the Wizard. Uncle Henry and Aunt Em sat in the next seat and the Shaggy Man and Omby Amby in the third seat. Of course Toto was with the party, curled up at Dorothy's feet, and just as they were about to start Billina came fluttering along the path and begged to be taken with them. Dorothy readily agreed, so the Yellow Hen flew up and perched herself upon the dashboard. She wore her pearl necklace and three bracelets upon each leg, in honor of the occasion.

Dorothy kissed Ozma good-bye, and all the people standing around waved their handkerchiefs, and the band in an upper balcony struck up a military march. Then the Wizard clucked to the Saw-Horse and said: "Gid-dap!" and the wooden animal pranced away and drew behind him the big red wagon and all the passengers, without any effort at all. A servant threw open a gate of the palace enclosure, that they might pass out; and so, with music and shouts following them, the journey was begun.

"It's almost like a circus," said Aunt Em, proudly. "I can't help feelin' high an' mighty in this kind of a turn-out."

Indeed, as they passed down the street, all the people cheered them lustily, and the Shaggy Man and the Wizard and the Captain-General all took off their hats and bowed politely in acknowledgment.

When they came to the great wall of the Emerald City the gates were opened by the Guardian who always tended them. Over the gateway hung a dull-colored metal magnet shaped like a horse-shoe, placed against a shield of polished gold.

"That," said the Shaggy Man, impressively, "is the wonderful Love

Magnet. I brought it to the Emerald City myself, and all who pass beneath this gateway are both loving and beloved."

"It's a fine thing," declared Aunt Em, admiringly. "If we'd had it in Kansas I guess the man who held a mortgage on the farm wouldn't have turned us out."

"Then I'm glad we didn't have it," returned Uncle Henry. "I like Oz better than Kansas, even; an' this little wood Saw-Horse beats all the critters I ever saw. He don't have to be curried, or fed, or watered, an' he's strong as an ox. Can he talk, Dorothy?"

"Yes, Uncle," replied the child. "But the Saw-Horse never says much. He told me once that he can't talk and think at the same time, so he prefers to think."

"Which is very sensible," declared the Wizard, nodding approvingly. "Which way do we go, Dorothy?"

"Straight ahead into the Quadling Country," she answered. "I've got a letter of interduction to Miss Cuttenclip."

"Oh!" exclaimed the Wizard, much interested. "Are we going there? Then I'm glad I came, for I've always wanted to meet the Cuttenclips."

"Who are they?" inquired Aunt Em.

"Wait till we get there," replied Dorothy, with a laugh; "then you'll see for yourself. I've never seen the Cuttenclips, you know, so I can't 'zactly 'splain 'em to you."

Once free of the Emerald City the Saw-Horse dashed away at tremendous speed. Indeed, he went so fast that Aunt Em had hard work to catch her breath, and Uncle Henry held fast to the seat of the red wagon.

"Gently—gently, my boy!" called the Wizard, and at this the Saw-Horse slackened his speed.

"What's wrong?" asked the animal, slightly turning his wooden head to look at the party with one eye, which was a knot of wood.

"Why, we wish to admire the scenery, that's all," answered the Wizard.

"Some of your passengers," added the Shaggy Man, "have never been out of the Emerald City before, and the country is all new to them."

"If you go too fast you'll spoil all the fun," said Dorothy. "There's no hurry."

"Very well; it is all the same to me," observed the Saw-Horse; and after that he went at a more moderate pace.

Uncle Henry was astonished.

"How can a wooden thing be so intelligent?" he asked.

"Why, I gave him some sawdust brains the last time I fitted his head with new ears," explained the Wizard. "The sawdust was made from hard knots, and now the Saw-Horse is able to think out any knotty problem he meets with."

"I see," said Uncle Henry.

"I don't," remarked Aunt Em; but no one paid any attention to this statement.

Before long they came to a stately building that stood upon a green plain with handsome shade trees grouped here and there.

"What is that?" asked Uncle Henry.

"That," replied the Wizard, "is the Royal Athletic College of Oz, which is directed by Professor H. M. Woggle-Bug, T. E."

"Let's stop and make a call," suggested Dorothy.

So the Saw-Horse drew up in front of the great building and they were met at the door by the learned Woggle-Bug himself. He seemed fully as tall as the Wizard, and was dressed in a red and white checked vest and a blue swallow-tailed coat, and had yellow knee-breeches and purple silk stockings upon his slender legs. A tall hat was jauntily set upon his head and he wore spectacles over his big bright eyes.

"Welcome, Dorothy," said the Woggle-Bug; "and welcome to all your friends. We are indeed pleased to receive you at this great Temple of Learning."

"I thought it was an Athletic College," said the Shaggy Man.

"It is, my dear sir," answered the Woggle-Bug, proudly. "Here it is that we teach the youth of our great land scientific College Athletics—in all their purity."

"Don't you teach them anything else?" asked Dorothy. "Don't they get any reading, writing and 'rithmetic?"

"Oh, yes; of course. They get all those, and more," returned the Professor. "But such things occupy little of their time. Please follow me and I will show you how my scholars are usually occupied. This is a class hour and they are all busy."

They followed him to a big field back of the college building, where several hundred young Ozites were at their classes. In one place they played football, in another baseball. Some played tennis, some golf; some were swimming in a big pool. Upon a river which wound through the grounds several crews in racing boats were rowing with great enthusiasm. Other groups of students played basketball and cricket, while in one place a ring was roped in to permit boxing and wrestling by the energetic youths. All the collegians seemed busy and there was much laughter and shouting.

"This college," said Professor Woggle-Bug, complacently, "is a great success. Its educational value is undisputed, and we are turning out many great and valuable citizens every year."

"But when do they study?" asked Dorothy.

"Study?" said the Woggle-Bug, looking perplexed at the question.

"Yes; when do they get their 'rithmetic, and jogerfy, and such things?"

"Oh, they take doses of those every night and morning," was the reply.

"What do you mean by doses?" Dorothy inquired, wonderingly.

"Why, we use the newly invented School Pills, made by your friend the Wizard. These pills we have found to be very effective, and they save a lot of time. Please step this way and I will show you our Laboratory of Learning."

He led them to a room in the building where many large bottles were standing in rows upon shelves.

"These are the Algebra Pills," said the Professor, taking down one of the bottles. "One at night, on retiring, is equal to four hours of study. Here are the Geography Pills—one at night and one in the morning. In this next bottle are the Latin Pills—one three times a day. Then we have the Grammar Pills—one before each meal—and the Spelling Pills, which are taken whenever needed."

"Your scholars must have to take a lot of pills," remarked Dorothy, thoughtfully. "How do they take 'em, in applesauce?"

"No, my dear. They are sugar-coated and are quickly and easily swallowed. I believe the students would rather take the pills than study, and certainly the pills are a more effective method. You see, until these School Pills were invented we wasted a lot of time in study that may now be better employed in practising athletics."

"Seems to me the pills are a good thing," said Omby Amby, who remembered how it used to make his head ache as a boy to study arithmetic.

"They are, sir," declared the Woggle-Bug, earnestly. "They give us an advantage over all other colleges, because at no loss of time our boys become thoroughly conversant with Greek and Latin, Mathematics and Geography, Grammar and Literature. You see they are never obliged to interrupt their games to acquire the lesser branches of learning."

"It's a great invention, I'm sure," said Dorothy, looking admiringly at the Wizard, who blushed modestly at this praise.

"We live in an age of progress," announced Professor Woggle-Bug, pompously. "It is easier to swallow knowledge than to acquire it laboriously from books. Is it not so, my friends?"

"Some folks can swallow anything," said Aunt Em, "but to me this seems too much like taking medicine."

"Young men in college always have to take their medicine, one way or another," observed the Wizard, with a smile; "and, as our Professor says, these School Pills have proved to be a great success. One day while I was making them I happened to drop one of them, and one of Billina's chickens gobbled it up. A few minutes afterward this chick got upon a roost and recited 'The Boy Stood on the Burning Deck' without making a single mistake. Then it recited 'The Charge of the Light Brigade' and afterward 'Excelsior.' You see, the chicken had eaten an Elocution Pill."

They now bade good bye to the Professor, and thanking him for his kind reception mounted again into the red wagon and continued their journey.

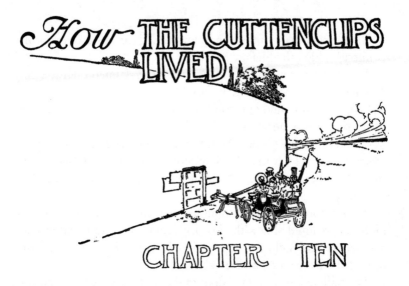

How THE CUTTENCLIPS LIVED

CHAPTER TEN

The travelers had taken no provisions with them because they knew that they would be welcomed wherever they might go in the Land of Oz, and that the people would feed and lodge them with genuine hospitality. So about noon they stopped at a farm-house and were given a delicious luncheon of bread and milk, fruits and wheat cakes with maple syrup. After resting a while and strolling through the orchards with their host—a round, jolly farmer—they got into the wagon and again started the Saw-Horse along the pretty, winding road.

There were sign-posts at all the corners, and finally they came to one which read:

☞ TAKE THIS ROAD TO THE CUTTENCLIPS

There was also a hand pointing in the right direction, so they turned the Saw-Horse that way and found it a very good road, but seemingly little traveled.

"I've never been to see the Cuttenclips before," remarked Dorothy.

"Nor I," said the Captain-General.

"Nor I," said the Wizard.

"Nor I," said Billina.

"I've hardly been out of the Emerald City since I arrived in this country," added the Shaggy Man.

"Why, none of us has been there, then," exclaimed the little girl. "I wonder what the Cuttenclips are like."

"We shall soon find out," said the Wizard, with a sly laugh. "I've heard they are rather flimsy things."

The farm-houses became fewer as they proceeded, and the path was at times so faint that the Saw-Horse had hard work to keep in the road. The wagon began to jounce, too; so they were obliged to go slowly.

After a somewhat wearisome journey they came in sight of a high wall, painted blue with pink ornaments. This wall was circular, and seemed to enclose a large space. It was so high that only the tops of the trees could be seen above it.

The path led up to a small door in the wall, which was closed and latched. Upon the door was a sign in gold letters reading as follows:

> *VISITORS are requested to* MOVE
> *SLOWLY and* CAREFULLY, *and to avoid*
> COUGHING *or making any* BREEZE *or*
> *DRAUGHT*

"That's strange," said the Shaggy Man, reading the sign aloud. "Who *are* the Cuttenclips, anyhow?"

"Why, they're paper dolls," answered Dorothy. "Didn't you know that?"

"Paper dolls! Then let's go somewhere else," said Uncle Henry. "We're all too old to play with dolls, Dorothy."

"But these are different," declared the girl. "They're alive."

"Alive!" gasped Aunt Em, in amazement.

"Yes. Let's go in," said Dorothy.

So they all got out of the wagon, since the door in the wall was not big enough for them to drive the Saw-Horse and wagon through it.

"You stay here, Toto!" commanded Dorothy, shaking her finger at the little dog. "You're so careless that you might make a breeze if I let you inside."

Toto wagged his tail as if disappointed at being left behind; but he made no effort to follow them. The Wizard unlatched the door, which opened outward, and they all looked eagerly inside.

Just before the entrance was drawn up a line of tiny soldiers, with uniforms brightly painted and paper guns upon their shoulders. They were exactly alike, from one end of the line to the other, and all were cut out of paper and joined together in the centers of their bodies.

As the visitors entered the enclosure the Wizard let the door swing back into place, and at once the line of soldiers tumbled over, fell flat upon their backs, and lay fluttering upon the ground.

"Hi, there!" called one of them; "what do you mean by slamming the door and blowing us over?"

"I beg your pardon, I'm sure," said the Wizard, regretfully. "I didn't know you were so delicate."

"We're not delicate!" retorted another soldier, raising his head from the ground. "We are strong and healthy; but we can't stand draughts."

"May I help you up?" asked Dorothy.

"If you please," replied the end soldier. "But do it gently, little girl."

Dorothy carefully stood up the line of soldiers, who first dusted their painted clothes and then saluted the visitors with their paper muskets. From the end it was easy to see that the entire line had been cut out of paper, although from the front the soldiers looked rather solid and imposing.

"I've a letter of introduction from Princess Ozma to Miss Cuttenclip," announced Dorothy.

"Very well," said the end soldier, and blew upon a paper whistle that hung around his neck. At once a paper soldier in a Captain's uniform came out of a paper house near by and approached the group at the entrance. He was not very big, and he walked rather stiffly and uncertainly on his paper legs; but he had a pleasant face, with very red cheeks and very blue eyes, and he bowed so low to the strangers that Dorothy laughed, and the breeze from her mouth nearly blew the Captain over. He wavered and struggled and finally managed to remain upon his feet.

"Take care, Miss!" he said, warningly. "You're breaking the rules, you know, by laughing."

"Oh, I didn't know that," she replied.

"To laugh in this place is nearly as dangerous as to cough," said the Captain. "You'll have to breathe very quietly, I assure you."

"We'll try to," promised the girl. "May we see Miss Cuttenclip, please?"

"You may," promptly returned the Captain. "This is one of her reception days. Be good enough to follow me."

He turned and led the way up a path, and as they followed slowly, because the paper Captain did not move very swiftly, they took the opportunity to gaze around them at this strange paper country.

Beside the path were paper trees, all cut out very neatly and painted a brilliant green color. And back of the trees were rows of cardboard houses, painted in various colors but most of them having green blinds. Some were large and some small, and in the front yards were beds of paper flowers quite natural in appearance. Over some of the porches paper vines were twined, giving them a cosy and shady look.

As the visitors passed along the street a good many paper dolls came to the doors and windows of their houses to look at them curiously. These dolls were nearly all the same height, but were cut into various shapes, some being fat and some lean. The girl dolls wore many beautiful costumes of tissue paper, making them quite fluffy; but their heads and hands were no thicker than the paper of which they were made.

Some of the paper people were on the street, walking along or congregated in groups and talking together; but as soon as they saw the strangers they all fluttered into the houses as fast as they could go, so as to be out of danger.

"Excuse me if I go edgewise," remarked the Captain, as they

came to a slight hill. "I can get along faster that way and not flutter so much."

"That's all right," said Dorothy. "We don't mind how you go, I'm sure."

At one side of the street was a paper pump, and a paper boy was pumping paper water into a paper pail. The Yellow Hen happened to brush against this boy with her wing, and he flew into the air and fell into a paper tree, where he stuck until the Wizard gently pulled him out. At the same time the pail went soaring into the air, spilling the paper water, while the paper pump bent nearly double.

"Goodness me!" said the Hen. "If I should flop my wings I believe I'd knock over the whole village!"

"Then don't flop them—please don't!" entreated the Captain. "Miss Cuttenclip would be very much distressed if her village was spoiled."

"Oh, I'll be careful," promised Billina.

"Are not all these paper girls and women named Miss Cuttenclips?" inquired Omby Amby.

"No, indeed," answered the Captain, who was walking better since he began to move edgewise. "There is but one Miss Cuttenclip, who is our Queen, because she made us all. These girls are Cuttenclips, to be sure, but their names are Emily and Polly and Sue and Betty and such things. Only the Queen is called Miss Cuttenclip."

"I must say that this place beats anything I ever heard of," observed Aunt Em. "I used to play with paper dolls myself, an' cut 'em out; but I never thought I'd ever see such things alive."

"I don't see as it's any more curious than hearing hens talk," returned Uncle Henry.

"You're likely to see many queer things in the Land of Oz, sir," said the Wizard. "But a fairy country is extremely interesting when you get used to being surprised."

"Here we are!" called the Captain, stopping before a cottage.

This house was made of wood, and was remarkably pretty in design. In the Emerald City it would have been considered a tiny dwelling, indeed; but in the midst of this paper village it seemed immense. Real flowers were in the garden and real trees grew beside it. Upon the front door was a sign reading:

MISS CUTTENCLIP.

Just as they reached the porch the front door opened and a little girl stood before them. She appeared to be about the same age as Dorothy, and smiling upon her visitors she said, sweetly:

"You are welcome."

All the party seemed relieved to find that here was a real girl, of flesh and blood. She was very dainty and pretty as she stood there welcoming them. Her hair was a golden blonde and her eyes turquoise blue. She had rosy cheeks and lovely white teeth. Over her simple white lawn dress she wore an apron with pink and white checks, and in one hand she held a pair of scissors.

"May we see Miss Cuttenclip, please?" asked Dorothy.

"I am Miss Cuttenclip," was the reply. "Won't you come in?"

She held the door open while they all entered a pretty sitting-room that was littered with all sorts of paper—some stiff, some thin, and some tissue. The sheets and scraps were of all colors. Upon a table were paints and brushes, while several pair of scissors, of different sizes, were lying about.

"Sit down, please," said Miss Cuttenclip, clearing the paper scraps off some of the chairs. "It is so long since I have had any visitors that I am not properly prepared to receive them. But I'm sure you will pardon my untidy room, for this is my workshop."

"Do you make all the paper dolls?" inquired Dorothy.

"Yes; I cut them out with my scissors, and paint the faces and some of the costumes. It is very pleasant work, and I am happy making my paper village grow."

"But how do the paper dolls happen to be alive?" asked Aunt Em.

"The first dolls I made were not alive," said Miss Cuttenclip. "I used to live near the castle of a great Sorceress named Glinda the Good, and she saw my dolls and said they were very pretty. I told her I thought I would like them better if they were alive, and the next day the Sorceress brought me a lot of magic paper. 'This is live paper,' she said, 'and all the dolls you cut out of it will be alive, and able to think and to talk. When you have used it all up, come to me and I will give you more.'

"Of course I was delighted with this present," continued Miss Cuttenclip, "and at once set to work and made several paper dolls, which, as soon as they were cut out, began to walk around and talk to me. But they were so thin that I found that any breeze would blow them over and scatter them dreadfully; so Glinda found this lonely place for me, where few people ever come. She built the wall to keep any wind from blowing away my people, and told me I could build a paper village here and be its Queen. That is why I came here and settled down to work and started the village you now see. It was many years ago that I built the first houses, and I've kept pretty busy and made my village grow finely; and I need not tell you that I am very happy in my work."

"Many years ago!" exclaimed Aunt Em. "Why, how old are you, child?"

"I never keep track of the years," said Miss Cuttenclip, laughing. "You see, I don't grow up at all, but stay just the same as I was when first I came here. Perhaps I'm older even than you are, madam; but I couldn't say for sure."

They looked at the lovely little girl wonderingly, and the Wizard asked:

"What happens to your paper village when it rains?"

"It does not rain here," replied Miss Cuttenclip. "Glinda keeps all the rain storms away; so I never worry about my dolls getting wet. But now, if you will come with me, it will give me pleasure to show you over my paper kingdom. Of course you must go slowly and carefully, and avoid making any breeze."

They left the cottage and followed their guide through the various streets of the village. It was indeed an amazing place, when one considered that it was all made with scissors, and the visitors were not only greatly interested but full of admiration for the skill of little Miss Cuttenclip.

In one place a large group of especially nice paper dolls assembled to greet their Queen, whom it was easy to see they loved dearly. These dolls marched and danced before the visitors, and then they all waved their paper handkerchiefs and sang in a sweet chorus a song called "The Flag of Our Native Land."

At the conclusion of the song they ran up a handsome paper flag on a tall flagpole, and all of the people of the village gathered around to cheer as loudly as they could—although, of course, their voices were not especially strong.

Miss Cuttenclip was about to make her subjects a speech in reply to this patriotic song, when the Shaggy Man happened to sneeze.

He was a very loud and powerful sneezer at any time, and he had tried so hard to hold in this sneeze that when it suddenly exploded the result was terrible.

The paper dolls were mowed down by dozens, and flew and fluttered in wild confusion in every direction, tumbling this way and that and getting more or less wrinkled and bent.

A wail of terror and grief came from the scattered throng, and Miss Cuttenclip exclaimed:

"Dear me! dear me!" and hurried at once to the rescue of her overturned people.

"Oh, Shaggy Man! How could you?" asked Dorothy, reproachfully.

"I couldn't help it—really I couldn't," protested the Shaggy Man, looking quite ashamed. "And I had no idea it took so little to upset these paper dolls."

"So little!" said Dorothy. "Why, it was 'most as bad as a Kansas cyclone." And then she helped Miss Cuttenclip rescue the paper folk and stand them on their feet again. Two of the cardboard houses had also tumbled over, and the little Queen said she would have to repair them and paste them together before they could be lived in again.

And now, fearing they might do more damage to the flimsy paper people, they decided to go away. But first they thanked Miss Cuttenclip very warmly for her courtesy and kindness to them.

"Any friend of Princess Ozma is always welcome here—unless he sneezes," said the Queen, with a rather severe look at the Shaggy Man, who hung his head. "I like to have visitors admire my wonderful village, and I hope you will call again."

Miss Cuttenclip herself led them to the door in the wall, and as they passed along the street the paper dolls peeped at them half fearfully from the doors and windows. Perhaps they will never forget the Shaggy Man's awful sneeze, and I am sure they were all glad to see the meat people go away.

How THE GENERAL MET THE FIRST AND FOREMOST

CHAPTER ELEVEN

On leaving the Growleywogs General Guph had to recross the Ripple Lands, and he did not find it a pleasant thing to do. Perhaps having his whiskers pulled out one by one and being used as a pincushion for the innocent amusement of a good natured jailor had not improved the quality of Guph's temper, for the old Nome raved and raged at the recollection of the wrongs he had suffered, and vowed to take vengeance upon the Growleywogs after he had used them for his purposes and Oz had been conquered. He went on in this furious way until he was half across the Ripple Land. Then he became seasick, and the rest of the way this naughty Nome was almost as miserable as he deserved to be.

But when he reached the plains again and the ground was firm under his feet he began to feel better, and instead of going back home he turned directly west. A squirrel, perched in a tree, saw him take this road and called to him warningly: "Look out!" But he paid no attention. An eagle paused in its flight through the air to look at him wonderingly and say: "Look out!" But on he went.

No one can say that Guph was not brave, for he had determined to visit those dangerous creatures the Phanfasms, who resided upon the very top of the dread Mountain of Phantastico. The Phanfasms were Erbs, and so dreaded by mortals and immortals alike that no one had been near their mountain home for several thousand years. Yet General Guph hoped to induce them to join in his proposed warfare against the good and happy Oz people.

Guph knew very well that the Phanfasms would be almost as dangerous to the Nomes as they would to the Ozites, but he thought himself so clever that he believed that he could manage these strange creatures and make them obey him. And there was no doubt at all that if he could enlist the services of the Phanfasms their tremendous power, united to the strength of the Growley-wogs and the cunning of the Whimsies would doom the Land of Oz to absolute destruction.

So the old Nome climbed the foothills and trudged along the wild mountain paths until he came to a big gully that encircled the Mountain of Phantastico and marked the boundary line of the dominion of the Phanfasms. This gully was about a third of the way up the mountain, and it was filled to the brim with red-hot molten lava, in which swam fire-serpents and poisonous salamanders. The heat from this mass and its poisonous smell were both so unbearable that even birds hesitated to fly over the gully, but circled around it. All living things kept away from the mountain.

Now Guph had heard, during his long lifetime, many tales of these dreaded Phanfasms; so he had heard of this barrier of melted lava, and also he had been told that there was a narrow bridge that spanned it in one place. So he walked along the edge until he found the bridge. It was a single arch of gray stone, and lying flat upon this bridge was a scarlet alligator, seemingly fast asleep.

When Guph stumbled over the rocks in approaching the bridge the creature opened its eyes, from which tiny flames shot in all directions, and after looking at the intruder very wickedly the scarlet alligator closed its eyelids again and lay still.

Guph saw there was no room for him to pass the alligator on the narrow bridge, so he called out to it:

"Good morning, friend. I don't wish to hurry you, but please tell me if you are coming down, or going up?"

"Neither," snapped the alligator, clicking its cruel jaws together. The General hesitated.

"Are you likely to stay there long?" he asked.

"A few hundred years or so," said the alligator.

Guph softly rubbed the end of his nose and tried to think what to do.

"Do you know whether the First and Foremost Phanfasm of Phantastico is at home or not?" he presently inquired.

"I expect he is, seeing he is always at home," replied the alligator.

"Ah; who is that coming down the mountain?" asked the Nome, gazing upward.

The alligator turned to look over its shoulder, and at once Guph ran to the bridge and leaped over the sentinel's back before it could turn back again. The scarlet monster made a snap at the Nome's left foot, but missed it by fully an inch.

"Ah ha!" laughed the General, who was now on the mountain path. "I fooled you that time."

"So you did; and perhaps you fooled yourself," retorted the alligator. "Go up the mountain, if you dare, and find out what the First and Foremost will do to you!"

"I will," declared Guph, boldly; and on he went up the path.

At first the scene was wild enough, but gradually it grew more and more awful in appearance. All the rocks had the shapes of frightful beings and even the tree trunks were gnarled and twisted like serpents.

Suddenly there appeared before the Nome a man with the head of an owl. His body was hairy, like that of an ape, and his only clothing was a scarlet scarf twisted around his waist. He bore a huge club in his hand and his round owl eyes blinked fiercely upon the intruder.

"What are you doing here?" he demanded, threatening Guph with his club.

"I've come to see the First and Foremost Phanfasm of Phantastico," replied the General, who did not like the way this creature looked at him, but still was not afraid.

"Ah; you shall see him!" the man said, with a sneering laugh. "The First and Foremost shall decide upon the best way to punish you."

"He will not punish me," returned Guph, calmly, "for I have come here to do him and his people a rare favor. Lead on, fellow, and take me directly to your master."

The owl-man raised his club with a threatening gesture.

"If you try to escape," he said, "beware—"

But here the General interrupted him.

"Spare your threats," said he, "and do not be impertinent, or I will have you severely punished. Lead on, and keep silent!"

This Guph was really a clever rascal, and it seems a pity he was so bad, for in a good cause he might have accomplished much. He realized that he had put himself into a dangerous position by coming to this dreadful mountain, but he also knew that if he showed fear he was lost. So he adopted a bold manner as his best defense. The wisdom of this plan was soon evident, for the Phanfasm with the owl's head turned and led the way up the mountain.

At the very top was a level plain, upon which were heaps of rock that at first glance seemed solid. But on looking closer Guph discovered that these rock heaps were dwellings, for each had an opening.

Not a person was to be seen outside the rock huts. All was silent.

The owl-man led the way among the groups of dwellings to one standing in the center. It seemed no better and no worse than any of the others. Outside the entrance to this rock heap the guide gave a low wail that sounded like "Lee-ow-ah!"

Suddenly there bounded from the opening another hairy man. This one wore the head of a bear. In his hand he bore a brass hoop. He glared at the stranger in evident surprise.

"Why have you captured this foolish wanderer and brought him here?" he demanded, addressing the owl-man.

"I did not capture him," was the answer. "He passed the scarlet alligator and came here of his own free will and accord."

The First and Foremost looked at the General.

"Have you tired of life, then?" he asked.

"No, indeed," answered Guph. "I am a Nome, and the Chief General of King Roquat the Red's great army of Nomes. I come of a long-lived race, and I may say that I expect to live a long time yet.

Sit down, you Phanfasms—if you can find a seat in this wild haunt—and listen to what I have to say."

With all his knowledge and bravery General Guph did not know that the steady glare from the bear eyes was reading his inmost thoughts as surely as if they had been put into words. He did not know that these despised rock heaps of the Phanfasms were merely deceptions to his own eyes, nor could he guess that he was standing in the midst of one of the most splendid and luxurious cities ever built by magic power. All that he saw was a barren waste of rock heaps, a hairy man with an owl's head and another with a bear's head. The sorcery of the Phanfasms permitted him to see no more.

Suddenly the First and Foremost swung his brass hoop and caught Guph around the neck with it. The next instant, before the General could think what had happened to him, he was dragged inside the rock hut. Here, his eyes still blinded to realities, he perceived only a dim light, by which the hut seemed as rough and rude inside as it was outside. Yet he had a strange feeling that many bright eyes were fastened upon him and that he stood in a vast and extensive hall.

The First and Foremost now laughed grimly and released his prisoner.

"If you have anything to say that is interesting," he remarked, "speak out, before I strangle you."

So Guph spoke out. He tried not to pay any attention to a strange rustling sound that he heard, as of an unseen multitude drawing near to listen to his words. His eyes could see only the fierce bear-man, and to him he addressed his speech. First he told of his plan to conquer the Land of Oz and plunder the country of its riches and enslave its people, who, being fairies, could not be killed. After relating all this, and telling of the tunnel the Nome King was building, he said he had come to ask the First and Foremost to join the Nomes, with his band of terrible warriors, and help them to defeat the Oz people.

The General spoke very earnestly and impressively, but when he had finished the bear-man began to laugh as if much amused, and his laughter seemed to be echoed by a chorus of merriment from an

unseen multitude. Then, for the first time, Guph began to feel a trifle worried.

"Who else has promised to help you?" finally asked the First and Foremost.

"The Whimsies," replied the General.

Again the bear-headed Phanfasm laughed.

"Any others?" he inquired.

"Only the Growleywogs," said Guph.

This answer set the First and Foremost laughing anew.

"What share of the spoils am I to have?" was the next question.

"Anything you like, except King Roquat's Magic Belt," replied Guph.

At this the Phanfasm set up a roar of laughter, which had its echo in the unseen chorus, and the bear-man seemed so amused that he actually rolled upon the ground and shouted with merriment.

"Oh, these blind and foolish Nomes!" he said. "How big they seem to themselves and how small they really are!"

Suddenly he arose and seized Guph's neck with one hairy paw, dragging him out of the hut into the open.

Here he gave a curious wailing cry, and, as if in answer, from all the rocky huts on the mountain top came flocking a horde of Phanfasms, all with hairy bodies, but wearing heads of various animals, birds and reptiles. All were ferocious and repulsive-looking to the deceived eyes of the Nome, and Guph could not repress a shudder of disgust as he looked upon them.

The First and Foremost slowly raised his arms, and in a twinkling his hairy skin fell from him and he appeared before the astonished Nome as a beautiful woman, clothed in a flowing gown of pink gauze. In her dark hair flowers were entwined, and her face was noble and calm.

At the same instant the entire band of Phanfasms was transformed into a pack of howling wolves, running here and there as they snarled and showed their ugly yellow fangs.

The woman now raised her arms, even as the man-bear had done, and in a twinkling the wolves became crawling lizards, while she herself changed into a huge butterfly.

Guph had only time to cry out in fear and take a step backward to avoid the lizards when another transformation occurred, and all returned instantly to the forms they had originally worn.

Then the First and Foremost, who had resumed his hairy body and bear head, turned to the Nome and asked:

"Do you still demand our assistance?"

"More than ever," answered the General, firmly.

"Then tell me: what can you offer the Phanfasms that they have not already?" inquired the First and Foremost.

Guph hesitated. He really did not know what to say. The Nome King's vaunted Magic Belt seemed a poor thing compared to the astonishing magical powers of these people. Gold, jewels and slaves they might secure in any quantity without especial effort. He felt that he was dealing with powers greatly beyond him. There was but one argument that might influence the Phanfasms, who were creatures of evil.

"Permit me to call your attention to the exquisite joy of making the happy unhappy," said he at last. "Consider the pleasure of destroying innocent and harmless people."

"Ah! you have answered me," cried the First and Foremost. "For that reason alone we will aid you. Go home, and tell your bandy-legged king that as soon as his tunnel is finished the Phanfasms will be with him and lead his legions to the conquest of Oz. The deadly desert alone has kept us from destroying Oz long ago, and your underground tunnel is a clever thought. Go home, and prepare for our coming!"

Guph was very glad to be permitted to go with this promise. The owl-man led him back down the mountain path and ordered the scarlet alligator to crawl away and allow the Nome to cross the bridge in safety.

After the visitor had gone a brilliant and gorgeous city appeared upon the mountain top, clearly visible to the eyes of the gaily dressed multitude of Phanfasms that lived there. And the First and Foremost, beautifully arrayed, addressed the others in these words:

"It is time we went into the world and brought sorrow and dismay to its people. Too long have we remained by ourselves upon this mountain top, for while we are thus secluded many nations have grown happy and prosperous, and the chief joy of the race of Phanfasms is to destroy happiness. So I think it is lucky that this messenger from the Nomes arrived among us just now, to remind us that the opportunity has come for us to make trouble. We will use King Roquat's tunnel to conquer the Land of Oz. Then we will destroy the Whimsies, the Growleywogs and the Nomes, and afterward go out to ravage and annoy and grieve the whole world."

The multitude of evil Phanfasms eagerly applauded this plan, which they fully approved.

I am told that the Erbs are the most powerful and merciless of all the evil spirits, and the Phanfasms of Phantastico belong to the race of Erbs.

How THEY MATCHED THE FUDDLES

CHAPTER TWELVE

Dorothy and her fellow travelers rode away from the Cuttenclip village and followed the indistinct path as far as the sign-post. Here they took the main road again and proceeded pleasantly through the pretty farming country. When evening came they stopped at a dwelling and were joyfully welcomed and given plenty to eat and good beds for the night.

Early next morning, however, they were up and eager to start, and after a good breakfast they bade their host good-bye and climbed into the red wagon, to which the Saw-Horse had been hitched all night. Being made of wood, this horse never got tired nor cared to lie down. Dorothy was not quite sure whether he ever slept or not, but it was certain that he never did when anybody was around.

The weather is always beautiful in Oz, and this morning the air was cool and refreshing and the sunshine brilliant and delightful.

In about an hour they came to a place where another road branched off. There was a sign-post here which read:

☛ THIS WAY TO FUDDLECUMJIG

"Oh, here is where we turn," said Dorothy, observing the sign.

"What! Are we going to Fuddlecumjig?" asked the Captain-General.

"Yes; Ozma thought we would enjoy the Fuddles. They are said to be very interesting," she replied.

"No one would suspect it from their name," said Aunt Em. "Who are they, anyhow? More paper things?"

"I think not," answered Dorothy, laughing; "but I can't say 'zactly, Aunt Em, what they are. We'll find out when we get there."

"Perhaps the Wizard knows," suggested Uncle Henry.

"No; I've never been there before," said the Wizard. "But I've often heard of Fuddlecumjig and the Fuddles, who are said to be the most peculiar people in all the Land of Oz."

"In what way?" asked the Shaggy Man.

"I don't know, I'm sure," said the Wizard.

Just then, as they rode along the pretty green lane toward Fuddlecumjig, they espied a kangaroo sitting by the roadside. The poor animal had its face covered with both its front paws and was crying so bitterly that the tears coursed down its cheeks in two tiny streams and trickled across the road, where they formed a pool in a small hollow.

The Saw-Horse stopped short at this pitiful sight, and Dorothy cried out, with ready sympathy:

"What's the matter, Kangaroo?"

"Boo-hoo! Boo-hoo!" wailed the kangaroo; "I've lost my mi—mi—mi— Oh, boo-hoo! Boo-hoo!"

"Poor thing," said the Wizard, "she's lost her mister. It's probably her husband, and he's dead."

"No, no, no!" sobbed the kangaroo. "It—it isn't that. I've lost my mi—mi— Oh, boo, boo-hoo!"

"I know," said the Shaggy Man; "she's lost her mirror."

"No; it's my mi—mi—mi— Boo-hoo! My mi— Oh, boo-hoo!" and the kangaroo cried harder than ever.

"It must be her mince-pie," suggested Aunt Em.

"Or her milk-toast," proposed Uncle Henry.

"I've lost my mi—mi—mittens!" said the kangaroo, getting it out at last.

"Oh!" cried the Yellow Hen, with a cackle of relief. "Why didn't you say so before?"

"Boo-hoo! I—I—couldn't," answered the kangaroo.

"But, see here," said Dorothy, "you don't need mittens in this warm weather."

"Yes, indeed I do," replied the animal, stopping her sobs and removing her paws from her face to look at the little girl reproachfully. "My hands will get all sunburned and tanned without my mittens, and I've worn them so long that I'll probably catch cold without them."

"Nonsense!" said Dorothy. "I never heard before of any kangaroo wearing mittens."

"Didn't you?" asked the animal, as if surprised.

"Never!" repeated the girl. "And you'll probably make yourself sick if you don't stop crying. Where do you live?"

"About two miles beyond Fuddlecumjig," was the answer. "Grandmother Gnit made me the mittens, and she's one of the Fuddles."

"Well, you'd better go home now, and perhaps the old lady will make you another pair," suggested Dorothy. "We're on our way to Fuddlecumjig, and you may hop along beside us."

So they rode on, and the kangaroo hopped beside the red wagon and seemed quickly to have forgotten her loss. By and by the Wizard said to the animal:

"Are the Fuddles nice people?"

"Oh, very nice," answered the kangaroo; "that is, when they're properly put together. But they get dreadfully scattered and mixed up, at times, and then you can't do anything with them."

"What do you mean by their getting scattered?" inquired Dorothy.

"Why, they're made in a good many small pieces," explained the kangaroo; "and whenever any stranger comes near them they have a habit of falling apart and scattering themselves around. That's when they get so dreadfully mixed, and it's a hard puzzle to put them together again."

"Who usually puts them together?" asked Omby Amby.

"Any one who is able to match the pieces. I sometimes put Grandmother Gnit together myself, because I know her so well I can tell every piece that belongs to her. Then, when she's all matched, she knits for me, and that's how she made my mittens. But it took a good many days hard knitting, and I had to put Grandmother together a good many times, because every time I came near she'd scatter herself."

"I should think she would get used to your coming, and not be afraid," said Dorothy.

"It isn't that," replied the kangaroo. "They're not a bit afraid, when they're put together, and usually they're very jolly and pleasant. It's just a habit they have, to scatter themselves, and if they didn't do it they wouldn't be Fuddles."

The travelers thought upon this quite seriously for a time, while the Saw-Horse continued to carry them rapidly forward. Then Aunt Em remarked:

"I don't see much use our visitin' these Fuddles. If we find them scattered, all we can do is to sweep 'em up, and then go about our business."

"Oh, I b'lieve we'd better go on," replied Dorothy. "I'm getting hungry, and we must try to get some luncheon at Fuddlecumjig. Perhaps the food won't be scattered as badly as the people."

"You'll find plenty to eat there," declared the kangaroo, hopping along in big bounds because the Saw-Horse was going so fast; "and they have a fine cook, too, if you can manage to put him together. There's the town now—just ahead of us!"

They looked ahead and saw a group of very pretty houses standing in a green field a little apart from the main road.

"Some Munchkins came here a few days ago and matched a lot of people together," said the kangaroo. "I think they are together yet, and if you go softly, without making any noise, perhaps they won't scatter."

"Let's try it," suggested the Wizard.

So they stopped the Saw-Horse and got out of the wagon, and, after bidding good bye to the kangaroo, who hopped away home, they entered the field and very cautiously approached the group of houses.

So silently did they move that soon they saw through the windows of the houses, people moving around, while others were passing to and fro in the yards between the buildings. They seemed much like other people, from a distance, and apparently they did not notice the little party so quietly approaching.

They had almost reached the nearest house when Toto saw a large beetle crossing the path and barked loudly at it. Instantly a wild clatter was heard from the houses and yards. Dorothy thought it sounded like a sudden hailstorm, and the visitors, knowing that caution was no longer necessary, hurried forward to see what had happened.

After the clatter an intense stillness reigned in the town. The strangers entered the first house they came to, which was also the largest, and found the floor strewn with pieces of the people who lived there. They looked much like fragments of wood neatly painted, and were of all sorts of curious and fantastic shapes, no two pieces being in any way alike.

They picked up some of these pieces and looked at them carefully. On one which Dorothy held was an eye, which looked at her pleasantly but with an interested expression, as if it wondered what she was going to do with it. Quite near by she discovered and picked up a nose, and by matching the two pieces together found that they were part of a face.

"If I could find the mouth," she said, "this Fuddle might be able to talk, and tell us what to do next."

"Then let us find it," replied the Wizard, and so all got down on their hands and knees and began examining the scattered pieces.

"I've found it!" cried the Shaggy Man, and ran to Dorothy with a queer-shaped piece that had a mouth on it. But when they tried to fit it to the eye and nose they found the parts wouldn't match together.

"That mouth belongs to some other person," said Dorothy. "You see we need a curve here and a point there, to make it fit the face."

"Well, it must be here some place," declared the Wizard; "so if we search long enough we shall find it."

Dorothy fitted an ear on next, and the ear had a little patch of red hair above it. So while the others were searching for the mouth she hunted for pieces with red hair, and found several of them which, when matched to the other pieces, formed the top of a man's head. She had also found the other eye and the ear by the time Omby Amby in a far corner discovered the mouth. When the face was thus completed all the parts joined together with a nicety that was astonishing.

"Why, it's like a picture puzzle!" exclaimed the little girl. "Let's find the rest of him, and get him all together."

"What's the rest of him like?" asked the Wizard. "Here are some pieces of blue legs and green arms, but I don't know whether they are his or not."

"Look for a white shirt and a white apron," said the head which had been put together, speaking in a rather faint voice. "I'm the cook."

"Oh, thank you," said Dorothy. "It's lucky we started you first, for I'm hungry, and you can be cooking something for us to eat while we match the other folks together."

It was not so very difficult, now that they had a hint as to how the man was dressed, to find the other pieces belonging to him, and as all of them now worked on the cook, trying piece after piece to see if it would fit, they finally had the cook set up complete.

When he was finished he made them a low bow and said:

"I will go at once to the kitchen and prepare your dinner. You will find it something of a job to get all the Fuddles together, so I advise you to begin on the Lord High Chigglewitz, whose first name is Larry. He's a bald-headed fat man and is dressed in a blue coat with brass buttons, a pink vest and drab breeches. A piece of his left knee is missing, having been lost years ago when he scattered himself too carelessly. That makes him limp a little, but he gets along very well with half a knee. As he is the chief personage in this town of Fuddle-cumjig, he will be able to welcome you and assist you with the others. So it will be best to work on him while I'm getting your dinner."

"We will," said the Wizard; "and thank you very much, Cook, for the suggestion."

Aunt Em was the first to discover a piece of the Lord High Chigglewitz.

"It seems to me like a fool business, this matching folks together," she remarked; "but as we haven't anything to do till dinner's ready we may as well get rid of some of this rubbish. Here, Henry, get busy and look for Larry's bald head. I've got his pink vest, all right."

They worked with eager interest, and Billina proved a great help to them. The yellow hen had sharp eyes and could put her head close to the various pieces that lay scattered around. She would examine the Lord High Chigglewitz and see which piece of him was next needed, and then hunt around until she found it. So before an hour had passed old Larry was standing complete before them.

"I congratulate you, my friends," he said, speaking in a cheerful voice. "You are certainly the cleverest people who ever visited us. I was never matched together so quickly in my life. I'm considered a great puzzle, usually."

"Well," said Dorothy, "there used to be a picture puzzle craze in

Kansas, and so I've had some 'sperience matching puzzles. But the pictures were flat, while you are round, and that makes you harder to figure out."

"Thank you, my dear," replied old Larry, greatly pleased. "I feel highly complimented. Were I not a really good puzzle there would be no object in my scattering myself."

"Why do you do it?" asked Aunt Em, severely. "Why don't you behave yourself, and stay put together?"

The Lord High Chigglewitz seemed annoyed by this speech; but he replied, politely:

"Madam, you have perhaps noticed that every person has some peculiarity. Mine is to scatter myself. What your own peculiarity is I will not venture to say; but I shall never find fault with you, whatever you do."

"Now, you've got your diploma, Em," said Uncle Henry, with a laugh, "and I'm glad of it. This is a queer country, and we may as well take people as we find them."

"If we did, we'd leave these folks scattered," she returned, and this retort made everybody laugh good-naturedly.

Just then Omby Amby found a hand with a knitting needle in it, and they decided to put Grandmother Gnit together. She proved an easier puzzle than old Larry, and when she was completed they found her a pleasant old lady who welcomed them cordially. Dorothy told her how the kangaroo had lost her mittens, and Grandmother Gnit promised to set to work at once and make the poor animal another pair.

Then the cook came to call them to dinner, and they found an inviting meal prepared for them. The Lord High Chigglewitz sat at the head of the table and Grandmother Gnit at the foot, and the guests had a merry time and thoroughly enjoyed themselves.

After dinner they went out into the yard and matched several other people together, and this work was so interesting that they might have spent the entire day at Fuddlecumjig had not the Wizard suggested that they resume their journey.

"But I don't like to leave all these poor people scattered," said Dorothy, undecided what to do.

"Oh, don't mind us, my dear," returned old Larry. "Every day or so some of the Gillikins, or Munchkins, or Winkies come here to amuse themselves by matching us together, so there will be no harm in leaving these pieces where they are for a time. But I hope you will visit us again, and if you do you will always be welcome, I assure you."

"Don't you ever match each other?" she inquired.

"Never; for we are no puzzles to ourselves, and so there wouldn't be any fun in it."

They now said good bye to the queer Fuddles and got into their wagon to continue their journey.

"Those are certainly strange people," remarked Aunt Em, thoughtfully, as they drove away from Fuddlecumjig, "but I really can't see what use they are, at all."

"Why, they amused us all for several hours," replied the Wizard. "That is being of use to us, I'm sure."

"I think they're more fun than playing solitaire or mumblety-peg," declared Uncle Henry, soberly. "For my part, I'm glad we visited the Fuddles."

How THE GENERAL TALKED TO THE KING

CHAPTER THIRTEEN

When General Guph returned to the cavern of the Nome King His Majesty asked:

"Well, what luck? Will the Whimsies join us?"

"They will," answered the General. "They will fight for us with all their strength and cunning."

"Good!" exclaimed the King. "What reward did you promise them?"

"Your Majesty is to use the Magic Belt to give each Whimsie a large, fine head, in place of the small one he is now obliged to wear."

"I agree to that," said the King. "This is good news, Guph, and it makes me feel more certain of the conquest of Oz."

"But I have other news for you," announced the General.

"Good or bad?"

"Good, Your Majesty."

"Then I will hear it," said the King, with interest.

"The Growleywogs will join us."

"No!" cried the astonished King.

"Yes, indeed," said the General. "I have their promise."

"But what reward do they demand?" inquired the King, suspiciously, for he knew how greedy the Growleywogs were.

"They are to take a few of the Oz people for their slaves," replied

Guph. He did not think it necessary to tell Roquat that the Growleywogs demanded twenty thousand slaves. It would be time enough for that when Oz was conquered.

"A very reasonable request, I'm sure," remarked the King. "I must congratulate you, Guph, upon the wonderful success of your journey."

"But that is not all," said the General, proudly.

The King seemed astonished.

"Speak out, sir!" he commanded.

"I have seen the First and Foremost Phanfasm of the Mountain of Phantastico, and he will bring his people to assist us."

"What!" cried the King. "The Phanfasms! You don't mean it, Guph!"

"It is true," declared the General, proudly.

The King became thoughtful, and his brows wrinkled.

"I'm afraid, Guph," he said rather anxiously, "that the First and Foremost may prove as dangerous to us as to the Oz people. If he and his terrible band come down from the mountain they may take the notion to conquer the Nomes!"

"Pah! That is a foolish idea," retorted Guph, irritably, but he knew in his heart that the King was right. "The First and Foremost is a particular friend of mine, and will do us no harm. Why, when I was there, he even invited me into his house."

The General neglected to tell the King how he had been jerked into the hut of the First and Foremost by means of the brass hoop. So Roquat the Red looked at his General admiringly and said:

"You are a wonderful Nome, Guph. I'm sorry I did not make you my General before. But what reward did the First and Foremost demand?"

"Nothing at all," answered Guph. "Even the Magic Belt itself could not add to his powers of sorcery. All the Phanfasms wish is to destroy the Oz people, who are good and happy. This pleasure will amply repay them for assisting us."

"When will they come?" asked Roquat, half fearfully.

"When the tunnel is completed," said the General.

"We are nearly half way under the desert now," announced the

King; "and that is fast work, because the tunnel has to be drilled through solid rock. But after we have passed the desert it will not take us long to extend the tunnel to the walls of the Emerald City."

"Well, whenever you are ready, we shall be joined by the Whimsies, the Growleywogs and the Phanfasms," said Guph; "so the conquest of Oz is assured without a doubt."

Again the King seemed thoughtful.

"I'm almost sorry we did not undertake the conquest alone," said he. "All of these allies are dangerous people, and they may demand more than you have promised them. It might have been better to have conquered Oz without any outside assistance."

"We could not do it," said the General, positively.

"Why not, Guph?"

"You know very well. You have had one experience with the Oz people, and they defeated you."

"That was because they rolled eggs at us," replied the King, with a shudder. "My Nomes cannot stand eggs, any more than I can myself. They are poison to all who live underground."

"That is true enough," agreed Guph.

"But we might have taken the Oz people by surprise, and conquered them before they had a chance to get any eggs. Our former defeat was due to the fact that the girl Dorothy had a Yellow Hen with her. I do not know what ever became of that hen, but I believe there are no hens at all in the Land of Oz, and so there could be no eggs there."

"On the contrary," said Guph, "there are now hundreds of chickens in Oz, and they lay heaps of those dangerous eggs. I met a goshawk on my way home, and the bird informed me that he had lately been to Oz to capture and devour some of the young chickens. But they are protected by magic, so the hawk did not get a single one of them."

"That is a very bad report," said the King, nervously. "Very bad, indeed. My Nomes are willing to fight, but they simply can't face hen's eggs—and I don't blame them."

"They won't need to face them," replied Guph. "I'm afraid of eggs myself, and don't propose to take any chances of being poisoned by them. My plan is to send the Whimsies through the tunnel first, and then the Growleywogs and the Phanfasms. By the time we Nomes get there the eggs will all be used up, and we may then pursue and capture the inhabitants at our leisure."

"Perhaps you are right," returned the King, with a dismal sigh. "But I want it distinctly understood that I claim Ozma and Dorothy as my own prisoners. They are rather nice girls, and I do not intend to let any of those dreadful creatures hurt them, or make them their slaves. When I have captured them I will bring them here and transform them into china ornaments to stand on my mantle. They will look very pretty—Dorothy on one end of the mantle and Ozma on the other—and I shall take great care to see they are not broken when the maids dust them."

"Very well, Your Majesty. Do what you will with the girls, for all I care. Now that our plans are arranged, and we have the three most powerful bands of evil spirits in the world to assist us, let us make haste to get the tunnel finished as soon as possible."

"It will be ready in three days," promised the King, and hurried away to inspect the work and see that the Nomes kept busy.

How THE WIZARD PRACTICED SORCERY

CHAPTER FOURTEEN

"Where next?" asked the Wizard, when they had left the town of Fuddlecumjig and the Saw-Horse had started back along the road.

"Why, Ozma laid out this trip," replied Dorothy, "and she 'vised us to see the Rigmaroles next, and then visit the Tin Woodman."

"That sounds good," said the Wizard. "But what road do we take to get to the Rigmaroles?"

"I don't know, 'zactly," returned the little girl; "but it must be somewhere just southwest from here."

"Then why need we go way back to the crossroads?" asked the Shaggy Man. "We might save a lot of time by branching off here."

"There isn't any path," asserted Uncle Henry.

"Then we'd better go back to the signposts, and make sure of our way," decided Dorothy.

But after they had gone a short distance farther the Saw-Horse, who had overheard their conversation, stopped and said:

"Here is a path."

Sure enough, a dim path seemed to branch off from the road they were on, and it led across pretty green meadows and past leafy groves, straight toward the southwest.

"That looks like a good path," said Omby Amby. "Why not try it?"

"All right," answered Dorothy. "I'm anxious to see what the Rig-maroles are like, and this path ought to take us there the quickest way."

No one made any objection to the plan, so the Saw-Horse turned into the path, which proved to be nearly as good as the one they had taken to get to the Fuddles.

At first they passed a few retired farm-houses, but soon these scattered dwellings were left behind and only the meadows and the trees were before them. But they rode along in cheerful content-ment, and Aunt Em got into an argument with Billina about the proper way to raise chickens.

"I do not care to contradict you," said the Yellow Hen, with dig-nity, "but I have an idea I know more about chickens than human beings do."

"Pshaw!" replied Aunt Em, "I've raised chickens for nearly forty years, Billina, and I know you've got to starve 'em to make 'em lay lots of eggs, and stuff 'em if you want good broilers."

"Broilers!" exclaimed Billina, in horror. "Broil my chickens!"

"Why, that's what they're for, ain't it?" asked Aunt Em, aston-ished.

"No, Aunt, not in Oz," said Dorothy. "People do not eat chickens here. You see, Billina was the first hen that was ever seen in this country, and I brought her here myself. Everybody liked her an' re-spected her, so the Oz people wouldn't any more eat her chickens than they would eat Billina."

"Well, I declare," gasped Aunt Em. "How about the eggs?"

"Oh, if we have more eggs than we want to hatch, we allow peo-ple to eat them," said Billina. "Indeed, I am very glad the Oz folks like our eggs, for otherwise they would spoil."

"This certainly is a queer country," sighed Aunt Em.

"Excuse me," called the Saw-Horse, "the path has ended and I'd like to know which way to go."

They looked around and, sure enough, there was no path to be seen.

"Well," said Dorothy, "we're going southwest, and it seems just as easy to follow that direction without a path as with one."

"Certainly," answered the Saw-Horse. "It is not hard to draw the wagon over the meadow. I only want to know where to go."

"There's a forest over there across the prairie," said the Wizard, "and it lies in the direction we are going. Make straight for the forest, Saw-Horse, and you're bound to go right."

So the wooden animal trotted on again and the meadow grass was so soft under the wheels that it made easy riding. But Dorothy was a little uneasy at losing the path, because now there was nothing to guide them.

No houses were to be seen at all, so they could not ask their way of any farmer; and although the Land of Oz was always beautiful, wherever one might go, this part of the country was strange to all the party.

"Perhaps we're lost," suggested Aunt Em, after they had proceeded quite a way in silence.

"Never mind," said the Shaggy Man; "I've been lost many a time—and so has Dorothy—and we've always been found again."

"But we may get hungry," remarked Omby Amby. "That is the worst of getting lost in a place where there are no houses near."

"We had a good dinner at the Fuddle town," said Uncle Henry, "and that will keep us from starving to death for a long time."

"No one ever starved to death in Oz," declared Dorothy, positively; "but people may get pretty hungry sometimes."

The Wizard said nothing, and he did not seem especially anxious. The Saw-Horse was trotting along briskly, yet the forest seemed farther away than they had thought when they first saw it. So it was nearly sundown when they finally came to the trees; but now they found themselves in a most beautiful spot, the wide-spreading trees being covered with flowering vines and having soft mosses underneath them.

"This will be a good place to camp," said the Wizard, as the Saw-Horse stopped for further instructions.

"Camp!" they all echoed.

"Certainly," asserted the Wizard. "It will be dark before very long and we cannot travel through this forest at night. So let us make a camp here, and have some supper, and sleep until daylight comes again."

They all looked at the little man in astonishment, and Aunt Em said, with a sniff:

"A pretty camp we'll have, I must say! I suppose you intend us to sleep under the wagon."

"And chew grass for our supper," added the Shaggy Man, laughing.

But Dorothy seemed to have no doubts and was quite cheerful.

"It's lucky we have the wonderful Wizard with us," she said; "because he can do 'most anything he wants to."

"Oh, yes; I forgot we had a Wizard," said Uncle Henry, looking at the little man curiously.

"I didn't," chirped Billina, contentedly.

The Wizard smiled and climbed out of the wagon, and all the others followed him.

"In order to camp," said he, "the first thing we need is tents. Will some one please lend me a handkerchief?"

The Shaggy Man offered him one, and Aunt Em another. He took them both and laid them carefully upon the grass near to the edge of the forest. Then he laid his own handkerchief down, too, and standing a little back from them he waved his left hand toward the handkerchiefs and said:

> "Tents of canvas, white as snow,
> Let me see how fast you grow!"

Then, lo and behold! the handkerchiefs became tiny tents, and as the travelers looked at them the tents grew bigger and bigger until in a few minutes each one was large enough to contain the entire party.

"This," said the Wizard, pointing to the first tent, "is for the accommodation of the ladies. Dorothy, you and your aunt may step inside and take off your things."

Every one ran to look inside the tent, and they saw two pretty white beds, all ready for Dorothy and Aunt Em, and a silver roost for Billina. Rugs were spread upon the grassy floor and some camp chairs and a table completed the furniture.

"Well, well, well! This beats anything I ever saw or heard of!" exclaimed Aunt Em, and she glanced at the Wizard almost fearfully, as if he might be dangerous because of his great powers.

"Oh, Mr. Wizard! How did you manage to do it?" asked Dorothy.

"It's a trick Glinda the Sorceress taught me, and it is much better magic than I used to practice in Omaha, or when I first came to Oz," he answered. "When the Good Glinda found I was to live in the Emerald City always, she promised to help me, because she said the Wizard of Oz ought really to be a clever Wizard, and not a humbug. So we have been much together and I am learning so fast that I expect to be able to accomplish some really wonderful things in time."

"You've done it now!" declared Dorothy. "These tents are just wonderful!"

"But come and see the men's tent," said the Wizard. So they went to the second tent, which had shaggy edges because it had been made from the Shaggy Man's handkerchief, and found that completely furnished also. It contained four neat beds for Uncle Henry, Omby Amby, the Shaggy Man and the Wizard. Also there was a soft rug for Toto to lie upon.

"The third tent," explained the Wizard, "is our dining room and kitchen."

They visited that next, and found a table and dishes in the dining tent, with plenty of those things necessary to use in cooking. The Wizard carried out a big kettle and set it swinging on a cross-bar before the tent. While he was doing this Omby Amby and the Shaggy Man brought a supply of twigs from the forest and then they built a fire underneath the kettle.

"Now, Dorothy," said the Wizard, smiling, "I expect you to cook our supper."

"But there is nothing in the kettle," she cried.

"Are you sure?" inquired the Wizard.

"I didn't see anything put in, and I'm almost sure it was empty when you brought it out," she replied.

"Nevertheless," said the little man, winking slyly at Uncle Henry, "you will do well to watch our supper, my dear, and see that it doesn't boil over."

Then the men took some pails and went into the forest to search for a spring of water, and while they were gone Aunt Em said to Dorothy:

"I believe the Wizard is fooling us. I saw the kettle myself, and when he hung it over the fire there wasn't a thing in it but air."

"Don't worry," remarked Billina, confidently, as she nestled in the grass before the fire. "You'll find something in the kettle when it's taken off—and it won't be poor, innocent chickens, either."

"Your hen has very bad manners, Dorothy," said Aunt Em, looking somewhat disdainfully at Billina. "It seems too bad she ever learned how to talk."

There might have been another unpleasant quarrel between Aunt Em and Billina had not the men returned just then with their pails filled with clear, sparkling water. The Wizard told Dorothy that she was a good cook and he believed their supper was ready.

So Uncle Henry lifted the kettle from the fire and poured its contents into a big platter which the Wizard held for him. The platter was fairly heaped with a fine stew, smoking hot, with many kinds of vegetables and dumplings and a rich, delicious gravy.

The Wizard triumphantly placed the platter upon the table in the dining tent and then they all sat down in camp chairs to the feast.

There were several other dishes on the table, all carefully covered, and when the time came to remove these covers they found bread and butter, cakes, cheese, pickles and fruits—including some of the luscious strawberries of Oz.

No one ventured to ask a question as to how these things came there. They contented themselves by eating heartily the good things provided, and Toto and Billina had their full share, you may be sure. After the meal was over Aunt Em whispered to Dorothy:

"That may have been magic food, my dear, and for that reason perhaps it won't be very nourishing; but I'm willing to say it tasted as good as anything I ever et." Then she added, in a louder tone: "Who's going to do the dishes?"

"No one, madam," answered the Wizard. "The dishes have 'done' themselves."

"La sakes!" ejaculated the good lady, holding up her hands in amazement. For, sure enough, when she looked at the dishes they had a moment before left upon the table, she found them all washed and dried and piled up into neat stacks.

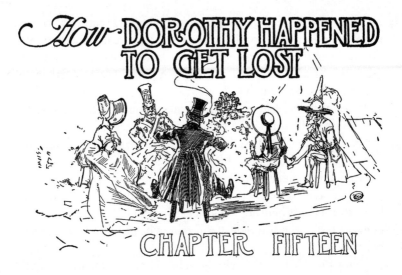

How DOROTHY HAPPENED TO GET LOST

CHAPTER FIFTEEN

It was a beautiful evening, so they drew their camp chairs in a circle before one of the tents and began to tell stories to amuse themselves and pass away the time before they went to bed.

Pretty soon a zebra was seen coming out of the forest, and he trotted straight up to them and said politely:

"Good evening, people."

The zebra was a sleek little animal and had a slender head, a stubby mane and a paint-brush tail—very like a donkey's. His neatly shaped white body was covered with regular bars of dark brown, and his hoofs were delicate as those of a deer.

"Good evening, friend Zebra," said Omby Amby, in reply to the creature's greeting. "Can we do anything for you?"

"Yes," answered the zebra. "I should like you to settle a dispute that has long been a bother to me, as to whether there is more water or land in the world."

"Who are you disputing with?" asked the Wizard.

"With a soft-shell crab," said the zebra. "He lives in a pool where I go to drink every day, and he is a very impertinent crab, I assure you. I have told him many times that the land is much greater in extent than the water, but he will not be convinced. Even this very evening, when I told him he was an insignificant creature who lived in a small pool, he asserted that the water was greater and more important than the land. So, seeing your camp, I decided to ask you to settle the dispute for once and all, that I may not be further annoyed by this ignorant crab."

When they had listened to this explanation Dorothy inquired:

"Where is the soft-shell crab?"

"Not far away," replied the zebra. "If you will agree to judge between us I will run and get him."

"Run along, then," said the little girl.

So the animal pranced into the forest and soon came trotting back to them. When he drew near they found a soft-shell crab clinging fast to the stiff hair of the zebra's head, where it held on by one claw.

"Now then, Mr. Crab," said the zebra, "here are the people I told you about; and they know more than you do, who live in a pool, and more than I do, who live in a forest. For they have been travelers all over the world, and know every part of it."

"There's more of the world than Oz," declared the crab, in a stubborn voice.

"That is true," said Dorothy; "but I used to live in Kansas, in the United States, and I've been to California and to Australia—and so has Uncle Henry."

"For my part," added the Shaggy Man, "I've been to Mexico and Boston and many other foreign countries."

"And I," said the Wizard, "have been to Europe and Ireland."

"So you see," continued the zebra, addressing the crab, "here are people of real consequence, who know what they are talking about."

"Then they know there's more water in the world than there is land," asserted the crab, in a shrill, petulant voice.

"They know you are wrong to make such an absurd statement, and they will probably think you are a lobster instead of a crab," retorted the animal.

At this taunt the crab reached out its other claw and seized the zebra's ear, and the creature gave a cry of pain and began prancing up and down, trying to shake off the crab, which clung fast.

"Stop pinching!" cried the zebra. "You promised not to pinch if I would carry you here!"

"And you promised to treat me respectfully," said the crab, letting go the ear.

"Well, haven't I?" demanded the zebra.

"No; you called me a lobster," said the crab.

"Ladies and gentlemen," continued the zebra, "please pardon my poor friend, because he is ignorant and stupid, and does not understand. Also the pinch of his claw is very annoying. So pray tell him that the world contains more land than water, and when he has heard your judgment I will carry him back and dump him into his pool, where I hope he will be more modest in the future."

"But we cannot tell him that," said Dorothy, gravely, "because it would not be true."

"What!" exclaimed the zebra, in astonishment; "do I hear you aright?"

"The soft-shell crab is correct," declared the Wizard. "There is considerably more water than there is land in the world."

"Impossible!" protested the zebra. "Why, I can run for days upon the land, and find but little water."

"Did you ever see an ocean?" asked Dorothy.

"Never," admitted the zebra. "There is no such thing as an ocean in the Land of Oz."

"Well, there are several oceans in the world," said Dorothy, "and people sail in ships upon these oceans for weeks and weeks, and never see a bit of land at all. And the joggerfys will tell you that all the oceans put together are bigger than all the land put together."

At this the crab began laughing in queer chuckles that reminded Dorothy of the way Billina sometimes cackled.

"*Now* will you give up, Mr. Zebra?" it cried, jeeringly; "now will you give up?"

The zebra seemed much humbled.

"Of course I cannot read geographys," he said.

"You could take one of the Wizard's School Pills," suggested Billina, "and that would make you learned and wise without studying."

The crab began laughing again, which so provoked the zebra that he tried to shake the little creature off. This resulted in more ear-pinching, and finally Dorothy told them that if they could not behave they must go back to the forest.

"I'm sorry I asked you to decide this question," said the zebra, crossly. "So long as neither of us could prove we were right we quite enjoyed the dispute; but now I can never drink at that pool again without the soft-shell crab laughing at me. So I must find another drinking place."

"Do! Do, you ignoramus!" shouted the crab, as loudly as his little voice would carry. "Rile some other pool with your clumsy hoofs, and let your betters alone after this!"

Then the zebra trotted back to the forest, bearing the crab with him, and disappeared amid the gloom of the trees. And as it was now getting dark the travelers said good night to one another and went to bed.

Dorothy awoke just as the light was beginning to get strong next morning, and not caring to sleep any later she quietly got out of bed, dressed herself, and left the tent where Aunt Em was yet peacefully slumbering.

Outside she noticed Billina busily pecking around to secure

bugs or other food for breakfast, but none of the men in the other tent seemed awake. So the little girl decided to take a walk in the woods and try to discover some path or road that they might follow when they again started upon their journey.

She had reached the edge of the forest when the Yellow Hen came fluttering along and asked where she was going.

"Just to take a walk, Billina; and maybe I'll find some path," said Dorothy.

"Then I'll go along," decided Billina, and scarcely had she spoken when Toto ran up and joined them.

Toto and the Yellow Hen had become quite friendly by this time, although at first they did not get along well together. Billina had been rather suspicious of dogs, and Toto had had an idea that it was every dog's duty to chase a hen on sight. But Dorothy had talked to them and scolded them for not being agreeable to one another until they grew better acquainted and became friends.

I won't say they loved each other dearly, but at least they had stopped quarreling and now managed to get on together very well.

The day was growing lighter every minute and driving the black shadows out of the forest; so Dorothy found it very pleasant walking under the trees. She went some distance in one direction, but not finding a path, presently turned in a different direction. There was no path here, either, although she advanced quite a way into the forest, winding here and there among the trees and peering through the bushes in an endeavor to find some beaten track.

"I think we'd better go back," suggested the Yellow Hen, after a time. "The people will all be up by this time and breakfast will be ready."

"Very well," agreed Dorothy. "Let's see—the camp must be over this way."

She had probably made a mistake about that, for after they had gone far enough to have reached the camp they still found themselves in the thick of the woods. So the little girl stopped short and looked around her, and Toto glanced up into her face with his bright little eyes and wagged his tail as if he knew something was wrong. He couldn't tell much about direction himself, because he had spent his time prowling among the bushes and running here and there; nor had Billina paid much attention to where they were going, being interested in picking bugs from the moss as they passed along. The Yellow Hen now turned one eye up toward the little girl and asked:

"Have you forgotten where the camp is, Dorothy?"

"Yes," she admitted; "have you, Billina?"

"I didn't try to remember," returned Billina. "I'd no idea you would get lost, Dorothy."

"It's the thing we don't expect, Billina, that usually happens," observed the girl, thoughtfully. "But it's no use standing here. Let's go in that direction," pointing a finger at random. "It may be we'll get out of the forest over there."

So on they went again, but this way the trees were closer together, and the vines were so tangled that often they tripped Dorothy up.

Suddenly a voice cried sharply:

"Halt!"

At first Dorothy could see nothing, although she looked around very carefully. But Billina exclaimed:

"Well, I declare!"

"What is it?" asked the little girl: for Toto began barking at something, and following his gaze she discovered what it was.

A row of spoons had surrounded the three, and these spoons stood straight up on their handles and carried swords and muskets. Their faces were outlined in the polished bowls and they looked very stern and severe.

Dorothy laughed at the queer things.

"Who are you?" she asked.

"We're the Spoon Brigade," said one.

"In the service of His Majesty King Kleaver," said another.

"And you are our prisoners," said a third.

Dorothy sat down on an old stump and looked at them, her eyes twinkling with amusement.

"What would happen," she inquired, "if I should set my dog on your Brigade?"

"He would die," replied one of the spoons, sharply. "One shot from our deadly muskets would kill him, big as he is."

"Don't risk it, Dorothy," advised the Yellow Hen. "Remember this is a fairy country, yet none of us three happens to be a fairy."

Dorothy grew sober at this.

"P'raps you're right, Billina," she answered. "But how funny it is, to be captured by a lot of spoons!"

"I do not see anything very funny about it," declared a spoon. "We're the regular military brigade of the kingdom."

"What kingdom?" she asked.

"Utensia," said he.

"I never heard of it before," asserted Dorothy. Then she added, thoughtfully, "I don't believe Ozma ever heard of Utensia, either. Tell me, are you not subjects of Ozma of Oz?"

"We never have heard of her," retorted a spoon. "We are subjects of King Kleaver, and obey only his orders, which are to bring all prisoners to him as soon as they are captured. So step lively, my girl, and march with us, or we may be tempted to cut off a few of your toes with our swords."

This threat made Dorothy laugh again. She did not believe she was in any danger; but here was a new and interesting adventure, so she was willing to be taken to Utensia that she might see what King Kleaver's kingdom was like.

How DOROTHY VISITED UTENSIA

CHAPTER SIXTEEN

There must have been from six to eight dozen spoons in the Brigade, and they marched away in the shape of a hollow square, with Dorothy, Billina and Toto in the center of the square. Before they had gone very far Toto knocked over one of the spoons by wagging his tail, and then the Captain of the Spoons told the little dog to be more careful, or he would be punished. So Toto was careful, and the Spoon Brigade moved along with astonishing swiftness, while Dorothy really had to walk fast to keep up with it.

By and by they left the woods and entered a big clearing, in which was the Kingdom of Utensia.

Standing all around the clearing were a good many cook-stoves, ranges and grills, of all sizes and shapes, and besides these there were several kitchen cabinets and cupboards and a few kitchen tables. These things were crowded with utensils of all sorts: frying pans, sauce pans, kettles, forks, knives, basting and soup spoons, nutmeg graters, sifters, colenders, meat saws, flat irons, rolling pins and many other things of a like nature.

When the Spoon Brigade appeared with the prisoners a wild shout arose and many of the utensils hopped off their stoves or their benches and ran crowding around Dorothy and the hen and the dog.

"Stand back!" cried the Captain, sternly, and he led his captives through the curious throng until they came before a big range that stood in the center of the clearing. Beside this range was a butcher's block upon which lay a great cleaver with a keen edge. It rested upon the flat of its back, its legs were crossed and it was smoking a long pipe.

"Wake up, Your Majesty," said the Captain. "Here are prisoners."

Hearing this, King Kleaver sat up and looked at Dorothy sharply.

"Gristle and fat!" he cried. "Where did this girl come from?"

"I found her in the forest and brought her here a prisoner," replied the Captain.

"Why did you do that?" inquired the King, puffing his pipe lazily.

"To create some excitement," the Captain answered. "It is so quiet here that we are all getting rusty for want of amusement. For my part, I prefer to see stirring times."

"Naturally," returned the cleaver, with a nod. "I have always said, Captain, without a bit of irony, that you are a sterling officer and a solid citizen, bowled and polished to a degree. But what do you expect me to do with these prisoners?"

"That is for you to decide," declared the Captain. "You are the King."

"To be sure; to be sure," muttered the cleaver, musingly. "As you say, we have had dull times since the steel and grindstone eloped and left us. Command my Counselors and the Royal Courtiers to attend me, as well as the High Priest and the Judge. We'll then decide what can be done."

The Captain saluted and retired and Dorothy sat down on an overturned kettle and asked:

"Have you anything to eat in your kingdom?"

"Here! Get up! Get off from me!" cried a faint voice, at which His Majesty the cleaver said:

"Excuse me, but you're sitting on my friend the Ten-quart Kettle."

Dorothy at once arose, and the kettle turned right side up and looked at her reproachfully.

"I'm a friend of the King, so no one dares sit on me," said he.

"I'd prefer a chair, anyway," she replied.

"Sit on that hearth," commanded the King.

So Dorothy sat on the hearth-shelf of the big range, and the subjects of Utensia began to gather around in a large and inquisitive throng. Toto lay at Dorothy's feet and Billina flew upon the range, which had no fire in it, and perched there as comfortably as she could.

When all the Counselors and Courtiers had assembled—and these seemed to include most of the inhabitants of the kingdom—the King rapped on the block for order and said:

"Friends and Fellow Utensils! Our worthy Commander of the Spoon Brigade, Captain Dipp, has captured the three prisoners you see before you and brought them here for—for—I don't know what for. So I ask your advice how to act in this matter, and what fate I should mete out to these captives. Judge Sifter, stand on my right. It is your business to sift this affair to the bottom. High Priest Colender, stand on my left and see that no one testifies falsely in this matter."

As these two officials took their places Dorothy asked:

"Why is the colender the High Priest?"

"He's the holiest thing we have in the kingdom," replied King Kleaver.

"Except me," said a sieve. "I'm the whole thing when it comes to holes."

"What we need," remarked the King, rebukingly, "is a wireless sieve. I must speak to Marconi about it. These old fashioned sieves talk too much. Now, it is the duty of the King's Counselors to counsel the King at all times of emergency, so I beg you to speak out and advise me what to do with these prisoners."

"I demand that they be killed several times, until they are dead!" shouted a pepper-box, hopping around very excitedly.

"Compose yourself, Mr. Paprica," advised the King. "Your remarks are piquant and highly-seasoned, but you need a scattering of commonsense. It is only necessary to kill a person once to make him dead; but I do not see that it is necessary to kill this little girl at all."

"I don't, either," said Dorothy.

"Pardon me, but you are not expected to advise me in this matter," replied King Kleaver.

"Why not?" asked Dorothy.

"You might be prejudiced in your own favor, and so mislead us," he said. "Now then, good subjects, who speaks next?"

"I'd like to smooth this thing over, in some way," said a flatiron, earnestly. "We are supposed to be useful to mankind, you know."

"But the girl isn't mankind! She's womankind!" yelled a corkscrew.

"What do you know about it?" inquired the King.

"I'm a lawyer," said the corkscrew, proudly. "I am accustomed to appear at the bar."

"But you're crooked," retorted the King, "and that debars you. You may be a corking good lawyer, Mr. Popp, but I must ask you to withdraw your remarks."

"Very well," said the corkscrew, sadly; "I see I haven't any pull at this court."

"Permit me," continued the flatiron, "to press my suit, Your Majesty. I do not wish to gloss over any fault the prisoner may have committed, if such a fault exists; but we owe her some consideration, and that's flat!"

"I'd like to hear from Prince Karver," said the King.

At this a stately carvingknife stepped forward and bowed.

"The Captain was wrong to bring this girl here, and she was wrong to come," he said. "But now that the foolish deed is done let us all prove our mettle and have a slashing good time."

"That's it! that's it!" screamed a fat choppingknife. "We'll make mincemeat of the girl and hash of the chicken and sausage of the dog!"

There was a shout of approval at this and the King had to rap again for order.

"Gentlemen, gentlemen!" he said, "your remarks are somewhat cutting and rather disjointed, as might be expected from such acute intellects. But you give no reasons for your demands."

"See here, Kleaver; you make me tired," exclaimed a saucepan, strutting before the King very impudently. "You're about the worst

King that ever reigned in Utensia, and that's saying a good deal. Why don't you run things yourself, instead of asking everybody's advice, like the big, clumsy idiot you are?"

The King sighed.

"I wish there wasn't a saucepan in my kingdom," he said. "You fellows are always stewing, over something, and every once in a while you slop over and make a mess of it. Go hang yourself, sir— by the handle—and don't let me hear from you again."

Dorothy was much shocked by the dreadful language the utensils employed, and she thought that they must have had very little proper training. So she said, addressing the King, who seemed very unfit to rule his turbulent subjects:

"I wish you'd decide my fate right away. I can't stay here all day, trying to find out what you're going to do with me."

"This thing is becoming a regular broil, and it's time I took part in it," observed a big gridiron, coming forward.

"What I'd like to know," said a can-opener, in a shrill voice, "is why the girl came to our forest, anyhow, and why she intruded upon Captain Dipp—who ought to be called Dippy—and who she is, and where she came from, and where she is going, and why and wherefore and therefore and when."

"I'm sorry to see, Sir Jabber," remarked the King to the can-opener, "that you have such a prying disposition. As a matter of fact, all the things you mention are none of our business."

Having said this the King relighted his pipe, which had gone out.

"Tell me, please, what *is* our business?" inquired a potato-masher, winking at Dorothy somewhat impertinently. "I'm fond of little girls, myself, and it seems to me she has as much right to wander in the forest as we have."

"Who accuses the little girl, anyway?" inquired a rolling-pin. "What has she done?"

"I don't know," said the King. "What has she done, Captain Dipp?"

"That's the trouble, Your Majesty. She hasn't done anything," replied the Captain.

"What do you want me to do?" asked Dorothy.

This question seemed to puzzle them all. Finally a chafingdish exclaimed, irritably:

"If no one can throw any light on this subject you must excuse me if I go out."

At this a big kitchen fork pricked up its ears and said in a tiny voice:

"Let's hear from Judge Sifter."

"That's proper," returned the King.

So Judge Sifter turned around slowly several times and then said:

"We have nothing against the girl except the stove-hearth upon which she sits. Therefore I order her instantly discharged."

"Discharged!" cried Dorothy. "Why, I never was discharged in my life, and I don't intend to be. If it's all the same to you, I'll resign."

"It's all the same," declared the King. "You are free—you and your companions—and may go wherever you like."

"Thank you," said the little girl. "But haven't you anything to eat in your kingdom? I'm hungry."

"Go into the woods and pick blackberries," advised the King, lying down upon his back again and preparing to go to sleep. "There isn't a morsel to eat in all Utensia, that I know of."

So Dorothy jumped up and said:

"Come on, Toto and Billina. If we can't find the camp we may find some blackberries."

The utensils drew back and allowed them to pass without protest, although Captain Dipp marched the Spoon Brigade in close order after them until they had reached the edge of the clearing.

There the spoons halted; but Dorothy and her companions entered the forest again and began searching diligently for a way back to the camp, that they might rejoin their party.

How THEY CAME TO BUNBURY

CHAPTER SEVENTEEN

Wandering through the woods, without knowing where you are going or what adventure you are about to meet next, is not as pleasant as one might think. The woods are always beautiful and impressive, and if you are not worried or hungry you may enjoy them immensely; but Dorothy was worried and hungry that morning, so she paid little attention to the beauties of the forest, and hurried along as fast as she could go. She tried to keep in one direction and not circle around, but she was not at all sure that the direction she had chosen would lead her to the camp.

By and by, to her great joy, she came upon a path. It ran to the right and to the left, being lost in the trees in both directions, and just before her, upon a big oak, were fastened two signs, with arms pointing both ways. One sign read:

☞ TAKE THE OTHER ROAD TO BUNBURY

and the second sign read:

☞ TAKE THE OTHER ROAD TO BUNNYBURY

"Well!" exclaimed Billina, eyeing the signs, "this looks as if we were getting back to civilization again."

"I'm not sure about the civil'zation, dear," replied the little girl; "but it looks as if we might get *somewhere*, and that's a big relief, anyhow."

"Which path shall we take?" inquired the Yellow Hen.

Dorothy stared at the signs thoughtfully.

"Bunbury sounds like something to eat," she said. "Let's go there."

"It's all the same to me," replied Billina. She had picked up enough bugs and insects from the moss as she went along to satisfy her own hunger, but the hen knew Dorothy could not eat bugs; nor could Toto.

The path to Bunbury seemed little traveled, but it was distinct enough and ran through the trees in a zigzag course until it finally led them to an open space filled with the queerest houses Dorothy had ever seen. They were all made of crackers, laid out in tiny squares, and were of many pretty and ornamental shapes, having balconies and porches with posts of bread-sticks and roofs shingled with wafer-crackers.

There were walks of bread-crusts leading from house to house and forming streets, and the place seemed to have many inhabitants.

When Dorothy, followed by Billina and Toto, entered the place, they found people walking the streets or assembled in groups talking together, or sitting upon the porches and balconies.

And what funny people they were!

Men, women and children were all made of buns and bread. Some were thin and others fat; some were white, some light brown and some very dark of complexion. A few of the buns, which seemed to form the more important class of the people, were neatly frosted. Some had raisins for eyes and currant buttons on their clothes; others had eyes of cloves and legs of stick cinnamon, and many wore hats and bonnets frosted pink and green.

There was something of a commotion in Bunbury when the strangers suddenly appeared among them. Women caught up their children and hurried into their houses, shutting the cracker doors carefully behind them. Some men ran so hastily that they tumbled over one another, while others, more brave, assembled in a group and faced the intruders defiantly.

Dorothy at once realized that she must act with caution in order not to frighten these shy people, who were evidently unused to the presence of strangers. There was a delightful fragrant odor of fresh bread in the town, and this made the little girl more hungry than ever. She told Toto and Billina to stay back while she slowly advanced toward the group that stood silently awaiting her.

"You must 'scuse me for coming unexpected," she said, softly, "but I really didn't know I was coming here until I arrived. I was lost in the woods, you know, and I'm as hungry as anything."

"Hungry!" they murmured, in a horrified chorus.

"Yes; I haven't had anything to eat since last night's supper," she explained. "Are there any eatables in Bunbury?"

They looked at one another undecidedly, and then one portly bun man, who seemed a person of consequence, stepped forward and said:

"Little girl, to be frank with you, we are all eatables. Everything in Bunbury is eatable to ravenous human creatures like you. But it is to escape being eaten and destroyed that we have secluded ourselves in this out-of-the-way place, and there is neither right nor justice in your coming here to feed upon us."

Dorothy looked at him longingly.

"You're bread, aren't you?" she asked.

"Yes; bread and butter. The butter is inside me, so it won't melt and run. I do the running myself."

At this joke all the others burst into a chorus of laughter, and Dorothy thought they couldn't be much afraid if they could laugh like that.

"Couldn't I eat something besides people?" she asked. "Couldn't I eat just one house, or a side-walk, or something? I wouldn't mind much what it was, you know."

"This is not a public bakery, child," replied the man, sternly. "It's private property."

"I know Mr.—Mr.—"

"My name is C. Bunn, Esquire," said the man. "C stands for Cinnamon, and this place is called after my family, which is the most aristocratic in the town."

"Oh, I don't know about that," objected another of the queer people. "The Grahams and the Browns and Whites are all excellent families, and there are none better of their kind. I'm a Boston Brown, myself."

"I admit you are all desirable citizens," said Mr. Bunn, rather stiffly; "but the fact remains that our town is called Bunbury."

"'Scuse me," interrupted Dorothy; "but I'm getting hungrier every minute. Now, if you're polite and kind, as I'm sure you ought to be, you'll let me eat *something*. There's so much to eat here that you never will miss it."

Then a big, puffed-up man, of a delicate brown color, stepped forward and said:

"I think it would be a shame to send this child away hungry, especially as she agrees to eat whatever we can spare and not touch our people."

"So do I, Pop," replied a Roll who stood near.

"What, then, do you suggest, Mr. Over?" inquired Mr. Bunn.

"Why, I'll let her eat my back fence, if she wants to. It's made of waffles, and they're very crisp and nice."

"She may also eat my wheelbarrow," added a pleasant looking Muffin. "It's made of nabiscos with a zuzu wheel."

"Very good; very good," remarked Mr. Bunn. "That is certainly very kind of you. Go with Pop Over and Mr. Muffin, little girl, and they will feed you."

"Thank you very much," said Dorothy, gratefully. "May I bring my dog Toto, and the Yellow Hen? They're hungry, too."

"Will you make them behave?" asked the Muffin.

"Of course," promised Dorothy.

"Then come along," said Pop Over.

So Dorothy and Billina and Toto walked up the street and the people seemed no longer to be at all afraid of them. Mr. Muffin's house came first, and as his wheelbarrow stood in the front yard the little girl ate that first. It didn't seem very fresh, but she was so hungry that she was not particular. Toto ate some, too, while Billina picked up the crumbs.

While the strangers were engaged in eating, many of the people came and stood in the street curiously watching them. Dorothy noticed six roguish looking brown children standing all in a row, and she asked:

"Who are you, little ones?"

"We're the Graham Gems," replied one; "and we're all twins."

"I wonder if your mother could spare one or two of you?" asked Billina, who decided that they were fresh baked; but at this dangerous question the six little gems ran away as fast as they could go.

"You mustn't say such things, Billina," said Dorothy, reprovingly. "Now let's go into Pop Over's back yard and get the waffles."

"I sort of hate to let that fence go," remarked Mr. Over, nervously, as they walked toward his house. "The neighbors back of us are Soda Biscuits, and I don't care to mix with them."

"But I'm hungry yet," declared the girl. "That wheelbarrow wasn't very big."

"I've got a shortcake piano, but none of my family can play on it," he said, reflectively. "Suppose you eat that."

"All right," said Dorothy; "I don't mind. Anything to be accommodating."

So Mr. Over led her into the house, where she ate the piano, which was of an excellent flavor.

"Is there anything to drink here?" she asked.

"Yes; I've a milk pump and a water pump; which will you have?" he asked.

"I guess I'll try 'em both," said Dorothy.

So Mr. Over called to his wife, who brought into the yard a pail made of some kind of baked dough, and Dorothy pumped the pail full of cool, sweet milk and drank it eagerly.

The wife of Pop Over was several shades darker than her husband.

"Aren't you overdone?" the little girl asked her.

"No indeed," answered the woman. "I'm neither overdone nor done over; I'm just Mrs. Over, and I'm the President of the Bunbury Breakfast Band."

Dorothy thanked them for their hospitality and went away. At the gate Mr. Cinnamon Bunn met her and said he would show her around the town.

"We have some very interesting inhabitants," he remarked, walking stiffly beside her on his stick-cinnamon legs; "and all of us who are in good health are well bred. If you are no longer hungry we will call upon a few of the most important citizens."

Toto and Billina followed behind them, behaving very well, and a little way down the street they came to a handsome residence where Aunt Sally Lunn lived. The old lady was glad to meet the little girl and gave her a slice of white bread and butter which had been used as a door-mat. It was almost fresh and tasted better than anything Dorothy had eaten in the town.

"Where do you get the butter?" she inquired.

"We dig it out of the ground, which, as you may have observed, is all flour and meal," replied Mr. Bunn. "There is a butter mine just at the opposite side of the village. The trees which you see here are all doughleanders and doughderas, and in the season we get quite a crop of dough-nuts off them."

"I should think the flour would blow around and get into your eyes," said Dorothy.

"No," said he; "we are bothered with cracker dust sometimes, but never with flour."

Then he took her to see Johnny Cake, a cheerful old gentleman who lived near by.

"I suppose you've heard of me," said old Johnny, with an air of pride. "I'm a great favorite all over the world."

"Aren't you rather yellow?" asked Dorothy, looking at him critically.

"Maybe, child. But don't think I'm bilious, for I was never in better health in my life," replied the old gentleman. "If anything ailed me, I'd willingly acknowledge the corn."

"Johnny's a trifle stale," said Mr. Bunn, as they went away; "but he's a good mixer and never gets cross-grained. I will now take you to call upon some of my own relatives."

They visited the Sugar Bunns, the Currant Bunns and the Spanish Bunns, the latter having a decidedly foreign appearance. Then they saw the French Rolls, who were very polite to them, and made a brief call upon the Parker H. Rolls, who seemed a bit proud and overbearing.

"But they're not as stuck up as the Frosted Jumbles," declared Mr. Bunn, "who are people I really can't abide. I don't like to be suspicious or talk scandal, but sometimes I think the Jumbles have too much baking powder in them."

Just then a dreadful scream was heard, and Dorothy turned hastily around to find a scene of great excitement a little way down the street. The people were crowding around Toto and throwing at him everything they could find at hand. They pelted the little dog with hard-tack, crackers, and even articles of furniture which were hard baked and heavy enough for missiles.

Toto howled a little as the assortment of bake stuff struck him; but he stood still, with head bowed and tail between his legs, until Dorothy ran up and inquired what the matter was.

"Matter!" cried a rye loafer, indignantly, "why the horrid beast has eaten three of our dear Crumpets, and is now devouring a Salt-rising Biscuit!"

"Oh, Toto! How could you?" exclaimed Dorothy, much distressed.

Toto's mouth was full of his salt-rising victim; so he only whined and wagged his tail. But Billina, who had flown to the top of a cracker house to be in a safe place, called out:

"Don't blame him, Dorothy; the Crumpets dared him to do it."

"Yes, and you pecked out the eyes of a Raisin Bunn—one of our best citizens!" shouted a bread pudding, shaking its fist at the Yellow Hen.

"What's that! What's that?" wailed Mr. Cinnamon Bunn, who had now joined them. "Oh, what a misfortune—what a terrible misfortune!"

"See here," said Dorothy, determined to defend her pets, "I think we've treated you all pretty well, seeing you're eatables, an' reg'lar food for us. I've been kind to you, and eaten your old wheelbarrows and pianos and rubbish, an' not said a word. But Toto and Billina can't be 'spected to go hungry when the town's full of good things they like to eat, 'cause they can't understand your stingy ways as I do."

"You must leave here at once!" said Mr. Bunn, sternly.

"Suppose we won't go?" asked Dorothy, who was now much provoked.

"Then," said he, "we will put you into the great ovens where we are made, and bake you."

Dorothy gazed around and saw threatening looks upon the faces of all. She had not noticed any ovens in the town, but they might be there, nevertheless, for some of the inhabitants seemed very fresh. So she decided to go, and calling to Toto and Billina to follow her she marched up the street with as much dignity as possible, considering that she was followed by the hoots and cries of the buns and biscuits and other bake stuff.

How OZMA LOOKED INTO THE MAGIC PICTURE

CHAPTER EIGHTEEN

Princess Ozma was a very busy little ruler, for she looked carefully after the comfort and welfare of her people and tried to make them happy. If any quarrels arose she decided them justly; if any one needed counsel or advice she was ready and willing to listen to them.

For a day or two after Dorothy and her companions had started on their trip, Ozma was occupied with the affairs of her kingdom. Then she began to think of some manner of occupation for Uncle Henry and Aunt Em that would be light and easy and yet give the old people something to do.

She soon decided to make Uncle Henry the Keeper of the Jewels, for some one really was needed to count and look after the bins and barrels of emeralds, diamonds, rubies and other precious stones that were in the Royal Storehouses. That would keep Uncle Henry busy enough, but it was harder to find something for Aunt Em to do. The palace was full of servants, so there was no detail of housework that Aunt Em could look after.

While Ozma sat in her pretty room engaged in thought she happened to glance at her Magic Picture.

This was one of the most important treasures in all the Land of

Oz. It was a large picture, set in a beautiful gold frame, and it hung in a prominent place upon a wall of Ozma's private room.

Usually this picture seemed merely a country scene, but whenever Ozma looked at it and wished to know what any of her friends or acquaintances were doing, the magic of this wonderful picture was straightway disclosed. For the country scene would gradually fade away and in its place would appear the likeness of the person or persons Ozma might wish to see, surrounded by the actual scenes in which they were then placed. In this way the Princess could view any part of the world she wished, and watch the actions of any one in whom she was interested.

Ozma had often seen Dorothy in her Kansas home by this means, and now, having a little leisure, she expressed a desire to see her little friend again. It was while the travelers were at Fuddle-cumjig, and Ozma laughed merrily as she watched in the picture her friends trying to match the pieces of Grandmother Gnit.

"They seem happy and are doubtless having a good time," the girl Ruler said to herself; and then she began to think of the many adventures she herself had encountered with Dorothy.

The images of her friends now faded from the Magic Picture and the old landscape slowly reappeared.

Ozma was thinking of the time when with Dorothy and her army she marched to the Nome King's underground cavern, beyond the Land of Ev, and forced the old monarch to liberate his captives, who belonged to the Royal Family of Ev. That was the time when the Scarecrow nearly frightened the Nome King into fits by throwing one of Billina's eggs at him, and Dorothy had captured King Roquat's Magic Belt and brought it away with her to the Land of Oz.

The pretty Princess smiled at the recollection of this adventure, and then she wondered what had become of the Nome King since then. Merely because she was curious and had nothing better to do, Ozma glanced at the Magic Picture and wished to see in it the King of the Nomes.

Roquat the Red went every day into his tunnel to see how the work was getting along and to hurry his workmen as much as possible. He was there now, and Ozma saw him plainly in the Magic Picture.

She saw the underground tunnel, reaching far underneath the deadly desert which separated the Land of Oz from the mountains beneath which the Nome King had his extensive caverns. She saw that the tunnel was being made in the direction of the Emerald City, and knew at once it was being dug so that the army of Nomes could march through it and attack her own beautiful and peaceful country.

"I suppose King Roquat is planning revenge against us," she said, musingly, "and thinks he can surprise us and make us his captives and slaves. How sad it is that any one can have such wicked thoughts! But I must not blame King Roquat too severely, for he is a Nome, and his nature is not so gentle as my own."

Then she dismissed from her mind further thought of the tunnel, for that time, and began to wonder if Aunt Em would not be happy as Royal Mender of the Stockings of the Ruler of Oz. Ozma wore few holes in her stockings; still, they sometimes needed mending. Aunt Em ought to be able to do that very nicely.

Next day the Princess watched the tunnel again in her Magic Picture, and every day afterward she devoted a few minutes to inspecting the work. It was not especially interesting, but she felt that it was her duty.

Slowly but surely the big arched hole crept through the rocks underneath the deadly desert, and day by day it drew nearer and nearer to the Emerald City.

How BUNNYBURY WELCOMED THE STRANGERS

CHAPTER NINETEEN

Dorothy left Bunbury the same way she had entered it and when they were in the forest again she said to Billina:

"I never thought that things good to eat could be so dis'gree'ble."

"Often I've eaten things that tasted good but were disagreeable afterward," returned the Yellow Hen. "I think, Dorothy, if eatables are going to act badly, it's better before than after you eat them."

"P'raps you're right," said the little girl, with a sigh. "But what shall we do now?"

"Let us follow the path back to the signpost," suggested Billina. "That will be better than getting lost again."

"Why, we're lost anyhow," declared Dorothy; "but I guess you're right about going back to that signpost, Billina."

They returned along the path to the place where they had first found it, and at once took "the other road" to Bunnybury. This road was a mere narrow strip, worn hard and smooth but not wide enough for Dorothy's feet to tread. Still it was a guide, and the walking through the forest was not at all difficult.

Before long they reached a high wall of solid white marble, and the path came to an end at this wall.

At first Dorothy thought there was no opening at all in the marble, but on looking closely she discovered a small square door about on a level with her head, and underneath this closed door was a bell-push. Near the bell-push a sign was painted in neat letters upon the marble, and the sign read:

No Admittance
Except on Business

This did not discourage Dorothy, however, and she rang the bell.

Pretty soon a bolt was cautiously withdrawn and the marble door swung slowly open. Then she saw it was not really a door, but a window, for several brass bars were placed across it, being set fast in the marble and so close together that the little girl's fingers might barely go between them. Back of the bars appeared the face of a white rabbit—a very sober and sedate face—with an eye-glass held in his left eye and attached to a cord in his button-hole.

"Well! what is it?" asked the rabbit, sharply.

"I'm Dorothy," said the girl, "and I'm lost, and—"

"State your business, please," interrupted the rabbit.

"My business," she replied, "is to find out where I am, and to—"

"No one is allowed in Bunnybury without an order or a letter of introduction from either Ozma of Oz or Glinda the Good," announced the rabbit; "so that that settles the matter," and he started to close the window.

"Wait a minute!" cried Dorothy. "I've got a letter from Ozma."

"From the Ruler of Oz?" asked the rabbit, doubtingly.

"Of course. Ozma's my best friend, you know; and I'm a Princess myself," she announced, earnestly.

"Hum—ha! Let me see your letter," returned the rabbit, as if he still doubted her.

So she hunted in her pocket and found the letter Ozma had given her. Then she handed it through the bars to the rabbit, who took it in his paws and opened it. He read it aloud in a pompous voice, as if to let Dorothy and Billina see that he was educated and could read writing. The letter was as follows:

"It will please me to have my subjects greet Princess Dorothy, the bearer of this royal missive, with the same courtesy and consideration they would extend to me."

"Ha—hum! It is signed 'Ozma of Oz,' " continued the rabbit, "and is sealed with the Great Seal of the Emerald City. Well, well, well! How strange! How remarkable!"

"What are you going to do about it?" inquired Dorothy, impatiently.

"We must obey the royal mandate," replied the rabbit. "We are subjects of Ozma of Oz, and we live in her country. Also we are under the protection of the great Sorceress Glinda the Good, who made us promise to respect Ozma's commands."

"Then may I come in?" she asked.

"I'll open the door," said the rabbit. He shut the window and disappeared, but a moment afterward a big door in the wall opened and admitted Dorothy to a small room, which seemed to be a part of the wall and built into it.

Here stood the rabbit she had been talking with, and now that she could see all of him she gazed at the creature in surprise. He was a good sized white rabbit with pink eyes, much like all other white rabbits. But the astonishing thing about him was the manner in which he was dressed. He wore a white satin jacket embroidered with gold, and having diamond buttons. His vest was rose-colored satin, with tourmaline buttons. His trousers were white, to correspond with the jacket, and they were baggy at the knees—like those of a zouave—being tied with knots of rose ribbons. His shoes were of white plush with diamond buckles, and his stockings were rose silk.

The richness and even magnificence of the rabbit's clothing made Dorothy stare at the little creature wonderingly. Toto and Billina had followed her into the room and when he saw them the rabbit ran to a table and sprang upon it nimbly. Then he looked at the three through his monocle and said:

"These companions, Princess, cannot enter Bunnybury with you."

"Why not?" asked Dorothy.

"In the first place they would frighten our people, who dislike dogs above all things on earth; and, secondly, the letter of the Royal Ozma does not mention them."

"But they're my friends," persisted Dorothy, "and go wherever I go."

"Not this time," said the rabbit, decidedly. "You, yourself, Princess, are a welcome visitor, since you come so highly recommended; but unless you consent to leave the dog and the hen in this room I cannot permit you to enter the town."

"Never mind us, Dorothy," said Billina. "Go inside and see what the place is like. You can tell us about it afterward, and Toto and I will rest comfortably here until you return."

This seemed the best thing to do, for Dorothy was curious to see how the rabbit people lived and she was aware of the fact that her friends might frighten the timid little creatures. She had not forgotten how Toto and Billina had misbehaved in Bunbury, and perhaps the rabbit was wise to insist on their staying outside the town.

"Very well," she said, "I'll go in alone. I s'pose you're the King of this town, aren't you?"

"No," answered the rabbit, "I'm merely the Keeper of the Wicket, and a person of little importance, although I try to do my duty. I must now inform you, Princess, that before you enter our town you must consent to reduce."

"Reduce what?" asked Dorothy.

"Your size. You must become the size of the rabbits, although you may retain your own form."

"Wouldn't my clothes be too big for me?" she inquired.

"No; they will reduce when your body does."

"Can *you* make me smaller?" asked the girl.

"Easily," returned the rabbit.

"And will you make me big again, when I'm ready to go away?"

"I will," said he.

"All right, then; I'm willing," she announced.

The rabbit jumped from the table and ran—or rather hopped—

to the further wall, where he opened a door so tiny that even Toto could scarcely have crawled through it.

"Follow me," he said.

Now, almost any other little girl would have declared that she could not get through so small a door; but Dorothy had already encountered so many fairy adventures that she believed nothing was impossible in the Land of Oz. So she quietly walked toward the door, and at every step she grew smaller and smaller until, by the time the opening was reached, she could pass through it with ease. Indeed, as she stood beside the rabbit, who sat upon his hind legs and used his paws as hands, her head was just about as high as his own.

Then the Keeper of the Wicket passed through and she followed, after which the door swung shut and locked itself with a sharp click.

Dorothy now found herself in a city so strange and beautiful that she gave a gasp of surprise. The high marble wall extended all around the place and shut out all the rest of the world. And here were marble houses of curious forms, most of them resembling overturned kettles but with delicate slender spires and minarets running far up into the sky. The streets were paved with white marble and in front of each house was a lawn of rich green clover. Everything was as neat as wax, the green and white contrasting prettily together.

But the rabbit people were, after all, the most amazing things Dorothy saw. The streets were full of them, and their costumes were so splendid that the rich dress of the Keeper of the Wicket was commonplace when compared with the others. Silks and satins of delicate hues seemed always used for material, and nearly every costume sparkled with exquisite gems.

But the lady rabbits outshone the gentlemen rabbits in splendor, and the cut of their gowns was really wonderful. They wore bonnets, too, with feathers and jewels in them, and some wheeled baby carriages in which the girl could see wee bunnies. Some were lying asleep while others lay sucking their paws and looking around them with big pink eyes.

As Dorothy was no bigger in size than the grown-up rabbits she had a chance to observe them closely before they noticed her presence. Then they did not seem at all alarmed, although the little girl naturally became the center of attraction and all regarded her with great curiosity.

"Make way!" cried the Keeper of the Wicket, in a pompous voice; "make way for Princess Dorothy, who comes from Ozma of Oz."

Hearing this announcement, the throng of rabbits gave place to them on the walks, and as Dorothy passed along they all bowed their heads respectfully.

Walking thus through several handsome streets they came to a square in the center of the city. In this square were some pretty trees and a statue in bronze of Glinda the Good, while beyond it were the portals of the Royal Palace—an extensive and imposing building of white marble covered with a filigree of frosted gold.

How DOROTHY LUNCHED WITH A KING

CHAPTER TWENTY

A line of rabbit soldiers was drawn up before the palace entrance, and they wore green and gold uniforms with high shakos upon their heads and held tiny spears in their hands. The Captain had a sword and a white plume in his shako.

"Salute!" cried the Keeper of the Wicket. "Salute Princess Dorothy, who comes from Ozma of Oz!"

"Salute!" yelled the Captain, and all the soldiers promptly saluted.

They now entered the great hall of the palace, where they met a gaily dressed attendant, from whom the Keeper of the Wicket inquired if the King were at leisure.

"I think so," was the reply. "I heard His Majesty blubbering and wailing as usual only a few minutes ago. If he doesn't stop acting like a cry-baby I'm going to resign my position here and go to work."

"What's the matter with your King?" asked Dorothy, surprised to hear the rabbit attendant speak so disrespectfully of his monarch.

"Oh, he doesn't want to be King, that's all; and he simply *has* to," was the reply.

"Come!" said the Keeper of the Wicket, sternly; "lead us to His Majesty; and do not air our troubles before strangers, I beg of you."

"Why, if this girl is going to see the King, he'll air his own troubles," returned the attendant.

"That is his royal privilege," declared the Keeper.

So the attendant led them into a room all draped with cloth-of-gold and furnished with satin-covered gold furniture. There was a throne in this room, set on a dais and having a big cushioned seat, and on this seat reclined the Rabbit King. He was lying on his back, with his paws in the air, and whining very like a puppy-dog.

"Your Majesty! Your Majesty! Get up. Here's a visitor," called out the attendant.

The King rolled over and looked at Dorothy with one watery pink eye. Then he sat up and wiped his eyes carefully with a silk handkerchief and put on his jeweled crown, which had fallen off.

"Excuse my grief, fair stranger," he said, in a sad voice. "You behold in me the most miserable monarch in all the world. What time is it, Blinkem?"

"One o'clock, Your Majesty," replied the attendant to whom the question was addressed.

"Serve luncheon at once!" commanded the King. "Luncheon for two—that's for my visitor and me—and see that the human has some sort of food she's accustomed to."

"Yes, Your Majesty," answered the attendant, and went away.

"Tie my shoe, Bristle," said the King to the Keeper of the Wicket. "Ah, me! how unhappy I am!"

"What seems to be worrying Your Majesty?" asked Dorothy.

"Why, it's this King business, of course," he returned, while the Keeper tied his shoe. "I didn't want to be King of Bunnybury at all, and the rabbits all knew it. So they elected me—to save themselves from such a dreadful fate, I suppose—and here I am, shut up in a palace, when I might be free and happy."

"Seems to me," said Dorothy, "it's a great thing to be a King."

"Were you ever a King?" inquired the monarch.

"No," she answered, laughing.

"Then you know nothing about it," he said. "I haven't inquired who you are, but it doesn't matter. While we're at luncheon, I'll tell you all my troubles. They're a great deal more interesting than anything you can say about yourself."

"Perhaps they are, to you," replied Dorothy.

"Luncheon is served!" cried Blinkem, throwing open the door, and in came a dozen rabbits in livery, all bearing trays which they placed upon the table, where they arranged the dishes in an orderly manner.

"Now clear out—all of you!" exclaimed the King. "Bristle, you may wait outside, in case I want you."

When they had gone and the King was alone with Dorothy he came down from his throne, tossed his crown into a corner and kicked his ermine robe under the table.

"Sit down," he said, "and try to be happy. It's useless for me to try, because I'm always wretched and miserable. But I'm hungry, and I hope you are."

"I am," said Dorothy. "I've only eaten a wheelbarrow and a piano to-day—oh, yes! and a slice of bread and butter that used to be a door-mat."

"That sounds like a square meal," remarked the King, seating himself opposite her; "but perhaps it wasn't a square piano. Eh?"

Dorothy laughed.

"You don't seem so very unhappy now," she said.

"But I am," protested the King, fresh tears gathering in his eyes. "Even my jokes are miserable. I'm wretched, woeful, afflicted, distressed and dismal as an individual can be. Are you not sorry for me?"

"No," answered Dorothy, honestly, "I can't say I am. Seems to me that for a rabbit you're right in clover. This is the prettiest little city I ever saw."

"Oh, the city is good enough," he admitted. "Glinda, the Good Sorceress, made it for us because she was fond of rabbits. I don't mind the city so much, although I wouldn't live here if I had my choice. It is being King that has absolutely ruined my happiness."

"Why wouldn't you live here by choice?" she asked.

"Because it is all unnatural, my dear. Rabbits are out of place in

such luxury. When I was young I lived in a burrow in the forest. I was surrounded by enemies and often had to run for my life. It was hard getting enough to eat, at times, and when I found a bunch of clover I had to listen and look for danger while I ate it. Wolves prowled around the hole in which I lived and sometimes I didn't dare stir out for days at a time. Oh, how happy and contented I was then! I was a real rabbit, as nature made me—wild and free!—and I even enjoyed listening to the startled throbbing of my own heart!"

"I've often thought," said Dorothy, who was busily eating, "that it would be fun to be a rabbit."

"It *is* fun—when you're the genuine article," agreed His Majesty. "But look at me now! I live in a marble palace instead of a hole in the ground. I have all I want to eat, without the joy of hunting for it. Every day I must dress in fine clothes and wear that horrible crown till it makes my head ache. Rabbits come to me with all sorts of troubles, when my own troubles are the only ones I care about. When I walk out I can't hop and run; I must strut on my rear legs and wear an ermine robe! And the soldiers salute me and the band plays and the other rabbits laugh and clap their paws and cry out: 'Hail to the King!' Now let me ask you, as a friend and a young lady of good judgment: isn't all this pomp and foolishness enough to make a decent rabbit miserable?"

"Once," said Dorothy, reflectively, "men were wild and un-clothed and lived in caves and hunted for food as wild beasts do. But they got civ'lized, in time, and now they'd hate to go back to the old days."

"That is an entirely different case," replied the King. "None of you Humans were civilized in one lifetime. It came to you by de-grees. But I have known the forest and the free life, and that is why I resent being civilized all at once, against my will, and being made a King with a crown and an ermine robe. Pah!"

"If you don't like it, why don't you resign?" she asked.

"Impossible!" wailed the Rabbit, wiping his eyes again with his handkerchief. "There's a beastly law in this town that forbids it. When one is elected a King there's no getting out of it."

"Who made the laws?" inquired Dorothy.

"The same Sorceress who made the town—Glinda the Good. She built the wall, and fixed up the city, and gave us several valuable enchantments, and made the laws. Then she invited all the pink-eyed white rabbits of the forest to come here, after which she left us to our fate."

"What made you 'cept the invitation, and come here?" asked the child.

"I didn't know how dreadful city life was, and I'd no idea I would be elected King," said he, sobbing bitterly. "And—and—now I'm It—with a capital I—and can't escape!"

"I know Glinda," remarked Dorothy, eating for dessert a dish of charlotte russe, "and when I see her again I'll ask her to put another King in your place."

"Will you? Will you, indeed?" asked the King, joyfully.

"I will if you want me to," she replied.

"Hurroo—hurray!" shouted the King; and then he jumped up from the table and danced wildly about the room, waving his napkin like a flag and laughing with glee.

After a time he managed to control his delight and returned to the table.

"When are you likely to see Glinda?" he inquired.

"Oh, p'raps in a few days," said Dorothy.

"And you won't forget to ask her?"

"Of course not."

"Princess," said the Rabbit King, earnestly, "you have relieved me of a great unhappiness, and I am very grateful. Therefore I propose to entertain you, since you are my guest and I am the King, as a slight mark of my appreciation. Come with me to my reception hall."

He then summoned Bristle and said to him: "Assemble all the nobility in the great reception hall, and also tell Blinkem that I want him immediately."

The Keeper of the Wicket bowed and hurried away, and His Majesty turned to Dorothy and continued: "We'll have time for a walk in the gardens before the people get here."

The gardens were back of the palace and were filled with beautiful flowers and fragrant shrubs, with many shade and fruit trees and marble paved walks running in every direction. As they entered this place Blinkem came running to the King, who gave him several orders in a low voice. Then His Majesty rejoined Dorothy and led her through the gardens, which she admired very much.

"What lovely clothes Your Majesty wears!" she said, glancing at the rich blue satin costume, embroidered with pearls, in which the King was dressed.

"Yes," he returned, with an air of pride, "this is one of my favorite suits; but I have a good many that are even more elaborate. We have excellent tailors in Bunnybury, and Glinda supplies all the material. By the way, you might ask the Sorceress, when you see her, to permit me to keep my wardrobe."

"But if you go back to the forest you will not need clothes," she said.

"N—o!" he faltered; "that may be so. But I've dressed up so long that I'm used to it, and I don't imagine I'd care to run around naked again. So perhaps the Good Glinda will let me keep the costumes."

"I'll ask her," agreed Dorothy.

Then they left the gardens and went into a fine big reception hall, where rich rugs were spread upon the tiled floors and the furniture was exquisitely carved and studded with jewels. The King's chair was an especially pretty piece of furniture, being in the shape of a silver lily with one leaf bent over to form the seat. The silver was everywhere thickly encrusted with diamonds and the seat was upholstered in white satin.

"Oh, what a splendid chair!" cried Dorothy, clasping her hands admiringly.

"Isn't it?" answered the King, proudly. "It is my favorite seat, and I think it especially becoming to my complexion. While I think of it, I wish you'd ask Glinda to let me keep this lily chair when I go away."

"It wouldn't look very well in a hole in the ground, would it?" she suggested.

"Maybe not; but I'm used to sitting in it and I'd like to take it with me," he answered. "But here come the ladies and gentlemen of the court; so please sit beside me and be presented."

How THE KING CHANGED HIS MIND

CHAPTER TWENTY-ONE

Just then a rabbit band of nearly fifty pieces marched in, playing upon golden instruments and dressed in neat uniforms. Following the band came the nobility of Bunnybury, all richly dressed and hopping along on their rear legs. Both the ladies and the gentlemen wore white gloves upon their paws, with their rings on the outside of the gloves, as this seemed to be the fashion here. Some of the lady rabbits carried lorgnettes, while many of the gentlemen rabbits wore monocles in their left eyes.

The courtiers and their ladies paraded past the King, who introduced Princess Dorothy to each couple in a very graceful manner. Then the company seated themselves in chairs and on sofas and looked expectantly at their monarch.

"It is our royal duty, as well as our royal pleasure," he said, "to provide fitting entertainment for our distinguished guest. We will now present the Royal Band of Whiskered Friskers."

As he spoke the musicians, who had arranged themselves in a corner, struck up a dance melody while into the room pranced the Whiskered Friskers. They were eight pretty rabbits dressed only in gauzy purple skirts fastened around their waists with diamond bands. Their whiskers were colored a rich purple, but otherwise they were pure white.

After bowing before the King and Dorothy the Friskers began their pranks, and these were so comical that Dorothy laughed with real enjoyment. They not only danced together, whirling and gyrating around the room, but they leaped over one another, stood upon their heads and hopped and skipped here and there so nimbly that it was hard work to keep track of them. Finally they all made double somersaults and turned handsprings out of the room.

The nobility enthusiastically applauded, and Dorothy applauded with them.

"They're fine!" she said to the King.

"Yes, the Whiskered Friskers are really very clever," he replied. "I shall hate to part with them when I go away, for they have often amused me when I was very miserable. I wonder if you would ask Glinda—"

"No, it wouldn't do at all," declared Dorothy, positively. "There wouldn't be room in your hole in the ground for so many rabbits, 'spec'ly when you get the lily chair and your clothes there. Don't think of such a thing, Your Majesty."

The King sighed. Then he stood up and announced to the company:

"We will now behold a military drill by my picked Bodyguard of Royal Pikemen."

Now the band played a march and a company of rabbit soldiers came in. They wore green and gold uniforms and marched very stiffly but in perfect time. Their spears, or pikes, had slender shafts of polished silver with golden heads, and during the drill they handled these weapons with wonderful dexterity.

"I should think you'd feel pretty safe with such a fine Bodyguard," remarked Dorothy.

"I do," said the King. "They protect me from every harm. I suppose Glinda wouldn't—"

"No," interrupted the girl; "I'm sure she wouldn't. It's the King's own Bodyguard, and when you are no longer King you can't have 'em."

The King did not reply, but he looked rather sorrowful for a time.

When the soldiers had marched out he said to the company: "The Royal Jugglers will now appear."

Dorothy had seen many jugglers in her lifetime, but never any so interesting as these. There were six of them, dressed in black satin embroidered with queer symbols in silver—a costume which contrasted strongly with their snow-white fur.

First they pushed in a big red ball and three of the rabbit jugglers stood upon its top and made it roll. Then two of them caught up a third and tossed him into the air, all vanishing, until only the two were left. Then one of these tossed the other upward and remained alone of all his fellows. This last juggler now touched the red ball, which fell apart, being hollow, and the five rabbits who had disappeared in the air scrambled out of the hollow ball.

Next they all clung together and rolled swiftly upon the floor. When they came to a stop only one fat rabbit juggler was seen, the others seeming to be inside him. This one leaped lightly into the air and when he came down he exploded and separated into the original six. Then four of them rolled themselves into round balls and the other two tossed them around and played ball with them.

These were but a few of the tricks the rabbit jugglers performed, and they were so skillful that all the nobility and even the King applauded as loudly as did Dorothy.

"I suppose there are no rabbit jugglers in all the world to compare with these," remarked the King. "And since I may not have the Whiskered Friskers or my Bodyguard, you might ask Glinda to let me take away just two or three of these jugglers. Will you?"

"I'll ask her," replied Dorothy, doubtfully.

"Thank you," said the King; "thank you very much. And now you shall listen to the Winsome Waggish Warblers, who have often cheered me in my moments of anguish."

The Winsome Waggish Warblers proved to be a quartette of rabbit singers, two gentlemen and two lady rabbits. The gentlemen Warblers wore full-dress swallow-tailed suits of white satin, with pearls for buttons, while the lady Warblers were gowned in white satin dresses with long trails.

The first song they sang began in this way:

"When a rabbit gets a habit
     Of living in a city
And wearing clothes and furbelows
     And jewels rare and pretty,
He scorns the Bun who has to run
     And burrow in the ground
And pities those whose watchful foes
     Are man and gun and hound."

Dorothy looked at the King when she heard this song and noticed that he seemed disturbed and ill at ease.

"I don't like that song," he said to the Warblers. "Give us something jolly and rollicking."

So they sang to a joyous, tinkling melody as follows:

"Bunnies gay
     Delight to play
In their fairy town secure;
     Ev'ry frisker
     Flirts his whisker
At a pink-eyed girl demure.
     Ev'ry maid
     In silk arrayed
At her partner shyly glances,
     Paws are grasped,
     Waists are clasped
As they whirl in giddy dances.
     Then together
     Through the heather
'Neath the moonlight soft they stroll;
     Each is very
     Blithe and merry,
Gamboling with laughter droll.
     Life is fun
     To ev'ry one
Guarded by our magic charm
     For to dangers

We are strangers,
Safe from any thought of harm."

"You see," said Dorothy to the King, when the song ended, "the rabbits all seem to like Bunnybury except you. And I guess you're the only one that ever has cried or was unhappy and wanted to get back to your muddy hole in the ground."

His Majesty seemed thoughtful, and while the servants passed around glasses of nectar and plates of frosted cakes their King was silent and a bit nervous.

When the refreshments had been enjoyed by all and the servants had retired Dorothy said:

"I must go now, for it's getting late and I'm lost. I've got to find the Wizard and Aunt Em and Uncle Henry and all the rest some-time before night comes, if I poss'bly can."

"Won't you stay with us?" asked the King. "You will be very wel-come."

"No, thank you," she replied. "I must get back to my friends. And I want to see Glinda just as soon as I can, you know."

So the King dismissed his court and said he would himself walk with Dorothy to the gate. He did not weep nor groan any more, but his long face was quite solemn and his big ears hung dejectedly on each side of it. He still wore his crown and his ermine and walked with a handsome gold-headed cane.

When they arrived at the room in the wall the little girl found Toto and Billina waiting for her very patiently. They had been lib-erally fed by some of the attendants and were in no hurry to leave such comfortable quarters.

The Keeper of the Wicket was by this time back in his old place, but he kept a safe distance from Toto. Dorothy bade good bye to the King as they stood just inside the wall.

"You've been good to me," she said, "and I thank you ever so much. As soon as poss'ble I'll see Glinda and ask her to put another King in your place and send you back into the wild forest. And I'll ask her to let you keep some of your clothes and the lily chair and one or two jugglers to amuse you. I'm sure she will do it, 'cause she's so kind she doesn't like any one to be unhappy."

"Ahem!" said the King, looking rather downcast. "I don't like to trouble you with my misery; so you needn't see Glinda."

"Oh, yes I will," she replied. "It won't be any trouble at all."

"But, my dear," continued the King, in an embarrassed way, "I've been thinking the subject over carefully, and I find there are a lot of pleasant things here in Bunnybury that I would miss if I went away. So perhaps I'd better stay."

Dorothy laughed. Then she looked grave.

"It won't do for you to be a King and a cry-baby at the same time," she said. "You've been making all the other rabbits unhappy and discontented with your howls about being so miserable. So I guess it's better to have another King."

"Oh, no indeed!" exclaimed the King, earnestly. "If you won't say anything to Glinda I'll promise to be merry and gay all the time, and never cry or wail again."

"Honor bright?" she asked.

"On the royal word of a King I promise it!" he answered.

"All right," said Dorothy. "You'd be a reg'lar lunatic to want to leave Bunnybury for a wild life in the forest, and I'm sure any rabbit outside the city would be glad to take your place."

"Forget it, my dear; forget all my foolishness," pleaded the King, earnestly. "Hereafter I'll try to enjoy myself and do my duty by my subjects."

So then she left him and entered through the little door into the room in the wall, where she grew gradually bigger and bigger until she had resumed her natural size.

The Keeper of the Wicket let them out into the forest and told Dorothy that she had been of great service to Bunnybury because she had brought their dismal King to a realization of the pleasure of ruling so beautiful a city.

"I shall start a petition to have your statue erected beside Glinda's in the public square," said the Keeper. "I hope you will come again, some day, and see it."

"Perhaps I shall," she replied.

Then, followed by Toto and Billina, she walked away from the high marble wall and started back along the narrow path toward the signpost.

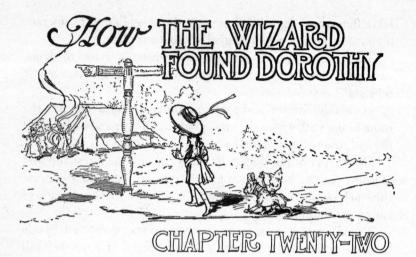

How THE WIZARD FOUND DOROTHY

CHAPTER TWENTY-TWO

When they came to the signpost, there, to their joy, were the tents of the Wizard pitched beside the path and the kettle bubbling merrily over a fire. The Shaggy Man and Omby Amby were gathering firewood while Uncle Henry and Aunt Em sat in their camp chairs talking with the Wizard.

They all ran forward to greet Dorothy, as she approached, and Aunt Em exclaimed: "Goodness gracious, child! Where have you been?"

"You've played hookey the whole day," added the Shaggy Man, reproachfully.

"Well, you see, I've been lost," explained the little girl, "and I've tried awful hard to find the way back to you, but just couldn't do it."

"Did you wander in the forest all day?" asked Uncle Henry.

"You must be a'most starved!" said Aunt Em.

"No," said Dorothy, "I'm not hungry. I had a wheelbarrow and a piano for breakfast, and lunched with a King."

"Ah!" exclaimed the Wizard, nodding with a bright smile. "So you've been having adventures again."

"She's stark crazy!" cried Aunt Em. "Whoever heard of eating a wheelbarrow?"

"It wasn't very big," said Dorothy; "and it had a zuzu wheel."

"And I ate the crumbs," added Billina, soberly.

"Sit down and tell us about it," begged the Wizard. "We've hunted for you all day, and at last I noticed your footsteps in this path—and the tracks of Billina. We found the path by accident, and seeing it only led to two places I decided you were at either one or the other of those places. So we made camp and waited for you to return. And now, Dorothy, tell us where you have been—to Bunbury or to Bunnybury?"

"Why, I've been to both," she replied; "but first I went to Utensia, which isn't on any path at all."

She then sat down and related the day's adventures, and you may be sure Aunt Em and Uncle Henry were much astonished at the story.

"But after seeing the Cuttenclips and the Fuddles," remarked her uncle, "we ought not to wonder at anything in this strange country."

"Seems like the only common and ordinary folks here are ourselves," rejoined Aunt Em, diffidently.

"Now that we're together again, and one reunited party," observed the Shaggy Man, "what are we to do next?"

"Have some supper and a night's rest," answered the Wizard promptly, "and then proceed upon our journey."

"Where to?" asked the Captain-General.

"We haven't visited the Rigmaroles or the Flutterbudgets yet," said Dorothy. "I'd like to see them—wouldn't you?"

"They don't sound very interesting," objected Aunt Em. "But perhaps they are."

"And then," continued the little Wizard, "we will call upon the Tin Woodman and Jack Pumpkinhead and our old friend the Scarecrow, on our way home."

"That will be nice!" cried Dorothy, eagerly.

"Can't say *they* sound very interesting, either," remarked Aunt Em.

"Why, they're the best friends I have!" asserted the little girl, "and you're sure to like them, Aunt Em, 'cause *ever'*-body likes them."

By this time twilight was approaching, so they ate the fine supper which the Wizard magically produced from the kettle and then went to bed in the cosy tents.

They were all up bright and early next morning, but Dorothy didn't venture to wander from the camp again for fear of more accidents.

"Do you know where there's a road?" she asked the little man.

"No, my dear," replied the Wizard; "but I'll find one."

After breakfast he waved his hand toward the tents and they became handkerchiefs again, which were at once returned to the pockets of their owners. Then they all climbed into the red wagon and the Saw-Horse inquired:

"Which way?"

"Never mind which way," replied the Wizard. "Just go as you please and you're sure to be right. I've enchanted the wheels of the wagon, and they will roll in the right direction, never fear."

As the Saw-Horse started away through the trees Dorothy said:

"If we had one of those new-fashioned airships we could float away over the top of the forest, and look down and find just the places we want."

"Airship? Pah!" retorted the little man, scornfully. "I hate those things, Dorothy, although they are nothing new to either you or me. I was a balloonist for many years, and once my balloon carried me to the Land of Oz, and once to the Vegetable Kingdom. And once Ozma had a Gump that flew all over this kingdom and had sense enough to go where it was told to—which airships won't do. The house which the cyclone brought to Oz all the way from Kansas, with you and Toto in it—was a real airship at the time; so you see we've had plenty of experience flying with the birds."

"Airships are not so bad, after all," declared Dorothy. "Some day they'll fly all over the world, and perhaps bring people even to the Land of Oz."

"I must speak to Ozma about that," said the Wizard, with a slight frown. "It wouldn't do at all, you know, for the Emerald City to become a way-station on an airship line."

"No," said Dorothy, "I don't s'pose it would. But what can we do to prevent it?"

"I'm working out a magic recipe to fuddle men's brains, so they'll never make an airship that will go where they want it to go," the Wizard confided to her. "That won't keep the things from flying, now and then, but it'll keep them from flying to the Land of Oz."

Just then the Saw-Horse drew the wagon out of the forest and a beautiful landscape lay spread before the travelers' eyes. Moreover, right before them was a good road that wound away through the hills and valleys.

"Now," said the Wizard, with evident delight, "we are on the right track again, and there is nothing more to worry about."

"It's a foolish thing to take chances in a strange country," observed the Shaggy Man. "Had we kept to the roads we never would have been lost. Roads always lead to some place, else they wouldn't be roads."

"This road," added the Wizard, "leads to Rigmarole Town. I'm sure of that because I enchanted the wagon wheels."

Sure enough, after riding along the road for an hour or two they

SOANDSO, AND SOANDSO, OH YES, I DON'T KNOW IT MIGHT BE SO I CALCULATE BUT I DON'T KNOW, IN TRE MINTRY CUTEYCORN APPLE SEEDS AND FLY AWAY JACK - - SIX SIXES ARE NOT SIXTY - SIX ? AND WE STILL HOLD TO FOLDEROL DE DOODLE ALL DAY, IF I HAD A DONKEY THAT WOULD'NT GO I'D BUY A FIDDLE FOR FIFTY CENTS AND RATTLE HIS BONES OVER THE STONES IT'S ONLY A BEGGAR WHOM NOBODY OWNS, LISTEN !?

entered a pretty valley where a village was nestled among the hills. The houses were Munchkin shaped, for they were all domes, with windows wider than they were high, and pretty balconies over the front doors.

Aunt Em was greatly relieved to find this town "neither paper nor patch-work," and the only surprising thing about it was that it was so far distant from all other towns.

As the Saw-Horse drew the wagon into the main street the travelers noticed that the place was filled with people, standing in groups and seeming to be engaged in earnest conversation. So occupied with themselves were the inhabitants that they scarcely noticed the strangers at all. So the Wizard stopped a boy and asked:

"Is this Rigmarole Town?"

"Sir," replied the boy, "if you have traveled very much you will have noticed that every town differs from every other town in one way or another and so by observing the methods of the people and the way they live as well as the style of their dwelling places it ought not to be a difficult thing to make up your mind without the trouble of asking questions whether the town bears the appearance of the one you intended to visit or whether perhaps having taken a different road from the one you should have taken you have made an error in your way and arrived at some point where—"

"Land sakes!" cried Aunt Em, impatiently; "what's all this rigmarole about?"

"That's it!" said the Wizard, laughing merrily. "It's a rigmarole because the boy is a Rigmarole and we've come to Rigmarole Town."

"Do they all talk like that?" asked Dorothy, wonderingly.

"He might have said 'yes' or 'no' and settled the question," observed Uncle Henry.

"Not here," said Omby Amby. "I don't believe the Rigmaroles know what 'yes' or 'no' means."

While the boy had been talking several other people had approached the wagon and listened intently to his speech. Then they began talking to one another in long, deliberate speeches, where many words were used but little was said. But when the strangers criticised them so frankly one of the women, who had no one else to talk to, began an address to them, saying:

"It is the easiest thing in the world for a person to say 'yes' or 'no' when a question that is asked for the purpose of gaining information or satisfying the curiosity of the one who has given expression to the inquiry has attracted the attention of an individual who may be competent either from personal experience or the experience of others to answer it with more or less correctness or at least an attempt to satisfy the desire for information on the part of the one who has made the inquiry by—"

"Dear me!" exclaimed Dorothy, interrupting the speech. "I've lost all track of what you are saying."

"Don't let her begin over again, for goodness sake!" cried Aunt Em.

But the woman did not begin again. She did not even stop talking, but went right on as she had begun, the words flowing from her mouth in a stream.

"I'm quite sure that if we waited long enough and listened carefully, some of these people might be able to tell us something, in time," said the Wizard.

"Don't let's wait," returned Dorothy. "I've heard of the Rigmaroles, and wondered what they were like; but now I know, and I'm ready to move on."

"So am I," declared Uncle Henry; "we're wasting time here."

"Why, we're all ready to go," added the Shaggy Man, putting his fingers to his ears to shut out the monotonous babble of those around the wagon.

So the Wizard spoke to the Saw-Horse, who trotted nimbly through the village and soon gained the open country on the other side of it. Dorothy looked back, as they rode away, and noticed that the woman had not yet finished her speech but was talking as glibly as ever, although no one was near to hear her.

"If those people wrote books," Omby Amby remarked with a smile, "it would take a whole library to say the cow jumped over the moon."

"Perhaps some of 'em do write books," asserted the little Wizard. "I've read a few rigmaroles that might have come from this very town."

"Some of the college lecturers and ministers are certainly related to these people," observed the Shaggy Man; "and it seems to me the Land of Oz is a little ahead of the United States in some of its laws. For here, if one can't talk clearly, and straight to the point, they send him to Rigmarole Town; while Uncle Sam lets him roam around wild and free, to torture innocent people."

Dorothy was thoughtful. The Rigmaroles had made a strong impression upon her. She decided that whenever she spoke, after this, she would use only enough words to express what she wanted to say.

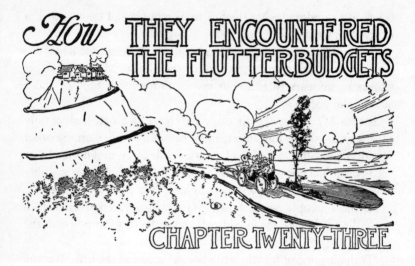

How THEY ENCOUNTERED THE FLUTTERBUDGETS

CHAPTER TWENTY-THREE

They were soon among the pretty hills and valleys again, and the Saw-Horse sped up hill and down at a fast and easy pace, the roads being hard and smooth. Mile after mile was speedily covered, and before the ride had grown at all tiresome they sighted another village. The place seemed even larger than Rigmarole Town, but was not so attractive in appearance.

"This must be Flutterbudget Center," declared the Wizard. "You see, it's no trouble at all to find places if you keep to the right road."

"What are the Flutterbudgets like?" inquired Dorothy.

"I do not know, my dear. But Ozma has given them a town all their own, and I've heard that whenever one of the people becomes a Flutterbudget he is sent to this place to live."

"That is true," Omby Amby added; "Flutterbudget Center and Rigmarole Town are called 'the Defensive Settlements of Oz.'"

The village they now approached was not built in a valley, but on top of a hill, and the road they followed wound around the hill like a corkscrew, ascending the hill easily until it came to the town.

"Look out!" screamed a voice. "Look out, or you'll run over my child!"

They gazed around and saw a woman standing upon the sidewalk nervously wringing her hands as she gazed at them appealingly.

"Where is your child?" asked the Saw-Horse.

"In the house," said the woman, bursting into tears; "but if it should happen to be in the road, and you ran over it, those great wheels would crush my darling to jelly. Oh, dear! oh dear! Think of my darling child being crushed to jelly by those great wheels!"

"Gid-dap!" said the Wizard, sharply, and the Saw-Horse started on.

They had not gone far before a man ran out of a house shouting wildly: "Help! Help!"

The Saw-Horse stopped short and the Wizard and Uncle Henry and the Shaggy Man and Omby Amby jumped out of the wagon and ran to the poor man's assistance. Dorothy followed them as quickly as she could.

"What's the matter?" asked the Wizard.

"Help! help!" screamed the man; "my wife has cut her finger off and she's bleeding to death!"

Then he turned and rushed back to the house, and all the party went with him. They found a woman in the front dooryard moaning and groaning as if in great pain.

"Be brave, madam!" said the Wizard, consolingly. "You won't die just because you have cut off a finger, you may be sure."

"But I haven't cut off a finger!" she sobbed.

"Then what *has* happened?" asked Dorothy.

"I—I pricked my finger with a needle while I was sewing, and—and the blood came!" she replied. "And now I'll have blood-poisoning, and the doctors will cut off my finger, and that will give me a fever and I shall die!"

"Pshaw!" said Dorothy; "I've pricked my finger many a time, and nothing happened."

"Really?" asked the woman, brightening and wiping her eyes upon her apron.

"Why, it's nothing at all," declared the girl. "You're more scared than hurt."

"Ah, that's because she's a Flutterbudget," said the Wizard, nodding wisely. "I think I know now what these people are like."

"So do I," announced Dorothy.

"Oh, boo-hoo-hoo!" sobbed the woman, giving way to a fresh burst of grief.

"What's wrong now?" asked the Shaggy Man.

"Oh, suppose I had pricked my foot!" she wailed. "Then the doctors would have cut my foot off, and I'd be lamed for life!"

"Surely, ma'am," replied the Wizard, "and if you'd pricked your nose they might cut your head off. But you see you didn't."

"But I might have!" she exclaimed, and began to cry again. So they left her and drove away in their wagon. And her husband came out and began calling "Help!" as he had before; but no one seemed to pay any attention to him.

As the travelers turned into another street they found a man walking excitedly up and down the pavement. He appeared to be in a very nervous condition and the Wizard stopped him to ask:

"Is anything wrong, sir?"

"Everything is wrong," answered the man, dismally. "I can't sleep."

"Why not?" inquired Omby Amby.

"If I go to sleep I'll have to shut my eyes," he explained; "and if I shut my eyes they may grow together, and then I'd be blind for life!"

"Did you ever hear of any one's eyes growing together?" asked Dorothy.

"No," said the man, "I never did. But it would be a dreadful thing, wouldn't it? And the thought of it makes me so nervous I'm afraid to go to sleep."

"There's no help for this case," declared the Wizard; and they went on.

At the next street corner a woman rushed up to them crying:

"Save my baby! Oh, good, kind people, save my baby!"

"Is it in danger?" asked Dorothy, noticing that the child was clasped in her arms and seemed sleeping peacefully.

"Yes, indeed," said the woman, nervously. "If I should go into the house and throw my child out of the window, it would roll way down to the bottom of the hill; and then if there were a lot of tigers and bears down there, they would tear my darling babe to pieces and eat it up!"

"Are there any tigers and bears in this neighborhood?" the Wizard asked.

"I've never heard of any," admitted the woman; "but if there were—"

"Have you any idea of throwing your baby out of the window?" questioned the little man.

"None at all," she said; "but if—"

"All your troubles are due to those 'ifs,' " declared the Wizard. "If you were not a Flutterbudget you wouldn't worry."

"There's another 'if,' " replied the woman. "Are you a Flutter-budget, too?"

"I will be, if I stay here long," exclaimed the Wizard, nervously.

"Another 'if'!" cried the woman.

But the Wizard did not stop to argue with her. He made the Saw-Horse canter all the way down the hill, and only breathed easily when they were miles away from the village.

After they had ridden in silence for a while Dorothy turned to the little man and asked:

"Do 'ifs' really make Flutterbudgets?"

"I think the 'ifs' help," he answered seriously. "Foolish fears, and worries over nothing, with a mixture of nerves and 'ifs,' will soon make a Flutterbudget of any one."

Then there was another long silence, for all the travelers were thinking over this statement, and nearly all decided it must be true.

The country they were now passing through was everywhere tinted purple, the prevailing color of the Gillikin Country; but as the Saw-Horse ascended a hill they found that upon the other side everything was of a rich yellow hue.

"Aha!" cried the Captain-General; "here is the Country of the Winkies. We are just crossing the boundary line."

"Then we may be able to lunch with the Tin Woodman," announced the Wizard, joyfully.

"Must we lunch on tin?" asked Aunt Em.

"Oh, no," replied Dorothy. "Nick Chopper knows how to feed meat people, and he will give us plenty of good things to eat, never fear. I've been to his castle before."

"Is Nick Chopper the Tin Woodman's name?" asked Uncle Henry.

"Yes; that's one of his names," answered the little girl; "and another of his names is 'Emp'ror of the Winkies.' He's the King of this country, you know, but Ozma rules over all the countries of Oz."

"Does the Tin Woodman keep any Flutterbudgets or Rigmaroles at his castle?" inquired Aunt Em, uneasily.

"No, indeed," said Dorothy, positively. "He lives in a new tin castle, all full of lovely things."

"I should think it would rust," said Uncle Henry.

"He has thousands of Winkies to keep it polished for him," explained the Wizard. "His people love to do anything in their power for their beloved Emperor, so there isn't a particle of rust on all the big castle."

"I suppose they polish their Emperor, too," said Aunt Em.

"Why, some time ago he had himself nickel-plated," the Wizard answered; "so he only needs rubbing up once in a while. He's the brightest man in all the world, is dear Nick Chopper; and the kindest-hearted."

"I helped find him," said Dorothy, reflectively. "Once the Scarecrow and I found the Tin Woodman in the woods, and he was just rusted still, that time, an' no mistake. But we oiled his joints, an' got 'em good and slippery, and after that he went with us to visit the Wizard at the Em'rald City."

"Was that the time the Wizard scared you?" asked Aunt Em.

"He didn't treat us well, at first," acknowledged Dorothy; "for he made us go away and destroy the Wicked Witch. But after we found out he was only a humbug wizard we were not afraid of him."

The Wizard sighed and looked a little ashamed.

"When we try to deceive people we always make mistakes," he said. "But I'm getting to be a real wizard now, and Glinda the Good's magic, that I am trying to practice, can never harm any one."

"You were always a good man," declared Dorothy, "even when you were a bad wizard."

"He's a good wizard now," asserted Aunt Em, looking at the little man admiringly. "The way he made those tents grow out of handkerchiefs was just wonderful! And didn't he enchant the wagon wheels so they'd find the road?"

"All the people of Oz," said the Captain-General, "are very proud of their Wizard. He once made some soap-bubbles that astonished the world."

The Wizard blushed at this praise, yet it pleased him. He no longer looked sad, but seemed to have recovered his usual good humor.

The country through which they now rode was thickly dotted with farm-houses, and yellow grain waved in all the fields. Many of the Winkies could be seen working on their farms and the wild and unsettled parts of Oz were by this time left far behind.

These Winkies appeared to be happy, light-hearted folk, and all removed their caps and bowed low when the red wagon with its load of travelers passed by.

It was not long before they saw something glittering in the sunshine far ahead.

"See!" cried Dorothy; "that's the Tin Castle, Aunt Em!"

And the Saw-Horse, knowing his passengers were eager to arrive, broke into a swift trot that soon brought them to their destination.

How THE TIN WOODMAN TOLD THE SAD NEWS

CHAPTER TWENTY-FOUR

The Tin Woodman received Princess Dorothy's party with much grace and cordiality, yet the little girl decided that something must be worrying her old friend, because he was not so merry as usual.

But at first she said nothing about this, for Uncle Henry and Aunt Em were fairly bubbling over with admiration for the beautiful tin castle and its polished tin owner. So her suspicion that something unpleasant had happened was for a time forgotten.

"Where is the Scarecrow?" she asked, when they had all been ushered into the big tin drawing-room of the castle, the Saw-Horse being led around to the tin stable in the rear.

"Why, our old friend has just moved into his new mansion," explained the Tin Woodman. "It has been a long time in building, although my Winkies and many other people from all parts of the country have been busily working upon it. At last, however, it is completed, and the Scarecrow took possession of his new home just two days ago."

"I hadn't heard that he wanted a home of his own," said Dorothy. "Why doesn't he live with Ozma in the Emerald City? He used to, you know; and I thought he was happy there."

"It seems," said the Tin Woodman, "that our dear Scarecrow cannot be contented with city life, however beautiful his surroundings might be. Originally he was a farmer, for he passed his early life in a corn-field, where he was supposed to frighten away the crows."

"I know," said Dorothy, nodding. "I found him, and lifted him down from his pole."

"So now, after a long residence in the Emerald City, his tastes have turned to farm life again," continued the tin man. "He feels that he cannot be happy without a farm of his own, so Ozma gave him some land and every one helped him build his mansion, and now he is settled there for good."

"Who designed his house?" asked the Shaggy Man.

"I believe it was Jack Pumpkinhead, who is also a farmer," was the reply.

They were now invited to enter the tin dining room, where luncheon was served.

Aunt Em found, to her satisfaction, that Dorothy's promise was more than fulfilled; for, although the Tin Woodman had no appetite of his own, he respected the appetites of his guests and saw that they were bountifully fed.

They passed the afternoon in wandering through the beautiful gardens and grounds of the palace. The walks were all paved with sheets of tin, brightly polished, and there were tin fountains and tin statues here and there among the trees. The flowers were mostly natural flowers and grew in the regular way; but their host showed them one flower bed which was his especial pride.

"You see, all common flowers fade and die in time," he explained, "and so there are seasons when the pretty blooms are scarce. Therefore I decided to make one tin flower bed all of tin flowers, and my workmen have created them with rare skill. Here you see tin camellias, tin marigolds, tin carnations, tin poppies and tin hollyhocks growing as naturally as if they were real."

Indeed, they were a pretty sight, and glistened under the sunlight like spun silver.

"Isn't this tin hollyhock going to seed?" asked the Wizard, bending over the flowers.

"Why, I believe it is!" exclaimed the Tin Woodman, as if surprised. "I hadn't noticed that before. But I shall plant the tin seeds and raise another bed of tin hollyhocks."

In one corner of the gardens Nick Chopper had established a fish-pond, in which they saw swimming and disporting themselves many pretty tin fishes.

"Would they bite on hooks?" asked Aunt Em, curiously.

The Tin Woodman seemed hurt at this question.

"Madam," said he, "do you suppose I would allow anyone to catch my beautiful fishes, even if they were foolish enough to bite on hooks? No, indeed! Every created thing is safe from harm in my domain, and I would as soon think of killing my little friend Dorothy as killing one of my tin fishes."

"The Emperor is very kind-hearted, ma'am," explained the Wizard. "If a fly happens to light upon his tin body he doesn't rudely brush it off, as some people might do; he asks it politely to find some other resting place."

"What does the fly do then?" enquired Aunt Em.

"Usually it begs his pardon and goes away," said the Wizard, gravely. "Flies like to be treated politely as well as other creatures, and here in Oz they understand what we say to them, and behave very nicely."

"Well," said Aunt Em, "the flies in Kansas, where I came from, don't understand anything but a swat. You have to smash 'em to make 'em behave; and it's the same way with 'skeeters. Do you have 'skeeters in Oz?"

"We have some very large mosquitoes here, which sing as beautifully as song birds," replied the Tin Woodman. "But they never bite or annoy our people, because they are well fed and taken care of. The reason they bite people in your country is because they are hungry—poor things!"

"Yes," agreed Aunt Em; "they're hungry, all right. An' they ain't very particular who they feed on. I'm glad you've got the 'skeeters educated in Oz."

That evening after dinner they were entertained by the Emperor's Tin Cornet Band, which played for them several sweet melodies. Also the Wizard did a few sleight-of-hand tricks to amuse the company; after which they all retired to their cosy tin bedrooms and slept soundly until morning.

After breakfast Dorothy said to the Tin Woodman:

"If you'll tell us which way to go we'll visit the Scarecrow on our way home."

"I will go with you, and show you the way," replied the Emperor; "for I must journey to-day to the Emerald City."

He looked so anxious, as he said this, that the little girl asked:

"There isn't anything wrong with Ozma, is there?"

He shook his tin head.

"Not yet," said he; "but I'm afraid the time has come when I must tell you some very bad news, little friend."

"Oh, what is it?" cried Dorothy.

"Do you remember the Nome King?" asked the Tin Woodman.

"I remember him very well," she replied.

"The Nome King has not a kind heart," said the Emperor, sadly, "and he has been harboring wicked thoughts of revenge, because we once defeated him and liberated his slaves and you took away his Magic Belt. So he has ordered his Nomes to dig a long tunnel underneath the deadly desert, so that he may march his hosts right into the Emerald City. When he gets there he intends to destroy our beautiful country."

Dorothy was much surprised to hear this.

"How did Ozma find out about the tunnel?" she asked.

"She saw it in her Magic Picture."

"Of course," said Dorothy; "I might have known that. And what is she going to do?"

"I cannot tell," was the reply.

"Pooh!" cried the Yellow Hen. "We're not afraid of the Nomes. If we roll a few of our eggs down the tunnel they'll run away back home as fast as they can go."

"Why, that's true enough!" exclaimed Dorothy. "The Scarecrow once conquered all the Nome King's army with some of Billina's eggs."

"But you do not understand all of the dreadful plot," continued the Tin Woodman. "The Nome King is clever, and he knows his

Nomes would run from eggs; so he has bargained with many terrible creatures to help him. These evil spirits are not afraid of eggs or anything else, and they are very powerful. So the Nome King will send them through the tunnel first, to conquer and destroy, and then the Nomes will follow after to get their share of the plunder and slaves."

They were all startled to hear this, and every face wore a troubled look.

"Is the tunnel all ready?" asked Dorothy.

"Ozma sent me word yesterday that the tunnel was all completed except for a thin crust of earth at the end. When our enemies break through this crust they will be in the gardens of the royal palace, in the heart of the Emerald City. I offered to arm all my Winkies and march to Ozma's assistance; but she said no."

"I wonder why?" asked Dorothy.

"She answered that all the inhabitants of Oz, gathered together, were not powerful enough to fight and overcome the evil forces of the Nome King. Therefore she refuses to fight at all."

"But they will capture and enslave us, and plunder and ruin all our lovely land!" exclaimed the Wizard, greatly disturbed by this statement.

"I fear they will," said the Tin Woodman, sorrowfully. "And I also fear that those who are not fairies, such as the Wizard, and Dorothy, and her uncle and aunt, as well as Toto and Billina, will be speedily put to death by the conquerors."

"What can be done?" asked Dorothy, shuddering a little at the prospect of this awful fate.

"Nothing can be done!" gloomily replied the Emperor of the Winkies. "But since Ozma refuses my army I will go myself to the Emerald City. The least I may do is to perish beside my beloved Ruler."

How THE SCARECROW DISPLAYED HIS WISDOM

Probably
The Wisest
Man in All
Oz.

CHAPTER TWENTY-FIVE

This amazing news had saddened every heart and all were now anxious to return to the Emerald City and share Ozma's fate. So they started without loss of time, and as the road led past the Scarecrow's new mansion they determined to make a brief halt there and confer with him.

"The Scarecrow is probably the wisest man in all Oz," remarked the Tin Woodman, when they had started upon their journey. "His brains are plentiful and of excellent quality, and often he has told me things I might never have thought of myself. I must say I rely a good deal upon the Scarecrow's brains in this emergency."

The Tin Woodman rode on the front seat of the wagon, where Dorothy sat between him and the Wizard.

"Has the Scarecrow heard of Ozma's trouble?" asked the Captain-General.

"I do not know, sir," was the reply.

"When I was a private," said Omby Amby, "I was an excellent army, as I fully proved in our war against the Nomes. But now there is not a single private left in our army, since Ozma made me the Captain-General, so there is no one to fight and defend our lovely Ruler."

"True," said the Wizard. "The present army is composed only of officers, and the business of an officer is to order his men to fight. Since there are no men there can be no fighting."

"Poor Ozma!" whispered Dorothy, with tears in her sweet eyes. "It's dreadful to think of all her lovely fairy country being destroyed. I wonder if we couldn't manage to escape and get back to Kansas by means of the Magic Belt? And we might take Ozma with us and all work hard to get money for her, so she wouldn't be so *very* lonely and unhappy about the loss of her fairyland."

"Do you think there would be any work for *me* in Kansas?" asked the Tin Woodman.

"If you are hollow, they might use you in a canning factory," suggested Uncle Henry. "But I can't see the use of your working for a living. You never eat or sleep or need a new suit of clothes."

"I was not thinking of myself," replied the Emperor, with dignity. "I merely wondered if I could not help to support Dorothy and Ozma."

As they indulged in these sad plans for the future they journeyed in sight of the Scarecrow's new mansion, and even though filled with care and worry over the impending fate of Oz, Dorothy could not help a feeling of wonder at the sight she saw.

The Scarecrow's new house was shaped like an immense ear of corn. The rows of kernels were made of solid gold, and the green upon which the ear stood upright was a mass of sparkling emeralds. Upon the very top of the structure was perched a figure representing the Scarecrow himself, and upon his extended arms, as well as upon his head, were several crows carved out of ebony and having ruby eyes. You may imagine how big this ear of corn was when I tell you that a single gold kernel formed a window, swinging outward upon hinges, while a row of four kernels opened to make the front entrance. Inside there were five stories, each story being a single room.

The gardens around the mansion consisted of corn-fields, and Dorothy acknowledged that the place was in all respects a very appropriate home for her good friend the Scarecrow.

"He would have been very happy here, I'm sure," she said, "if only the Nome King had left us alone. But if Oz is destroyed of course this place will be destroyed too."

"Yes," replied the Tin Woodman, "and also my beautiful tin castle, that has been my joy and pride."

"Jack Pumpkinhead's house will go too," remarked the Wizard, "as well as Professor Woggle-Bug's Athletic College, and Ozma's royal palace, and all our other handsome buildings."

"Yes, Oz will indeed become a desert when the Nome King gets through with it," sighed Omby Amby.

The Scarecrow came out to meet them and gave them all a hearty welcome.

"I hear you have decided always to live in the Land of Oz, after this," he said to Dorothy; "and that will delight my heart, for I have greatly disliked our frequent partings. But why are you all so downcast?"

"Have you heard the news?" asked the Tin Woodman.

"No news to make me sad," replied the Scarecrow.

Then Nick Chopper told his friend of the Nome King's tunnel, and how the evil creatures of the North had allied themselves with the underground monarch for the purpose of conquering and destroying Oz. "Well," said the Scarecrow, "it certainly looks bad for Ozma, and all of us. But I believe it is wrong to worry over anything before it happens. It is surely time enough to be sad when our country is despoiled and our people made slaves. So let us not deprive ourselves of the few happy hours remaining to us."

"Ah! that is real wisdom," declared the Shaggy Man, approvingly. "After we become really unhappy we shall regret these few hours that are left to us, unless we enjoy them to the utmost."

"Nevertheless," said the Scarecrow, "I shall go with you to the Emerald City and offer Ozma my services."

"She says we can do nothing to oppose our enemies," announced the Tin Woodman.

"And doubtless she is right, sir," answered the Scarecrow. "Still, she will appreciate our sympathy, and it is the duty of Ozma's friends to stand by her side when the final disaster occurs."

He then led them into his queer mansion and showed them the beautiful rooms in all the five stories. The lower room was a grand reception hall, with a hand-organ in one corner. This instrument the Scarecrow, when alone, could turn to amuse himself, as he was very fond of music. The walls were hung with white silk, upon which flocks of black crows were embroidered in black diamonds. Some of the chairs were made in the shape of big crows and uphol-stered with cushions of corn-colored silk.

The second story contained a fine banquet room, where the Scarecrow might entertain his guests, and the three stories above that were bed-chambers exquisitely furnished and decorated.

"From these rooms," said the Scarecrow, proudly, "one may ob-tain fine views of the surrounding corn-fields. The corn I grow is always husky, and I call the ears my regiments, because they have so many kernels. Of course I cannot ride my cobs, but I really don't care shucks about that. Taken altogether, my farm will stack up with any in the neighborhood."

The visitors partook of some light refreshment and then hurried away to resume the road to the Emerald City. The Scarecrow found a seat in the wagon between Omby Amby and the Shaggy Man, and his weight did not add much to the load because he was stuffed with straw.

"You will notice I have one oat-field on my property," he re-marked, as they drove away. "Oat-straw is, I have found, the best of all straws to re-stuff myself with when my interior gets musty or out of shape."

"Are you able to re-stuff yourself without help?" asked Aunt Em. "I should think that after the straw was taken out of you there wouldn't be anything left but your clothes."

"You are almost correct, madam," he answered. "My servants do the stuffing, under my direction. For my head, in which are my excellent brains, is a bag tied at the bottom. My face is neatly painted upon one side of the bag, as you may see. My head does not need re-stuffing, as my body does, for all that it requires is to have the face touched up with fresh paint occasionally."

It was not far from the Scarecrow's mansion to the farm of Jack Pumpkinhead, and when they arrived there both Uncle Henry and Aunt Em were much impressed. The farm was one vast pumpkin field, and some of the pumpkins were of enormous size. In one of them, which had been neatly hollowed out, Jack himself lived, and he declared that it was a very comfortable residence. The reason he grew so many pumpkins was in order that he might change his head as often as it became wrinkled or threatened to spoil.

The pumpkin-headed man welcomed his visitors joyfully and offered them several delicious pumpkin pies to eat.

"I don't indulge in pumpkin pies myself, for two reasons," he said. "One reason is that were I to eat pumpkins I would become a cannibal, and the other reason is that I never eat, not being hollow inside."

"Very good reasons," agreed the Scarecrow.

They told Jack Pumpkinhead the dreadful news about the Nome King, and he decided to go with them to the Emerald City and help comfort Ozma.

"I had expected to live here in ease and comfort for many centuries," said Jack, dolefully; "but of course if the Nome King destroys everything in Oz I shall be destroyed too. Really, it seems too bad, doesn't it?"

They were soon on their journey again, and so swiftly did the Saw-Horse draw the wagon over the smooth roads that before twilight fell they had reached the royal palace in the Emerald City, and were at their journey's end.

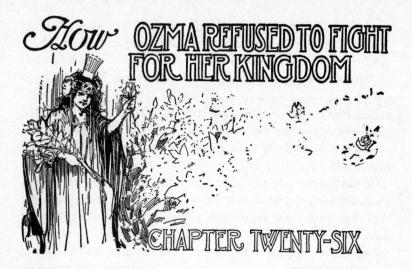

How OZMA REFUSED TO FIGHT FOR HER KINGDOM

CHAPTER TWENTY-SIX

Ozma was in her rose garden picking a bouquet when the party arrived, and she greeted all her old and new friends as smilingly and sweetly as ever.

Dorothy's eyes were full of tears as she kissed the lovely Ruler of Oz, and she whispered to her:

"Oh, Ozma, Ozma! I'm *so* sorry!"

Ozma seemed surprised.

"Sorry for what, Dorothy?" she asked.

"For all your trouble about the Nome King," was the reply.

Ozma laughed with genuine amusement.

"Why, that has not troubled me a bit, dear Princess," she replied. Then, looking around at the sad faces of her friends, she added: "Have you all been worrying about this tunnel?"

"We have!" they exclaimed in a chorus.

"Well, perhaps it is more serious than I imagined," admitted the fair Ruler; "but I haven't given the matter much thought. After dinner we will all meet together and talk it over."

So they went to their rooms and prepared for dinner, and Dorothy dressed herself in her prettiest gown and put on her coronet, for she thought that this might be the last time she would ever appear as a Princess of Oz.

The Scarecrow, the Tin Woodman and Jack Pumpkinhead all sat at the dinner table, although none of them was made so he could eat. Usually they served to enliven the meal with their merry talk, but to-night all seemed strangely silent and uneasy.

As soon as the dinner was finished Ozma led the company to her own private room in which hung the Magic Picture. When they had seated themselves the Scarecrow was the first to speak.

"Is the Nome King's tunnel finished, Ozma?" he asked.

"It was completed to-day," she replied. "They have built it right under my palace grounds, and it ends in front of the Forbidden Fountain. Nothing but a crust of earth remains to separate our enemies from us, and when they march here they will easily break through this crust and rush upon us."

"Who will assist the Nome King?" inquired the Scarecrow.

"The Whimsies, the Growleywogs, and the Phanfasms," she replied. "I watched to-day in my Magic Picture the messengers whom the Nome King sent to all these people to summon them to assemble in his great caverns."

"Let us see what they are doing now," suggested the Tin Woodman.

So Ozma wished to see the Nome King's cavern, and at once the landscape faded from the Magic Picture and was replaced by the scene then being enacted in the jeweled cavern of King Roquat.

A wild and startling scene it was which the Oz people beheld.

Before the Nome King stood the Chief of the Whimsies and the Grand Gallipoot of the Growleywogs, surrounded by their most skillful generals. Very fierce and powerful they looked, so that even the Nome King and General Guph, who stood beside his master, seemed a bit fearful in the presence of their allies.

Now a still more formidable creature entered the cavern. It was the First and Foremost of the Phanfasms and he proudly sat down in King Roquat's own throne and demanded the right to lead his forces through the tunnel in advance of all the others. The First and Foremost now appeared to all eyes in his hairy skin and the bear's head. What his real form was even Roquat did not know.

Through the arches leading into the vast series of caverns that

lay beyond the throne room of King Roquat, could be seen ranks upon ranks of the invaders—thousands of Phanfasms, Growley-wogs and Whimsies standing in serried lines, while behind them were massed the thousands upon thousands of General Guph's own army of Nomes.

"Listen!" whispered Ozma. "I think we can hear what they are saying."

So they kept still and listened.

"Is all ready?" demanded the First and Foremost, haughtily.

"The tunnel is finally completed," replied General Guph.

"How long will it take us to march to the Emerald City?" asked the Grand Gallipoot of the Growleywogs.

"If we start at midnight," replied the Nome King, "we shall ar-rive at the Emerald City by daybreak. Then, while all the Oz peo-ple are sleeping, we will capture them and make them our slaves. After that we will destroy the city itself and march through the Land of Oz, burning and devastating as we go."

"Good!" cried the First and Foremost. "When we get through with Oz it will be a desert wilderness. Ozma shall be my slave."

"She shall be *my* slave!" shouted the Grand Gallipoot, angrily.

"We'll decide that by and by," said King Roquat, hastily. "Don't let us quarrel now, friends. First let us conquer Oz, and then we will divide the spoils of war in a satisfactory manner."

The First and Foremost smiled wickedly; but he only said:

"I and my Phanfasms go first, for nothing on earth can oppose our power."

They all agreed to that, knowing the Phanfasms to be the might-iest of the combined forces. King Roquat now invited them to attend a banquet he had prepared, where they might occupy themselves in eating and drinking until midnight arrived.

As they had now seen and heard all of the plot against them that they cared to, Ozma allowed her Magic Picture to fade away. Then she turned to her friends and said:

"Our enemies will be here sooner than I expected. What do you advise me to do?"

"It is now too late to assemble our people," said the Tin Woodman, despondently. "If you had allowed me to arm and drill my Winkies we might have put up a good fight and destroyed many of our enemies before we were conquered."

"The Munchkins are good fighters, too," said Omby Amby; "and so are the Gillikins."

"But I do not wish to fight," declared Ozma, firmly. "No one has the right to destroy any living creatures, however evil they may be, or to hurt them or make them unhappy. I will not fight—even to save my kingdom."

"The Nome King is not so particular," remarked the Scarecrow. "He intends to destroy us all and ruin our beautiful country."

"Because the Nome King intends to do evil is no excuse for my doing the same," replied Ozma.

"Self-preservation is the first law of nature," quoted the Shaggy Man.

"True," she said, readily. "I would like to discover a plan to save ourselves without fighting."

That seemed a hopeless task to them, but realizing that Ozma was determined not to fight, they tried to think of some means that might promise escape.

"Couldn't we bribe our enemies, by giving them a lot of emeralds and gold?" asked Jack Pumpkinhead.

"No, because they believe they are able to take everything we have," replied the Ruler.

"I have thought of something," said Dorothy.

"What is it, dear?" asked Ozma.

"Let us use the Magic Belt to wish all of us in Kansas. We will put some emeralds in our pockets, and can sell them in Topeka for enough to pay off the mortgage on Uncle Henry's farm. Then we can all live together and be happy."

"A clever idea!" exclaimed the Scarecrow.

"Kansas is a very good country. I've been there," said the Shaggy Man.

"That seems to me an excellent plan," approved the Tin Woodman.

"No!" said Ozma, decidedly. "Never will I desert my people and leave them to so cruel a fate. I will use the Magic Belt to send the rest of you to Kansas, if you wish, but if my beloved country must be destroyed and my people enslaved I will remain and share their fate."

"Quite right," asserted the Scarecrow, sighing. "I will remain with you."

"And so will I," declared the Tin Woodman and the Shaggy Man and Jack Pumpkinhead, in turn. Tiktok, the machine man, also said he intended to stand by Ozma. "For," said he, "I should be of no use at all in Kansas."

"For my part," announced Dorothy, gravely, "if the Ruler of Oz must not desert her people, a Princess of Oz has no right to run away, either. I'm willing to become a slave with the rest of you; so all we can do with the Magic Belt is to use it to send Uncle Henry and Aunt Em back to Kansas."

"I've been a slave all my life," Aunt Em replied, with considerable cheerfulness, "and so has Henry. I guess we won't go back to Kansas, anyway. I'd rather take my chances with the rest of you."

Ozma smiled upon them all gratefully.

"There is no need to despair just yet," she said. "I'll get up early to-morrow morning and be at the Forbidden Fountain when the fierce warriors break through the crust of earth. I will speak to them pleasantly and perhaps they won't be so very bad, after all."

"Why do they call it the Forbidden Fountain?" asked Dorothy, thoughtfully.

"Don't you know, dear?" returned Ozma, surprised.

"No," said Dorothy. "Of course I've seen the fountain in the palace grounds, ever since I first came to Oz; and I've read the sign which says: 'All Persons are Forbidden to Drink at this Fountain.' But I never knew *why* they were forbidden. The water seems clear and sparkling and it bubbles up in a golden basin all the time."

"That water," declared Ozma, gravely, "is the most dangerous thing in all the Land of Oz. It is the Water of Oblivion."

"What does that mean?" asked Dorothy.

"Whoever drinks at the Forbidden Fountain at once forgets everything he has ever known," Ozma asserted.

"It wouldn't be a bad way to forget our troubles," suggested Uncle Henry.

"That is true; but you would forget everything else, and become as ignorant as a baby," returned Ozma.

"Does it make one crazy?" asked Dorothy.

"No; it only makes one forget," replied the girl Ruler. "It is said that once—long, long ago—a wicked King ruled Oz, and made himself and all his people very miserable and unhappy. So Glinda, the Good Sorceress, placed this fountain here, and the King drank of its water and forgot all his wickedness. His mind became innocent and vacant, and when he learned the things of life again they were all good things. But the people remembered how wicked their King had been, and were still afraid of him. Therefore he made them all drink of the Water of Oblivion and forget everything they had known, so that they became as simple and innocent as their King. After that they all grew wise together, and their wisdom was good, so that peace and happiness reigned in the land. But for fear some one might drink of the water again, and in an instant forget all he had learned, the King put that sign upon the fountain, where it has remained for many centuries up to this very day."

They had all listened intently to Ozma's story, and when she finished speaking there was a long period of silence while all thought upon the curious magical power of the Water of Oblivion.

Finally the Scarecrow's painted face took on a broad smile that stretched the cloth as far as it would go.

"How thankful I am," he said, "that I have such an excellent assortment of brains!"

"I gave you the best brains I ever mixed," declared the Wizard, with an air of pride.

"You did, indeed!" agreed the Scarecrow, "and they work so splendidly that they have found a way to save Oz—to save us all!"

"I'm glad to hear that," said the Wizard. "We never needed saving more than we do just now."

"Do you mean to say you can save us from those awful Phanfasms, and Growleywogs and Whimsies?" asked Dorothy eagerly.

"I'm sure of it, my dear," asserted the Scarecrow, still smiling genially.

"Tell us how!" cried the Tin Woodman.

"Not now," said the Scarecrow. "You may all go to bed, and I advise you to forget your worries just as completely as if you had drunk of the Water of Oblivion in the Forbidden Fountain. I'm going to stay here and tell my plan to Ozma alone, but if you will all be at the Forbidden Fountain at daybreak, you'll see how easily we will save the kingdom when our enemies break through the crust of earth and come from the tunnel."

So they went away and left the Scarecrow and Ozma alone; but Dorothy could not sleep a wink all night.

"He is only a Scarecrow," she said to herself, "and I'm not sure that his mixed brains are as clever as he thinks they are."

But she knew that if the Scarecrow's plan failed they were all lost; so she tried to have faith in him.

How THE FIERCE WARRIORS INVADED OZ

CHAPTER TWENTY-SEVEN

The Nome King and his terrible allies sat at the banquet table until midnight. There was much quarreling between the Growleywogs and Phanfasms, and one of the wee-headed Whimsies got angry at General Guph and choked him until he nearly stopped breathing. Yet no one was seriously hurt, and the Nome King felt much relieved when the clock struck twelve and they all sprang up and seized their weapons.

"Aha!" shouted the First and Foremost. "Now to conquer the Land of Oz!"

He marshaled his Phanfasms in battle array and at his word of command they marched into the tunnel and began the long journey through it to the Emerald City. The First and Foremost intended to take all the treasures in Oz for himself; to kill all who could be killed and enslave the rest; to destroy and lay waste the whole country, and afterward to conquer and enslave the Nomes, the Growleywogs and the Whimsies. And he knew his power was sufficient to enable him to do all these things easily.

Next marched into the tunnel the army of gigantic Growleywogs, with their Grand Gallipoot at their head. They were dreadful beings, indeed, and longed to get to Oz that they might begin to pilfer and destroy. The Grand Gallipoot was a little afraid of the First and Foremost, but had a cunning plan to murder or destroy that powerful being and secure the wealth of Oz for himself. Mighty little of the plunder would the Nome King get, thought the Grand Gallipoot.

The Chief of the Whimsies now marched his false-headed forces into the tunnel. In his wicked little head was a plot to destroy both the First and Foremost and the Grand Gallipoot. He intended to let them conquer Oz, since they insisted on going first; but he would afterward treacherously destroy them, as well as King Roquat, and keep all the slaves and treasure of Ozma's kingdom for himself.

After all his dangerous allies had marched into the tunnel the Nome King and General Guph started to follow them, at the head of fifty thousand Nomes, all fully armed.

"Guph," said the King, "those creatures ahead of us mean mischief. They intend to get everything for themselves and leave us nothing."

"I know," replied the General; "but they are not as clever as they think they are. When you get the Magic Belt you must at once wish the Whimsies and Growleywogs and Phanfasms all back into their own countries—and the Belt will surely take them there."

"Good!" cried the King. "An excellent plan, Guph. I'll do it. While they are conquering Oz I'll get the Magic Belt, and then only the Nomes will remain to ravage the country."

So you see there was only one thing that all were agreed upon—that Oz should be destroyed.

On, on, on the vast ranks of invaders marched, filling the tunnel from side to side. With a steady tramp, tramp, they advanced, every step taking them nearer to the beautiful Emerald City.

"Nothing can save the Land of Oz!" thought the First and Foremost, scowling until his bear face was as black as the tunnel.

"The Emerald City is as good as destroyed already!" muttered the Grand Gallipoot, shaking his war club fiercely.

"In a few hours Oz will be a desert!" said the Chief of the Whimsies, with an evil laugh.

"My dear Guph," remarked the Nome King to his General, "at last my vengeance upon Ozma of Oz and her people is about to be accomplished."

"You are right!" declared the General. "Ozma is surely lost."

And now the First and Foremost, who was in advance and nearing the Emerald City, began to cough and to sneeze.

"This tunnel is terribly dusty," he growled, angrily. "I'll punish that Nome King for not having it swept clean. My throat and eyes are getting full of dust and I'm as thirsty as a fish!"

The Grand Gallipoot was coughing too, and his throat was parched and dry.

"What a dusty place!" he cried. "I'll be glad when we reach Oz, where we can get a drink."

"Who has any water?" asked the Whimsie Chief, gasping and choking. But none of his followers carried a drop of water, so he hastened on to get through the dusty tunnel to the Land of Oz.

"Where did all this dust come from?" demanded General Guph, trying hard to swallow but finding his throat so dry he couldn't.

"I don't know," answered the Nome King. "I've been in the tunnel every day while it was being built, but I never noticed any dust before."

"Let's hurry!" cried the General. "I'd give half the gold in Oz for a drink of water."

The dust grew thicker and thicker, and the throats and eyes and noses of the invaders were filled with it. But not one halted or turned back. They hurried forward more fierce and vengeful than ever.

How THEY DRANK AT THE FORBIDDEN FOUNTAIN

CHAPTER TWENTY-EIGHT

The Scarecrow had no need to sleep; neither had the Tin Woodman or Tiktok or Jack Pumpkinhead. So they all wandered out into the palace grounds and stood beside the sparkling water of the Forbidden Fountain until daybreak. During this time they indulged in occasional conversation.

"Nothing could make me forget what I know," remarked the Scarecrow, gazing into the fountain, "for I cannot drink the Water of Oblivion or water of any kind. And I am glad that this is so, for I consider my wisdom unexcelled."

"You are cer-tain-ly ve-ry wise," agreed Tiktok. "For my part, I can on-ly think by ma-chin-er-y, so I do not pre-tend to know as much as you do."

"My tin brains are very bright, but that is all I claim for them," said Nick Chopper, modestly. "Yet I do not aspire to being very wise, for I have noticed that the happiest people are those who do not let their brains oppress them."

"Mine never worry me," Jack Pumpkinhead acknowledged. "There are many seeds of thought in my head, but they do not sprout easily. I am glad that it is so, for if I occupied my days in thinking I should have no time for anything else."

In this cheery mood they passed the hours until the first golden streaks of dawn appeared in the sky. Then Ozma joined them, as fresh and lovely as ever and robed in one of her prettiest gowns.

"Our enemies have not yet arrived," said the Scarecrow, after greeting affectionately the sweet and girlish Ruler.

"They will soon be here," she said, "for I have just glanced at my Magic Picture, and have seen them coughing and choking with the dust in the tunnel."

"Oh, is there dust in the tunnel?" asked the Tin Woodman.

"Yes; Ozma placed it there by means of the Magic Belt," explained the Scarecrow, with one of his broad smiles.

Then Dorothy came to them, Uncle Henry and Aunt Em following close after her. The little girl's eyes were heavy because she had had a sleepless and anxious night. Toto walked by her side, but the little dog's spirits were very much subdued. Billina, who was always up by daybreak, was not long in joining the group by the fountain.

The Wizard and the Shaggy Man next arrived, and soon after appeared Omby Amby, dressed in his best uniform.

"There lies the tunnel," said Ozma, pointing to a part of the ground just before the Forbidden Fountain, "and in a few moments the dreadful invaders will break through the earth and swarm over the land. Let us all stand on the other side of the fountain and watch to see what happens."

At once they followed her suggestion and moved around the fountain of the Water of Oblivion. There they stood silent and expectant until the earth beyond gave way with a sudden crash and up leaped the powerful form of the First and Foremost, followed by all his grim warriors.

As the leader sprang forward his gleaming eyes caught the play of the fountain and he rushed toward it and drank eagerly of the sparkling water. Many of the other Phanfasms drank, too, in order to clear their dry and dusty throats. Then they stood around and looked at one another with simple, wondering smiles.

The First and Foremost saw Ozma and her companions beyond

the fountain, but instead of making an effort to capture her he merely stared at her in pleased admiration of her beauty—for he had forgotten where he was and why he had come there.

But now the Grand Gallipoot arrived, rushing from the tunnel with a hoarse cry of mingled rage and thirst. He too saw the fountain and hastened to drink of its forbidden waters. The other Growleywogs were not slow to follow suit, and even before they had finished drinking the Chief of the Whimsies and his people came to push them away, while they one and all cast off their false heads that they might slake their thirst at the fountain.

When the Nome King and General Guph arrived they both made a dash to drink, but the General was so mad with thirst that he knocked his King over, and while Roquat lay sprawling upon the ground the General drank heartily of the Water of Oblivion.

This rude act of his General made the Nome King so angry that for a moment he forgot he was thirsty and rose to his feet to glare upon the group of terrible warriors he had brought here to assist him. He saw Ozma and her people, too, and yelled out:

"Why don't you capture them? Why don't you conquer Oz, you idiots? Why do you stand there like a lot of dummies?"

But the great warriors had become like little children. They had forgotten all their enmity against Ozma and against Oz. They had even forgotten who they themselves were, or why they were in this strange and beautiful country. As for the Nome King, they did not recognize him, and wondered who he was.

The sun came up and sent its flood of silver rays to light the faces of the invaders. The frowns and scowls and evil looks were all gone. Even the most monstrous of the creatures there assembled smiled innocently and seemed light-hearted and content merely to be alive.

Not so with Roquat, the Nome King. He had not drunk from the Forbidden Fountain and all his former rage against Ozma and Dorothy now inflamed him as fiercely as ever. The sight of General Guph babbling like a happy child and playing with his hands in the cool waters of the fountain astonished and maddened Red Roquat.

Seeing that his terrible allies and his own General refused to act, the Nome King turned to order his great army of Nomes to advance from the tunnel and seize the helpless Oz people.

But the Scarecrow suspected what was in the King's mind and spoke a word to the Tin Woodman. Together they ran at Roquat and grabbing him up tossed him into the great basin of the fountain.

The Nome King's body was round as a ball, and it bobbed up and down in the Water of Oblivion while he spluttered and screamed with fear lest he should drown. And when he cried out his mouth filled with water, which ran down his throat, so that straightway he forgot all he had formerly known just as completely as had all the other invaders.

Ozma and Dorothy could not refrain from laughing to see their dreaded enemies become as harmless as babes. There was no danger now that Oz would be destroyed. The only question remaining to solve was how to get rid of this horde of intruders.

The Shaggy Man kindly pulled the Nome King out of the fountain and set him upon his thin legs. Roquat was dripping wet, but he chattered and laughed and wanted to drink more of the water. No thought of injuring any person was now in his mind.

Before he left the tunnel he had commanded his fifty thousand Nomes to remain there until he ordered them to advance, as he wished to give his allies time to conquer Oz before he appeared with his own army. Ozma did not wish all these Nomes to overrun her land, so she advanced to King Roquat and taking his hand in her own said gently:

"Who are you? What is your name?"

"I don't know," he replied, smiling at her. "Who are you, my dear?"

"My name is Ozma," she said; "and your name is Roquat."

"Oh, is it?" he replied, seeming pleased.

"Yes; you are King of the Nomes," she said.

"Ah; I wonder what the Nomes are!" returned the King, as if puzzled.

"They are underground elves, and that tunnel over there is full of them," she answered. "You have a beautiful cavern at the other end of the tunnel, so you must go to your Nomes and say: 'March home!' Then follow after them and in time you will reach the pretty cavern where you live."

The Nome King was much pleased to learn this, for he had forgotten he had a cavern. So he went to the tunnel and said to his army: "March home!" At once the Nomes turned and marched back through the tunnel, and the King followed after them, laughing with delight to find his orders so readily obeyed.

The Wizard went to General Guph, who was trying to count his fingers, and told him to follow the Nome King, who was his master. Guph meekly obeyed, and so all the Nomes quitted the Land of Oz forever.

But there were still the Phanfasms and Whimsies and Growleywogs standing around in groups, and they were so many that they filled the gardens and trampled upon the flowers and grass because they did not know that the tender plants would be injured by their clumsy feet. But in all other respects they were perfectly harmless and played together like children or gazed with pleasure upon the pretty sights of the royal gardens.

After counseling with the Scarecrow Ozma sent Omby Amby to

the palace for the Magic Belt, and when the Captain-General returned with it the Ruler of Oz at once clasped the precious Belt around her waist.

"I wish all these strange people—the Whimsies and the Growleywogs and the Phanfasms—safe back in their own homes!" she said.

It all happened in a twinkling, for of course the wish was no sooner spoken than it was granted.

All the hosts of the invaders were gone, and only the trampled grass showed that they had ever been in the Land of Oz.

How GLINDA WORKED A MAGIC SPELL

CHAPTER TWENTY-NINE

"That was better than fighting," said Ozma, when all our friends were assembled in the palace after the exciting events of the morning; and each and every one agreed with her.

"No one was hurt," said the Wizard, delightedly.

"And no one hurt us," added Aunt Em.

"But, best of all," said Dorothy, "the wicked people have all forgotten their wickedness, and will not wish to hurt any one after this."

"True, Princess," declared the Shaggy Man. "It seems to me that to have reformed all those evil characters is more important than to have saved Oz."

"Nevertheless," remarked the Scarecrow, "I am glad Oz is saved. I can now go back to my new mansion and live happily."

"And I am glad and grateful that my pumpkin farm is saved," said Jack.

"For my part," added the Tin Woodman, "I cannot express my joy that my lovely tin castle is not to be demolished by wicked enemies."

"Still," said Tiktok, "o-ther en-e-mies may come to Oz some day."

"Why do you allow your clock-work brains to interrupt our joy?" asked Omby Amby, frowning at the machine man.

"I say what I am wound up to say," answered Tiktok.

"And you are right," declared Ozma. "I myself have been thinking of this very idea, and it seems to me there are entirely too many ways for people to get to the Land of Oz. We used to think the deadly desert that surrounds us was enough protection; but that is no longer the case. The Wizard and Dorothy have both come here through the air, and I am told the earth people have invented airships that can fly anywhere they wish them to go."

"Why, sometimes they do, and sometimes they don't," asserted Dorothy.

"But in time the airships may cause us trouble," continued Ozma, "for if the earth folk learn how to manage them we would be overrun with visitors who would ruin our lovely, secluded fairyland."

"That is true enough," agreed the Wizard.

"Also the desert fails to protect us in other ways," Ozma went on, thoughtfully. "Johnny Dooit once made a sandboat that sailed across it, and the Nome King made a tunnel under it. So I believe something ought to be done to cut us off from the rest of the world entirely, so that no one in the future will ever be able to intrude upon us."

"How will you do that?" asked the Scarecrow.

"I do not know; but in some way I am sure it can be accomplished. To-morrow I will make a journey to the castle of Glinda the Good, and ask her advice."

"May I go with you?" asked Dorothy, eagerly.

"Of course, my dear Princess; and also I invite any of our friends here who would like to undertake the journey."

They all declared they wished to accompany their girl Ruler, for this was indeed an important mission, since the future of the Land of Oz to a great extent depended upon it. So Ozma gave orders to her servants to prepare for the journey on the morrow.

That day she watched her Magic Picture, and when it showed her that all the Nomes had returned through the tunnel to their underground caverns, Ozma used the Magic Belt to close up the tunnel, so that the earth underneath the desert sands became as solid as it was before the Nomes began to dig.

Early the following morning a gay cavalcade set out to visit the famous Sorceress, Glinda the Good. Ozma and Dorothy rode in a chariot drawn by the Cowardly Lion and the Hungry Tiger, while the Saw-Horse drew the red wagon in which rode the rest of the party.

With hearts light and free from care they traveled merrily along through the lovely and fascinating Land of Oz, and in good season reached the stately castle in which resided the Sorceress.

Glinda knew that they were coming.

"I have been reading about you in my Magic Book," she said, as she greeted them in her gracious way.

"What is your Magic Book like?" inquired Aunt Em, curiously.

"It is a record of everything that happens," replied the Sorceress. "As soon as an event takes place, anywhere in the world, it is immediately found printed in my Magic Book. So when I read its pages I am well informed."

"Did it tell how our enemies drank the Water of 'Blivion?" asked Dorothy.

"Yes, my dear; it told all about it. And also it told me you were all coming to my castle, and why."

"Then," said Ozma, "I suppose you know what is in my mind, and that I am seeking a way to prevent any one in the future from discovering the Land of Oz."

"Yes; I know that. And while you were on your journey I have thought of a way to accomplish your desire. For it seems to me unwise to allow too many outside people to come here. Dorothy, with her uncle and aunt, has now returned to Oz to live always, and there is no reason why we should leave any way open for others to travel uninvited to our fairyland. Let us make it impossible for any one ever to communicate with us in any way, after this. Then we may live peacefully and contentedly."

"Your advice is wise," returned Ozma. "I thank you, Glinda, for your promise to assist me."

"But how can you do it?" asked Dorothy. "How can you keep every one from ever finding Oz?"

"By making our country invisible to all eyes but our own," replied the Sorceress, smiling. "I have a magic charm powerful enough to accomplish that wonderful feat, and now that we have been warned of our danger by the Nome King's invasion, I believe we must not hesitate to separate ourselves forever from all the rest of the world."

"I agree with you," said the Ruler of Oz.

"Won't it make any difference to us?" asked Dorothy, doubtfully.

"No, my dear," Glinda answered, assuringly. "We shall still be able to see each other and everything in the Land of Oz. It won't affect us at all; but those who fly through the air over our country will look down and see nothing at all. Those who come to the edge of the desert, or try to cross it, will catch no glimpse of Oz, or know in what direction it lies. No one will try to tunnel to us again because we cannot be seen and therefore cannot be found. In other words, the Land of Oz will entirely disappear from the knowledge of the rest of the world."

"That's all right," said Dorothy, cheerfully. "You may make Oz invis'ble as soon as you please, for all I care."

"It is already invisible," Glinda stated. "I knew Ozma's wishes, and performed the Magic Spell before you arrived."

Ozma seized the hand of the Sorceress and pressed it gratefully.

"Thank you!" she said.

How THE STORY OF OZ CAME TO AN END

CHAPTER THIRTY

The writer of these Oz stories has received a little note from Princess Dorothy of Oz which, for a time, has made him feel rather discontented. The note was written on a broad white feather from a stork's wing, and it said:

> *"You will never hear anything more about Oz, because we are now cut off forever from all the rest of the world. But Toto and I will always love you and all the other children who love us.*
>
> "DOROTHY GALE."

This seemed to me too bad, at first, for Oz is a very interesting fairyland. Still, we have no right to feel grieved, for we have had enough of the history of the Land of Oz to fill six story books, and from its quaint people and their strange adventures we have been able to learn many useful and amusing things.

So good luck to little Dorothy and her companions. May they live long in their invisible country and be very happy!

THE END

A Highly Condensed History of Oz

As a special addendum, we append four pages culled from Baum's fourth Oz book. Despite his official position as "The Royal Historian of Oz," Baum was about as capable of chronological consistency as the Wizard was of doing real magic. Still, for those readers raised on the chronicles of Narnia and Middle-earth who are desperate for a little background to this generally ahistorical, live-in-the-moment magic land, we include this tourist pamphlet's summary of some high points of Oz history, pre-Wizard. It is reproduced from Chapter 15 of Dorothy and the Wizard in Oz.

Dorothy sprang up and ran to seize her friend's hand, drawing him impulsively toward the lovely Princess, who smiled most graciously upon her guest. Then the Wizard entered, and his presence relieved the boy's embarrassment. The little man was clothed in black velvet, with many sparkling emerald ornaments decorating his breast; but his bald head and wrinkled features made him appear more amusing than impressive.

Ozma had been quite curious to meet the famous man who had built the Emerald City and united the Munchkins, Gillikins, Quadlings and Winkies into one people; so when they were all four seated at the dinner table the Princess said:

"Please tell me, Mr. Wizard, whether you called yourself Oz after this great country, or whether you believe my country is called Oz after you. It is a matter that I have long wished to enquire about, because you are of a strange race and my own name is Ozma. No one, I am sure, is better able to explain this mystery than you."

"That is true," answered the little Wizard; "therefore it will give me pleasure to explain my connection with your country. In the first place, I must tell you that I was born in Omaha, and my father, who was a politician, named me Oscar Zoroaster Phadrig Isaac Norman Henkle Emmannuel Ambroise Diggs, Diggs being the last name because he could think of no more to go before it. Taken altogether, it was a dreadfully long name to weigh down a poor innocent child, and one of the hardest lessons I ever learned was to remember my own name. When I grew up I just called myself O. Z., because the other initials were P-I-N-H-E-A-D; and that spelled 'pinhead,' which was a reflection on my intelligence."

"Surely no one could blame you for cutting your name short," said Ozma, sympathetically. "But didn't you cut it almost too short?"

"Perhaps so," replied the Wizard. "When a young man I ran away from home and joined a circus. I used to call myself a Wizard, and do tricks of ventriloquism."

"What does that mean?" asked the Princess.

"Throwing my voice into any object I pleased, to make it appear that the object was speaking instead of me. Also I began to make balloon ascensions. On my balloon and on all the other articles I used in the circus I painted the two initials: 'O. Z.,' to show that those things belonged to me.

"One day my balloon ran away with me and brought me across the deserts to this beautiful country. When the people saw me come from the sky they naturally thought me some superior creature, and bowed down before me. I told them I was a Wizard, and showed them some easy tricks that amazed them; and when they saw the initials painted on the balloon they called me Oz."

"Now I begin to understand," said the Princess, smiling.

"At that time," continued the Wizard, busily eating his soup while talking, "there were four separate countries in this Land, each one of the four being ruled by a Witch. But the people thought my power was greater than that of the Witches; and perhaps the Witches thought so too, for they never dared oppose me. I ordered the Emerald City to be built just where the four countries cornered together, and when it was completed I announced myself the Ruler of the Land of Oz, which included all the four countries of the Munchkins, the Gillikins, the Winkies and the Quadlings. Over this Land I ruled in peace for many years, until I grew old and longed to see my native city once again. So when Dorothy was first blown to this place by a cyclone I arranged to go away with her in a balloon; but the balloon escaped too soon and carried me back alone. After many adventures I reached Omaha, only to find that all my old friends were dead or had moved away. So, having nothing else to do, I joined a circus again, and made my balloon ascensions until the earthquake caught me."

"That is quite a history," said Ozma; "but there is a little more history about the Land of Oz that you do not seem to understand—perhaps for the reason that no one ever told it to you. Many years before you came here this Land was united under one Ruler, as it is now, and the Ruler's name was always 'Oz,' which means in our language 'Great and Good'; or, if the Ruler happened to be a woman, her name was always 'Ozma.' But once upon a time four Witches leagued together to depose the King and rule the four parts of the kingdom themselves; so when the Ruler, my grandfather, was hunting one day, one Wicked Witch named Mombi stole him and carried him away, keeping him a close prisoner. Then the Witches divided up the kingdom, and ruled the four parts of it until you came here. That was why the people were so glad to see you, and why they thought from your initials that you were their rightful ruler."

"But, at that time," said the Wizard, thoughtfully, "there were two Good Witches and two Wicked Witches ruling in the land."

"Yes," replied Ozma, "because a good Witch had conquered Mombi in the North and Glinda the Good had conquered the evil Witch in the South. But Mombi was still my grandfather's jailor, and afterward my father's jailor. When I was born she transformed me into a boy, hoping that no one would ever recognize me and know that I was the rightful Princess of the Land of Oz. But I escaped from her and am now the Ruler of my people."

"I am very glad of that," said the Wizard, "and hope you will consider me one of your most faithful and devoted subjects."

"We owe a great deal to the Wonderful Wizard," continued the Princess, "for it was you who built this splendid Emerald City."

"Your people built it," he answered. "I only bossed the job, as we say in Omaha."

"But you ruled it wisely and well for many years," said she, "and made the people proud of your magical art. So, as you are now too old to wander abroad and work in a circus, I offer you a home here as long as you live. You shall be the Official Wizard of my kingdom, and be treated with every respect and consideration."

"I accept your kind offer with gratitude, gracious Princess," the little man said, in a soft voice, and they could all see that tear-drops were standing in his keen old eyes. It meant a good deal to him to secure a home like this.

"He's only a humbug Wizard, though," said Dorothy, smiling at him.

"And that is the safest kind of a Wizard to have," replied Ozma, promptly.

Traveling On?

Suggested Further Reading

If you enjoyed the magical fantasy of the Oz books, and have not read widely in other literature of magic realms, consider the books referred to in the introductory essay, and some others appended here, too. Most are published for children, though not all of them—be forewarned!

⬧ *Peter Pan* (known also as *Peter and Wendy*), J. M. Barrie

⬧ *Alice's Adventures in Wonderland* and *Through the Looking-Glass,* Lewis Carroll

⬧ The Chronicles of Prydain, Lloyd Alexander

⬧ The Chronicles of Narnia, C. S. Lewis

⬧ *Winnie-the-Pooh* and *The House at Pooh Corner,* A. A. Milne

⬧ *Mistress Masham's Repose,* T. H. White

⬧ *The Children of Green Knowe* and sequels, L. M. Boston

⬧ *The Diamond in the Window* and sequels, Jane Langton

⬧ *The Inferno,* Dante

⬧ "The Lord of the Rings" sequence, J.R.R. Tolkien

- *The Once and Future King,* T. H. White
- *The Marriage of Cadmus and Harmony,* Roberto Calasso
- *Titus Groan* and sequels, Mervyn Peake
- *A Christmas Carol,* Charles Dickens
- *Harry Potter and the Sorcerer's Stone* and sequels, J. K. Rowling
- *A Wizard of Earthsea* and sequels, Ursula K. Le Guin
- *The Wolves of Willoughby Chase* and sequels, Joan Aiken
- "His Dark Materials" sequence, Philip Pullman
- Classic fairy tales of Charles Perrault and the Brothers Grimm
- *The Collected Tales of Hans Christian Andersen*
- Aesop's Fables
- *The Metamorphoses,* Ovid
- *The Water-Babies,* Charles Kingsley

Not to forget these, equally good and worthwhile:

- *The Princess and the Goblin* and *The Princess and Curdie,* George Macdonald
- *At the Back of the North Wind,* George Macdonald
- *The Jungle-Books,* Rudyard Kipling
- *Five Children and It* and sequels, E. Nesbit
- *The Book of Dragons,* E. Nesbit
- "The Dark is Rising" sequence, Susan Cooper
- *A Wrinkle in Time* and sequels, Madeleine L'Engle
- *The Wee Free Men* and sequels, Terry Pratchett
- *The Mouse and His Child,* Russell Hoban
- *Howl's Moving Castle,* Diana Wynne Jones
- *The Ear, the Eye, and the Arm,* Nancy Farmer

Some flitches from the great Oz cycle, interesting and heretical:

◇ *Wicked* and *Son of a Witch*, by Gregory Maguire
Also "Scarecrow" from *Half-Human*, edited by Bruce Coville

◇ *A Barnstormer in Oz*, Philip José Farmer

◇ *Was*, Geoff Ryman

◇ *Seven-Day Magic*, Edward Eager

New York City is home to a children's bookstore called Books of Wonder—a rather fabulous place in its own right. Its owner, Peter Glassman, has been instrumental in keeping the series of Oz books in print; he's written new essays on L. Frank Baum and reissued classics that continue to bring new readers to the Wonderful Land of Oz. For further reading, you could do no better than to get yourself there, or check out the website at www.booksofwonder.com, and continue your exploration of the fabulous Land of Oz whenever the world at large (and sometimes it does seem quite at large) becomes a bit much.

LET'S TALK ABOUT OZ
A READER'S GUIDE

One of the joys of travel is discussing the journey. Now that you have ventured further abroad in Oz, let's talk about it. . . .

1. Many readers come to know Oz through the famous 1939 Technicolor film starring Judy Garland. Keep in mind that the film was made after the books collected here had become beloved by thousands of readers. In what way does the film version interfere with, correct, or otherwise vary Baum's conception of his land of Oz? Building on that point, in other entertainments based on Baum's work—like the play or film of *The Wiz*, or the film *Return to Oz*, or the musical *Wicked*—what is the sine qua non of Oz? What are the consistent features, and what might, if anything could, constitute a betrayal of Baum's vision?

2. In his original introduction to *The Wonderful Wizard of Oz*, L. Frank Baum remarked that "the winged fairies of Grimm and Andersen have brought more happiness to childish hearts than all other human creations. Yet the old time fairy tale...may now be classed as 'historical' in the children's library; for the time has come for a series of newer 'wonder tales' in which the

stereotyped genie, dwarf, and fairy are eliminated, together with all the horrible and blood-curdling incident devised by their authors to point a fearsome moral of each tale.... *The Wonderful Wizard of Oz*...aspires to being a modernized fairy tale, in which the wonderment and joy are retained and the heart-aches and nightmares are left out." If that was Baum's aspiration in writing *Wizard*, did he achieve his aims? How about in the later books? What do you see in *Land, Ozma,* and *Emerald City* that points to Baum's admiration for earlier fairy tales? What changes on them has he rung? Is it true that he avoided tacking morals on, or is it just that the morals are not "fearsome" but pleasant?

3. Erik Christian Haugaard, a highly regarded translator of Andersen's tales from the Danish into English, once wrote "The fairy tale belongs to the poor.... I know of no fairy tale which upholds the tyrant, or takes the part of the strong against the weak." What about political power in Baum's Oz? Who has it, and who should have it? What about poverty and what about privilege? What about charity? Are the social dilemmas of our own day reflected in Baum's depiction of life in Oz?

4. Geoff Ryman begins his 1992 adult novel *Was*—which concerns an invented history for a girl named Dorothy and a writer named L. Frank Baum—with a scene in which his protagonist, Jonathan, is entranced by the fellow at the Hertz car rental desk in Manhattan, Kansas. "He reminded Jonathan of the farmer in the painting *American Gothic*" (p. 4). In what ways does Oz comment on Midwestern values, or East Coast social conventions, or West Coast libertarianism—either of its time (turn of the twentieth century) or of now?

5. Now you've read about Tip's transformation. Put rather clumsily, has Baum bitten off more than he can chew? Transformations are popular in children's literature, and in all the literatures that became children's stories in the nineteenth century. Ovid's metamorphoses, Galatea and Pygmalion, Kingsley's water-babies, Lewis Carroll's endless shape-shifting, Pinocchio from a wooden puppet to a boy, Ruskin's older sons in *The King of the Golden River,* Macdonald's humans-to-animals in *The*

Princess and Curdie, the Velveteen Rabbit, Sylvester in William Steig's *Sylvester and the Magic Pebble*...the list is endless. None of these is like what happens to Tip. What do you make of it? Can you breathe? Take a sip of water.

6. In his essay "A Short Text about Magic" (British Film Institute, London, 1992), Salman Rushdie remarks about the 1939 MGM film *The Wizard of Oz,* "Glinda and the Witch of the West are the only two symbols of power in a film which is largely about the powerless, and it's instructive to 'unpack' them. They are both women, and a striking aspect of *The Wizard of Oz* is its lack of a male hero.... The power of men, it is suggested, is illusory; the power of women is real." Do the three Oz books republished here concern themselves with differences between illusion and reality, or, more to the point, between the reality of feminine power and the illusion of male power? Is this really Baum's point, or was it MGM's point? Or is it merely Rushdie's point? How do Ozma, Glinda, and Dorothy measure up on these scores?

7. When Baum wrote the Oz books, there was little else like them: an extended series of adventures about a fantastic land created by a single artist. Surely there'd be no Chronicles of Narnia without Oz, and perhaps no Middle-earth either, even though Narnia is mapped out with the sextants of Christianity, and Middle-earth with even more arcane instruments of philology. Is it fair to consider Oz in the same breath with Narnia and Middle-earth, Prydain and Earthsea, or does it more reasonably share the shelf with Edward Lear in such works as "The Dong with the Luminous Nose" and Lewis Carroll's "Jabberwocky"? Put otherwise, what might Baum's inspirations actually be?

8. Is there such a thing as too much inventiveness? Does too much zany drollery tend to paralyze the underlying consistency of a land that is presented as a universe unto itself? Think of the nonsense of Mother Goose—"the dish ran away with the spoon"—where every new rhyme posits a new condition of life, just as every new country in Oz seems to have its own laws and to be largely self-contained. Or is Oz an early version of Douglas

Adams's galaxy, the one the hitchhiker so needed a guide for—a place that is characterized by inconsistency, surreal incompatibility?

9. In *The New Yorker*, John Updike once published a consideration of Oz that was called "OZ IS US." Updike's critical mind and his poetic sensibility invent a relationship among those words that begin with vowels and end in sibilants: *Oz, is, us.* Or is that not *us* but the U.S.? Is Oz the U.S.? Does Oz rely for its essential characteristic on the notion of a land of plenty, of harmony, all personal satisfactions fulfilled, all inequities resolved? In what ways are these Oz narratives derived from how America dreams of itself?

MODERN LIBRARY IS ONLINE AT WWW.MODERNLIBRARY.COM

MODERN LIBRARY ONLINE IS YOUR GUIDE TO CLASSIC LITERATURE ON THE WEB

THE MODERN LIBRARY E-NEWSLETTER

Our free e-mail newsletter is sent to subscribers, and features sample chapters, interviews with and essays by our authors, upcoming books, special promotions, announcements, and news. To subscribe to the Modern Library e-newsletter, visit **www.modernlibrary.com**

THE MODERN LIBRARY WEBSITE

Check out the Modern Library website at **www.modernlibrary.com** for:

- The Modern Library e-newsletter
- A list of our current and upcoming titles and series
- Reading Group Guides and exclusive author spotlights
- Special features with information on the classics and other paperback series
- Excerpts from new releases and other titles
- A list of our e-books and information on where to buy them
- The Modern Library Editorial Board's 100 Best Novels and 100 Best Nonfiction Books of the Twentieth Century written in the English language
- News and announcements

Questions? E-mail us at **modernlibrary@randomhouse.com**. For questions about examination or desk copies, please visit the Random House Academic Resources site at **www.randomhouse.com/academic**